NEW YORK TIMES BESTSELLING AUTHOR

LINDSAY McKENNA

&

USA TODAY BESTSELLING AUTHOR

BARB HAN

TEXAS PROTECTOR

2 Thrilling Stories
Solitaire & Texas Abduction

HARLEQUIN®

ISBN-13: 978-1-335-50838-6

Recycling programs for this product may not exist in your area.

Texas Protector

Copyright © 2023 by Harlequin Enterprises ULC

Solitaire
First published in 1987. This edition published in 2023.
Copyright © 1987 by Nauman Living Trust

Texas Abduction
First published in 2021. This edition published in 2023.
Copyright © 2021 by Barb Han

For questions and comments about the quality of this book, please contact us at CustomerService@Harlequin.com.

Harlequin Enterprises ULC
22 Adelaide St. West, 41st Floor
Toronto, Ontario M5H 4E3, Canada
www.Harlequin.com

Printed in U.S.A.

CONTENTS

Lindsay McKenna is proud to have served her country in the US Navy as an aerographer's mate third class—also known as a weather forecaster. She was a pioneer in the military romance subgenre and loves to combine heart-pounding action with soulful and poignant romance. True to her military roots, she is the originator of the long-running and reader-favorite Morgan's Mercenaries series. She does extensive hands-on research, including flying in aircraft such as a P3-B Orion sub-hunter and a B-52 bomber. She was the first romance writer to sign her books in the Pentagon bookstore. Visit her online at lindsaymckenna.com.

Books by Lindsay McKenna

Visit the Author Profile page
at Harlequin.com for more titles.

SOLITAIRE

Lindsay McKenna

Chapter 1

"Don't go in there. It's too dangerous." A large hand splayed across on the blueprint of the emerald mine in Hampton, Maine, that Cat was studying. Her concentration broken, she blinked. Thinking it was the owner of the gem mine, she slowly stood up and turned.

Normally, she barely had to lift her eyes to look into those of a man, so she was momentarily disconcerted to find herself eye to eye with a khaki-covered chest. She brought her gaze up and looked into dark blue eyes the color of midnight sapphire and equally breathtaking. The man's stubborn jaw accentuated the intensity of his gaze, and if it weren't for the laugh lines bracketing his mouth and the crinkles at the corners of his eyes, she would have bet he never smiled.

"I beg your pardon," Cat said coolly.

"I've already been in that mine. It isn't safe."

Her mouth curved into a knowing smile. "What mine is?"

Impatience flared in his eyes. "This is no time for jokes, Ms. Kincaid. I was in that dump this morning and the owner is crazy to ask anyone to actually inspect that worthless pit. The timbers are not only rotted, but there's water in the sedimentary manging wall above those timbers that's weakened the entire crosscut."

"You're obviously not Mr. Graham," Cat returned testily. "So perhaps you'd be good enough to tell me who you are, and how you know my name."

"No, I'm not the owner of this worthless excuse for a mine. And everyone in our business knows the name Cat Kincaid." His eyes grew warm and he extended his hand. "My name is Slade Donovan. I'm a geologist."

Cat shook his hand, finding his grip firm but not overpowering. "I don't understand, Mr. Donovan. Has Mr. Graham hired you to help assess the condition of the Emerald Lady Mine?" She stole a look at her watch. She didn't have much time and she couldn't waste what she had on social amenities.

Slade had the good grace to look sheepish. "Well, not exactly, Ms. Kincaid. Oh, hell, do you mind if I call you Cat? That's what most people call you, right? I don't like standing on formality any more than I have to."

Wariness returned to Cat's eyes. "Slade Donovan. Where have I heard that name before?"

He colored slightly, heightening the ruddy glow already in his cheeks. "Mining engineers and geologists are a pretty close group on the international circuit," he parried. "I've worked a few gem mines in Africa and South America."

Cat pushed a few dark brown strands of hair from her

forehead and took a step back, gauging him closely in the interim. "I know I've heard of you…"

"That's not really important right now; you are." He pointed out the grimy window of the old shack. "Lionel Graham has a poor reputation among geologists. You can't trust him." His voice, naturally low and with an obvious Texas accent, deepened with urgency. "He's waited too long for a mine inspection into that crosscut. Those post and stull timbers would crack if someone were to breathe on them the wrong way, Cat."

"Ms. Kincaid, please, Mr. Donovan. If the owner hasn't hired you, then what are you doing here?" It was on the tip of her tongue to ask just who he thought he was to be telling her, a mining engineer, whether she should go into a mine or not. Staring at him critically, she guessed his age to be around her own thirty-three years. He managed to look both rugged and boyish, a combination helped by the lock of rebellious brown hair lying on his broad brow.

He suddenly offered her a devastating smile, obviously meant to melt the heart of any woman he wanted to charm. The smile, however, had the opposite effect on her. Placing her hands on her hips, she stood waiting for an explanation.

"Actually, I flew in from Bogota when I heard you were coming here." Slade brushed the errant lock back in one quick motion. "I've been trying to track you down for days. I got in last night and—"

"Ah, there you are, Ms. Kincaid." Lionel Graham, a portly man dressed impeccably in a gray suit, entered the office. His balding head shone beneath the naked light bulb suspended above them, and his brow wrinkled as he turned to the tall man standing beside her. "What are you doing here, Donovan? I thought you were still in South America."

Slade scowled back at Graham and drew himself up to his full six-foot-four. "I was in Tunnel B this morning, Graham, the crosscut. I can't say I liked what I saw."

Graham frowned, sucking in his potbelly. "Now see here, Donovan, I don't know what you're doing here, but no one is allowed inside the Emerald Lady unless I authorize it."

"I can see why," Slade shot back. "That mine's back is broken. Someone hasn't been following proper pumping practices, and you've got nothing but rotting posts and stulls weighed down by a ceiling ready to collapse on anyone stupid enough to go in there."

Graham colored fiercely. "What does a geologist know about engineering matters?" he challenged.

"A damn good geologist, Graham." Slade glanced over his shoulder toward Cat. "I know emerald mines, Graham, and you have no business sending anyone down in that shaft."

Cat moved forward, her anger finally at the boiling point. She didn't have time to stand there listening to these two. "Mr. Donovan, your opinion is not wanted or needed. That's why I'm here. I troubleshoot bad mines for a living. Do you?"

Struggling to contain his temper, Slade asked, "Ever hear of taking a bath, Ms. Kincaid?" Although not a common practice, some unscrupulous mine owners would put very little money into a supposedly rich gem site, then declare it a catastrophic business loss to collect a healthy tax return. Well, the Emerald Lady was a lost cause and both Slade and Graham knew it. The only one who didn't was Cat Kincaid, and he wasn't going to let her find out the hard way if he had anything to say about it.

"I fail to see what that has to do with this situation, Mr.—"

"My friends call me Slade. And the Emerald Lady is nothing more than a nice, juicy business loss just waiting to be picked up by Graham."

Graham flushed scarlet. "You've gone too far this time, Donovan," he sputtered. "Unless you're suddenly working with the U.S. Mine Safety—"

Slade turned conspiratorially to Cat for a moment. "That's who ought to be called in to handle this situation. Tunnel B is just begging to fall. But then, Graham—" he turned to the red-faced man "—you wouldn't stand to get as much of a tax loss if you didn't have someone of Ms. Kincaid's stature sign on the bottom line, stating that your mine is not only inoperable, but a disaster of the first degree."

"Look, Donovan, you've no right," began a riled Graham.

Slade, ignoring him, swung his attention back to Cat. "You've been a mining engineer for over ten years. And there isn't anyone in our business who doesn't respect or admire your work in constructing mines under almost impossible circumstances." Slade jabbed a finger toward the Emerald Lady mine. "But your life and your knowledge, not to mention your neck, aren't worth risking for that pit. I'm telling you, that shaft is deadly. Don't go in there. Let Graham get the U.S. mining officials to do it instead."

Cat was momentarily swayed by the fervor of his request; Donovan's deep Texas accent flowed through her like a cool breeze on a hot jungle night. Then she blinked, realizing that he had literally spun her into his web with his husky, coaxing voice. Irritated that she had let him affect her at all, she said, "Mr. Donovan, I think Mr. Graham and I can handle this. In case you forgot, mine inspection is part of being a mining engineer."

Graham pulled out a white silk handkerchief and mopped his perspiring brow. "It most certainly is! Ms. Kincaid's specialty is troublesome mines; that's why I called her. And I resent your inference, Donovan, that I'm doing this for a business loss. Nothing could be further from my mind. The Emerald Lady is the best, and we'll hire only the best if we get into trouble."

Slade snorted. Graham was lying through his perfectly capped teeth. Slade wondered briefly why Cat couldn't see through Graham's ploy. Who had raised her to never question another person's motives?

"Please—" he opened both his callused hands out toward Cat in a final, pleading gesture "—don't go in there. There was a heavy rain here last night. Give the mine another day to settle down. Water's leaking like a sieve in there, and in the crosscut. The supporting timbers are rotted. A day. Just one."

There simply wasn't enough time for this, and Cat stepped up to Donovan, her jaw set. "My schedule doesn't permit the luxury of an extra day. I intend to inspect this mine right now, Mr. Donovan. I don't have time to stand here and discuss this issue. By this afternoon—" she looked at the gold Rolex watch on her darkly tanned left wrist "—at 2:00 p.m., to be precise, I have a flight back to New York City. I have to be in Australia by tomorrow evening."

Rain began falling at a steady clip, spreading a gray pall over the heavily forested area that surrounded the mine. Slade interpreted this as a warning. Cat merely regarded it as an inconvenience.

She picked up her white miner's hard hat, which had accumulated scratches and dents from many years of use. Each depression was from a rock large enough to have injured her. Cat tested the light strapped to the front of the hat before settling it on her sable-colored hair. Then she plugged the jack into a battery pack that she carried on a web belt around her waist. As she finished her preparations, Cat tried to ignore Donovan, whose tightly throttled energy had the room in a state of electric tension.

"Donovan," Graham began, "I don't care who you think you are. You're trespassing on private property." He glanced around. "If you don't leave, I'll call the sheriff on my car telephone and have you booted out of here on your—"

"Save your threats, Graham. I'm staying until Ms. Kincaid is safely out of that mine." His blue eyes narrowed on Graham's porcine face. "And there's not a damn thing you can do about it unless you think you're big enough to throw me out of here."

Cat shook her head and picked up a safety lamp. Lighting the regulation-size lantern, she watched with satisfaction as the yellow flame grew. She straightened up.

"You going in with her, Graham?" Slade prodded savagely.

"Of course not. She's the mining expert."

Slade's mouth twisted into a lethal line. "You wouldn't be caught dead in there because you know just how unsafe that pit is."

Cat opened the door and nailed both men with a look of authority. "You two can stay here and argue about the mine's merits, but I'm going into it." She looked directly at Slade. "And don't follow me in. Understand?"

He grimaced and nodded. "Whatever you say, lady." Then his icy composure gave way to concern. "But I'd like to see you come back in one piece."

Cat tilted her head, a question in her eyes. What had the scuttlebutt been about the man named Slade Donovan? Later, after the mine inspection was over, she'd search her memory. The name sounded familiar, but was he tied to good news or bad? Judging from his bull-in-the-china-shop tactics, it probably wasn't very good.

"I'll be out in about an hour, Mr. Graham, unless I find something, then it will take a bit longer."

"Fine, fine. Take your time. I'll be waiting."

Slade took a step toward her. "Get in and then get the hell out. Any miner with an ounce of brains could tell twenty minutes after entering it that the mine's broken."

Cat gave him a cool look, then pulled the miner's hat brim a little lower across her eyes. "In about an hour, Mr. Graham…"

Helplessly Slade watched her leave and move out into the downpour. The lightweight pale blue canvas jacket she wore darkened immediately with splotches of rain. Muttering a curse, Slade elbowed past Graham. Cat was halfway across the empty, muddy expanse, heading toward the yawning dark hole of the mine shaft, when Slade caught up with her.

"Ms. Kincaid—Cat—here, take this with you." He thrust a portable radio into her hand. "It's waterproof," he quickly explained. The rain slashed across his face, and his hair darkened as it became plastered against his skull. "Just in case, okay? Don't give me that look, either. This is a safety measure. There's no one here to help you in case something does go wrong." He drew to a halt just inside the shaft. Slade gave her a pleading look, knowing he couldn't intimidate or push Cat into doing what he wanted. He'd heard she had a mind of her own and now he had to deal with that.

Cat stuffed the radio inside her jacket to protect it. The damp, stale air flowing out of the mine swept around them and a chill worked its way up her back. "Okay," she said, "I'll take it with me. But you stay here. I've had enough of your strong-arm tactics, Mr. Donovan. You're just lucky Mr. Graham didn't call the sheriff. You could be in a lot of hot water. He's a fairly influential man in mining, even if his reputation is less than virtuous."

"Lady," Slade confirmed, grinning, "Graham's sunk more worthless pits around the world than I've sampled ore."

"Let me get on with my business, Donovan."

"Yeah, go ahead. How about if I buy you a steak for lunch when you're done?"

There was something intriguing about Slade Donovan that Cat couldn't quite put her finger on; her sixth sense—or was it female curiosity—urged her to accept. "Lunch," she grudgingly agreed. "But a short one."

"I know, you've got a plane to catch." He smiled, the tension in his face easing momentarily.

Cat flipped on her helmet light, holding the safety lamp out in front of her. "See you later, Donovan." Watching where she placed her rubber-booted feet, Cat began her trek down the gentle incline of the adit, or main shaft. Darkness closed around her like a consuming embrace, and the only light was the muted yellow glow of the safety lamp. She inhaled the dankness of the silent shaft. Like most emerald mines, it wasn't deep; it ran shallow, following either sedimentary or pegmatite veins that hid the green rock in calcite nests. The floor was littered profusely with limestone slabs, evidence that the mine hadn't been worked in quite a while.

Cat stopped at every few timbers and studied them carefully with her practiced eye. The overhead roof, or manging wall, of pale green limestone dripped constantly. Most of it was due to the dampness inherent in a mine. But Slade had been right: trickles of water had followed fissures in the sediment and wound their way down into the mine itself. Rock bolts should have been placed in the wall to strengthen it. Without them the wetness would weaken the wall. As Cat ran practiced fingers across the stull, or timbers, supporting the limestone roof, she saw that the main shoring points would have to be immediately replaced and new ones installed.

The thin beam of light from her helmet probed the blackness as Cat raised her head to assess the damage to each post and stull. The adit split into a Y, known to miners as a crosscut. This was the beginning of Tunnel B. The air leaving the shaft was desultory and pregnant with a stale, musty odor. Cat wondered if the dew point was high enough for it to actually rain within the mine. Again, Slade had been right: Graham hadn't even begun to put the necessary care into this mine to make it a decent place to work. If Graham was as knowledgeable as Donovan had said he was, he had no excuse to have skimped on proper ventilation and pumping equipment. Moisture was eating away at the powerful oak and hardwood beams that kept the walls from collapsing and the roof from dropping, and some unlucky miner could lose his life beneath it. She turned down the crosscut, a secondary tunnel off the main adit, and carefully in-

spected each support. The limestone had turned a rust
color where water had leaked through from above, indicating iron in the sediment above the exposed vein. Cat
smiled grimly. Slade had accurately predicted the condition of the shaft: there was no way emeralds were going
to be found in this kind of rock. The only type that held
emeralds was calcite limestone, and none was in evidence here. Even though she wasn't a geologist, she'd
seen plenty of rock, and she was knowledgeable enough
to make the assessment on her own.

The deeper she went, the more oppressive the air became. The incline became vertical—what miners called
a winze. Cat halted at the lip of the winze. She held the
safety lamp high, looking for the reason for the vertical
descent of the shaft. Normally, it was because the vein
of calcite or pegmatite went off in an unexpected direction. But judging from the iron-marked limestone, Cat
could see no discernible reason for it. She ran her fingers
lightly over the hardwood timber; the surface was slick
with algae and wet from the constant leakage of water.
Above, the main horizontal stull was fully cracked and
sagging. Again, Slade's words came to her about the back
of the mine being broken.

Cat's lips tightened and she stood quietly. All around
her, she could hear the plunk, plunk, plunk of water. The
passage gleamed from the liquid seeping in through the
walls. Should she go on? Chances were, if one timber
was cracked, the others would be, too, indicating that the
entire roof was caving in. It was only a matter of time
until the limestone, weakened by water flow through the
natural fissures, would collapse. Why did Graham want
her to investigate the worthiness of this mine? It was
a total loss. So much money would have to be poured

into shoring up the crosscut alone, she wondered if the mine's calculated yield was worth that kind of expense. Cat thought not, but that wasn't any of her business; that was Graham's decision to make.

The floor of the mine was slippery with mud and slime. Cat took each step carefully, for she had no wish to cause any undue vibration that might further weaken the supports. Automatically, she pressed her wet fingers against her jacket where the radio lay next to her heart. Slade was turning out to be a pretty decent person after all; his advice had been good, and the radio was a definite asset.

Pushing thoughts of Slade aside, Cat concentrated on the overhead stulls. She stopped every ten feet and examined each one thoroughly. About three hundred feet into the winze, Cat crouched by the left wall. The limestone had cracked, and a healthy spring of water gushed through the opening, running down into the shaft. That wasn't good. It indicated a major structural weakness in the rock wall glistening beneath her fingertips. Slowly rising, Cat cautiously moved to the other side of the mine and continued her inspection.

She had gone another two hundred feet, almost to the end of Tunnel B according to the map, when a sickening crack echoed through the shaft. In one motion, Cat turned, sprinting back toward the beginning of the crosscut. Suddenly, a rumbling sound began. The hollow, drumlike roar rolled through the shaft like mounting thunder. She couldn't tell whether the winze was caving in behind or in front of her. Water several inches deep rushed down the shaft, and she splashed through it. She leaped to the lip that signaled an end to the winze. Slipping, Cat skidded to her knees in the muck and mud of the crosscut. The safety lamp bounced twice and then the flame went out.

Loud snapping and groaning noises followed. Cat's breath tore from her as she scrambled to her feet; the only light left was the one on her helmet. Water was rapidly rising from foot to ankle level; she knew a crack in the wall up ahead had given way. Had the entire wall caved in, leaving her no escape?

Behind her, Cat heard the limestone manging wall grate, and she automatically ducked her head, keeping one hand on her helmet as she raced toward the intersection of the adit. Only two hundred feet more, she guessed, gasping for breath. A crash caromed beside her, and rocks began falling. She halted, breathing hard. Should she retreat or—fist-size pieces of limestone began raining down around her. She was trapped! Cat shielded her face and lurched forward, dust and rock hailing down as she slogged forward, staggering and stumbling.

Suffocating dust filled Cat's mouth, nose and lungs. She coughed violently, unable to breathe. Blinded by the dust, which was thicker than smoke, she tripped. As she did, the manging wall where she had stood seconds before dropped to the floor. A rock the size of a baseball crashed onto her hard hat, knocking it off her head. The hat and light bounced crazily, sending a skittering beam of light through the dense grayness. Another rock struck her shoulder, spinning her around. Cat threw her hands up to protect her head as she pitched backward. She slammed into the jagged rocks, the breath ripped out of her. Seconds later, more than a ton of rock and soil filled the chamber where she was trapped. A cry tore from her as the rest of the other wall collapsed, nearly burying her. Pain lanced up her right side and Cat sank back, unconscious.

* * *

With a violent oath, Slade raced down the mine shaft. He had heard the ominous crack of timbers, sounding one after another like breaking matchsticks. He shouted for Cat, but his voice was drowned out by a deep roar that sent icy fear up his spine. A rolling cloud of dust engulfed him and he turned back, hacking and coughing, his hand across his nose and mouth as he stumbled out.

Lionel Graham came lumbering out of the mine shack, his eyes round with shock. Slade ran toward him and grabbed him by the lapel of his expensive English raincoat.

"Damn you, Graham, it's happened! Now you get on that car phone and call for help. Now!"

"Y-yes, of course. Of course," he sputtered, and hurried toward his car.

Slade spun around and ran back to the mine opening, pulling out the radio he kept in a leather carrying case on his hip. The red light blinked on, indicating that the battery was sufficiently charged and ready to be used.

"Cat? Cat, can you hear me? This is Slade. Over." He released the button. All he could hear was static. His mind whirled. Was she dead? Buried alive? Or had she been given a reprieve, and been trapped in a chamber? If so, how much air was left? He knew from his own grim experience that dust could suffocate a person. He ran into the mine and went as far as he could before the choking wall of limestone dust stopped him. Again, he called her. Again, no answer. Damn it to hell! He wanted to wrap his fingers around Graham's fleshy throat and strangle the bastard. He might as well have set Cat up to be murdered. But right now, Slade needed Graham's influence to get local miners together to begin excavating the mine to search for Cat.

Slade wasn't one to pray often, not that he didn't believe in God, but he more or less used Him in emergencies only. Well, this was an emergency, and as he pressed the radio's On button once again, he prayed that Cat would hear him this time.

"Cat? Cat Kincaid, can you hear me? This is Slade Donovan. If you can hear me, depress the handset. Show me you're alive. Over."

The constant static of the portable radio now lodged between her rib cage and the wall of rocks slowly brought Cat back to consciousness. Blood trickled from her nose and down her lips. She tried to lick them, but her tongue met a thick caking of dust. Suddenly a sharp, riveting pain brought her fully conscious; it felt as if her right side were on fire. Dully, Cat tried to take stock of herself. She was buried up to her thighs in rubble. The weak light from her helmet lay to the left, barely visible through the curtain of dust that hung in the chamber.

The radio static continued, and dazedly Cat reached into her jacket. It hurt to breathe. It hurt to move. Dizziness washed over her and she knew that she was injured. How badly she didn't know. Not yet. And maybe never. She had no idea how large or small was the chamber where she was buried. If it was too small, and there wasn't sufficient oxygen, she would die of suffocation sooner, rather than later. If she was lucky, oxygen might be trickling through the walls blocking her escape, and she wouldn't suffocate.

Her fingers closed over the radio. Twisting slightly, she pulled it out of her jacket. A gasp tore from her and a tidal wave of pain caused her to black out for several seconds.

When she came to, she took light, shallow breaths of the murky air. To breathe deep meant suffering a knifelike pain ripping up her right side. Busted ribs, she thought, slowly pulling the radio out of the jacket.

The light from her hard hat was slowly dimming, but she focused on first things first: the radio. Would it work? Was Donovan still out there? Her hand trembled badly as she fumbled to turn the radio on. The red light blinked on, and a rough, scratchy noise greeted her. Finally, she fine-tuned it with the other dial.

Her fingers, now bruised and bloodied, slipped on the button she hoped would link her with the outside world. Cat depressed it and tried to speak, but the only sound that came from her throat was a low croak. If only she could have some water! She could hear it all around her, the same rushing sound as before. Had that wall collapsed behind her where the limestone had cracked and separated?

"D-Donovan…" Her voice was barely a hoarse whisper. Dust clogged her throat and she wanted to cough, but didn't dare for fear of disturbing her broken ribs. Then the radio crackled and an incredible surge of relief flowed through her as she heard Donovan's Texas baritone come scratchily over the handset.

"Cat! I can barely hear you. Give me a report on your condition."

"I—I'm trapped between a double cave-in. My legs are under rubble, but if I can move off my belly, I can free myself. Chamber is—dust too thick to tell how small or large it is yet."

"Injuries?"

"Right lung hurts…can't breathe very well. Legs are numb but I think if I get the rocks off, they'll be okay."

Terror leaked through Slade's voice. "Head injury?"

Cat had to wait a minute to assess herself. She slowly raised her hand, feeling her dust-laden hair, and met warm stickiness as she felt across her scalp. Her head was throbbing as if it might split into a hundred pieces, like the limestone around her. "Maybe a mild concussion. Dizzy—"

"Oxygen?"

"Let me radio back. Got to try and reach my hard hat."

"All right, just take it easy. We're going to get you out of there. Just hang on. Graham's phoned for help. We expect miners and excavation equipment within the next hour. Get back to me on the size of the place you're trapped in. Over."

Just the reassuring sound of Slade's voice kept her panic from exploding. There was something about him that instilled faith in his promise to get her out of there. Gently, Cat set down the radio. What she would do for some water now! Dizziness came and went and Cat felt nausea clawing up her throat—she had all the symptoms of a concussion. Stretching her left hand out, fingers extended, she reached for her hard hat. There! Her fingers closed over the hat and she pulled it back to her.

As the dust slowly settled around her, Cat got an idea of the chamber's size. Rocks ranging from the size of her fist to huge sheets that easily weighed half a ton were lodged all around her. She had been lucky: if she had not tripped and fallen where she now lay, a sheet of limestone nearby would have sheared right through her. She'd be dead. The drenching reality washed through her and she closed her eyes, exhausted. *I shouldn't be tired. Got to get these rocks off my legs and move around. Maybe I can find some water...* Then drowsiness overwhelmed her.

Slade paced back and forth in front of the mine like an infuriated lion. He gripped the radio tightly in his fist. The rain was continuing to fall at a steady rate; the sky had become a dismal gray. Angrily, he shook off the thought and the feeling. Cat was alive, and that was all that mattered. No one should die alone in that godforsaken place. He wanted to vent his anger on Graham, who sat in his silver Mercedes looking pasty from the turn of events. The frightened mine owner had gone to extraordinary measures to call in local workers who had once toiled in the worthless mine, and to order heavy equipment from a nearby town. The local fire department would arrive shortly with oxygen tanks, masks and rescue apparatus. As soon as they came, Slade was going to borrow a tank and mask and make his way down the shaft to locate Cat's chamber. He halted. Cat should have called in by now.

Slade called her five times and there was no answer. Was Cat unconscious? Had she died because of oxygen deprivation? Torn between staying and going deeper, he stared down the black maw of the shaft. Maybe her radio was on the blink. He tried to ignore his memory of the slur of Cat's words and the pain he'd heard with each breath she had taken. He had a gut feeling she was in a lot more serious condition than she was revealing.

He called again. This time, he got an answer. "Cat, how are you?"

"Uhh, dizzy. Sorry, didn't mean to black out."

Slade's mouth thinned, his eyes reflecting his anxiety, but he kept it out of his voice as he depressed the On button. "You're doing fine. Did you get a look at the chamber?"

"Twenty feet long and ten feet wide. The manging

wall is holding. I'm under a stull that's stopping it from falling on top of me."

Relief flowed through him. "Great. Any indication of air supply?"

"Dust still too thick. I'm turning off my light to conserve it. Need water worse."

"I know. Look, you just rest."

"C-can't. Got to try and get rocks off legs."

Slade nodded. "The fire department is coming with oxygen gear. As soon as they arrive, I'm going to find you, Cat. For now, just conserve your energy."

She knew Slade was right, but she was shivering from the overwhelming dampness around her. As dry as her mouth and throat were, the moisture was seeping through to her bones. She shut off the light and slowly began to remove one rock at a time from the back of her legs. Only her left hand was undamaged. Movement of her right arm sent such a spasm of pain up Cat's side that she lost consciousness.

Cat was used to darkness; when she constructed a mine shaft, she was constantly in the darkened earth with only a safety lamp and lighted hard hat to illuminate her way. But rarely had she gone without any light at all, and now the dark was as suffocating as the dust that hung around her. A shiver rippled through her, the darkness like fingers of fear closing around her throat. Cat tasted her panic and concentrated on removing the rocks from her thigh, gradually releasing herself from the entrapment.

Minutes dragged by. *And each minute seems like a lifetime,* Cat realized. She clung to the hope that Slade would call again. Just to hear another human voice eased the terror that was intensified by the dark. Her breath came in painful, ragged gasps; each one feeling as if a knife was being plunged through her lungs. Sweat mingled with dust as it trickled down her face, stinging her eyes. Resting until the dizziness passed, Cat knew she would have to use her right hand to start removing the debris from her right leg. An involuntary cry tore from her contorted lips as she pushed the first rock off her thigh. Blackness closed in on her and she rested her brow against her left arm, sobbing.

"Over here!" Slade motioned the first of two arriving volunteer fire department pumpers toward the opening of the mine. Graham reluctantly got out of his car and met the chief, who was dressed in a white helmet and turn-out gear. *Finally,* Slade thought, moving toward the fire chief. In moments he had established his identity and was given an air pack and mask. He took a safety lamp and settled the hard hat on his head, then entered the mine. His heart rate picked up. How far down the crosscut had the cave-in taken place? He mentally began to calculate the possible scenarios he might find. If there was a huge wall of debris, it might take days before they could reach Cat. He prayed it was the opposite—that the bulk of the cave-in had occurred behind her and only a thin wall stood between her and freedom.

Chapter 2

Slade found the wall of rock near the second timber support in the crosscut and carefully examined the timbers around him. They were sturdy and did not appear stressed. That meant mining equipment such as drills and augers could be moved into the mine to begin removing the debris without fear of another avalanche. The dust was still thick as Slade breathed in the sweet flow of oxygen through his face mask. Sweat trickled down his temples, following the line of his jaw. Some of his fear for Cat slipped away; most of the rock and dirt that had fallen was in small chunks, and easily handled by picks, shovels and wheelbarrows. Rescue would come more quickly.

Slade crouched by one wall of the crosscut, watching as a constant stream of water disappeared into the wall. He knew that if it was getting through, life-bearing oxygen could also be carried into the chamber where Cat was trapped. Pulling out the radio, Slade attempted contact with her. He waited patiently, repeating his call three times before she answered. Cat's voice was tight and hoarse, and Slade knew she was in a hell of a lot of pain.

"How's my girl doing?"

A choked sound came over the radio. "Hanging—in there."

"Mining engineers always did have more guts than brains," he told her wryly. "I'm outside the wall where you're trapped, Cat. Give me a status report."

"Oxygen level seems the same. There's—running water to my left."

"Outstanding. How about you?"

"Would it do any good to tell you?"

"Don't play that game with me. I know I can't get to you yet, but I want to know the extent of your injuries and if you're feeling worse."

"I'll bet you use that line on every woman you meet, Donovan."

He grinned, but it didn't reach his narrowed eyes as he continued to appraise the wall of debris before him. "With you, I wouldn't use a line. Come on, level with me. How are you doing?"

"I've got the rocks off my legs and I managed to turn over. The right side of the tunnel wall looks weak and the stull above my head keeps creaking and groaning."

Slade scowled. That meant that even Cat's chamber could cave in, burying her under tons of rubble. Urgency thrummed through him. "How's that concussion you're sporting?"

"Not—good. I keep passing out. Very sleepy when I shouldn't be. I was sleeping until you called. The scratchy sounds from the radio woke me up."

Damn it! She had suffered a worse head injury than he had first thought. "Okay," Slade soothed, keeping his voice steady. "How's your ribs?"

"If I don't breathe, I feel great."

She had spunk, he'd give her that. "And when you do?"

"Feels like someone's shoved a knife up under my right rib cage."

"Think you've got compound fractures?" If she did, the broken bone could conceivably puncture the lung if she moved around too much.

"I can feel blood there. I don't know. It hurts too much to touch the area and find out."

"Stay still if you can." It was either busted ribs or a punctured lung. Or both.

"Right."

"Do you have a water source?" If she had oxygen and water, Cat could last a long time. But if she had undetected internal injuries, time could prove to be their enemy. Cat needed immediate medical attention.

"Y-yes, a small stream along the left wall. All the amenities, Donovan."

"Except you don't have me. And I intend to remedy that situation shortly. Tell me, how many posts are in your chamber?" There was a post for every ten feet of spacing.

"One, Donovan. And it's not looking very healthy."

"You know enough to place yourself under it, with your back up against it, don't you?"

"Y-yes. Once I feel up to crawling over there, I'll do it."

"Can't you walk over to it?"

"Too dizzy. I'd fall and skin my knees."

He almost smiled. "Wouldn't want you to skin up those pretty knees."

"You're full of Texas baloney, Donovan."

He laughed. "I told you before, Cat, with you, I'm honest."

"Sure, an honest geologist. That'll be the day."

"Guess I'll have to prove it to you, won't I?"

"Right now I need a knight on a white charger. Come and get me, Donovan."

"Would you settle for thirty firemen, fifty miners and some drilling equipment instead?"

"Sounds wonderful."

He heard the sudden wobble in Cat's voice, as if she were close to tears. Slade tightened his grip around the radio. "Look, it appears that about ten feet of earth and rock are separating us, Cat. Unless we run into some limestone sheets weighing a ton or more, we ought to be able to reach you within twenty-four hours."

"Slade?"

Slade blinked the sweat from his eyes, hearing the fear in Cat's voice for the first time. "What is it, sweetheart?"

"C-could you contact my parents? Tell them what's happened? Especially my brother Rafe? They live in Colorado. The Triple K Ranch. If I give you the phone number, could you call them? Please?"

"Sure, anything you want."

Relief cracked her voice. "T-thanks. Here's the number."

Slade committed it to memory. "I'm signing off, Cat. The miners will be here any minute. I've got Graham's permission to organize and run this rescue operation. If you need anything, call. Otherwise I'll contact you in about an hour."

"Just let me know if you can reach my family."

"I'll personally make the call. Graham's got a phone in his car."

"Thanks, Slade. It means a lot to me…."

"I can tell." As he left the dankness of the mine, his mind shifted to another matter. Slade knew very few geologists or mining engineers who had sunk roots and had a family or children. He also knew from reading articles on Cat Kincaid that she wasn't married. As Slade got to his feet and began his trek to the adit, he wondered what man in his right mind would let someone as rare as Cat Kincaid out of his sight, much less out of his life. There was a special quality about her that he longed to explore. She was like an emerald mine waiting to be discovered: enticing, mysterious and filled with rich promise.

Gray light filtered through the adit, telling him he was near the opening. Well, he'd discovered one thing about Cat: family meant a great deal to her. Rafe was obviously a brother she could look up to, admire and lean on in times of trouble. Lucky guy, he told himself enviously.

As Slade walked out into the pall of rain, he glared at the gray sky overhead. They didn't need more water; it would loosen more dirt and the rain would trickle through the weakened limestone, making the rescue effort even more precarious than before. Slade had good instincts, and his gut sense had often saved his life in the past. Now, that voice screamed out that another cave-in was near. His instincts also warned him that if this was Cat's first cave-in, she would need emotional support to get back the courage to someday walk into the darkness of another mine.

Cat could barely move her head. She sat with her back against the rough, splintered surface of the post. Five hours had elapsed. Slade had called once an hour and sweet God in heaven, how she came to rely on him; he was her support system against the fear that threatened to consume her. Each passing hour made it become harder to control her rising panic.

Her spirits had plummeted when Slade had not been able to raise anyone at her parents' ranch right away. Cat felt alone and vulnerable in a way she'd never before experienced. Rafe—she needed Rafe's steadying presence. He was always the one to get them out of a jam when they were kids growing up in the Rocky Mountain wilderness. There had been times when she was scared to death, but because Rafe reassured her that it would be all right, she took dangerous chances with him. When Slade informed her he couldn't reach anyone at the Triple K, her fears loomed up again.

Slade had told her he had the first shift with the miners clearing away the debris. Cat couldn't hear the strike of pickaxes or the grind of huge auger drill bits boring holes to loosen the soft base so it could be shoveled away. The wall, Slade had said, was at least ten feet thick, perhaps twenty. It could, at worst, be days before she could be rescued.

At 10:00 a.m., Slade was able to make contact with the Kincaid Ranch. After a tense conversation, he made his way to the wall and called Cat. After four tries, she still didn't answer and Slade grew worried. Another five calls. Nothing. Had Cat passed out? Was she sleeping because of the concussion? Slade tried to contain his apprehension.

Cat finally floated out of unconsciousness and weakly raised her left arm. The luminous dials on her Rolex told her she had been asleep for nearly six hours. She lay on the hard pebbled floor on her left side to ease the pressure on her right. Experimentally, Cat lightly ran her fingers over her ribs, feeling how swollen her flesh had become beneath her damp canvas jacket. Not good, she thought blearily. The radio clicked, telling her that Slade was trying to contact her.

The radio lay near her head and she depressed the button. "S-Slade?"

"Cat? My God, are you all right?"

A grimace pulled at her lips. "Fine. Went to sleep, didn't I?"

"Yeah. Six hours. You scared the hell out of me."

"S-sorry."

"Don't worry about it. Listen, I got hold of your family and everyone's flying out here to see you. They'll be landing soon and I've arranged to have someone meet them at the nearest airport. Your parents, brother, sister and her husband are coming."

Tears leaked down her face and she couldn't trust her voice.

"The whole family's coming?"

He laughed. "Yeah. I'm impressed. Not many families would fly to the rescue."

"We're close."

"How are you holding up?"

"I've had better days, Donovan. How are things out there?"

"We've got thirty men on line for you, sweetheart. We're hauling about a ton of dirt and rock an hour. I'm shoring the shaft up with new post and stull every three feet as we go."

Cat nodded, trying to lick her dry lips. "How many tons do you figure is between you and me?"

Slade's voice was apologetic. "About fifty tons of material. If we can keep up the pace I've set, we'll have you out of there in roughly fifty hours."

Fifty more hours in the damp darkness. It seemed like an eternity. Could she control her fear? It was so black, she couldn't even see her hand if she held it up in front of her nose. And she was thirsty. Her tongue felt swollen, her throat rough as sandpaper. She would have to crawl the width of the footwall to sip that trickle of life-giving water along the opposite wall.

"You're doing a good job, Donovan. I'm going to owe you a lot by the time you get me out of here."

"Don't worry, I intend to collect for my services, lady."

Cat smiled, allowing his voice to cover her like a blanket of balm. "Whatever you want, Donovan, within reason."

Slade chuckled indulgently. "Don't worry, the price won't be so high you won't want to pay it. Look, I'll check in on you an hour from now."

Panic nibbled at her crumbling control and Cat gripped the radio, dreading the return to silence. "For some reason, I trust you, Donovan. I shouldn't, but I do."

His voice came back, husky but velvet to soothe her shattered composure. "Hold that thought, Cat. I'll be here for you, that's a promise."

Two things happened in the next hour. The entire Kincaid family arrived at the Emerald Lady, and Slade could not raise Cat again on his radio. Rafe Kincaid, the brother, was close to exploding, firing questions faster than Slade could answer them. The tall, strapping Colorado rancher took off his Stetson, rolled up his sleeves, grabbed a hard hat and went into the mine to help in the rescue effort. So did Jim Tremain, Dal's husband. Slade liked Cat's family; Sam and Inez Kincaid, Cat's parents, and Dal Tremain, Cat's younger sister, helped to set up a place where coffee could be dispensed in the nearby shack and sandwiches could be made for the hardworking rescue crews. Millie, the Kincaid's housekeeper, who was apparently an integral part of the family, watched Dal's months-old baby, Alessandra, while Dal worked.

Within an hour of their arrival, the Kincaid family had organized chow lines for the hungry miners. Meanwhile, Slade had returned to the mine to continue directing the rescue. Slade tried to reassure Rafe that his sister had probably lost consciousness again due to her concussion. Rafe glowered at him, as if it were his fault, but Slade shrugged it off. Let the rancher expend his anger on the pickax he was wielding, instead of blowing up at him.

Cat tasted blood. She lay on her left side, shivering. What time was it? How many hours had passed since she had last lost consciousness? The luminous dials of her watch blurred and she blinked. Her vision was being affected and that frightened her. The radio was pressed protectively to her breast and she shakily turned it on, the red light glowing brightly in the darkness. Almost immediately, Slade's voice came through, soothing her fragmented nerves.

"Cat?"

She heard the anxiety in Slade's voice and was grateful for his undiminished caring.

"I'm alive," she announced, her voice weaker than it had been earlier.

"Thank God. What happened? You've been out ten hours."

"I can't hang on to consciousness, Slade. Keep blacking out."

"Don't worry about it. Let me go get your parents. Your family arrived some time ago. They're helping in the relief efforts. Rafe and Jim Tremain have been using a pickax and shovel the last ten hours. That's quite a family you've got. Hold on…"

Tears began to stream down her grimy cheeks when she heard her father's gruff voice, and then her mother's. Cat tried not to cry. She tried to sound brave and calm and steady, everything she wasn't. But when Rafe was put on, her voice cracked, betraying her real emotions. Whether it was the avalanche of tightly withheld feelings or the strain of her entrapment, Cat was barely coherent. There was so much she wanted to say; instead tears flowed in a warm stream down her cheeks, and her voice was wobbly and fragmented.

"S-Slade…" she choked.

"He's done a fine job, Cat," Rafe came back. "He knows what he's doing. Look, you just hang on. We've got an ambulance and paramedic crew standing by to take you to the closest hospital. Keep your chin up, Baby Sis. We all love you. Just remember all the times you and I dared danger and won. It'll be the same this time. I promise you."

Rafe grimly handed the radio back to Donovan. Neither man looked at the other; if they had, they would have seen tears forming in the corners of their eyes. Slade's face was slack with exhaustion and streaked with dirt and mud. He took the radio from Rafe.

"Cat?"

"Y-yes?"

"Thirty-five hours to go, sweetheart. You've got a passel of people out here who love you. Just remember that."

Grim, unshaven men, their eyes bloodshot and red-rimmed from too much dust, their hands bruised and bloodied with scrapes and cuts, continued on. Day had turned to night and then day again. The rain had stopped and so had Cat's infrequent radio exchanges. Yet, the Kincaids' courage inspired the rescuers, and there wasn't a man among them who slept more than a few hours between the mandatory six-hour shifts at the end of a shovel, a wheelbarrow or pickax. No one complained, and Slade found that phenomenal.

Rubbing his bleary eyes, Slade held up his watch. A portable generator provided light in the damp expanse of the mine. Five hours…five hours before they broke through and made contact. Was Cat on the left wall near the stream? No stranger to cave-ins, he worried about her dehydrating. The people who knew of his escapes had said he'd had nine lives. Well, Cat had better have nine lives; she'd need them to survive this one.

Cat wasn't sure what pulled her from her floating state. Was it the whoosh of fresh air into the staleness of the chamber or the frantic sound of steel-bladed shovels tearing a hole through the last of the wall that held her captive? Or was it actually recognizing Rafe's hushed voice, and Slade's? Whatever it was, she pulled on the last of her reserves and turned her head, which was now lying in a trickle of water, toward the men's urgent voices.

The light from Slade's helmet slashed through the thick silence of the chamber. His eyes widened as he

found Cat covered with filth and dust, her hair caked with
mud around her pale, translucent face. She lay on her left
side, stretched out across the stream of water. Thank God
she'd had the foresight to move to the water; all she had
to do was turn her face and sip from the shallow stream.
His admiration for her survival instincts rose. Next, Rafe
came through the six-foot opening, followed by a paramedic with a thin oak body board and a neck brace.

Slade reached her first, his hand closing protectively
over Cat's shoulder. He leaned over from his kneeling
position, his face close to hers. He whispered her name
twice before he saw her long dark lashes flutter and
barely open.

Cat saw a lopsided smile pull at Slade's mouth; his face
was tense, his eyes burned out with bone-deep exhaustion. She saw a flame of hope in them, too. She tried to
form his name on her parched, cracked lips, but only a
hoarse sound issued forth.

"Shh, sweetheart. Your knights in shining armor have
arrived. All I want you to do is lie very still while we get
you on this body board and truss you up like a Christmas goose."

She wasn't able to comprehend all that Slade said as
he leaned over her. The warmth of his breath coupled
with his husky voice flowed like balm across her, filling her with new strength. A small smile tugged at Cat's
mouth. She felt Slade's long fingers close gently across
her shoulder, and she knew he understood.

An incredible aura of care surrounded Cat during
those twenty minutes when the three men worked on
her. She was conscious for minutes at a time, lapsing
in and out of the arms of darkness. Rafe's voice or his
familiar touch on her hair would draw her back to con-

sciousness. She began to anticipate Slade's knowing, professional touch as he and the paramedic turned her over, placing her on the body board. She had grown used to the pain in her right side, but the callused pressure of Slade's fingers as he fitted the brace around her neck brought tears to her eyes.

The jab of a needle brought her to greater awareness, but once they had her strapped securely to the thin oak board Cat lost consciousness again.

Slade handed Sam Kincaid another cup of coffee as they stood in the waiting room of the surgical floor of the hospital. He wasn't sure who looked worse: he or Rafe. They were muddy, their hair plastered down from untold hours of sweat. Every muscle in Slade's body screamed for rest and the luxury of a hot shower. He wrinkled his nose; the brackish odor of the mine and his sour sweat smell surrounded him. He glanced at his watch. An hour ago Cat had been taken to the emergency room, attended by a number of physicians and nurses. None of the family had been allowed to go with her. Why didn't someone come out and tell them how she was?

Slade hadn't tried to hide his own emotions as he'd sat alongside Rafe in the ambulance. Cat had been chalk white; even her freckles had looked washed out. Her once-beautiful sable-brown hair was a stringy mat of mud and blood. There'd been a three-inch gash across her scalp, and she had bled heavily, but he was more worried about the skull beneath her scalp. Just how bad was her concussion? Judging from Cat's pallor and her prolonged bouts of unconsciousness, it was serious.

A doctor came through the double swinging doors, his face unreadable. He headed for the elder Kincaid. The entire family, with Millie and Slade, surrounded the doctor before he drew to a stop.

"Mr. Kincaid?"

Sam Kincaid nodded. "Doctor? How's my girl?"

"I'm Dr. Scott," he said, extending his hand. "Cathy is in serious condition, Mr. Kincaid. She's suffered two broken ribs. She's extremely dehydrated and we've got her on two I.V.s to restabilize her."

Slade closed his fist. His voice was strained. "And her head injury, Dr. Scott?"

Scott's narrow face became impassive. "Severe concussion. She keeps lapsing in and out of consciousness." His brow furrowed. "Is your name Slade?"

"Yes. Slade Donovan."

"Cathy is asking for you. We need to try and keep her awake. I want to keep her from going into a coma."

Inez Kincaid's thin face grew still. "A coma, doctor?"

"Yes. If I can keep Slade with her, she might rally enough to fight back and stay awake. We've got that portion of her head packed in dry ice to reduce the swelling." He looked up at Slade. "Let's get you cleaned up a little, son, and then, if you don't mind, I'd like you to remain with Cathy for a while."

Slade nodded. He followed Dr. Scott down the immaculate hall to a lounge. A nurse gave him a green surgical shirt and a pair of trousers to replace his filthy clothes. Slade took a quick hot shower and fought the deep drowsiness that tried to claim him. It wasn't yet time to sleep off the past forty-eight hours he'd been awake.

The nurse, a petite blonde with blue eyes, smiled once he emerged from the lounge. "Now you look like a doctor, Mr. Donovan. Follow me, please." She took him to the intensive-care unit, where each patient's room was enclosed on three sides with glass panels. Cathy looked dead. She matched the color of her sheets. Her hair had been washed clean and an ice pack placed carefully against her skull. The sigh of oxygen and the beeps of the cardiac unit made Slade grow wary. So many machines to monitor her fragile hold on life, he thought.

The nurse drew up a chair alongside Cat's bed. "You can sit here, Mr. Donovan."

Slade thanked her, but moved to the bed. He reached out and slipped his hand across Cat's limp, cool fingers. They had washed her free of all the filth.

"You look a little on the thin side, Mr. Donovan. They said you and the Kincaids worked but didn't eat. I'll have someone run down to the cafeteria and bring you dinner."

Slade smiled, grateful for the nurse's thoughtfulness. "Thanks," he replied. Then he shifted his attention to Cat. Funny, Slade told Cat silently as he cupped her fingers between his to warm them, you were a stranger to me three days ago. A lump rose in his throat. What is it about you that touches me so?

Perhaps it was the vulnerability of her features. Or the lips that reminded him of a lush, exotic jungle orchid he'd seen in Brazil—cherry red, even now in her present condition. Or perhaps it was her heart-shaped face, or the wide cheekbones that gave her eyes an almost tilted look. A smile eased the taut planes of Slade's face as he followed the coverlet of freckles from one cheek across her broken nose to the other cheek.

Slade reached over, lightly tracing the bump on her nose. How did she break such a pretty nose? And when had she broken it? He had so many questions to ask her, so much he didn't know about her that he wanted to know. "Cat?" he said softly. "Can you hear me? It's Slade. I've come for you. I want you to fight back." His fingers tightened against hers as he reluctantly straightened up. He blinked. Was he imagining things, or had her lashes fluttered in response to his hushed request?

When Cat awoke, she was clear at once as to where she was. The murmuring of the equipment caught her attention first. Then she forced open her weighted lids. She became aware of the broken snore of a man nearby. And then she felt the warm, callused fingers that enclosed her hand. Despite the pain, Cat turned her head to the right. Her eyes widened. Slade Donovan lay slumped in a chair, snoring, his chin sagging toward his chest and his hand gripping hers. A flood of warmth coursed through her and Cat closed her eyes. She was alive. Slade had dragged her back from the depths of the mine.

Her voice cracked when she tried to call his name. Cat used what little strength she had in her hand and squeezed Slade's fingers. She watched him awaken from the heavy sleep. Her heart wrenched as she saw the darkness shadowing his red-rimmed eyes. His face was gaunt and she saw the stress plainly carved on the stubbled, angular planes of his face.

Slade blinked, his hand tightening on her fingers. "Cat?" He whispered her name unbelievingly. Standing, he leaned over the bed, one hand cupping her cheek as he gazed disbelievingly into her barely opened eyes. "I'll be damned, you're awake."

She gave him a weak smile. "I-is this a dream?"

Slade laughed unsurely, his blue eyes burning fiercely with happiness. "If it is, sweetheart, then we're dreaming together." He reached over and pressed a buzzer to alert the nurse's desk. "Hold on, there's a whole passel of doctors who are anxious to see you awake."

Cat was thirsty, her mouth gummy. "What about my family?"

"They're here, waiting for you to open those beautiful emerald eyes of yours." He pressed a kiss to her cool, damp brow. "Welcome back to the world of the living. This calls for one hell of a celebration."

In the next two days, Slade was absorbed into the Kincaid clan. He ate with the family and shared rooms with them at a local motel. At breakfast on the third morning, Sam Kincaid sat with his family, a frown marring his features.

"Dr. Scott says Cat will need a place to recuperate. He's worried about her concussion and thinks she ought to be under some kind of supervision for at least eight weeks." Sam gave his wife a tender look. "With your hip operation coming up in two weeks, we won't be able to give Cat the care she needs."

Rafe's mouth twisted. "I've got the room; it's just the timing, Dad. We've had these Bureau of Land Mines investigations going on for the past few months, and they've thrown off our schedule for a while. Family comes first. I'll take Cat in; she's more important. If I made the time for the BLM, I can sure as hell make time for my sister."

Slade suddenly brightened. "I can help. I think, under the circumstances, Cat would be better off with me." The corners of Rafe's mouth turned down and Slade knew instinctively that Rafe felt this was strictly a family matter; outsiders weren't needed. Slade directed the remainder of his proposal to Rafe to win his approval, knowing the family would then agree to Cat's staying with him. He folded his large hands on the table. This reminded Slade of poker games. Some he had lost; others he had won. This time, the stakes were high, and he had never wanted to win more. Slade didn't question why he wanted Cat on his ranch to recuperate. Since the beginning, Cat had touched some inner chord of his. He wanted—no—demanded the opportunity to get to know her. His reasons for meeting her in the first place would take secondary importance. He put on his most serious expression and spoke in a low voice.

"I know you've only been allowed fifteen minutes at a time to visit with Cat. And she may or may not have been conscious enough to mention our relationship. I have a small ranch in southwest Texas. Del Rio, to be exact. In addition, my next-door neighbors, Matt and Kai Travis, can be of great help, if we need them. Kai's a physiotherapist and a nurse for the local grade school. I have a qualified nurse three miles down the road from my ranch and the perfect place for Cat to stay." Slade's voice dropped. "I think Cat's going to take a lot of attention in order to get back on her feet. I've been in three mine cave-ins myself and I know what they do up here," he said, pointing to his head.

"I care a hell of a lot for Cat. Those hours spent with her while she was buried were some of the worst of my life." He felt a tinge of guilt for implying that he and Cat had a relationship. But it wasn't a total lie, he rationalized. "Having been buried myself, I'm in a pretty good position to help Cat." His voice grew tight with undisguised emotion. "I can help her. I can get her up and over some of the reactions she's going to have because of this experience."

Rafe rubbed his recently shaven jaw. "Kinda like falling off a horse and getting scared to mount up afterward?"

Slade nodded, sensing the subtle shift of acceptance to his proposal. "Yes, only worse. Cave-ins affect everyone differently. Nightmares are common, and with her concussion, someone is going to have to monitor her closely so she doesn't sleepwalk or something. And that does happen." He looked at father and son. "I realize this is a family matter, but in this case, I think I can provide the type of care Cat is going to need."

Sam glanced over at his son. "Why don't we let Cat have a say in this before we decide for her?"

Slade held up his hand. "I really don't think that's necessary. I'm positive Cat will want to come home with me. Besides, I've got my twin-engine plane at the airport ten miles from here. I could fly her back in comfort while you'd have to make an awful lot of special arrangements to try the same thing. I'm sure Cat would like to be with me. I know how close she is with the family, but each of you have a lot of things going on right now. Hell, I'm between job assignments. And even if I wasn't, I'd drop what I was doing to come and take care of Cat."

Rafe looked hesitant, but shrugged his powerful shoulders. "Sounds like it may be the best thing for Cat, and that's the most important thing right now, Dad."

Sam Kincaid stared at Slade for a long time, mulling over the request. "It's settled then. Cat will go home with you, Slade."

Slade felt heat rise in his cheeks as he grasped the rancher's hand. "Thanks, Sam. None of you will regret your decision, believe me." A fierce wave of protectiveness nearly overwhelmed Slade as he rose from the table. He was shocked by his offer to care for Cat, yet nothing he'd ever done had ever felt so right. Gratefully, he shook each man's hand.

* * *.

Inez kissed her daughter's cheek. Cat had been transferred to a private room and the entire family, minus Millie, who, since the baby wasn't allowed in the room, was in the lounge, stood around her bed.

"You take care, honey," Inez said. She patted Cat's hand gently.

Cat blinked up at her mother. "You're all leaving?" There was a catch in her voice. She saw Rafe nod, his cowboy hat clasped between his roughened fingers.

Slade went to the other side of the bed and grasped Cat's left hand, while giving her a devastating smile meant to neutralize her questions. He hadn't talked to her about the arrangements and he knew the Kincaids hadn't either. Cat wasn't even aware of the agreement, but in all honesty, Slade felt Cat would thrive in the environment he could provide her. His initial reason for contacting her had been to offer her a lucrative business deal. Now, that all seemed unimportant.

"Everything's been taken care of, Cat. All you have to do is just lie there, look beautiful and heal up." He patted her hand, giving her a conspiratorial wink. Her green eyes widened as she stared blankly up at him.

Rafe leaned down, kissing her hair. "I'll be in touch, Cat. Slade's given us your phone number and I'll give you a call every couple of days to see how you're coming along." He smiled. "I'll keep you posted on what Goodyear and Nar are up to. They've had a lot of run-ins with each other lately."

Sam Kincaid was next, giving his daughter a slight smile. "You're in the best of hands, Cat."

"But—"

"Now, now," Slade soothed, "just relax, Cat." He

wished they would hurry through their farewells and leave before Cat upset his carefully constructed applecart. Dal and Jim Tremain came over, saying goodbye.

"Slade promised us you'd be in good hands," Dal told her sister. "We'd love to have you stay with us, but I don't think you'd get any rest with the baby around. I hope you understand."

Cat looked from Dal to Slade. His features looked suspiciously beatific.

"Well, uh, sure I understand. And Alessandra probably takes up all your time, anyway."

Dal looked relieved that she understood and pressed another kiss on Cat's waxen cheek. "Listen, we'll call you once you get to Texas. Slade's ranch sounds perfect for you."

Slade's ranch? Cat turned too quickly, pain causing her to gasp. She shut her eyes, all the questions purged from her mind. Slade gave her a game smile and waved goodbye to the departing family.

"Well, we'll be seeing you, Cat," her dad said, opening the door. "We'll call you once a week and see how you're comin' along. Bye, honey…"

Cat tried to speak, to beg them to stay. When the pain finally subsided, the door had shut and silence filled the void. She looked up at Slade, her eyes narrowed. Slade was still holding her left hand, his fingers warming her cooler ones. She wanted to jerk out of his grasp but had better sense than to try it, knowing what the movement would cost her in terms of pain.

"All right, Donovan, what is going down?"

"Donovan? You were calling me Slade before."

Cat compressed her lips, and set her jaw in a well-known Kincaid line that spelled trouble. "What cards do you have up that sleeve of yours? Everyone thinks I'm going to your ranch. No one's asked me. If you think you can shanghai me, you've got another thing coming."

Slade tried to look properly chastised and continued to run his thumb in a feather-light circle on the back of her hand. "Shanghai you?" He groaned and raised his eyes dramatically to the ceiling. "Cat, I simply volunteered my plane and my ranch as a place where you can properly recuperate." He stole a glance at her to see what effect his teasing was having. Absolutely none, he realized with a lurch. Slade girded himself for battle as spots of color came to Cat's cheeks and an emerald flame leaped to life in her eyes. She might be sick, but she wasn't helpless.

Slade tried to nip her reaction in the bud. "Listen to me, this is no time to get upset, Cat. I told your family that a nurse is three miles away from my ranch. Kai Travis and her husband, Matt, are good friends of mine. Dr. Scott said you'd need a warm, dry climate and the help of a nurse from time to time. Plus," he went on quickly, trying to stay ahead of her opposition, "your brother, Rafe, has been under a BLM investigation for the past few months and he's got his hands full trying to catch up on the ranch work. He wouldn't be able to devote enough time to you. Your mother's hip operation is in two weeks." Slade shrugged and managed a hopeful smile. "I offered my ranch because I can take good care of you, Cat, while you convalesce. I did what I felt was best for us at the time."

"Us?" came the strangled response. "There is no 'us'!"

Looking contrite, Slade released her hand and walked to the end of the bed, holding her outraged stare. "Yes, us."

Cat's mouth dropped open. And then she quickly closed it into a thin line. "You and I are complete strangers."

Slade had the good grace to look embarrassed. "Maybe we were a week ago, but I don't feel that way about you now. Not after everything we've gone through together." His voice became husky. "Before, I respected your work as a mining engineer. And then, when you were trapped, I saw and felt your courage. We both know the chances of your surviving that cave-in were pretty slim."

At the mention of the cave-in, a chill wound through Cat. She tried to throw it off, but a suffocating fear rose up into her throat, choking her. Panic followed on its heels and Cat struggled to pretend nothing was wrong. My God, she was breaking out in a cold sweat! What was wrong with her? The fear she felt was all-consuming as it flowed darkly through her. Shakily, she wiped her sweaty brow, refusing to look at Slade.

Finally back in control, she spoke. "That still doesn't give you any right to tell my family that they aren't needed, Donovan!" Her voice cracked. "I want my family, not you."

His face softened and Slade came to her side, brushing his knuckles lightly against her tear-stained cheek. "I know how fragile you really are, Cat, remember? I've been in cave-ins myself and lived to tell about it. I told your family that I knew what you were going to go through and I felt I was the best one for the job."

"I'm not your responsibility, damn it!"

"Don't get excited, Cat. The doctors want you to rest."

"Then you shouldn't have bullied your way into a family situation and taken over like you did!" She was breathing hard, each expansion of her ribs a fiery agony. Sweat glistened on her taut features and she lay back, her fists clenched. She turned her stormy green gaze on him. "You're not doing this out of the kindness of your heart.

I wish I could remember where I'd heard your name before. Then, I could put this together."

Slade winced. He wasn't sure himself why he was doing it. Sure, there was his business proposition, but that wasn't his primary reason for wanting her nearby. He felt like a greedy robber, stealing time to get to know Cat on a personal level. "You've a right to be upset and angry," Slade said, choosing his words carefully. "Rafe wanted to ask you if you wanted to go with me or come to the Triple K. For that, we owe you an apology. Rather, I do. Because I persuaded them that you'd be happy to come to Del Rio, Texas, with me." He held her angry gaze. "I may kick around the world, Cat, but I do have some roots. The ranch is nothing fancy, but it's nice. You're not out of the woods yet with your injuries, and I convinced your family that with qualified medical help nearby, my ranch would be better for you. Besides, when you get better, there's a business deal I'd like to discuss with you."

Cat eyed him suspiciously, somewhat mollified by his explanation. "I don't know... Let me think for a moment, Donovan."

He shrugged shyly. "All I'm asking is to be allowed to help you for eight weeks, Cat. Hey, this isn't a jail sentence. If you don't like the place, you can leave. No hard feelings. It's just that you can't be by yourself and I have the time plus the room."

Cat could have cried with frustration, but she had to admit that Slade was right. He had saved her life, and if she hadn't been so arrogant, she'd have listened to his warning.

"All right, Donovan," she muttered, "you saved my life. I didn't realize my mother was going to have an operation so soon." She rubbed the tears out of her eyes. "I hate feeling like an invalid! I don't like to be a burden on anyone, especially you. I don't call getting a crabby, sick mining engineer just payment for all that you've done for me."

His serious face creased in a boyish smile. "I happen to like crabby, sick mining engineers. For the next few months you're going to rest and get plied with a lot of stories told by one of the best storytellers in west Texas: me. You're to be a guest at my ranch, Cat. I just hope you like my company as much as I'm going to enjoy yours."

Cat refused to look at him. "I'm not a small child that needs to be told bedtime stories."

Slade's grin was wide, revealing white teeth. "We'll see," was all he said. He glanced at his watch. "Time for a nap. You close those beautiful eyes, and I'm going to talk with Dr. Scott about what time we can get you out of this godforsaken cell."

Cat wrinkled her nose. "Why should I be so anxious to trade one kind of prison for another?"

Slade came around and pressed a quick kiss to her fragrant hair. "It's really me who is your prisoner."

"Want to bet?" And yet, another part of her relaxed. If nothing else, the cave-in had taught Cat how alone a person could really be. Slade had reached her during those terrible hours, and her heart knew it even if her mind tried to tell her differently. "Don't mind me," she muttered in apology. "I'm not normally this crabby. I do appreciate your offer to take me in."

Slade enjoyed her pout; her lower lip was full and petulant. The urge to capture her mouth and gentle it beneath his was growing, but Slade gently tucked the desire aside. "I understand your apprehension, Cat. Things have moved mighty fast today. But you sit back and concentrate on getting well. Let me take care of you for a while."

With a merry look, Slade opened her door. "Rest. You're getting dark shadows beneath those lovely eyes of yours. Just dream of the Mourning Dove Ranch."

Cat watched Slade leave, enjoying his irrepressible, little-boy spirit that magically coaxed her out of her darkest moments. She shut her eyes, aware that the monstrous fear she had wanted to bury had miraculously vanished. Was it because of Slade? With a groan, Cat tried to look objectively at her motives for capitulating to him. He had vaguely mentioned discussing a business deal with her when she was better. Cat clung to that bare-branch offering and turned away from other feelings toward him.

Since when had she ever backed down from the demands of life? Only once. When she and geologist Greg Anderson had called off their relationship. But this was different, a voice whispered to Cat. Not only that, she reluctantly conceded, she didn't have the emotional fortitude it took to wage the necessary battle to get out of Donovan's clutches. And clutches they were, Cat thought grimly. Or were they? She couldn't ignore the tender light that burned in his sapphire eyes every time he looked at her. Right now, as never before in her life, Cat needed help from someone other than herself. And Slade had offered that help to her. Instinctively, Cat knew that Slade could help rebuild her strength from the rubble of the mine cave-in.

Chapter 3

"Well, Cathy, you're certainly going to be in good hands." Dr. Scott smiled as he looked through the release forms, while Cat sat patiently on the edge of the bed. With the help of one of the nurses, she had awkwardly pulled on a pair of cinnamon-colored slacks and a white tank top. Maine's summer weather was usually on the cool side, but at eight o'clock this bright August morning, it was already a sunny seventy degrees.

"We'll see about that, doctor," she told him dryly. Cat automatically touched her tightly taped ribs. Two of the lowest had been broken and if the break had been any higher, her breasts would have prevented the elastic torso wrap from being applied.

"Mr. Donovan's a paramedic, you know," the physician said, hurriedly scribbling his signature on the last paper.

"Is he?" Cat looked up with interest.

"Yes, a very capable one. I've given him a list of all the prescriptions you might need, Cathy. He's going to be watching you rather closely for the next couple of weeks because of your head injury. Let him know if you ever get dizzy."

Dizzy? The first time she'd sat up, she'd nearly keeled over. If it hadn't been for Slade's quick action, she would have fallen off the bed. At first, Cat had retreated from his watchfulness; she was unused to being confined by an ailing body and resented being taken care of. But after three days, Slade had remained his cheerful, positive self and Cat had had to beg him not to tell any more jokes. She had feared she would laugh out loud, and that awful, ripping pain would take her breath away. Slade's normally ebullient personality had sobered slightly, then shifted into a new gear—that of charming conversationalist.

A nurse arrived with the wheelchair for Cat's ride to the front doors of the hospital. "The dizziness may or may not be permanent," Dr. Scott warned, helping her into the chair. "The next two weeks will tell us quite a lot. Off you go, now. I understand you've an air trip ahead. Mr. Donovan's quite a good pilot."

Cat couldn't resist a smile. "Did he tell you that?"

"No, I saw his flight logbook sitting with some other items. Being a pilot myself, I got him talking. He's not only multiengine rated, he's up on all the instrumentation demands, too. Judging from the hours he's flown, I'll lay you odds he flies around the world. He certainly has a lot of stories to tell."

"Slade Donovan is a born storyteller, I suspect. Thank you, doctor, for everything."

"Have a good flight, Cathy. We'll be eager to hear how you're progressing."

At the curbside outside the hospital, the nurse eased the wheelchair to a halt. Slade was waiting next to the rental car for her. He was dressed in a freshly pressed blue shirt with epaulets on each shoulder. The shirt matched the color of his eyes, Cat thought. She had to stop herself from staring as if she were a gawky teenager instead of a woman older than thirty. His hair was dark and shining from a recent shower, his skin smooth of the stubble that always gave him a five o'clock shadow by four o'clock.

As Cat took his large hand and stood up, she suddenly saw Slade in a new light. His touch, as always, sent a warm rush through her. He had brought sunshine to her during her recent exile to Hades. She closed her eyes, allowing a fleeting feeling of dizziness to pass. Slade, observing her hesitation, moved closer to her left side, in case she should fall. Cat opened her eyes and raised her face to the sun.

"Do you know how good it feels to be outside again?" she asked, drawing in a deep breath of fresh air.

"Spoken like a true tunneler," Slade replied. His fingers tightened on her elbow. "Ready? I've got Maggie all fueled and waiting."

"Maggie?" Cat looked up at Slade tentatively.

Slade helped her into the front seat of the rental car and then shut the door. "Yeah, Maggie's my twin-engine Cessna. And she's as pretty as her name."

The sun shone warmly through the windows and a fragrant scent of pine drifted in, making the day magical for Cat. As Slade eased into the car, he flashed her a heart-stopping smile. "You'll like Maggie. She's built like a sleek greyhound. Red and white, lean and mean."

"The way you like your women, Donovan?" Now why had she made that remark? He had looked absolutely

elated, as if flying were going to release him from his
captive state on earth. Cat felt like a genuine wet blanket,
but Donovan cheerfully snapped the safety belt across
his lap and chest.

"Jealousy will get you nowhere. Maggie's big-hearted
enough to embrace both of us. Now, young lady, we've
got a light westerly wind and clear skies waiting for us.
Ready?"

Yes, she was ready, Cat realized. Perhaps it was partly
relief that they were putting miles between her and the
mine that had almost claimed her life, but another part
of her was ready for a new adventure. Cat closed her
eyes, allowing the wind to flow across her, moving her
hair languidly against her temple and neck. Slade's hand
settled momentarily on her own.

"Okay?"

The concern in his voice soothed her. "I'm fine. Just
enjoying my freedom, Donovan."

There was hurt evident in his voice. "My friends call
me Slade."

Cat opened her eyes and studied his clean profile, from
his straight brows to his finely shaped nose and mobile
mouth. "After all we've been through together, I guess
friend is a good word to use for us."

His hand left her fingers and he concentrated on his
driving. Friend was only one term he applied to Cat. He
also wanted to explore other possibilities. She affected
him as no woman ever had before. "Friends," Slade murmured. "That's a good place for us to start."

"I hope you have a lot of patience," she warned, feeling suddenly awkward.

Slade pinned her with an intense look. "Why?"

"Because I'm not myself, Slade. I'm jumpy and I snap when I don't mean to."

He smiled. "Lady, I've been snapped at by the best of them. I regard our two-month vacation at my ranch as just one more adventure."

"Normally I'd agree with you. But I'm afraid you're getting the raw end of this deal, Slade. I'll give you one more chance to back off from your offer to let me use your ranch as my hospital for two months."

The road spilled out of the small town, a narrow gray asphalt ribbon among the pine-clad hills. "Not on your life, Cat. I like a woman who has wanderlust in her soul!"

A smile shadowed Cat's mouth as she met Slade's merry glance. "Folks like us have it in their blood, don't we? What's so surprising about finding someone like yourself?"

"You try so hard to hide what's deep inside you, Cat Kincaid. I keep trying to figure out who closed you up like a book under lock and key. But I know you're not like those rocks I hunt, without feeling." He laughed, a deep, resonant laugh. "You're like an elusive emerald: hard to find, dangerous to extract and fragile when being cut and polished into a gem."

Cat felt the heat rise in her cheeks. "It's the nature of my work that makes me quiet. You're a geologist, you should know that."

Slade knew, but he couldn't resist teasing her. She responded so quickly to the slightest amount of goading. He really shouldn't, because she was far from well and Dr. Scott had warned him about overtaxing Cat. "I know what you're saying, Cat, but I like to see that green fire leap into your eyes. I'll let you off the hook, though.

Dr. Scott gave me a stern lecture about not picking on you…for now."

Cat closed her eyes, resting comfortably despite the tightness of the rib wrap. "That's big of you," she parried. "I suppose I ought to count my lucky stars for the reprieve."

"It's going to be a short one," he warned, shooting her a mischievous look.

Cat smiled. She knew he was baiting her again. He's good for me, she suddenly realized. But if the big, arrogant Texan knew that, he'd gloat. "What kind of pilot are you?" she asked, changing the subject.

"I got my license at Disneyland. Does that impress you?"

Laughter bubbled up in her throat but she squelched it, trying to avoid the subsequent pain. "You're so full of baloney. Come on, level with me."

"And if I did, would it make any difference?"

"My level of comfort would increase markedly if I knew more of your nefarious credentials." She suspected his credentials were far from nefarious, but enjoyed turning the tables on him for a change.

Slade appeared momentarily wounded. "Well, I have exactly 3,212 hours on my multiengine and I.F.R. ratings and have been qualified in twelve different aircraft during my short experience of flying."

"My comfort level is increasing," she admitted with a smile.

"Let's see. What else? The pilot is thirty-five, six feet four inches tall, single, roguishly handsome, makes a decent living, doesn't have any outstanding debts to speak of and currently is unattached." He looked squarely at her. "How's your comfort level now?"

"It just nosedived."

"Oh."

"I'd have felt better if you'd told me that you've flown around the world and are an excellent navigator."

"Well, I'm that, too."

"But for some reason, you thought your personal stats would be of more interest to me?"

"I don't want you to worry that you'd be a third wheel at the Mourning Dove Ranch. You're lucky—you'll be the only woman there besides Pilar, my manager's wife."

"Somehow, I don't quite know if that's lucky or unlucky, Donovan."

He grinned. "It's definitely lucky, Ms. Kincaid. Wait and see."

"Is that a threat or a promise?"

"Your choice. Which do you want it to be?"

"You're impossible, Slade, certifiably impossible."

"Yeah, that's what I've been told. But then, because of my impossible qualities, I did discover a couple of gem deposits over in Brazil." His voice grew softer. "Ever heard of the El Camino Mine, Ms. Kincaid?"

Cat blinked. The El Camino Mine had been splashed across all the mining and geology magazines two years earlier. It was, according to most geologists, one of the finest tourmaline discoveries in the world. The quality of the precious stones was almost flawless, and had sent excitement through the gem community. One fine deposit of watermelon tourmaline had set everyone on their ears. The pink stones without fractures were as rare as emeralds without flaws. She saw Slade's smile widen.

"Don't tell me...wait...you discovered that deposit! That's where I've heard your name before." Her thump-

ing heart underscored her awe. "I almost ended up working at that site," Cat added in disbelief.

"I know. I was the one who tried to persuade the owners to hire you to sink the shafts." Slade shrugged. "But
contracts are contracts; you were still building a mine
shaft in Austria at the time. Just think, we almost rubbed
elbows two years ago."

Cat was still shaking her head. "You discovered El
Camino. I can't believe it."

"You'll wound my poetic soul with barbs like that."

"Somehow, I think very little penetrates that thick
skin of yours."

"Mmm, careful. The right woman has open access to
my tender heart and loving soul."

"You're going to make me laugh whether I want to or
not, Slade. Now stop it."

He saw the faint smile at the corners of her lush mouth,
an unspoiled mouth that needed taming. Cat wasn't like
most women, he suspected. But then, he didn't expect
her to be. She lived in a world of brawny miners, skilled
in the reshaping of the earth, but resistant to women
who chose to be more than bed partners and housekeep-
ers. Slade knew by the set of Cat's jaw that she had endured much to succeed in her career, and he admired her
for that. Like the roses that grew wild behind his ranch
house, Cat had not only flowered, she had blossomed in
the harsh environment.

Slade cornered the car gently, turning into the flight-
service area of the airport. He pointed toward the tarmac.
"Say hello to my number-two gal, Maggie."

Cat's eyes widened in appreciation as she stared at the
sleek, aerodynamically designed Cessna. Slade might
appear laid back, but he took good care of his airplane.

Its gleaming white surface looked recently waxed, and the graceful red stripe running from the tail to the nose was a dark ruby color. The name on the fuselage read: Donovan's Services, Inc.

"Just what services do you perform?" she couldn't resist asking.

Slade put the car in park and pulled the key from the ignition. His grin was infuriating. "What service would you like rendered?"

Cat clamped her mouth shut, fiercely aware of the innuendo in his voice.

"If Maggie's number two, who's number one?" she persisted.

Slade released his seat belt and opened his door. Still grinning, he replied, "I'm holding that position open for a woman who wants to share my name and put her shoes under my bed and has as much wanderlust in her soul as I do."

"Chances are, like every other engineer and geologist I've met, you've got a woman in every port."

Donovan winked. "Maybe," was all he said, before he walked off to the flight office. Within ten minutes he had returned with his flight plan in hand. Then he helped Cat out of the car, remaining close beside her, their bodies almost touching.

"Maggie's beautiful," Cat told him admiringly.

"I knew you had a fine eye for beauty. Ready?"

Cat was as excited as if she were heading off to a new mining site in a new land. Slade's smile told her he understood the tremor of excitement in her voice when she said, "Yes, I'm ready."

Some of Cat's initial exuberance turned to gratitude when she entered the spacious cabin of the aircraft. Slade had taken out three seats on the starboard side. In their place was a comfortable-looking cot, complete with a pillow, blankets and sheets. He motioned her toward it.

"Dr. Scott said that you wouldn't be able to withstand a trip sitting up all the time. It's going to take us ten hours to reach the ranch."

She slid him a glance. "Do you spoil all your women this way? So much attention to detail?"

"Just for you, Cat. Just you."

"One part of me believes you; the other doesn't," she said lightly. Her expression, however, was thoughtful.

"You wound my Texas spirit," Slade complained. "Perhaps I'm your knight in shining armor carrying you off to my castle to live happily ever after. Would that be so bad?"

His wistfulness moved through her like a lover's caress. My God, the man could weave a spell with his intimate talk—something Cat had not often found in men she'd met during her travels. She'd been handed most of their lines, but Slade was different. The feeling was good, however, so she didn't really want to fight it.

"You have been my knight, Slade," she admitted shyly. "You saved my life."

He preened beneath her compliment, his careless grin spreading across his face. "Well, my lady, you have a choice: sit up in the copilot's seat for a while and keep me company, or lie down and enjoy the scenery."

"I'd like to sit up in the cockpit."

"Ah, to be with me. Good choice."

"No, I want to see how you handle this plane." Mustn't let him get too cocky, she reminded herself.

"Oh." A shadow crossed his face.

Cat had never run into a man who showed such a

range of feelings so easily. Most men stonewalled their emotions and responses, which was why she had found little incentive to establish an enduring relationship with any of them. With Slade, it was just the opposite. He was so obviously rattled by her reason for coming into the cockpit. Feeling more than a little guilty, Cat muttered, "I don't feel like being relegated to the rear just yet. I'm hungry for some good conversation."

Slade brightened and motioned her to move in front of him. "So, you'll even settle for me, hmm?"

Choosing not to reply, Cat sat down and observed Slade's attention to detail as he checked her seat belt before revving up the aircraft's two engines. Once he put on the headset, with the slender mike close to his lips, Slade was in another world. But even then, he made Cat feel as though they were a team, putting a headset on her and showing her where the volume dial was located.

She was entranced by Slade's hands: despite their size and roughness, there was a touching grace to their movements as they went through the preflight check. Heat unexpectedly moved through her. Slade was affecting her on levels she hadn't anticipated.

Meanwhile, Slade was receiving clearance to take off, and launched into a nonstop commentary about how Maggie was just as alive as they were, in her own way. Cat noticed how his fingers wrapped gently around the twin throttles positioned on the console between them, and she wondered what it would be like to be similarly stroked by this man. A slight smile hovered around her mouth as a fantasy began to take shape.

Suddenly, they were lifting off. All else was forgotten as Slade shot her a joyous look. She smiled back. Maggie sliced through the blue skies of Maine, her nose pointed in a southwesterly direction, toward Texas. Slade adjusted the fuel mixture and the engines began their deep, throbbing growl. Then the vibration minimized and peace blanketed the cabin.

"Maggie's crew will now ask their esteemed and illustrious passenger if she would like some coffee."

"I don't know about the esteemed and illustrious part—" she grinned "—but yes, the passenger would love a cup of coffee. Where is it? I can get it."

Slade held up his hand. "No, don't move." He reached down and retrieved a battered aluminum thermos from behind his seat. Setting the plane on autopilot, he expertly poured a cup and handed it to her. Cat's otherwise pale cheeks flamed as their fingertips met and touched. "You look more relaxed," Slade commented. "Is it because we didn't crash on takeoff or because you're on another adventure?"

"You have the disturbing ability to read my mind," she muttered, disconcerted.

Slade poured himself some coffee and recapped the thermos. Then, taking Maggie off autopilot, he wrapped his fingers lightly around the yoke. "Why does that bother you?"

"In my experience," she said thoughtfully, "few men look farther than the wrapping."

"You can't blame any of us poor males for looking, after spending months in some foreign jungle or godforsaken desert. Especially when someone as exotic-looking as you comes along."

Heat flowed up her neck. "I'm hardly exotic." Cat held up her left hand, showing him the calluses on her palm. "That's not exotic, Donovan. I've got hands like millions of women in Third World countries who wash and beat their family's clothes on some rock in a stream. I've got more muscle than women who work out daily at a health spa." She touched her hair. "I have to wear my hair so short that sometimes I'm mistaken for a man from the rear." She grimaced. "I'm hardly exotic, as you put it."

"So you think I'm handing you a line?"

Cat sighed, then admitted warily, "The way you talk, I almost believe you mean it."

Slade gave her a smoldering look. "I do mean it. Someday," he drawled in his thick Texan accent, "I'll show you why you're such an incredibly exotic woman."

Cat avoided his gaze as molten weakness again flowed through her like light refracting through a diamond. "If there is an enigma here," she said, laughing, "it's you. Tell me about yourself. And none of your Texas tall tales."

Slade laughed good-naturedly, then finished off his coffee and set the cup aside. "Now, there isn't a Texan alive who can resist embellishing the truth a bit."

"Try."

Slade scanned the instrument panel. They had climbed to fifteen thousand feet, the skies were azure and the sunlight bright. He pulled a pair of aviator's sunglasses from the pocket of his shirt and put them on. "I was born in Galveston, Texas, thirty-five years ago. My Irish father emigrated to the U.S. when he was a lad and he's still a fisherman in Galveston. My mother—she's the native-born Texan—owns a small shop at an exclusive mall, importing products from Ireland."

"Sisters? Brothers?"

"Seven. I'm the fifth-oldest, with three brothers and three beautiful sisters."

"Not exotic sisters?"

He tilted his head toward her and his voice lowered to an intimate tone. "No, you're exotic. They aren't."

He had such a convincing line, Cat thought, secretly delighted with his opinion that she was exotic and, of course, keeping in mind that it was just that. "I see. How did you get into geology?"

"I decided I didn't want to fish for a living like the rest of my family. I used to stand in the boat and watch the waves and wonder where they had come from. What far shore had they left? What ships did they encounter on their journey? Or what fish or mammals had graced them with their presence?" Slade shook his head. "No, my father told me when I was only this high—" he pointed to his knee "—that I was like my great-grandfather, who was the family adventurer. He could never stay in one place more than a few months at a time, either."

"And you have that same restlessness?" Cat offered. She handed him her empty cup.

Slade shrugged. "Restlessness? No. Life to me is one constant, nonstop adventure. I always want to know what lies over the next hill or wander through the next valley to see what and who is living there."

"Why the fascination with geology then? You could have been in the merchant marine instead, sailing the seas."

Slade smiled at her question. "Rocks held a special fascination for me. As a kid, when I finished my fishing chores, I used to pick stones up from the beach and study them. I'd wonder why one was black and another striated with pink and white. I used to hold them in my hand, trying to communicate with them and asking them their names and where they had come from."

Cat closed her eyes, resting against the seat. She could

imagine a dark-haired boy crouched on the ground, holding in his palm a rock that stirred his curiosity, staring at it with intense fascination. Slade was like a child who had never closed off his ability to dream and spin stories. He was special, Cat admitted, a rare being who still had the ability to fantasize, to ignore the limitations in a rationally constructed society. "And did any of them talk to you?" she asked softly.

"Of course they did," he said with a laugh. "That was what led me to ask my teachers about the life of a rock. Eventually they got tired of all my questions and ordered special books on rock hunting for me."

"And are you still like that little boy, always asking questions?"

"I haven't changed at all," Slade confirmed with satisfaction. "Today, I drive mining engineers to the edge of distraction."

"Where did you take your geology schooling?" she asked, curious to know more about his past.

"Is there any other place? Colorado."

"Like me. I'm impressed."

He feigned drama, his hand across his heart. "Finally! We have something in common."

"Oh, come on, it's not that bad."

"You made it seem that way, Ms. Kincaid."

She shot him a wry glance. "Despite any possible ulterior motives, you did save my life. The least I could be is a decent guest."

"Did I slip something into the coffee?"

Cat chortled. "Come on, I'm not always a stick-in-the-mud."

"Did I accuse you of that? No way, sweetheart. You're

a risk taker because your career demands it. It makes you an interesting and exotic woman. One of a kind."

"Oh, please! Get off the exotic kick, Slade."

"I can't help it if you're not a regular hothouse flower. That's your fault."

"Let's steer the conversation back to you. A four-year degree out of Colorado and then what?"

"Just kicked around the world prospecting like any other crazy rock hound."

"What kind of rocks? Is your specialty igneous?" she asked, remembering his tourmaline discovery.

"Why? Do I remind you of an igneous type?"

She smiled. Geologists usually chose one of three of the different rock types to specialize in: igneous, metamorphic or sedimentary. "You know what they say about the igneous type: they run hot and molten."

"So that's how you see me, eh?"

"I see you being bored by sedimentary exploration. You're strong and robust; you're the sort who would challenge igneous rock and tackle it with ease. Although we both know sinking mine shafts into rock that doesn't want to be penetrated isn't easy."

"Granted. Or should I say: granite."

"Slade, I'm not even going to laugh because that's a sick rock joke you'd use on a freshman in geology."

"Nobody said my humor was always in top form." He gave her his innocent little-boy look.

"Do people always forgive your transgressions?"

"More importantly, will you?"

"I don't hold grudges."

"But you'll remember."

Her voice grew soft. "I'll remember."

"Well, enough of me," Slade countered. "How about

yourself? I had the pleasure of meeting your entire family, so I got an idea of what you're like."

"I'm sure Dal and Rafe gave you an earful about me."

"Don't sound so wary."

With a grimace, Cat pretended to pay more attention to the sky around them. "All right, you tell me what they said."

"Let's see, what adjectives should I use?"

"If you use exotic, I'm going to take everything you're saying as one-hundred percent baloney, Donovan," she warned him.

"Texans can be serious at times, too," he reassured her, attempting a somber look.

"We'll see. So what do you think of me, now that you've learned all from my family?"

"You're a daredevil. Rafe told me how you two jumped your horses between two cliffs."

"Did he also tell you that my horse stumbled on the other side and fell? I broke my arm and nose."

Slade shook his head. He saw and felt Cat relaxing. She had been so long in isolation with men that she was closed up. He saw the softening of her lips, heard new life in her voice and saw more color stain her cheeks. If nothing else, during the next eight weeks of recuperation, Slade would remind Cat of her decidedly female side, gently drawing all of it to the surface. He knew he could do it; there was a chemistry between them.

"Rafe said you and he made the jump, but that Dal had chickened out. I'd probably be with Dal." Slade paused and looked at her. "What you did matches the kind of career you chose. Mining engineers have to be a blend of conservatism and daring."

"What I did didn't take much brains—is that what you're saying?"

"Hey, we were all young once and we all pulled our share of foolish stunts. I'm chalking up your wild ride to youth."

"If the truth be known, I was scared spitless. Rafe was angry because Dal wouldn't go and he—well, I let him coerce me into doing it."

"But you didn't want to?"

"Are you kidding me? That was an eight-foot leap. I was riding a green four-year-old quarter horse who'd never seen a cliff, much less jumped one. I didn't know if he was going to jump it, skid to the edge, fall into it or what."

Slade pursed his lips, going for a second cup of coffee and offering her some. She declined. "Interesting," he murmured.

"Oh?"

Slade put the plane back on autopilot and sipped his coffee. "That gives me a useful piece of information about you."

"Uh-oh…"

He grinned. "It's not bad. What it tells me is that despite an overwhelming fear, you did what had to be done and carried it out successfully. I call that courage."

"That particular stunt was called stupid. What took courage was to tell Dad how I broke my arm and nose. Rafe got the belt on his behind. I would've gotten a licking, too, if I hadn't gotten broken bones."

Savoring the hot liquid before he spoke, Slade commented, "You can still take that basic premise about yourself and apply it like a formula to any other type of situation. No, there's a basic vein of courage in you. I like that."

Cat warmed beneath Slade's compliment; the obvious pleasure in his voice was like a physical caress. She rarely enjoyed men in the field. But she wasn't in the field; her contract assignment had been delayed because of her injury. Cat's brows dipped.

"What's bothering you?" Slade asked.

"Hmm? Oh, I was just thinking that because of this accident, I've blown my next assignment." She had talked briefly to Ian Connors, the man who had hired her. Technically, because of her unexpected injuries, she didn't have to honor the contract. Cat had managed to hold off giving him an answer on whether she'd fulfill the contract or not. Just the bare thought of entering another mine made her break into a cold sweat.

"In Australia?"

"Yes. A two-year contract."

"You needed a vacation anyway, Cat."

He was right. She hadn't walked away from work for five years now. "Work is play for me," she tried without enthusiasm. How could one mine cave-in turn her life-long love into a terrorizing nightmare she never wanted to experience again?

"Still, we all need time away, Cat."

"Do you?" Cat asked, trying to deflect talk of her going back to work. Specifically, into a mine.

"Sure, I'm only human. I can stand the jungle or being a sand rat for only so long and then I have to get back to civilization and get human again."

"Are you between assignments?"

"Yeah. I was heading home to Texas for a couple of months."

"How long since you were home?"

"One year. I think you'll like Mourning Dove. For west Texas, it's a nice spot."

"A lot of sand, scrub brush, jackrabbit and deer?"

"That, too."

"Tell me about the ranch. Is it a working one?"

"Not anymore. I've more or less created a deer preserve out of it and sold off all the cattle. I have a Mexican family who lives nearby who takes care of it during my absences. Carlos and his wife, Pilar, are the caretakers." His voice grew warmer. "Pilar is the best cook this side of the Mexican border. I can hardly wait to get home and fatten up on her cooking." He patted his hard, lean stomach meaningfully.

Cat understood; she was underweight as well. Perhaps the Mourning Dove Ranch wasn't going to be all that bad after all. Slade wasn't the womanizer she had first thought. As a matter of fact, she was going to have to reevaluate many things about Slade. Cat couldn't apply her earlier experiences to him because he didn't fit into the categories of men she had known before. She slid him a warm look.

"Has anyone ever accused you of being different?"

Slade laughed solidly, flipped a switch to take the plane off autopilot and resumed the task of flying. "Many times. Why? Does it bother you?"

"You are a bit disconcerting." And disturbing. Every movement he made reminded Cat that Slade was a consummate athlete; there was never a wasted motion and he had a coordination that at times took her breath away.

"But not threatening?"

She paused a moment before answering, "No."

"What took you so long to answer my question?"

Cat refused to be baited by him. "Nothing."

"You were trying to decide whether to be wary of me or not, weren't you?"

"Quit being such a know-it-all."

"Your brother, Rafe, spoke a lot about you." He added in a gentler voice, "Good things. How you love the land and the animals. How easily you were moved by a sunset. Or by a foal being born. I like my woman to be easily touched by everything around her."

A tremor vibrated through her and Cat discreetly did not ask what Slade meant when he called her his woman. His ability to put everything, including their conversation, on intensely personal terms rattled her. "Life, to me, is a continual blossoming," she admitted, her eyes darkening with fervor. "All we have to do is keep our hearts and minds open to receive its gifts."

Slade's mouth curved into a knowing smile. "Why are you so afraid to show that side of yourself?"

"I think all of us hide parts of ourselves," Cat said defensively.

"I'm an open book."

"Sure you are. That's why you unexpectedly dropped into my life."

Slade glanced quickly at her. "Best thing I ever did."

Cat shook her head. "So, if you aren't an igneous type, what are you?" she asked, ignoring his innuendo.

"I'm a sedimentary man. Ah, the eyebrows lift and the eyes go wide. What do you know, I finally got a rise out of you."

"You get a rise out of me every time we spar," Cat parried.

"I don't see us as sparring."

"Call it whatever you want."

Slade scratched his head. "Somehow, I'm going to have to instill some trust into our relationship."

Cat almost blurted out, "What relationship?" But she bit back the response. "Why sedimentary rock? Most geologists are bored stiff by that type."

"You find a fair amount of gem-quality stone in sediment, that's why."

"Ah, now you're beginning to make sense. You're more a gem hunter than a geologist." Cat eyed him speculatively. "You're a prospector in search of the mother lode, aren't you?"

Slade checked the instruments, a smile pulling at his mouth. "You mean a treasure hunter? A modern-day gold miner?"

"You said it; I didn't."

"I hear distaste in your voice." Slade's voice was deceptively noncommittal.

Cat tried to evade his comment. Greg had done this to her; he had placed the mining of precious gems over their love for one another. And it had killed their relationship. Struggling not to let her past experience taint her idea of Slade, she said, "There's nothing wrong with finding the world's major tourmaline deposits. It can make you a very rich man."

Slade looked at her a long time. He saw the discomfort in every line of Cat's mobile face. "And you think that's why I go chasing after gem mines?" he probed.

"I don't know. Why do you? You don't strike me as the typical treasure hunter." Which was true. Slade was unlike Greg in many ways, and for the better.

Slade was glad that Cat had asked instead of just assumed why he specialized in precious stones. Even he had to admit that most of the gem hunters he knew were like the old-timers during the gold rush. They were loners to begin with, shaped by the roughness of their life-style. Most of the men he knew carried pistols on their hips and knives in their belts. And they all had one driving force in common: they wanted to get rich. Money took precedence over anything else that life might offer them.

"Gems hold a special fascination for me, Cat. In a way, they're like people: when you first discover them, put a miner's light on them, they're rough and unpolished. Then, as you take the time to gently loosen them from the matrix of pegmatite or sediment, you can carry them to the surface. It's exciting to realize that what you carry in the palm of your hand hasn't ever seen sunlight. As you bring it to the surface to watch the light refract through it for the first time, you're the first one to ever witness it." Slade gave her a soft smile. "It's much like watching a person unfold in front of you, watching how they react and respond. Later, a jeweler will look at that rough specimen with a knowing eye, spot its inclusions and watch how the light refracts through it. He'll cut it to bring out all of the natural fire and brilliance that has waited millions of years to be brought to life."

"That's an inspiring view." At least he hadn't mentioned money as his prime goal, Cat thought.

The corners of his eyes crinkled and he shared a look with her. "I'm comfortable with it. Although there are some people who are always going to be as impenetrable as iron ore."

"How many diamonds have you met in your life, as opposed to plain old iron ore?" she asked curiously.

Slade laughed, enjoying her easy acceptance of how he saw the world. "I've met many an uncut gemstone in both men and women."

"And a few iron-ore types?"

"Sometimes. In my business, as you already know, we're a pretty interesting lot to begin with."

Cat closed her eyes, suddenly exhausted for no reason.

"Tired?" Slade guessed. "Or bored with this piece of iron ore?"

"You're hardly iron ore, Slade Donovan. But right now I think I'd better get some sleep before my opinions get me in trouble. I feel so tired all of a sudden."

"Maybe it's the company you've been keeping."

"Now, Slade," she reassured him, her eyes sparkling mischievously, "you're hardly a bore, and you know it."

A slow smile touched his strong mouth. "Just wanted to make sure."

"You're such an egotist," Cat said, yawning, and slowly rose, then made her way from the cockpit to the cot in the cabin. Carefully, she lay down on her left side, then closed her eyes and spiraled into sleep.

Chapter 4

There was a mild bumping. Cat heard a change in the aircraft's engines and stirred. She had fallen asleep just as they had flown over Pennsylvania's border. Now they seemed to be landing. Probably refueling, she thought groggily, closing her eyes once again. With a sigh, she slid back into sleep.

Slade quietly made his way from the cockpit. It was early evening and the shadows were long as the sun edged toward the western horizon. Cat lay on her back, still sleeping soundly. He'd made a feather-light landing, the wheels gently kissing the parched Texas airstrip. Now they were home. Home... The feeling moved powerfully through him as he gazed down at Cat. Yes, they were home.

He approached the cot, noting that Cat's skin was stretched tautly across her cheekbones and dark shadows lay beneath her thick lashes. It was her mouth, however, that made his body tighten with sudden, almost painful awareness of just how much this woman affected him. He felt the same kind of excitement that thrummed through him when he was close to finding the one rock leading him to a vein of hidden treasure.

Cat was a treasure, Slade had decided. He crouched down, one hand resting near her head and the other on her slender arm. Hungrily, he brought her close to him, breathing in her sweet scent. How vulnerable she was. Leaning over, Slade gently caressed her parted lips with his.

Cat's lashes fluttered as she felt the warmth and pressure of Slade's mouth molding to hers. Heat spiraled through her like a ribbon, flooding upward on its dizzying course. Slade's breath fanned lightly across her cheek. Her heart pounded as his mouth coaxed her lips open, and she responded to him unquestioningly.

The instant Slade felt her returning pressure, his mouth worshipped her as if she were a fragile gift that would shatter if mishandled.

Cat drowned in Slade's honeyed invitation, her nipples hardening against the confines of her blouse. He was strong and good and tasted wonderful. Her nostrils flared as she drank in the scent of his special blend of male aroma combined with a slight hint of shaving cream.

"Sweet," he whispered against her wet, responsive lips. "God, you're sweet emerald fire."

Cat forced her lashes open, and became hotly aware of the naked desire in Slade's face. His eyes held her captive with a look that went straight to her heart. This man was supremely confident of his masculinity.

"Did I turn into a frog or something while I slept?" she asked huskily, smiling.

Slade caressed her hair. "Hardly. You're more like Sleeping Beauty!"

It was too much for her and Cat could barely think. Suddenly aware they were on the ground, she glanced around. "Where are we?"

Slade slowly moved out of his crouched position, knowing that if he didn't, he'd be sorely tempted to kiss Cat again. "We're in Del Rio, Texas. We've landed at Mourning Dove Ranch in time to see the sun set in a couple of hours."

"We're at the ranch? Already?"

"Sure." Could she be as shaken as he was by that kiss? he speculated. Or was it simply that her bearings were off?

"How long did I sleep?" Cat looked at him shyly. Slade had his answer.

"A long time." He reached out, brushing her flushed cheek. "But you needed it. Come on, I'll help you up."

Cat took his hand, biting back a cry of pain when Slade carefully levered her into a sitting position. Her face ashen, Cat thanked him and gripped the edges of the cot. Slade went to the hatch and opened it. The early evening sun and a slice of blue sky showed through the door. Dry Texas heat flowed through the cabin. Cat took a deep breath, then released it, feeling the tension pour out of her.

Slade grinned and lifted his hand in welcome as Carlos, his manager, came down the long, narrow dirt strip in a beat-up Jeep. "Our chariot has arrived, my lady," Slade announced to Cat. "Are you ready to go to your castle?"

"Lead on, my prince," she said with a flourish, moving

to the door. "I'm rather curious to see this castle you've hidden in the desert."

And desert it was. The earth was the color of bone, and was strewn with twisted, jade-green sagebrush. A few long-eared, black-tipped jackrabbits were in evidence, and the sun was strong and bright.

Cat gripped Slade's hand as he led her down the stairs. She stood back and watched as Carlos climbed out of the olive-colored Jeep. He greeted them in Spanish, waving his straw cowboy hat exuberantly. As the men heartily embraced each other, Cat smiled. Carlos and Slade acted more like family than employer and employee.

With one arm around Carlos, Slade turned and introduced her to his number-one man. Carlos bowed grandly, then took her hand and kissed it.

"Señorita Kincaid, welcome to Mourning Dove. We've been expecting you for some time now." Carlos's coffee-colored face beamed with genuine sincerity as he released her hand.

Cat slid Slade a glance. "You've been expecting me for some time?"

Slade shifted awkwardly.

"Si, señorita," Carlos confirmed, seemingly unaware of his friend's discomfort. "Come! My wife, Pilar, has your room ready. Señor Slade told us of your injuries and Pilar can hardly wait to mother you as she has our other six children. She even has chicken soup waiting."

Cat smiled and walked with Slade toward the Jeep. "Six kids?"

"Si. Señor Slade has sent two of them to college already. He's practically their uncle. The other four are helping with the ranch when they're not in school."

Cat's luggage, which had once been destined for Australia, was carefully placed in the Jeep. Slade sat in back, perched precariously between all the bags, while Cat sat in front. She was grateful that Carlos carefully negotiated the dirt road leading from the airstrip to a rambling adobe brick ranch house surrounded by sturdy cottonwood trees. Cat tried to ignore the aggravating rib pain that seemed to be settling in for good, and concentrated on the ranch instead. The house was a testimonial to Texas's tradition of spaciousness. She noticed solar reflectors on the roof, and the number of windows made her gape. She turned her head slightly to Slade, who sat behind her.

"You wouldn't have had something to do with the design of this house, would you?" she asked sweetly.

His teeth were white against his tanned skin. "Why? Does it show?"

"Yes. How much reconstruction did you do after you moved in?"

"After I made my fortune from the El Camino, I was able to afford the walls of windows facing east and west. There's more, but you'll see it all when we get inside."

Cat guessed that there were at least fifteen rooms in the house. Four chimney stacks rose from the roof. It would be fun to tour this house, she thought. What would it reveal of Slade?

Carlos parked the Jeep beneath a cedar-topped garage with no sides. Next to it stood a woman who looked to be in her forties, and whom Cat assumed to be Pilar. Her black hair was tightly wound into a crown of braids and she wore a simple white peasant blouse and a scarlet skirt. Her welcoming smile reminded Cat of Slade's, and she smiled in return, feeling lighter and happier than she had in a long while.

Pilar gripped Cat's left hand and squeezed it gently,

introducing herself in halting English. Her warm brown eyes sparkled as she motioned for Cat to follow her.

If Cat could have taken a deep breath, she would have. The ranch reminded her of a geode: plain, gray and undistinguished on the outside, but once opened, a crystalline palace of shimmering beauty. Cat walked from the foyer and into the expansive living room. A slanting cathedral ceiling rose skyward with windows facing west to catch the late-afternoon and setting sun's light. In one corner a floor-to-ceiling granite chimney, glinting with feldspar and mica, rose like a speckled black-and-white giant.

Trees and jungle foliage grew along a waterfall and stream winding through the living room. The wall opposite the windows held ten long shelves with a gem collection that took her breath away. Cat automatically held her ribs as she walked to the wall. Strategically placed lights brought out the rough, unpolished gems that ranged in size from as small as her fist to as large as a watermelon.

"Oh, Slade…" she whispered, entranced as she stood staring at them. She felt him come to her side.

"Like the collection?"

"Like it? This would rival some of the better museums I've been in."

"Each specimen is from one of my trips."

Cat couldn't resist stroking a cantaloupe-size blue topaz crystal growing out of brown colored lepidolite rock. "And I'll bet each one is a story," she said, grinning, and returned the gem to its niche.

Slade tried to look serious. "I told you, I'm a master spinner of tales. True tales, I might add."

"I intend to take you up on some of them, believe me," Cat said, while inwardly estimating that this gem collection was easily worth at least a quarter of a million dollars.

"Not today, however." He led her across handwoven Navaho and Hopi rugs and out of the living room. "Pilar's already giving me dirty looks because I haven't taken you to your room and gotten you into bed to rest."

"Slade, I'm not an invalid. As a matter of fact, I hate being sick and I can't stand being bed bound. Busted ribs might prevent me from riding one of those horses in the corral, but they can't stop me from being mobile."

He motioned down a wide hall and opened the first door on the left. Sunlight spilled into the room and one wall was composed all of glass supported by weathered cedar spars. Palms, their fronds grazing the slanted ceiling, graced each corner. A handwoven multicolored quilt covered the cedar double bed. The dresser and drawers were also of cedar and, if Cat wasn't mistaken, hand carved. The room was spare, but homey.

"Over here is a desk, should you feel the urge to write a letter," Slade said, motioning toward it, "or make phone calls. There's also a stereo and a TV hidden in the cabinet over there, should you get bored with our company."

"Slade, what a thought!"

"Carlos will bring your luggage in a minute. In the meantime, the bathroom's over there and if you want to sweat out anything, the spa is directly outside the glass doors, across that brick patio and straight ahead. I'll see you later."

Cat turned as Slade quietly slipped out the door, leaving her to get adjusted to her new surroundings. She was grateful for this act of consideration. In fact, she felt better already. A knock on her door announced Carlos with her bags. Pilar arrived moments later to put all her clothes away for her, leaving Cat feeling extremely pampered and a little helpless. To remedy that feeling, she decided on a hot shower. Stepping to the dresser, she chose a pair of pale blue cotton pants and a dainty, short-sleeved turquoise blouse. Now that she was between jobs, she could allow herself to dress more femininely. On the job she always wore khaki pants, a T-shirt or a short-sleeved blouse.

Alone again, Cat stripped down, gently pulling apart the Velcro binding around her rib cage. The cloth bandage that had surrounded her torso fell away, leaving a welt-like imprint on her flesh. She reveled in the hot shower and wrapped herself with a white towel afterward. Relaxed, she padded into the bedroom to face the chore of getting dressed. No longer was she in the hospital where one of the nurses could help her get into her bra and then expertly wrap the elastic bandage around her ribs. Slade had discussed it with her earlier, saying that he was sure Pilar could do it for her instead.

Pilar was eager to help and understood Cat's instructions fully. She hooked Cat's lacy white bra and helped her into her slacks. Despite all her well-meaning attempts, however, Pilar could not rewrap the torso bandage properly. By the fourth try, Cat was sweating from the pain while Pilar tried futilely to maneuver and close it.

"I'm so sorry, *señorita*. Perhaps you can go without it?"

"I wish I could, Pilar. Would you go get Slade, please? He knows how to close it."

Pilar's eyes widened slightly as she set the wrap aside, but she said, "I'll get him right away, *señorita. Uno momento,* eh?"

"Si," Cat agreed. Already, she could feel a flush crawl-

ing up her neck and into her face. Slade would see her blushing. Well, what else could she do? Wear the bandage, not bathe and smell? No way. Slade was a paramedic: he would know how to rewrap her quickly and expertly.

There was a brief knock at the door and Slade entered. "Pilar said you're in trouble," he said, slipping through the door. He saw Cat's red cheeks, and knew at once that she was having problems.

"Pilar gave the bandage the old college try, but it didn't work. Would you mind wrapping it around me?"

Slade nodded, deliberately keeping his gaze above her neck as he approached her. "I'd ask Kai Travis to do this, but I just called their ranch and they won't be home for two more hours, according to their maid, Maria."

Cat watched him pick up the bandage and she stood, carefully raising her arms so that he could place it around her. "That's all right. Pilar did her best. I guess we both should have expected this. Wrapping ribs is an art."

Slade leaned down, perusing the large black-and-blue bruise that covered most of her right side. He gently touched the outer edges of the area. Cat inhaled slightly. "Hurt?"

"It's okay."

"Lie to anyone but me, Cat."

"It hurts like hell."

Slade grimaced. "And Pilar's handling of the situation hasn't helped, has it?"

"Hindsight. Don't be upset with her. Can you get it on?"

"I'm not upset with Pilar. Grip my shoulder with your left hand and hold on." He noticed a thin white scar that traversed the left side of her rib cage. "Looks like you've

taken your share of rib injuries before," he commented.
"All right, exhale. I'll make this as fast as possible."

Cat did as Slade requested, her fingers sinking into
the folds of his blue chambray cotton shirt. She tried to
steel herself against the coming pain. Slade was quick
and efficient. She felt his other arm go around her shoulders the instant he closed the Velcro on the left side of
her ribs, below her bra.

"You're a good patient, Cat Kincaid," he praised huskily, watching all the color drain from her face. Despite
the pain, she hadn't moaned or complained. Slade guided
her to the edge of the bed to sit down. Picking up her
blouse, he helped her slip it on. Then he crouched down
in front of her, buttoning it for her.

Cat forced a slight smile. "Thanks…" Each touch of
his fingers on the pearl-shaped buttons sent a tremor
through her, erasing the pain, fanning a liquid flame
higher and brighter within her.

"We can do one of two things," he told her. "I can
try to teach Pilar the art of wrapping or do it myself."
He glanced up at her. "Frankly, I don't think your ribs
need extra punishment while Pilar learns. You have any
qualms about me doing this for you once a day?"

Cat shook her head. "No. Anything's better than having someone learn to do this right now. It's just too painful for me."

"It's my fault. I thought anyone could wrap ribs."

Relaxing as the pain lessened, Cat managed a slight
smile. "It's nobody's fault, Slade. I'm not upset if you
aren't."

Slade captured the top button, just above the slight
swell of her cleavage. "We'll manage this together,"
he promised, noting that his voice had thickened. He

couldn't react like this to Cat, or she'd choose to suffer through Pilar's attempts, no matter what the cost to herself. No, when he kissed her again, Slade wanted her to know it wouldn't be an occasion for pain. He wanted her to be totally willing and if he had read the sultry look in her half-closed green eyes correctly, they were both anticipating when it would happen again.

"You're done," he said briskly. "Now, I was making a pitcher of 'welcome to Texas' margaritas out at the bar. Care to join me?" Slade stood and held out his hand to her. He saw disbelief in Cat's eyes, as if she'd expected him to take advantage of the situation. His smile broadened.

Cat gripped his hand, watching as her fingers were swallowed up in his palm. Tiny shivers raced up her arm as she rose.

"Do you make a mean margarita, Slade?"

"How mean do you want it?"

"Make mine a double."

"For the pain or for the embarrassment?"

Cat wondered when he was going to let go of her hand as he led her to the door. He seemed reluctant to relinquish her fingers. "You're less of a brigand than I first thought," she confessed.

"Didn't you know? Texans are the epitome of discretion. Not to mention being gallant gentlemen."

"Careful, or you'll start believing your own tales."

His laughter floated down the hall as they walked toward the living room. "Caught. Again."

Cat followed him to a cedar bar that sat opposite the huge fireplace. Sunlight lanced through the area, setting the honey-colored cedar aglow. She took a seat on one of the leather-upholstered black bar stools while Slade went behind the bar and finished making the promised pitcher of margaritas. Pouring two, he placed them on a tray then motioned her to follow him out to the screened-in porch.

The breeze was dry and lifted a few errant strands of her damp hair. Slade pulled out a chair and she sat down, taking the proffered drink.

Slade sat opposite her, crossing one leg over the other. A hundred feet from the porch, a slender ribbon of water wound its way through a line of cottonwoods. He sighed happily. Everything he valued most was right here before him—including this slender young woman he had promised to nurse back to health.

"What did you use, 150-proof tequila?" Cat grinned, a sweet shiver rippling through her.

"You asked for a double," he reminded her innocently. "I took you at your word."

Cat eyed the cold, beaded glass. "This would neutralize a tank," she grumbled good-naturedly.

"Drink it slowly. Texas is like the Caribbean or South America; you're living at a different pace than most Americans."

She sipped the tart drink and nodded. "I've served my fair share of time on those kinds of jobs, too. I call it Bahama time."

Slade grinned. "Yeah. If you ask, 'How far is it?' they'll say, 'Not far, not far.' And if you ask, 'When?' they'll say, 'Soon, soon.'"

"Maybe those people have the right attitude, Slade. Maybe we westerners are too driven and don't know how to relax." She stretched luxuriously.

"Do you know how?" he asked, holding her amused gaze.

"No. I keep looking at this enforced eight-week convalescence and see myself going crazy. What will I do?"

Slade gave her an eloquent shrug. "I've got plenty of work waiting—assay reports, charting, core samples to check." Slade slid her a careful glance. "If you get bored, you might want to pitch in..." he baited.

Cat chuckled and raised her glass in toast. "Not a chance, Slade. Not a chance."

Cat couldn't get to sleep, no matter how hard she tried. Each time she closed her eyes, images of her entrapment in the mine loomed before her. Thank God, Slade had kept her going, or she'd have given up all hopes of rescue. Slade. Almost immediately, she felt relief from the terror gnawing away at her. She drifted off to sleep, remembering how his lips had felt....

Toward 4:00 a.m., Cat jerked awake. Shakily she got up and pulled on her white cotton robe. Making her way through the still house, Cat stood at the screen doors. Although she was cold, sweat bathed her brow. How long she stood there, her forehead resting against the cool aluminum molding, she didn't know. Only when she heard a door open and then quietly close did she straighten up, her attention drawn to the hallway.

Slade rubbed his face wearily as he padded into the living room. Seeing Cat standing forlornly near the doors, he halted abruptly.

"Cat?"

"I'm all right," she replied faintly.

He heard the strain in her voice and walked over. Even in the dim light, he could see the tension etched in Cat's somber features. "Bad dreams?" he guessed, moving toward the bar.

With a shaky laugh, Cat followed him. "Yes. In it, my Australian contractor was calling me to find out where the hell I was. What about that contract we signed, he kept saying." That was one of her dreams. The one that had awakened her involved the mine cave-in. Pride stopped her from admitting as much to Slade. She sat down on the bar stool and watched as he began making a small pot of coffee. Just having him nearby eased some of the fear ripping through her.

Slade pushed the errant strands of his hair off his brow and turned around to retrieve two earthenware mugs. Then he leaned against the counter that stood between them.

"How can you fulfill your contract now?" he demanded. Concern was evident in his voice. "You're going to be laid up for two months solid. Isn't there a clause somewhere that refers to acts of God or some such thing to get you off the hook?"

Cat turned away. Right now, Slade looked endearingly mussed and she had a powerful desire to slip her arms around his broad, capable shoulders and seek the solace he was offering. Without a doubt, Slade would hold her if she wanted and give her the peace she sought. Torn by so many conflicting emotions and her fears of ever entering a mine again, Cat remained silent.

"Hey…" Slade gently touched her arm. "What is it, Cat? Come on, you can tell me…"

Cat hung her head, not wanting Slade to see the stinging tears blurring her vision. "I, uh…"

"Great start," he teased, "what else?"

With a loud sniff, Cat managed a half laugh and half sob. "You'll think it's stupid. Childish."

As much as Slade wanted to continue touching her

soft, warm skin, he forced his hand to drop away. Leaning against the bar, his head bent forward almost touching hers, he said, "Okay, straight-arrow, shoot. I don't think a contract is the reason you're crying." His voice lowered to a velvet coaxing. "Fear of entering a mine is probably more like it. Right?"

Cat nodded slowly. "Oh, I feel so damn stupid, Slade." She raised her head, dabbed away at the evidence of the tears and stared at him. "Here I am, a grown woman— not a scared little child. So I was in a mine cave-in; big deal. I ought to be able to face my fear of going in again instead of shriveling up and dying inside whenever I think about it. Or dream about it."

With a slight smile, Slade shook his head. "As a kid, I was always afraid of thunderstorms. I still am to this day. Get a lightning strike too close and this guy cringes and ducks."

"I doubt you're afraid of anything, Slade."

"Think I'm fibbing?"

"I don't know. These days, I'm one knot of confusion." Cat smiled slightly at him. "Maybe you'd say something like that just to make me feel better. I don't know…"

Slade had to physically stop himself from pulling Cat close to him. Right now, she was very, very fragile. "Look," he began softly, "you're going to go through all kinds of daily and nightly hell with this fear. Get used to it. More important, don't close up. Talk about those fears, Cat. That's one of the reasons I wanted you with me: I've survived more than my fair share of cave-ins. I know what you're going through and I can help you if you'll let me." He reached out, capturing her tightly knotted hands on the bar. Gently, he pried each of her fingers free until they were relaxed between his own larger hands.

His warmth spread through her, enveloping her pounding heart. Cat met his tender expression. "Was anyone there to help you through nights like…this?"

"Most of the time, no. And I'm not ashamed to admit that after the first cave-in, I hit alcohol to escape from the same type of hell you're going to experience." Slade grimaced. "After a few bad weeks, I got off the booze and cleaned up my act. I crawled through it and survived, just like you will."

Her heart wrenched at his admission. "I don't know how you stood it, Slade. Right now I don't want to be alone. That's a first for me; practically all my life I've been alone or lived in remote places. I liked it. But now…"

He squeezed her hands. "We all have barriers we can't overcome alone, sweetheart. And I promised you, you won't have to go through this alone…"

She mustered a tender smile. "I told you I was a bad patient. Thanks for being here for me, Slade. The next step is to stop having nightmares about Ian Connors trying to pressure me into fulfilling that contract."

Chapter 5

A week later, Cat's worst fears came true when she received the dreaded call from Ian Connors, owner of the Australian mining company. She had been drinking her third cup of morning coffee, reading a book Slade had written on sedimentary gemstones, when the phone rang. Pilar answered it and pointed to the phone sitting near Cat's elbow.

"A Mr. Connors, *señorita*?"

Cat felt a sharp stab in her stomach as all her carefully hidden fears exploded within her. Pilar shot her a look of concern as Cat picked up the extension.

Closing her eyes, Cat took the call, too occupied to see Pilar quietly slip from the kitchen and hurry across the patio toward Slade's hobby shop. Mouth dry, heart pounding at the base of her throat, Cat barely got out a civil hello to Ian.

Pilar, alarmed by Cat's unexpected behavior, rushed

out to Slade's shop to tell him that Cat had turned alarmingly pale. He followed her back without delay. Folding his arms against his chest, he grimly watched Cat as he eavesdropped on the heated conversation.

"Look, Mr. Connors," she was explaining, a hint of tremor in her voice. "I simply can't come. I'm under doctor's orders to rest for two months. There are a number of other highly qualified mining engineers who can take my place. You don't need me."

Slade's eyes narrowed as he saw Cat nervously wipe her perspiring brow. In the past week, she had tried so valiantly to fight her inner battle with fear. And yet, he had sensed her aching need to lean on him, to trust him to help her. His mouth flattened into a thin line as he pondered the situation.

"I know what my contract says, Mr. Connors. You don't need to remind me. Look, there's no use shouting! That's not going to get us anywhere. I'm no happier than you are that that mine caused me so much injury." She twisted around on the stool, uncomfortable. "And no, I'm not going to fulfill the terms of the contract. You what? Are you joking?" Cat rolled her eyes and stifled the urge to swear. "You're going to sue me?" She clenched her teeth momentarily. "Okay, you go right ahead and try. But before you do, let me give you the phone number of the surgeon who saved my life! He can fill you in on all the gory details."

She was breathing hard by the time the call was completed. Slamming down the phone, Cat regretted the action instantly. Holding her right side, she slipped off the chair and headed out of the house and onto the screen-enclosed patio.

A few minutes later, Slade ambled out with two glasses

of cool, frosty lemonade. Cat's lower lip was compressed into a tight line, and her eyes flashed with emerald fire as she glared over at him.

"I suppose you heard?"

"He's just upset. Here, this is nice and cool. Come and sit down with me here and let's discuss it."

Unable to contain her anger, Cat put the lemonade down and began pacing the entire length of the porch. "Of all things, Slade. Ian Connors thinks he's going to sue me for breach of contract!"

Slade rose to his feet, holding out his hand to her. "Come on," he coaxed, "let's go for a walk down by the stream."

It seemed natural for Cat to slip her hand into Slade's. As they wandered down the stone path toward the stand of cottonwoods and the ribbon of water, she relaxed even more. She gave Slade a warm look.

"You're good for me."

"I try to be, Cat. You deserve it."

She shook her head. "I wish Greg had felt that way." Then she added, "We almost got married."

Slade slowed down as they neared the stream. Multicolored rocks peeked out from just below the water's surface and shimmered in the early-morning sun. He motioned for Cat to sit against the trunk of a cottonwood and then joined her. "Want to tell me about it?"

Cat chose two stalks of grass and plucked them. She handed one to Slade and then put the other into the corner of her mouth. Tipping her head back, she stared up through the dark green, sunlit foliage.

"It's the closest I ever came to marriage."

"You make it sound like a disease." Slade watched as the tension drained from Cat's features.

"I don't mean it to sound like that. I fell head over heels in love with Greg. Imagine, at twenty-seven taking the blind nosedive of an eighteen-year-old girl."

Slade smiled slightly. "There must have been some chemistry there to have done it."

With a painful nod, Cat said, "There was. Or I thought there was."

"What went wrong?" Slade resisted taking the small, graceful hand that lay so close to his. Was she even aware of her sensuality? He loved the feminine swing of her hips and the luscious mouth that begged to be kissed. And sometimes her breathless laughter sent a keen ache through him.

"Greg was a geologist, like you. He was thirty, single and had been knocking around in the industry since he was twenty-four. His whole life revolved around finding the mother lode."

Slade heard the disgust in her voice. "A treasure hunter?"

"Of the first order. Gold, platinum or any kind of precious gem mining. It didn't matter to him. He lived for that find of a lifetime."

Slade suddenly recalled their conversation when they had flown in from Maine, and remembered how Cat had reacted to the possibility that he might also be a treasure hunter. He certainly didn't want Cat to place him in Greg's category. Had she already? Clearing his throat, he asked, "Greg put money before people?"

Throwing the chewed stalk of grass away, Cat picked another. A frown creased her brow. "Yes. Only I didn't realize the depth of his treasure fever. The whole thing came to a head when he found gold on some land he had purchased near the Kalgoorlie mines."

With a whistle, Slade turned around, facing her. "The Kalgoorlie gold mines are among the best in Australia."

"Overnight, Greg became a very rich man," she recalled, bitterness staining her words.

Slade picked up her hand. "But?"

"What we had became second best," she admitted hoarsely. "Greg put gold above us. He really didn't need what I had to offer him. Gold fever became his wife, friend and lover."

Slade ran his thumb across her soft cheek. How he wanted to gather Cat into his arms and hold her! He could see tears glistening in her eyes and he gently placed his hands on her shoulders.

"Listen to me, Cat," Slade said in a low voice charged with emotion. "Greg didn't deserve you. Anyone who puts money ahead of the most priceless gift in the world hasn't got his head screwed on straight."

Cat fought back the tears and met Slade's level look. "Do you, Slade?"

He shook his head. "I may have green-fire fever, but it has never come between me and the woman in my life." His hands tightened momentarily on her shoulders. It was important that Cat believe him. "I do know what money can and cannot buy. Do you understand that?" *Please, say you do,* he begged silently.

Impulsively, Cat leaned forward, placing a kiss on his cheek. Slade smelled male, of sunshine and perspiration. "I believe you," she said huskily, smiling up at his surprised expression. Running her fingers down his left arm, she sat back.

Shaken by her spontaneity, Slade felt a molten heat spread through his hardening body because of her touch. He gave her a shy smile, the words coming haltingly. "I hope, Cat, that you always know you're more important to me than any business concern." Gathering his courage, he added, "I like what you and I have. Money can't buy that."

Without a word, Cat rested her hand in his. "I like what we have, too, Slade. But I don't know where it's going."

"Is that important right now?" He tried to brace himself for an answer he did not want to hear.

"No," Cat said softly. "My entire life's in a tailspin professionally. The only good thing to come out of all this is what we share. And for that, I'm grateful. You're steady and you've offered me someone to lean on. And right now, I need that." She smiled tenderly. "Maybe this restless, globe-trotting mining engineer needed that all along and was too blind to realize it."

"Well," Slade said huskily, "a crisis has a funny way of putting things into proper perspective. Having you here is like sunlight to me, Cat. I don't know where we're going, either, but I like it. I like what you bring out in me, and the talks we have. You're important to me…"

Leaning toward him, Cat placed her arms around Slade's shoulders. She wasn't able to give very much of a hug because of her healing ribs. "You have a funny way of making yourself a part of my life, Slade," she whispered near his ear.

Gently, Slade placed his hands on her waist. "You're more valuable than any gold mine, sweetheart. Believe that with all your heart and soul." As he got to his feet and helped Cat to stand, a sweet euphoria swept through him.

Three days later, Slade was still remembering their conversation as he doodled absently on a note pad. There was plenty of work clamoring for his attention, but he

had a hard time concentrating on anything except Cat.
Slade turned around in his leather chair, staring out of the
window toward the patio below. Suddenly Cat appeared,
dressed in a pair of kelly-green shorts and a white tank
top. She was slowly taking her afternoon stroll across the
brick-topped patio. She looked lonely—just as lonely as
he felt. Slade, restless, tossed the pencil onto the desk.
Getting to see Cat for a few minutes each morning to
help her with the rib wrap, and then for an hour at lunch,
wasn't enough. Not anymore. The eight hours a day demanded of him to coordinate the opening of the Verde
mine held less and less interest for him.

With a snort, Slade got up, moving to the window to
watch Cat as she wandered aimlessly on her way. Questions raced through his mind. When should he broach the
fact that he wanted Cat to work for him? Right now, she
wasn't even sure she wanted to continue being a mining
engineer. Cave-ins had a way of forcing one to look at
fear. How each individual handled it was another question. The past weeks had effectively erased Slade's original reason for wanting Cat to recover at Mourning Dove.
No, more and more, Slade wanted *her*. Each morning he
awoke he was happy as never before because of Cat's
quiet presence.

Glancing down at his watch, he saw it was two-thirty.
To hell with work; he wanted to spend the rest of the afternoon with Cat. It was too late for the picnic they had
talked about earlier. But there was still time to take her to
a fishing pond nearby. Whistling softly, pleased with the
idea, Slade shut off the light and strolled out of his office.

"There you are," he greeted her cheerfully.

Cat lifted her head. She sat in a lounge chair beneath
a trellis shelter of bougainvillea vines. Her pulse began

to pound as she met Slade's blue gaze. She closed the magazine on her lap as he approached.

"Uh-oh, you look like you're on the prowl." She eyed him with wary appreciation.

Slade sat down at the end of the chair, staring admiringly at her long legs, now tanned gold from days in the sun. He longed to run his hands all the way up them and feel her response. Tucking his torrid thoughts away, he met her teasing look.

"I am," he warned her. "I was hunting for you." He gestured toward the Travis ranch in the distance. "Figured the day was too nice to waste working. How'd you like to catch our dinner tonight?"

Cat hesitated, wanting to contain her eagerness. "Fishing?"

"Sure. Matt and Kai have a nice little river that's filled with bass. I've got the fishing tackle. All I need is my favorite lady to come along. Game?"

Cat gave up trying to disguise her delight. "You bet. But I'm not a good fisherman. My brother Rafe's an ace at it. If I hook anything, it's by sheer dumb luck."

Slade grinned and stood, offering Cat his hand. She took it without hesitation. The sun had tanned Cat's once-pale face, and her green eyes sparkled with good health once again. He hoped part of her happiness was due to his presence. "I suspect you're a lot better than you let on," replied Slade, gently pulling her up. "Come on, you can help me get the tackle and we'll be on our way. Maybe if Kai's home, she can join us."

"Wonderful!"

As they drove to the Travis ranch, Cat confided, "I'm glad you can pull away from work every once in a while."

The wind was hot and dry against his face. "I'm not a workaholic like some people you might have known."

Cat recognized the reference to Greg, but made no comment.

"Gold fever has a way of demanding your body and soul," Slade continued. He caught her thoughtful expression. "So, you like your man to be spontaneous and not hooked into the work harness all the time. What else do you like?"

Caught up in his expansive mood, Cat relaxed as they drove slowly down the dirt road. "My dream man would cherish our relationship above anything else."

"Even if you were pauper poor?"

"Poor in one way, but rich in another," she agreed with a laugh. "But this is a fantasy, remember? There's no such thing as a dream man—or woman, for that matter. But I'd like him to take me on picnics out in the wilderness where we could share a bottle of cold white wine or join me in the kitchen to bake chocolate-chip cookies."

"Hey, let's do that when we get back. I love chocolate-chip cookies."

Cat went warm inside. She could barely tear her gaze from Slade's wonderfully shaped mouth. She longed to have him kiss her again, but he'd been treading so carefully. His touch was nearly impersonal when he helped her with the rib wrap. Only lately had he even held her hand and, once, embraced her briefly. She wanted more, Cat realized. Much more. "Are you serious?" she challenged.

Giving her a hurt look, Slade held up his hand, as if swearing to his statement. "No kidding, I'm a sucker for cookies. And ice cream. And one particular exotic woman…"

Heat flamed into her cheeks and Cat allowed it to sweep straight through her. "Thank you," she managed, unable to hold his penetrating look. Both of them were tautly aware of the tension that crackled between them. Never had a man made Cat feel more like a woman.

Slade, unable to resist, picked up her hand and placed a gentle kiss on her palm. "You're welcome…"

Unstrung by Slade's sudden shift in mood, Cat fished quietly beside him at the river. The tall, stately pecan trees hugged their side of the bank, providing welcome shade. Kai Travis had greeted them when they'd arrived, provided icy lemonade, but had declined joining them. If Cat had looked closer, she would have seen a merry look in Kai's wide eyes that spoke volumes. Why did she feel Kai was deliberately leaving them alone?

"Hey! There goes your bobber!"

Cat jerked upright. She had been lounging half asleep against a pecan tree, rod in hand, when the red-and-white bobber at the end of her line was pulled down beneath the jade depths of the river. Slade's excitement sizzled through her and Cat scrambled to her feet. He was at her side as she gave a firm jerk upward on the pole. Immediately, the rod tip bent nearly double as the fish on the other end was hooked.

"I got him, Slade!" She struggled to flip off the safety on the reel. It had been years since she had gone fishing and she was rusty and clumsy. Slade stood nearby, excitement in his voice.

"Looks big. Hold on, I'll get the net. Keep tension on that line or he'll flip out of the water and shake the hook loose."

Cat looked out of the corner of her eye as Slade swept

the net into his hand and walked to the edge of the bank. "What a fighter," she gasped, slowly reeling the fish closer.

"You're doing fine, sweetheart. Hey…he's a grand-pappy. Why, that bass must weigh close to five pounds. Okay, bring him in nice and slow…"

With a triumphant laugh, Cat set the rod aside after Slade had captured the bass. He expertly slid the hook out of the paper-thin mouth of the fish. Proudly he held the fish up for her to examine.

"For someone who hasn't fished much, you've got some kind of luck," he congratulated her. Slade put the bass on the stringer, then placed it back into the water to keep it alive until they were ready to go home. He knelt down and washed his hands. Cat stood beside him, her cheeks flushed with victory. Her smile went straight to Slade's heart.

His sapphire eyes darkened with intent as he stood up. Sweeping Cat into his arms, he held her gently against his damp, hard body. "You," he whispered thickly, "are something else." Then he claimed her parted lips.

Instinctively, Cat slid her arms across his shoulders. Slade's mouth was strong, cherishing. He ran his tongue in an outlining motion, placing small kisses at each corner of her lips. A soft moan welled up within her and Cat trusted her full weight to Slade, lost in the growing fire of their mutual explorations.

"Sweet," he said in a rush, framing her face, lost in the tide of her returning kiss. The smoldering heat exploded violently within Slade as her mouth met and equaled the pressure of his own. Gripping her shoulders, Slade drowned in Cat, all thoughts taking flight. Feelings were what counted with him. He followed the inner yearnings of his heart, drinking deeply of Cat, losing himself in her womanliness.

Disappointed when Slade's mouth left hers, Cat looked up and was enveloped in the cobalt intensity of his gaze as he stared down at her. The world swayed and she gripped his arms.

"Cat? Are you all right?"

All right? She was delirious. Trying to smile, she nodded. "D-do you always catch a woman off guard like this, Slade?"

He groaned softly, cupping her chin, holding her dreamy expression. "There's just one woman I want to catch off guard, and that's you, sweetheart. No one else… just you…"

Waves of tidal strength rocked through her and Cat closed her eyes, pressing her cheek against his palm. "No one has ever made me dizzy, Slade Donovan. Ever."

Dizzy himself, Slade reveled in her openness and honesty with him. Here was the woman he had always known existed, and she was sharing herself with him. Lightheaded and a little shaky, Slade gently drew Cat into his arms. The day was hot, their shirts damp from perspiration, but he didn't care. "It's your fault, you know."

"What is? The kiss?"

Slade rubbed his jaw against the softness of her sablecolored hair. "Definitely."

Cat pulled away, laughing at his teasing. "How could it be?"

Mirth danced in his features. "You promised me chocolate-chip cookies, remember? I go crazy when a woman offers to bake me cookies."

With a playful look, Cat stepped out of his arms. "You're so full of it, Slade Donovan."

He recaptured Cat's hand, pulling her to a halt before she could escape completely. "Now wait a minute, I was kidding about the cookies, not the kiss."

"Really?"

Slade gave her a measuring look, wondering if Cat was serious or if she was just giving him a good dose of his own medicine. "I can do without the cookies, but I can't do without you."

"That's nice to know, Donovan; I rate higher than a chocolate-chip cookie."

He wanted to throttle her. "You rate a hell of a lot higher than that and you know it."

Merrily, Cat slipped from his grasp and retrieved her rod. "Really? Well, we'll see." She gave him a look filled with challenge. "I'm going to put you to the test, Slade."

"Oh?"

Satisfaction wreathed Cat's smile as she baited the hook and then tossed the bobber back into the river. "Tonight, after dinner, I'm going to bake you three dozen chocolate-chip cookies. I'll use my mom's recipe, and they're better than any other kind you've ever eaten."

He brightened. "Great."

"There's only one catch to all this, Donovan."

He frowned. "What?"

Cat sat back down, her back against the pecan tree, grinning. "You have a choice: a kiss from me or those three dozen cookies tonight. Which will it be, I wonder?"

Slade gave in to her teasing. There was no question in his mind that he'd rather have the kiss. Still, he couldn't resist playing Cat's game. "Cat, how can you do this to me? Do you realize how rare it is that I get homemade chocolate-chip cookies?"

Choking back her laughter, Cat tried very hard to

keep a straight face and appear to concentrate on fishing. "Didn't you just say I rated higher than a cookie?"

"This isn't fair! Of course you're more important than a cookie." Slade stood over her, hoping to intimidate her into thinking twice about the choice she offered him.

Cat looked up, giving him an innocent look. "If that's true, then you'll settle for a good-night kiss instead of those cookies I'm going to bake."

"What will happen to those cookies, then?"

"I'm sure Pilar's children would love them, aren't you?"

Groaning, Slade stalked over to his rod. "You don't fight fair, you know that?"

Barely able to keep the smile from pulling up the corners of her mouth, Cat nodded. "Neither do you. You're just getting a taste of your own medicine, Donovan. How does it feel?"

Slade sat down, balancing the rod on his knees, and gave her a devilish look. "You're going to pay for this, Ms. Kincaid."

"Uh-oh, threats! Threats!"

Joy swept through Slade as he watched Cat laugh like a delighted child. She was beautiful in so many ways. And grudgingly, he admitted he'd finally met his match. The little vixen. Well, he'd win the last round in this sparring between them. And what sweet, luscious revenge it would be.

That evening, after Pilar had left for the night, Cat went to the kitchen to bake. Slade hung around, watching closely as she made her mother's recipe for chocolate-chip cookies. Every now and again, Slade would lean over her shoulders and swipe a bite of the dough.

And then he would steal a light kiss from Cat. Tinkering with the cappuccino maker, Slade worked nearby on the tile drain board. Cat looked soft and feminine in a pale pink sundress. The square neck on the dress showed off her recent tan to a decided advantage.

"Did I tell you how pretty you look in that dress?"

Cat began to drop the cookie dough onto the sheet. The corners of her mouth lifted slightly and she pinned Slade's longing gaze. "Is this your way of getting a cookie? Flattery?"

Slade placed the lid on the cappuccino machine, screwing it down tightly. He met her smile. "Cookies can't hold a flame to you."

Laughing lightly, she murmured, "Why, thank you. Can I help it if I think you have ulterior motives designed to weaken my resolve?"

"Sweetheart, if I want to weaken your resolve, I'll be a hell of a lot more straightforward about it."

"Uh-oh, Texans are rather brash, aren't they?" Cat walked around Slade and moved to the oven. He leaned petulantly against the drain board, watching her through half-closed eyes. She found it hard to fight the attraction he always generated in her. Eyeing the oven's temperature control, Cat straightened up. She brushed away strands of damp hair from her brow.

"Texans are honest," Slade defended, eagerly absorbing her every movement.

Placing the sheet of cookies in the oven, Cat closed the door. "Even if it kills them," she agreed. "There. In about ten minutes, the first dozen will be ready. How's our cappuccino coming?"

Slade roused himself from staring at her. Her flushed cheeks and the serenity surrounding her made her just that much more enticing. Everything was happening so quickly. He didn't want to rush Cat or make her feel as if he was stalking her.

"Here," Slade said, handing her a large mug of the steaming brew, frothy with hot milk. Then he joined her on the living-room couch. The last of the cookies had been baked and were set out to cool. The merriment in Cat's eyes as she took the cup made him smile. With a contented sigh, Slade sat back, his shoulders almost touching hers.

"How are you doing?" Cat asked, sipping contentedly at her cappuccino.

Slade rolled his head to the left, drinking in her smiling features. "Okay."

"You're holding up amazingly well for a Cookie Monster."

"Yeah, I know it."

"I've got them counted, Slade. So don't come sneaking out here in the middle of the night to steal one. Or two. Probably half a dozen."

Slade joined her laughter and picked up her hand. "I've got something even better than that, Cat."

"What?" She loved the feel of his big, firm hand.

"I was privileged to see you working in the kitchen."

"Being a mining engineer doesn't mean I can't do anything else."

"Now, don't go getting contrary. That was a compliment. You looked kind of pretty and at home in there. I liked the feeling." His voice lowered. "For the first time since I bought this place, it feels like a home." And then he met Cat's sober gaze. "Do you know what I mean?"

Her voice was barely above a whisper. "Yes, I know…"

Reluctantly, Slade released her hand. "What we... share...is so good, Cat."

Cat set her mug on the coffee table. Slade gave her a puzzled look as she rose and walked to the kitchen.

"Now what did I say?" he demanded, sitting up. "Cat?"

Cat returned with a saucer stacked with cookies. She handed them to Slade. "Nothing's wrong," she told him, sitting back down beside him. "Everything's right..."

Delighted with her change of heart, Slade picked up a cookie. He was about to take a bite out of it, then hesitated. "Does this mean I still get my kiss?"

"I hereby release you from having to make a choice," Cat said, her eyes sparkling.

"Here, this one's for the cook. She's one hell of a fine lady."

Cat took the proffered cookie, giving Slade a tender smile. Holding up her cookie in a toast, she murmured, "And here's to one hell of a fine man."

Happily, Slade touched her cookie with his. He consumed four of them without another word.

Laughing, Cat snuggled into the couch, her legs tucked beneath her. The beatific look of pleasure on Slade's face made her feel good. She reached out, resting her hand against his shoulder. "You're such an easy person to please, Slade Donovan. Does it always take so little to make you happy?"

He glanced over at Cat, matching her smile. "That's me in a nutshell, sweetheart. Small, simple things in life are the best. Like that kiss we shared this afternoon..."

"Or the cookies..."

"Yeah, them too. But the kiss was sweeter. Better." And then he brightened. "This is pretty good—not only do I get these great-tasting cookies, but I also get to give you a good-night kiss."

"Don't gloat, Slade."

"Was I gloating?"

"You know you are. You're as bad as Rafe when it comes to getting everything your way."

Rafe called her less than a week later. Joyfully, Cat picked up the phone when Pilar told her who it was. The early-afternoon sunlight spilled through the windows as Cat took the phone into the living room, making herself comfortable on the apricot-colored couch.

"How are you?" Cat asked, barely able to contain her happiness.

"Things could be going a hell of a lot better, Cat."

Her brows dipped. "Oh, no. What's wrong, Rafe?"

"You remember I told you about Jessica?"

"The lady investigator from the Bureau of Land Mines?"

"Same one," he said gruffly.

Gripping the phone, Cat felt her brother's unspoken anguish. "Oh, Rafe, what happened? I know how much you love her. Didn't you fly up to Wyoming to see her?"

"Yes…but…things just didn't work out for us, Cat. Not the way I wanted, at least. Listen, enough of my troubles. How are you? You sound better. Happier."

Her heart bled for Rafe. How many times had he talked of Jessie to her? Any fool could see that Rafe was head over heels in love with the woman. Shutting her eyes, Cat had no defense against her brother's pain. "Oh, I'm surviving."

"Isn't Slade Donovan treating you right?"

The threat in Rafe's voice made her laugh softly. "Now

don't go getting growly like an old bear just waking up from hibernation. Slade is—well, he's wonderful, Rafe."

"Then what's the problem? You're worried. I can hear it in your voice."

"It's just the calls I'm getting from mining companies who want to hire me. Seems like everyone knows I can't fulfill the terms of the Australian contract and they're trying to entice me into other jobs. They're like Nar hunting down a rabbit."

Rafe's laughter was explosive. "That damned eagle. Speaking of hunting, did you know he grabbed Goodyear the other day?"

Buoyed by Rafe's sudden good humor, Cat was swept along by it. "Oh, no. What happened? Did Millie get on her broomstick and fly after him?"

Chuckling, Rafe recounted the latest escapade of the golden eagle and the nearly-thirty-pound, overfed cat, Goodyear. "Well, you know how Nar dive-bombs the chicken coop every once in a while to keep everyone on their toes?"

"Yes, the little turkey."

"Now, Nar would be insulted if you called him a turkey."

"Jim Tremain calls him a flying pig and he's right! Well, go on. What happened?"

"Pig is right. Anyway, Nar spotted the Goodyear blimp outside the horse-paddock area. I guess Goodyear had caught his first mouse ever."

"As fat as that cat is, I'm surprised he's caught one. Sure the mouse wasn't crippled, blind and already dead from old age?"

"Who knows?" Rafe laughed. "Anyway, I was saddling Flight up to help herd some cattle to the south range when I saw Nar land about ten feet away from Good-year. The cat hadn't hurt the mouse. He was just hold-ing it between his front paws gloating over it. Frankly, I don't think Goodyear knew what to do with it. Millie feeds him so many table scraps he's never had to hunt a day in his life."

"What did Nar do?"

"He flapped his wings and came clucking and chutting up to Goodyear. The cat flattened his ears and crouched over his mouse. He wasn't going to give up his feast to that brazen bird."

Cat could barely stifle her giggles, and held a protec-tive arm across her stomach. "Did Nar take the mouse?"

"No. He made a lightning strike for Goodyear's tail and picked him right up off the ground. You should have heard the racket. The mouse squeaked and ran. Goodyear was shrieking like a scalded cat. Nar lumbered toward the meadow, trying to get airborne, dragging Goodyear in a wake of dust. Can you imagine a thirteen-pound eagle trying to lift off with a thirty-pound fatso? I was laugh-ing so hard, tears were running down my face. Goodyear was digging into the grass and dirt trying to stop Nar from moving forward. Nar kept getting jerked around until finally he crashed. Both he and the cat hit the dirt at the same time. You should have seen it—dust, feath-ers and cat fur were flying everywhere."

Crying with laughter, Cat couldn't speak for almost a minute. "Oh, no! What happened? Did Millie ever get wind of it?"

"Nah, I ran out of the barn to stop Nar from dragging the damn idiot cat around by the tail. There was a huge cloud of dust and all these screams from Nar and snarls from Goodyear. Just as I got there, Goodyear shot out like a fired cannonball with a couple of feathers in his mouth. Nar limped out the other side with a real hurt look on his face. I stood there laughing. That cat finally got even for all the times Nar teased and chased him. Last I saw, Goodyear was rolling at high speed toward the safety of the chicken coop, Nar's tail feathers in his mouth."

Wiping the tears from her eyes, Cat said with a giggle, "Finally, after all these years, Goodyear evens the score! Did you tell Dal that her eagle got the worst end of the confrontation?"

"Yeah, I did. I don't know who laughed harder, Dal or me."

Cat smiled tenderly, cradling the phone. "You're so good for me, Rafe. All I have to do is remember Nar and Goodyear's latest battle and I'll die laughing."

Suddenly shifting gears, Rafe asked, "Have you heard anything about the Emerald Lady Mine or what they were going to do with the owner?"

Cat sobered slightly. "Lionel Graham has been handed a large fine by the government."

"Well deserved," Rafe applauded.

"I don't think he'll be able to build any more mines in the U.S. without the government watching him closely. He got what was coming to him."

"Slade had been right about him all the time," Rafe added.

Cat made a wry face. "Tell me about it. If I had listened to him in the first place, I wouldn't have gotten into my present bind."

"But then, you wouldn't have met Slade."

Rafe was right. Cat closed her eyes for a moment. "And I'm very glad we've had the time together."

"Good," Rafe rumbled, his voice warm and pleased, "you deserve some happiness."

"Between you, Slade and Kai Travis, I'm surrounded by people who make me smile and laugh."

"So, you like the Travis gal, eh?"

"Yes. She and her husband, Matt, are wonderful. Slade has had them over here for dinner once a week and we have a great time. You should see their one-year-old, Josh. I've never seen a cuter tyke." And then Cat cringed. Why did she have to bring up the subject of babies to Rafe? She knew how much he'd wanted kids before his wife had died in childbirth.

There were a few awkward moments of silence, then Rafe cleared his throat. "You sound better now, Cat. I'll give you a call in a week and see if you're still improving."

Trying to rally for his sake, Cat murmured, "Don't worry. Between Slade and Kai I have to get better."

Chapter 6

Kai loosened the blood-pressure cuff from around Cat's left arm. "Perfectly healthy and normal. Not bad after four weeks." She set the cuff aside and examined the nearly healed scar along Cat's scalp. "You're just as tough as Slade," she teased. "Are all you rock-hunting miners built out of the same genetic material?"

Cat met her smile. Kai had a genuine warmth emanating from her that made Cat feel good. "I'm not as tough as I look."

"Nonsense. Come on, let's go enjoy a late-morning margarita on Slade's back porch. It's almost noon and I can't stay long. Maria is watching Josh until I get back. Let's spend a few minutes catching up on what we've been doing the past few days." Kai reached for her hand, giving it a squeeze. "I'm really glad you're here, Cat. Out on this Texas desert, I get a little lonely for feminine company."

Cat followed Kai out into the living room and sat down at the bar. Kai made a mean margarita, almost as good as Slade's. "I don't know what I'd have done without you, Kai," Cat admitted.

Kai dropped the ice cubes into the blender, shut the lid and turned it on. "Slade would have been utterly lost without your help."

"What do you mean?"

Kai poured the margaritas into two long-stemmed glasses, her eyes sparkling. "I'm sure he's told you why he flew up to Maine to find you. After all, he wanted only the best engineer to build that mine of his down in Colombia. He'd talked for months of a way to lure you away from your other commitments. Believe me when I tell you that when Slade wants something, he doesn't take no for an answer." Kai added a slice of lime to the drinks. "But then, you've experienced his persuasive sales abilities, so you know what I'm talking about. I don't think I've ever seen Slade as intense as he was about hiring you. He wanted the best." Her eyes twinkled and she leaned forward, her long auburn hair falling around her face. "Just between us, I think Slade's enjoying your company so much he's forgotten about the mine. When I talk to him, he always speaks of you, never about the Verde."

Cat nearly choked on Kai's statement. She barely tasted the tart drink, thrown as she was into a maelstrom of powerful emotions. Slade had wanted to hire her to build him a mine? He had hinted about a business deal, but she had forgotten all about it. Maybe his offer to have her recuperate at the ranch was just part of his business plan. Why hadn't she questioned Slade more closely? But then, how could she? As badly injured as she was, she had willingly accepted Slade's offer to recuperate here. What an idealistic fool she had been.

"It's good," Cat forced out in a tight voice, all her focus on the unannounced business deal.

Kai smiled and came around to join her. The white slacks and bright green blouse did nothing but bring out her natural beauty. "Great! Hey, you know we should go shopping soon. Slade could fly us into Houston for the day. He always has business with Alvin, his partner, there. I'm sure he wouldn't mind if we tagged along."

Slade had a partner. A business partner. Cat didn't like what she was hearing. Was Slade's care and seeming desire nothing more than a means to get her to work with him on his mine? A knifelike pain tore through her. Had Slade's kisses only been a disguise for what he really wanted? No wonder he'd downplayed her problems with Ian Connors. If Slade wanted her services, he'd gladly tell her to drop Connors.

Her fingers tightened around the frosty stem of the glass. Shaken, Cat took another gulp of the margarita. *One way or another, I have to find out why Slade really brought me here. Maybe it wasn't out of the kindness of his heart, as I thought.* Inwardly, Cat died. Until that moment, she had never really gotten in touch with the depth of her feelings for Slade. And now it was sheer, aching torture to admit just how much he had come to mean to her.

After Kai had gone, Cat sat in the silence of the living room. *I've just found out why I'm here at Mourning Dove Ranch,* Cat grimly told herself. She gingerly ran her hands over her healing ribs and went to the kitchen, where Pilar was starting preparation for lunch.

"Did you want coffee, Señorita Cat?" she greeted her, lifting one soapy hand.

Cat managed a smile and went over to a large pot, pouring herself a cup of coffee. "I can get it, Pilar. Thank you." She needed time to think. "Is Slade in his office?"

"Either his office or hobby shop," Pilar replied. "Would you like an early lunch?"

"No, thank you. I'll just go out to the porch for a while." She had no appetite.

Cat sat down at the table, staring beyond the screened-in porch. Absently, she smoothed the burgundy skirt that was imprinted with a profusion of white, pink and lavender orchid blooms. Kai had insisted over the weeks that she have something other than pants to wear and had given her a gift of the Mexican skirt and blouse. Cat fingered the lace of the boat-necked white blouse she wore, her mind spinning.

Cat's mind focused on Slade. Was he planning to send men and machinery down to Colombia to gear up for the mine he wanted to build? For eight hours each day he would disappear into his office. Was Slade playing a waiting game with her? Cat tried to search her memory for some betraying facts. Slade would join her, like clockwork, at noon, for an hour-long lunch. She could never quite get used to his devastating effect on her— that special warmth flowing up through her, the added beat to her heart when she first saw him crossing the living room and moving to the porch where Pilar served lunch. Merriment was usually lurking in his eyes when he approached her. Cat frowned, the coffee tasting bitter. Right or wrong, she was drawn powerfully to Slade, and it was more than physical. How she felt about him and what he wanted from her warred within her. She had to talk to Slade and clear the air.

Cat rose, her mouth set in a determined line. She wanted to do something—anything—to settle what lay between them. In another few weeks she would be fit and ready to work again. Cat set the coffee cup on the drain board, gathering her courage. Padding silently through the house, she walked across the garden and patio. The palms of her hands grew damp as she followed the left fork. Cat tried out a number of opening lines in her head as she walked along the path to Slade's shop. She slowed, coming to a sliding-glass door that was partially open.

Slade was bent over what she recognized to be a multi-wheel gem polisher. He had a gem in a brown, waxlike substance known as dop, and was grinding the shape of the gem against the spinning wheel. His long work-bench, to the right, was strewn with a can of dop sticks that would hold a rough-cut cabachon-shaped gem. Facet-ing equipment, which would shape a gem to blinding brilliance, was nearby. Cat stood in the doorway, tense.

Sensing her presence, despite the level of noise, Slade turned around. "Come in…if you can find a place to sit down." Taking off his safety glasses, Slade leaned over, pulling a stool toward him, motioning for Cat to join him.

"I—thanks." Cat sat down.

"Looks like you're a little bored."

Somehow, he looked more pulse-poundingly hand-some than usual to her. Slade wore a faded red T-shirt that emphasized the powerful breadth of his chest and tight muscles. His jeans were streaked with dust and soiled across the thighs, where he obviously wiped his fingers as he worked.

"I didn't know you were a jeweler," Cat began lamely, unsure how to begin her preamble.

Slade grinned, putting the glasses back on and returning to the work at hand, turning on the polisher again. He expertly positioned the cabachon he held on the stick between his hands. "Making jewelry is my hobby."

Cat leaned forward, fascinated. "An unusual hobby for a man."

"But not a geologist," Slade corrected, lightly pressuring the stone against the wheel. A whirring sound continued for several seconds before he lifted the stone away. Slade dipped it into some water, and rubbed away the accumulated material that resulted when the rock was polished. There was satisfaction mirrored in his face. He held the stick out to her. "Take a look. That's pink tourmaline from the El Camino mine. Beautiful specimen, isn't it?"

Cat held the stick, observing the gem. Slade was no amateur in his fashioning of the stone. The tourmaline was at least four carats in size, and Slade had used the oval cut to bring out the breathtaking pink fire from the depths of the stone. "It's lovely," she whispered.

Slade smiled. "There's no color on earth like this," he agreed, running his callused finger over the gem.

"You're hardly a novice," Cat accused, handing the stick back to him.

His smile broadened as he set it down on the table next to the lathe. "No, but my mother taught me to be modest about my talents. So what did you think I was doing back here?"

"Working on the latest geology reports, collecting data for a place where you might want to go next," she hinted, waiting to see if he would take the bait.

"I wanted to get this ring finished in time for my mother's birthday. It's only ten days away," he murmured, taking off his safety glasses.

"It's a lovely stone. I'm sure your mother will be thrilled with it."

"I sure hope you're right. So, you're itching to get back into the mining mode?"

Cat froze internally. "Not yet."

"Let's change our schedule, then. How would you like to go on a picnic with me today?"

Caught off guard, Cat repeated, "A picnic?" It sounded wonderful and she knew the sudden catch in her voice showed her surprise. She saw Slade smile as he got up and rinsed his hands off in a basin nearby.

"Well—I—there's something we have to discuss, Slade."

"Great. I'm cashing in on that rain check I promised you, Cat. We can talk over lunch. Why don't you tell Pilar we're going? She'll be happy to fix something for us."

Cat slid off the stool. Maybe a picnic would be the right place to broach the subject. "Oh? Does she want to get us out from underfoot?"

"She's been after me for the past two weeks to take you on one. I couldn't because it's hell traveling with taped ribs any more than necessary. Now, you're almost as good as new and I think it's just what we both need."

Cat turned away, feeling heat in her cheeks. "Have you had broken ribs before, Slade?"

He chuckled. "Yeah, when I was at the university I played football. One game I took three hits simultaneously and ended up under a pile of opposing players. I came out with four busted ribs. Needless to say, I didn't play the rest of the season." He lifted his head and turned toward her. "That's how I knew how much pain you were in this past month. You're a pretty brave lady, you know that?"

With a wan smile, Cat stepped out the sliding-glass doors. "Don't put me on a pedestal, Slade. I'll fall off before you can blink twice. I've got enough inclusions in me to match any emerald you find." Inclusions were the hairline fissures that could flaw the otherwise clear surface of a gem. In other words, they were mistakes, and she made her own fair share. And so did Slade.

"Inclusions make you interesting, sweetheart. Who wants a flawless gem? They're rather boring in comparison."

"You're a glutton for punishment, then. I'll tell Pilar of our lunch plans." Cat tried to stop the fear expanding within her. In the weeks they had lived together under the same roof, peace had reigned, not irritation or tension. No, Cat thought wryly to herself, the only tension her heart felt was a longing to draw closer to Slade. Toward the end of the picnic, Cat could talk to Slade about the mine.

Packing the wicker basket in the back of the Jeep, Slade guided Cat into the front seat. He wanted to tell her how beautiful she had become in the past month; her sable hair shone with gold highlights, and though it was a bit shaggy, it was more appealing as it grew longer. She was, by anyone's standards, a woman to be recognized. Pilar had given her a broad-brimmed straw hat to protect her face from the harsh sun overhead. Slade got into the driver's seat, and the Jeep started up with a cough and sputter.

"Where are we going?" Cat asked.

"A special place for a special lady," Slade answered. He pointed the Jeep down the flat expanse of dirt road, driving slowly and avoiding most of the holes in the road that might jar Cat. "It's on Kai and Matt's ranch. I only took you by one part of the river before. The part we're going to now has about four thousand pecan trees planted along it. And there's a beautiful spot near the water where they placed a picnic table. I thought you might enjoy a change of scenery."

The sun was warm and Cat held the hat on with one hand. "Kai wanted to know if I'd go into Houston with her to shop for a day."

Slade made a chortling sound. "Uh-oh. Women going shopping spells disaster. Houston will never be the same. Did you tell her you'd go?"

Cat shrugged. "I told her I'd think about it."

He heard the hesitancy in her voice, but didn't understand it. Usually, most women would give their right arm to go shopping in such a cosmopolitan and sophisticated city as Houston. But then, Cat wasn't the average female, Slade reminded himself. He almost sensed that Cat didn't want to leave the ranch, whatever her reasons. Had her nightmares dampened her otherwise keen traveling spirit? He decided to pursue that at an opportune time, later.

Slade spread the red cotton tablecloth across the green picnic table while Cat brought over the basket. Pilar had packed beef sandwiches, potato salad, some apples and a bottle of zinfandel, Slade's favorite white wine. The pecan trees rose straight and tall, already bearing a quantity of fruit. In the fall, they would be harvested during a five-day celebration. The noontime heat was well over ninety. Beneath the trees, with a cool breeze rippling off the small, quiet river that languidly flowed past them, it was an acceptable eighty degrees. Slade motioned for Cat to come and sit down. When she did, he sat next to her, something he rarely did at the ranch.

His move hadn't been missed by Cat, either. At first, she was going to say something, and then thought better of it. She wondered perversely if he had deliberately used reverse psychology on her so she would willingly welcome his advances. Cat shook her head, angry with herself. Slade had been the perfect host since she had come to his ranch. She decided to drop her wariness and simply enjoy him for the duration of the picnic.

"I didn't realize how skilled you were at jewelry making. Do you work on it every day?"

Slade handed Cat a plastic cup half-filled with the delicate white wine. "Yes. After I get caught up on paperwork, I head over to the shop. I use the samples I collect from my job assignments and play treasure hunter, stalking the gems I know are buried deep within the matrix."

"I'd like to see some of your finished work. Is that possible?"

"Sure. I keep all my fledgling attempts and mistakes in the back room."

"Knowing you as I do, I doubt if you've got any 'mistakes.'"

Slade set a plate loaded with food in front of her. "I've got plenty of mistakes. I just don't go around showing them to everyone."

"Why to me?" she asked, meeting and holding his gaze.

"What if I told you I wanted you to know me with and without mistakes?"

Cat's heart pumped hard to underscore the implications of his question. "Then I'd ask why you're according me that privilege." Was he going to tell her about his mine?

"Would you?" He looked at her closely.

She nodded, sipping the spicy, clear wine. "I think it signals a certain change in a relationship when both people let down their guard and allow the other to see all their qualities."

Slade took her statement seriously, biting into a sandwich. He was having trouble keeping the conversation light. The past week had been pure hell on him. He wanted to do something about the longing in Cat's eyes as she looked up at him. Food was the last thing on his mind right now. "That's another thing I like about you, Ms. Kincaid; you don't play the games men and women play so well with one another."

"But you play games, Slade."

He winced inwardly at the sudden sadness in her voice. He wiped his mouth and then his fingers on a paper napkin. He captured her hand, squeezing it gently. "Not with you, sweetheart." He saw the unsureness in her emerald eyes as she studied him in the intervening silence.

Cat swallowed a sudden lump in her throat. Tears pricked her eyes. Angrily she shoved these unexpected feelings back down inside, to be dealt with later, and shook her head. "I just don't know what to think, Slade. Ever since we met, I felt as though you wanted something from me. At first, I thought it was just because you were interested in me—as a woman. But later, once we developed a friendship, I changed my mind about that. Right now, I'm not sure what you want from me." She sat rigidly. "Kai mentioned you had a mine down in Colombia. By any chance does that explain why I'm here at your ranch?" She prayed it wasn't so. Slade's brows dipped. He shoved the plate aside, concentrating on Cat, hearing the pain in her voice. "I'm sorry, Cat. I really screwed up, then. Yeah, I had flown to Maine to try and persuade you to come and work for me. But—" he managed a shy smile "—when I saw you all my logic went out the door. I hadn't expected you to affect me like you did." He picked up her hand, cradling it gently. "I wanted you to come here for personal motives, not professional ones. Please, believe me." Slade refused to relinquish her hand. He reached out with the other, lightly tracing her cheek and delicate jawline. "And when it comes to you on a personal level..." His voice turned harsh. "Do you know how damned hard it's been to keep my hands off you so you could heal? As much as I wanted to put my arms around you, hold you tight against me and kiss the hell out of you, I knew I couldn't." He saw hope suddenly spring like an emerald flame into her widening eyes.

"Look, let's untangle our communication with one another. Yes, I came hunting you down." He halted, struggling with words. "I'm lousy at talk, Cat. Let me show you how I feel about you." Slade leaned down, wanting, needing to feel her lips once again beneath his. "I've been wanting to do this for so damn long..." He molded his mouth to hers. An explosion of need reeled through Slade as her soft, pliant lips yielded to him. He felt her arm sliding around his neck and he groaned as she lightly swayed against his chest. He had to forcibly stop his hands from following her curves upward to the small, firm breasts resting against him. Instead, Slade framed her face, cherishing her wine-bathed lips, using his tongue to probe the corners of her mouth.

"You make a man thirsty for more," he groaned as he probed the inner, moist recesses of her mouth. A column of need roared through him, his body hardening with a fire of its own. Cat's breath was moist and ragged against him and Slade reveled in her ardor. He allowed his hands to trail down her slender neck and cup her shoulders. Reluctantly, he eased away, then stared down hungrily at Cat. She was his, all of her.

As Slade drew back, his hands captured hers. "Listen to me," he told her roughly, his voice heavy with desire. "I want you like I've never wanted another woman, Cat. And it's not because of what I need from you professionally." Slade caressed her cheek, reveling in her luminous eyes. "Can you separate the issues? It's important to me that you can."

Cat was barely coherent after the branding kiss that had seared her lips. She hadn't been merely hungry for Slade's touch, she'd been starved, and her returning fervor had caught her totally off guard. Never had a man affected her so profoundly as did Slade. Touching Slade physically was merely an extension of everything else Cat already felt in her heart.

Her heart? Cat was careful not to place any emphasis on that unexpected and unknown quantity right now. If age had taught her nothing else, it had taught her that time would reveal what was real in their burgeoning relationship. Now, Slade was waiting for an answer from her. She stared into his eyes, seeing fear mingled with hope. Fear?

"I want to separate these things, Slade. Why don't you tell me what you want from me and then we can clear the air. I don't want to suspect your every move or intention. You can't blame me for reacting like this. Put yourself in my place."

Slade refused to allow Cat to reclaim her hands. He gave her all his attention. "Professionally, I want you to think about building a mine for me. That's all. The decision is up to you and I'm not going to pressure you about it." He gently squeezed her fingers. "But some of your reaction isn't warranted. At least, not with me and what we share."

She hung her head for an instant, wanting to believe Slade. "Maybe all the years of being in the field have made me more isolated than I wanted to be." She sighed. "Maybe I just need someplace I can go to when it all becomes too much to take."

"Don't you have a permanent address? An apartment on the coast? A condo?" Slade ran his thumb gently in small circles on the back of her hand.

Cat shook her head, relaxing beneath Slade's ministrations, wonderful tingling sensations fleeing up her arm as he lightly stroked her. "The Triple K is home."

"That's the family homestead. What about some place special for you?"

"No. The mine I'm building on my next assignment becomes my home. I live in a tent or trailer just like everyone else."

"Well, you apparently need more. I noticed you called the ranch your home today for the first time."

A shiver of longing moved through her and Cat acknowledged his statement. "I did, didn't I?"

"Yes."

Cat gave a rueful shake of her head. "I think I'm burned out and haven't even recognized my own symptoms."

Slade reluctantly let her go and brought their plates back over so that they could finish lunch. He wasn't hungry, but he recognized the need to step back and talk about their other problems. "I think this accident has helped open you up to some of your feelings," he said quietly, wanting to find a way to probe the content of her restless nights.

"I can't shake the nightmares, Slade."

He treaded lightly, sipping his wine. "Have you figured out why they're still with you?"

Cat picked up a ripe red apple, the surface slick and polished as she slowly turned it around between her hands. "As stupid as this sounds, I find myself standing at the opening to a mine. And then, I break out into a cold sweat."

"Afraid to enter it?"

Cat gnawed on her lower lip. "Yes. Of all things, Slade, I'm afraid to go down into an adit. I've spent the past ten years of my life in shafts, even those that miners were afraid to go into, and I never thought anything of it. Can you believe that? It's just blown me away." She looked down at her hands, closed tightly around the apple. "More important, it shouldn't affect me like it has. It's stupid."

"Ever fallen off a horse?"

"More times than I can count. Why?"

"Rafe said you can apply the same logic to a mine. There isn't a miner, an engineer or geologist who's been trapped who hasn't experienced that same strangling fear."

Relief was mirrored in Cat's features. "You're using the right word: strangling. Sometimes, when I think about it, I can barely breathe. I feel as if an invisible hand is choking off my breath and I'm slowly suffocating."

"Like you were in that cave-in."

Cold fear took away the heat within her. "Yes."

"Well," Slade said slowly, "there are two things you can do, Cat. One is to never enter another mine and give up a good portion of your work. Or you can go face that fear by entering a mine again. It's like getting thrown off a horse and then climbing right back on. The sooner you do it, the quicker the fear recedes."

"Does the fear ever go away?"

"It's different for everyone."

"You've been trapped. How does it affect you when you go into a shaft?"

"There's always a thread of fear deep down in me," Slade admitted. "But then, I swing my focus to why I'm down there, and the fever of finding a gem outweighs my fear."

"What have three cave-ins taught you?"

A slight smile pulled at his mouth. "To value each minute of each day like there will never be another. I used to live in the future; I don't anymore."

Cat closed her eyes, relief washing through her. "I'm so glad you understand." Her voice held a tremor. "Every day I find myself enjoying little things I overlooked before. I used to ignore so much, Slade."

"But you don't anymore," he said softly, giving her a tender smile that promised so much.

They finished lunch and Slade repacked the basket, placing it in the Jeep. Cat stood near the river, watching a bass leap out at a dragonfly that had flown too close to his lily-pad home beneath the water. As he turned back to her, Slade read the sad expression on her face. She was allowing him to sense her feelings, no longer hiding so much of herself from him. He found himself smiling. Each time they shared an encounter, it was as if another petal of their relationship had opened.

Slade's feelings were strong toward Cat and he didn't fight them. How many nights had he lain awake, thinking of her? She was like him in some respects, always traveling the world in search of a new adventure. Cat was also strong and independent, and he liked that about her. Yet, as he studied her profile, he was achingly aware of her vulnerability.

Cat was pleasantly surprised as Slade gently drew her back against him. Her lips parted as he brushed her hair with a kiss. "Slade…" She whispered his name.

"This is what I wanted to do," he told her in a low voice, his fingers gently massaging her shoulders. Her skin was soft and firm beneath his explorations. "The sunlight dances off your hair and I can see the gold in it."

Cat's smile softened. "Pyrite. Fool's gold."

"No way, lady. You're a rare vein of gold that few are ever privileged to see."

Her nostrils flared as she inhaled his salty, masculine scent. "I'm afraid, Slade."

He opened his eyes, holding her a little more firmly, disturbed by the tremulous quality in her tone. "Of what?"

"Of you."

"I won't hurt you."

"Not intentionally."

"Have you always run, Cat?"

She shook her head, glorying in his male strength, the tenderness he offered her. She needed it badly. "No, but you're different."

He rested his mouth against the silky strands of her hair. "Explain."

"You show how you feel. Most of the men I know are

closed up like the mines we dig. I haven't had much experience with a man of your openness."

"Ah, I see." He pressed a kiss to her temple. "Never
took on a Texan?" He deliberately teased her, feeling the
tension in her shoulders. Then, almost as quickly, her tension dissolved beneath his cajoling tone.

"No. Never."

"What else bothers you about me?"

"Just that." Cat tilted her head, catching his teasing expression. "And what you wanted from me professionally."

Slade smiled, feeling the softness of her cheek against
his sandpapery one. "I'm sorry I didn't discuss the matter
sooner, Cat. The mine became secondary to your coming here to the ranch. You were what was important to
me. I'm not lying, nor am I playing a game with you. If
this has been on your mind, though, I wish you'd asked
sooner."

"I was afraid of the answer, Slade," Cat admitted
hoarsely. "No one likes to think they're manipulated or
strung along."

Slade sighed deeply. "I guess I deserve that from you.
My intentions were to discuss the mine when you were
ready. Right now, you're still healing." He kissed her
temple.

Cat leaned back against him. "What I want to know
is, why aren't you married? A man with your attributes
would turn any woman's head."

His smile disappeared and he gently folded his arms
around her as they stood at the bank of the river. "Came
close a couple of times," Slade admitted.

"But?"

"What woman was going to accept my traveling life-
style and stay at home without me for months at a time?"

"She could go with you."

He shook his head. "Not the women I fell in love with. They wanted a home and a family. Until recently, I couldn't provide the kind of security they wanted. You know how geologists bum around the world. There aren't many women willing to make a home in the desert for a year, or live in a jungle in Thailand while you hunt for gems. Women get the worst end of the deal: loneliness. I can understand their position and that's the main reason I haven't married." Slade gazed down at her. "I told you before: I'm looking for a woman who's as footloose as I am."

Cat ignored the invitation in his voice. She was thinking along similar lines. Finding a man who would accept her vocation and allow her to travel had slimmed candidates to a bare minimum. "I don't find many men willing to let me roam, either."

"Just two old travel-weary vets of the rock industry, huh?"

Cat smiled. "With at least another couple of decades of bumming around left in them." If she could control her fear of mine entry.

"I think when I'm eighty, I'll still be a rock hound at heart."

"The earth is too alive to us to ever walk away from," Cat agreed. And knowing that, she suddenly vowed to overcome her fear. The earth had always been good to her.

"I like your attitude, lady. Come to think of it, I haven't seen much not to like about you."

"Wait." Cat laughed. "I get in a blue funk every once in awhile."

"And when you do, what happens?"

"I get crabby and crawl into my shell."

"Retreat is the better part of valor, maybe?"

"You understand."

"I try," Slade whispered, pressing one last kiss on her temple before he released her. *Soon,* he promised Cat softly, *soon you'll be in my arms like I've been dreaming for the past month.*

As they walked back toward the Jeep, Slade stole a look at her. "How'd you like me to tell you about my mine, sometime? When you're up to it, that is."

Cat stared nonplussed at him for a moment, digesting his question. "Let me think about it."

Slade held up both hands in a gesture of friendly surrender. "Great. I just don't want any more misunderstandings between us, Cat. You tell me when you're ready, and I'll spill out everything."

Cat nodded and slipped into the seat of the Jeep. "Fair enough."

Slade accepted her dictate and turned the key. The Jeep roared to life and they followed the dirt road beneath the thousands of pecan trees, heading back to Mourning Dove Ranch.

Cat mulled over his explanation about the mine and was relieved. He hadn't asked her to the ranch just to get her professional services. The intimacy Slade had established with her after lunch had sent such sharp longing through her, it was worse than the pain she had experienced with her broken ribs. Cat forced herself to think of other matters. Casting a glance over at Slade, she decided to find out more about his mysterious mining project.

Chapter 7

As they got out of the Jeep and walked into the house, Cat gathered all that was left of her nerve and spoke up.

"Slade?"

"Yes?"

"I don't want to wait to hear the story of your mine." She came to a halt and rested her fingers lightly on his upper arm. "Do you have some time this afternoon?"

Pleasure shone in his eyes as he looked down at her. "That took a lot of courage, Cat. I was hoping you'd ask."

He guided Cat to the kitchen and gave Pilar the basket. Then Slade poured them some fragrant coffee and stole some date-nut bread that Pilar had just baked. He sat down next to Cat on the back porch, his long legs spread out in front of him.

She cast a glance over at him. "Why were you hoping I'd ask?"

"A long time ago, Cat, I found that people really didn't want something unless they asked for it. My mother used to shake her finger at me and tell me to hold my own counsel, opinions and advice unless someone asked for them." Slade gave her a little-boy grin as he polished off his chunk of warm bread. "Over the years, I've found my mother to be right—as usual."

"Wise words from your mother," Cat agreed solemnly. She wanted to rest against him and smiled to herself. "Tell me about your mine, oh weaver of spells and fables."

Slade nodded and settled back. "A long time ago, back in 1531, the Spanish conquistador, Francisco Pizarro, landed on the coast of Peru. To his delight and greed, he found fabulous emeralds there, and in Chile and Ecuador. He became entranced with where these emeralds had come from and tortured countless Indians to get this information.

"Finally, in 1537, the conquistadors had the answer they sought: Chivor, Colombia. There they found emeralds in feldspar-rich veins of yellow-gray shale or limestone. Chivor's crystal-clear emeralds made the conquistadors bend the backs of every Indian they could find and put them into slavery to work the mine. Twelve hundred Indians were kept caged in Chivor's tunnels on a food ration that even a rat couldn't subsist on. Spain's monarchy couldn't tolerate the conditions the Indians were placed in, and ordered them freed of further enslavement. Eventually, production dropped off and the jungle reclaimed Chivor. The mine became 'lost.'

"Then, in 1896, Chivor was rediscovered by a Colombian mining engineer who used a three-hundred-year-old map he had found in an old manuscript. Chivor now operates as one of the largest privately owned emerald mines in the world."

Cat smiled wistfully. "You sound as if you wished you had been that Colombian mining engineer to have found Chivor again."

Slade nodded, thinking how beautiful Cat looked when she was relaxed. "You'd better believe it. There's another well-known emerald site in Colombia. Chivor sits up where a breeze will stir and the temperature is cooler on the slopes of the jungle-capped mountains. The Muzo Valley, which sits in the Cordillera Oriental, an extension of the Andes Mountain chain, is hot, humid and insect-infested. The emeralds at Muzo are found in white calcite veins between beds of black shale.

"At Muzo, the emeralds are flawed heavily with inclusions, making them look cloudy. Chivor's emeralds are clear in comparison but lack the range of color that Muzo's hold. Muzo's emeralds are considered far more valuable because of this color range. Personally, I disagree. I'll take a less-inclusioned emerald over a cloudy one with color any day. Anyway, Muzo's reputation is that of greed, murder and thievery run amok. It got so bad that it was shut down in 1970 because of the number of murders and crimes. The mines of Muzo had been privately owned up until that time. The owners feared for their lives and the yield of their mines. They begged for government protection in the form of soldiers. The private companies agreed to lease their mines to the government in return for protection and guarding of their emerald treasure by the national police."

Slade glanced over at Cat. "The guaqueros, or treasure hunters, went on digging their rat tunnels into the emerald mines anyway. Cave-ins kill a lot of them. So does suffocation, because these rat holes aren't properly ventilated. The guaquero who manages to tunnel into one of the emerald mines then begins to steal. If he finds a stone, he must risk his own life trying to get it to an emerald dealer, known as an esmeraldero, who waits at the Rio Itoco, the river at the bottom of the Muzo Valley, to sell it."

"And have the police stopped some of the bloodshed, Slade?"

He grimaced. "To a degree, they have. But what has happened is that the police are either paid off by the guaqueros to look the other way while they steal from the mines or they just plain feel sorry for the tens of thousands of starving humans who have flocked from the squalor of Bogotá out into the field in search of their personal fortune."

"That's the history. How do you fit into this interesting puzzle?" Cat asked, watching his blue eyes grow warm with a smile. Slade made her feel good and she couldn't conceive of being away from his sunny presence.

"Let me tell you about my colorful partner who lives in Houston. Once upon a time, there was this grizzled old Texas diehard. His name was Alvin Moody and he made his fortune gambling on oil wells instead of dry holes. Pretty soon, his oil discoveries outweighed the dry holes he found, so he became one of the Texas elite money-wise. He's about six-foot-four and even taller in the stories told about him. Alvin's a meek name, and it doesn't fit him as far as I'm concerned. That aside, Alvin got restless with the gas-and-oil game. He wanted to stretch himself and had always had a fascination for gems. He'd heard of Chivor, Cosquez and Muzo in Colombia. And being the street-smart, junkyard dog that he was, he figured there were more emeralds than just in those three areas."

"How old is Alvin?" Cat asked, enjoying Slade's story.

Slade rubbed his jaw. "Let's see…somewhere around seventy-three. He's got snow-white hair, squinty blue eyes that'll drop you at thirty feet if you cross him the wrong way and a voice that booms like a bear."

"Sounds like a real character," she said with a chuckle.

"I think Texas glories in them," Slade agreed. "I was down in a sleazy bar at the bad end of Bogotá when I ran into Alvin."

"I won't ask what you were doing there," Cat said dryly.

"Same thing he was: looking for stories about the emerald-rich mountains of Colombia. I'd been there seven days and picked up quite a bit of bull. In between, I'd play rounds of poker with the emerald dealers, listen, learn and store it."

"You a good poker player, Slade?" Cat knew the answer to that without asking, but couldn't resist teasing him.

Slade grinned. "Wait and see. Alvin came into this dirty, smoky bar, twice as big as life, all decked out in a khaki safari suit, Texas cowboy hat and boots. He spotted our game and invited himself to sit down. There were four scruffy-looking esmeralderos who smelled of the Rio Itoco, plus me in my usual grubby geology gear and Alvin. Everyone in the bar stopped talking and gawked when he rolled on in and invited himself to our table. It was a hell of a sight."

"And so you all played poker?"

Slade hedged and held up his hand. "A fifth esmeraldero sat down. Juan Cortez was his name. He was a slimy-looking character; looked as if somebody was hunting him. He didn't have any money but we let him join the game because he said he owned three hundred and forty acres near Muzo and had a map where he knew emeralds were located. Whoever won, and believe me, he was planning on winning, would get the map. Cortez was hungry for some capital to start his venture into the area. That's why he wanted into the game."

"How did Cortez get this map?"

His eyes darkened. "Cat, you never ask an esmeraldero where he got anything or you're liable to be lookin' down the barrel of his pistol."

"Oh."

"The stakes got high. A lot higher than the cash I was carrying on me. I saw that glimmer in Alvin Moody's eyes. He, like I, believed that Cortez had the real thing by the way the guy was acting. I didn't want to fold my hand and Cortez wouldn't take my American Express credit card as a promise of cash."

Cat laughed. "Smart man! You might not be paid up or it could be stolen for all Cortez knew."

"Fortunately, Alvin came to my rescue. He didn't have to stake me but he said he'd loan me the money I wanted. If I won, he'd get half the mine." Slade's eyes twinkled. "Alvin had a busted card hand, so he was smart enough to sense that I was holding some pretty good ones or he wouldn't have made the offer."

"It wasn't out of the generosity of his heart, was it?"

"Hell, no. Alvin's a businessman. I'd have done the same thing."

"Cortez must have been holding some good cards, too."

"He was," Slade admitted, flashing a smile. "Alvin

staked me. By this time, there was twenty thousand dollars on the table. Everyone in El Toro Posada was crowded around our table: farmers, miners and drifters. It was getting pretty tense, so I laid my pearl-handled Colt .45 revolver on the table close to my right hand where everyone could see it. The crowd stepped back a couple of paces. Alvin grinned. Cortez sweated. The other four esmeralderos all bowed out with a curse as the ante continued upward. In another ten minutes, there was forty thousand dollars lying on the table with just Cortez and myself still in the game. Alvin kept peeling off thousand-dollar bills from that wad of money he had pulled out of his pocket; cool as hell."

Cat sat up, rapt. "Well, what happened?"

Slade pushed an errant lock of hair off his brow. "I called Cortez's hand. He grinned that evil little smile of his. He had pointy teeth that reminded me of a weasel's. He said, '*Señores*, I'm happy to take your money,' and laid out a ten of clubs, jack of diamonds, queen of clubs, king of spades and an ace of clubs."

"A straight, ace high," Cat acknowledged, breath lodged in her throat. "And then what happened, Slade?"

"Cortez grinned wider and threw his hands over the pile of money and raw emeralds sitting in the middle of the table. Alvin said, 'Hold it, snake breath.' And he gripped both of Cortez's hands and then looked straight at me. 'Your turn,' he told me. So, I began laying out my cards one at a time. I started with a ten of hearts, jack of hearts, queen of hearts, king of hearts and finally, the ace of hearts."

"My God," Cat whispered, "a royal flush. What a time to get one." And then she gave him a hard look. "You didn't cheat, did you?"

Slade looked momentarily wounded. "Me?" A devastating smile pulled at his mouth. Slade held up both his hands. "Sweetheart, I'm the luckiest damn bastard you've ever seen. Even luckier than Alvin, and he's not too shabby, either."

Cat laughed with him. "So what did Cortez do? Cry?"

Slade snorted. "I can tell you've got a lot to learn about these snake pits in Colombia. No, he lunged for my revolver. Alvin jerked him up like a rat out of a lab jar, holding him while he screamed all kinds of curses at us. I put all our hard-earned money into every pocket I had. I even stuffed it into Alvin's safari jacket and into that ten-gallon hat he was wearing. I knew we were in a hell of a lot of trouble. Any moment, any one of those men could jump us. I grabbed my revolver, firing it three times into the air. Everyone stepped back, eyeing us like a pack of wolves.

"Alvin held Cortez by his ragged clothes at each shoulder while I searched the little guy for his map. I found it, opened it up to make sure it wasn't a blank piece of paper. It wasn't. As far as I could tell, it was genuine. Cortez grudgingly signed the land deed over to us. We really didn't have the time to stop and check it out. We had to get out of there or we'd be dead meat. Alvin dropped Cortez and then unpacked that big, evil-looking .360 Magnum, Dirty Harry type of revolver he carries, and pointed it at the crowd while we backed out of the bar.

"Outside, we hightailed it for my Jeep and dug holes getting out of there. Alvin was staying at the Tequendama Hotel, so we went over there to rest up, have a tall, cool one and see if the deed had been worth all our efforts."

Cat stood, suddenly excited and unable to sit still any longer. "This is all true, Slade?"

"Yes. It gets better. Want a drink?"

"I could use one."

Slade slowly uncoiled from his relaxed position and guided her back into the house. Cat sat on the stool while he went behind the bar to mix up a pitcher of margaritas. She put both elbows on the polished cedar.

"How could you verify if the map was genuine?"

"We went to the deeds office in Bogotá and checked it out. Cortez had been as good as his word. As to the possibility of emeralds on it, we had to go to the location and find out. For all we knew, Cortez could have sold us a bunch of jungle with nothing but mosquitoes and anacondas crawling all over it. We packed up the Jeep the next day and took off for the Silla de Montar Valley."

"Where was it located?" Cat wanted to know, thanking him as he handed her a margarita.

Slade rested easily against the bar, sipping his drink. "How about two valleys over from the Muzo mines?"

Cat's eyes widened. "That close to another emerald field?" she gasped.

"Yes, ma'am. When we located Cortez's landholding, it was in the saddle between Caballo and Lazo Mountain. That's how the valley got its name. Alvin and I spent a month out there."

"What kind of rock base, Slade?"

He had her, he thought, seeing the sudden interest in Cat's eyes. Now she was starting to ask a mining engineer's questions.

"Calcite limestone. Prime sedimentary rock for emeralds. But then, you know that."

"Not the black shale of Muzo?"

"No. From the core samples I took, there is a thick base of limestone just beneath the topsoil and subsoil strata." He took a pencil from his pocket and reached for a small notepad, drawing her a quick illustration. "Perfect limestone for emeralds here," he said. "Beneath it, black shale. My guess is that it's the same stratum that has been pushed to the surface at Muzo." He tapped the limestone stratum with the pencil. "Here, at our location, it's still buried pretty deeply."

"Why are you saying calcite limestone when all evidence points to the shale bearing the emeralds instead, Slade?"

He straightened up. "Wait here," was all he said, and he disappeared out the door through the kitchen.

Cat sat there for what seemed a long time. By her watch, it was only five minutes, but it felt like hours. Slade came back, an enigmatic look on his face and a kidskin leather pouch in his left hand. He gently handed her the pouch.

"Open it."

She hadn't realized that she was holding her breath as she loosened the drawstrings. Then she drew out five uncut emeralds still embedded in the white rock known as calcite. They completely took her breath away. The perfect, six-sided green crystals were buried in the surrounding matrix, glinting with staggering color beneath the light at the bar.

"Incredible, Slade…"

"Green fire," he whispered, leaning close to her, their heads nearly touching as they both stared down at the matrix. "Gem of the gods, something mere mortals would murder their best friend for and sell their soul to the devil to possess. Green fire…"

"I—it's simply beautiful." She held it up to the light. "From what I know of Colombian emeralds, these uncut emeralds have far fewer inclusions than most." Cat leveled a look at him. "Emeralds of this quality are worth a fortune, Slade."

"They came from the land we won from Cortez, Cat. Take a good look at this, hold it and let it burn into your memory."

She didn't have to be told to hold it. Automatically, Cat could swear she felt a shimmering vibrancy that only a true gem possessed. What she held in her hands was priceless, the dark green vivid against the pure white calcite. "They're too beautiful for words," she whispered, turning them slowly, watching the light refract through the clear, near-perfect depths of each crystal.

Slade cupped his hands around hers, holding her gaze. "Your eyes are even more beautiful than they are, did you know that? Now, maybe you can appreciate what I see when I look at you."

Shaken by the intimacy of his voice, Cat's lips parted. She felt the roughness of his hands holding hers, sending flames of longing through her. "W-what are you going to do with this?"

Slade released her and straightened up. "Put it on the shelf over there. Another story to tell my next guest or visitor," he said. "What would you do with it?"

Cat carefully placed the matrix back in the pouch and sat it on the bar between them. "Most men would have sold it."

"I always save the first gems I find at a new site." He gave her an intense look. "Remember what I said before: money isn't everything. This may be worth two hundred thousand on the open market, but that doesn't matter."

Slade watched Cat nod in understanding. An odd smile tugged at his mouth. "I told Alvin I wanted the best for this project. The limestone deposit is almost a flaky kind of black shale. The chances of cave-in are great. I wanted someone who was used to dealing with unusual mine situations. You were the only one I wanted for the job, Cat." He picked up the bag that contained the matrix of emeralds and set it aside. "Your reputation far preceded you, and I told Alvin that we're dealing with a mine in a country that's used to volcanic and earthquake potential. I didn't want just any mining engineer. There are special stresses and environmental items to be considered in how the mine will be constructed. That's where your special talents come in."

The idea was initially exciting to Cat. Seconds later, the pit of her stomach became a knot of cold, drenching fear. Yes, from what she knew of the rock strata of Colombia, earthquakes were always a hazard to a mine shaft sunk into the unstable earth. She broke into a sweat, focused on the fear that was now gobbling her up whole.

Slade frowned, noticing the sheen on Cat's forehead. The color had drained from her cheeks and the excitement he had seen in her eyes had flickered and died. Automatically, he reached across to close his hand over hers. "What is it?" he coaxed.

A lump grew in her throat. "I'm scared, Slade."

His fingers tightened. "Look at me, Cat. Come on now, listen carefully; the only way to conquer that fear is to face it. I know it's not easy. And it won't be pleasant. But I'll be there, if that makes any difference to you."

Oh, yes, that would make a difference, Cat wanted to blurt out. But the words were frozen in her aching throat.

Slade's low-timbred voice moved through her.

"Cat, if I didn't think this was best for you, I wouldn't even suggest it. Aside from my wanting you to sink that shaft, you have to enter a mine somewhere in the world. I'd rather it be ours. I can be with you. I can help you cope with that fear."

"I'll think about it," she whispered, taking her cold hands from his warm ones.

Slade measured Cat's hesitancy, trying to ferret out the reason for her behavior. He had seen the glow of adventure in her face minutes before, the promise of another challenge to be reckoned with and tamed. And he had also seen the fear swallow up that glow like dark thunderclouds rolling threateningly across the horizon. He placed both elbows on the bar and hunkered down.

"Cat, I don't have much time. While you've been recovering here the past six weeks, I've been in my office coordinating the leasing of heavy earth-moving equipment. Alvin's down in Bogotá right now directing the effort." Slade released a breath of air, his gaze moving over her pensive features. "You know as well as anyone what kind of effort it takes to get equipment, construction supplies and a host of other essential items into a jungle area."

Cat nodded, biting her lower lip. As much as she wanted to ignore Slade's persuasive words, she couldn't. She could no longer tell herself she was immune to Slade on a personal level, either. "It's tough any way you want to cut it," she agreed.

Slade absently moved the pouch around on the polished surface of the bar. "We're trying to be discreet about the movement of the equipment. If word gets out in Bogotá about our possible find, we'll have hundreds of treasure-hungry guaqueros following us." He snorted softly. "And that's just the tip of the iceberg. Once they know we've got something, all hell will break loose. We're trying to keep a lid on it, but time's short."

Raising her chin, Cat met Slade's sober blue gaze. "As much as I would like to help you, Slade, I don't know if I can walk back into a mine. And I couldn't stand outside a shaft that's being built by laborers and not go inside to check their work." She bowed her head. "I feel so humiliated. I've never admitted I was scared to anyone."

"You've never been brought to your knees before, Cat," he began quietly. "Most of us get the hell knocked out of us long before you took your turn. It's not the end of the world, even though I know it looks like it to you. And as for having no guts or backbone, you've got more than most. The cave-in is going to show you how to reach down inside yourself and find a new wellspring of strength, Cat."

She sniffed, tears rolling down her cheeks. "I'm empty, Slade. How can you draw on nothing?" she whispered painfully.

His smile was gentle as he leaned forward, kissing her closed eyes, tasting the saltiness of her tears. "Trust me, it's there. And you can draw on it when you have to face walking into a shaft again."

A sob broke from deep inside her, and Cat felt Slade's hands slide from her face. She sat there all alone on the stool, hurting and feeling more alone than she ever had in all her life. She had thought she knew what loneliness was, but she hadn't—not like this. When she felt Slade's arms go around her, drawing her against the warm hardness of his body, Cat abandoned herself to his strength. She had none of her own left; she took what he offered her of his, instead.

Slade pressed a kiss to her hair, aware of the subtle

fragrance of jasmine around her. He held Cat while she wept, rocking her as he would rock a hurt child, allowing her to release the pent-up anguish she had tried to ignore. He felt his own eyes mist, and shut them, resting his jaw lightly against Cat's hair, murmuring words of comfort to her. The power of his emotions stunned even him; the protectiveness he felt toward Cat took him by surprise. He wanted to ease her hurt, absorb it so she could be cleansed of all the horror he knew stalked her twenty-four hours a day. Finally, her sobs lessened and Slade dug a handkerchief from his back pocket, lifted her chin and dried her face of tears.

Slade nudged stray wisps of damp hair from Cat's cheek and temple, easing them behind her delicate ears. His mouth worked to hold back a barrage of feelings. "When I first met you, something happened. And I know you feel it, too. There's a chemistry between us and I want a chance to explore that with you. Hell, we're not kids anymore, Cat. The rose-colored glasses were taken away from us a long time ago. I'm putting you between a rock and a hard place and I know it. I won't let you go, no matter how frightened you are of entering a mine. You can learn to trust me and lean on me. I won't let you down."

Cat let him hold her, unable to respond, yet desperate to believe him.

"I'll help you get back on your feet in two ways," Slade went on. "I'll provide a mine to work in and I'll be there to help you fight your fear." Slade caressed her flaming red cheeks. "Together, we're strong, Cat, and we both know that. Don't run and hide from this." Slade's heart fell when he saw that Cat remained numb in his arms. What else could he do or say?

Cat's eyes reflected the confusion she felt. Could her feelings for Slade heal this overwhelming fear of another cave-in?

Slade, feeling her slip away, groped to find something that would force her to stay. "If you can't agree to do it for the reasons I've just laid out for you, then do it because you owe me. I saved your life and this is what I'm asking in return: I want you to build me a mine in Colombia. An even and fair trade for saving your life. What do you say?" Slade held his breath, watching the shock register on Cat's face. He groaned inwardly. God, what had he done by blurting out the first thing that came to mind? Was he wrong to use her own sense of duty to blackmail her into conquering her fear?

Miserably, Cat looked away, far too uncertain of herself to deal with Slade's overture. She had to escape that wall of pain, run and hide in the quiet confines of her room. "Let me go, Slade. I've got to rest..."

He took a step back, allowing his hands to slip from her shoulders. Slade felt Cat withdrawing her temporary trust from him. He had blown it by telling her she owed him. Suddenly, he was afraid. Would he be willing to lose her to make her whole again? As he stood there, Slade knew the answer: he cared enough to risk everything to make Cat whole.

"Go ahead," he coaxed in a strained voice. "You're tired and you've been through hell today. Just lie down and sleep on it, Cat."

Sleep? How? Cat had walked to the sanctuary of her peaceful room, but despite the dizzying brilliance of the sun slanting through the trellis overhead, she felt as if she were again in the dark pit. Her conscience warred with her fear. Slade was right: she owed him. Then why had it hurt so much when he'd said it? Cat lay on her stomach, clutching the pillow between her arms, head buried in its goosedown folds. *I'm a mess inside. I can't think straight, I can't get a hold on my emotions. Why can't I just let my logic sort all this out?*

She lay there for almost an hour, an internal battle waging between her malfunctioning mental faculties and the tumult of emotions that refused to be ignored any longer. Cat cried some more, terrible animal sounds torn from her soul. They were sounds she'd heard others make, but never her. Finally, her eyes red-rimmed and the pillow soaked, Cat fell into an exhausted, dreamless sleep, an empty vessel floating aimlessly on a sea of dark, turbulent emotions.

Slade was frowning heavily, holding a tumbler of whiskey between his hands, when Pilar padded into the living room. She hovered near the bar where he sat.

"Señor Slade?"

He barely looked up. "Yes?"

"The *señorita*, she weeps like a woman who has lost everything." Pilar shrugged her delicate shoulders, then gave him a beseeching look. "I just passed her room on the way to the linen closet."

Slade's hands tightened around the heavy glass. "Thank you, Pilar."

She hesitated, tilting her head. "You are not going to see if she needs help?"

His mouth worked into a thin line, holding back the emotions that threatened to overtake him. "No," he said harshly, and then gave Pilar an apologetic look. He hadn't meant to take his anger out on Pilar because of his own stupidity. "No," he repeated more gently.

Pilar frowned, her huge brown eyes searching his for a long moment. *"Si, señor,"* she said, then turned away, going back to the kitchen.

Slade swore under his breath, scraping the stool loudly against the cedar floor as he moved. He stalked through the room, going out to the porch. Continuing outdoors, he opened the screen, striding down the slight incline toward the small stream winding lazily through the cottonwoods. Slade finally came to a halt at the edge of the clear green water, staring angrily down at the sun-dappled surface. Throwing down the last of the whiskey, his knuckles whitened as he gripped the tumbler. The whiskey was hot, searing, like the pain he felt for Cat.

I should go to her; she needs me. No, that's not true. If she needed me, she'd have stayed. She wouldn't have run to her bedroom. Slade snorted violently, his blue eyes icy with anger aimed at himself. *You blew it, Donovan. You dumb son of a bitch, why did you have to tell her she owed you?* He raked his fingers through his hair, unable to contain his inner fury over his desperate action.

Miserably, Slade allowed the full weight of what he'd just done to Cat overtake him. *I did it for her,* he told himself. But his cartwheeling mind wasn't sure. Confused and upset, he knew he needed some counsel. Kai Travis had always been his sounding board when he got into a bind. He needed her common sense, because he didn't know how to untie the knot he'd just created between Cat and himself.

Kai met him at the sliding screen door as he walked up the steps.

"Slade? You look awful. What's wrong?"

Self-consciously, Slade thrust his hands into the pockets of his jeans, looking down at Kai. "I'm sorry to ride over unannounced, Kai."

She took him by the arm, leading him into the living room and to the couch. "Since when did you need an invitation? What's going on? Is something wrong with Cat?"

He shrugged and sat down. "I really screwed up this afternoon with her, Kai." He rubbed his face tiredly.

Kai sat on the small hassock in front of him. "Tell me what happened."

The quiet tenor of Kai's voice shook loose all his suppressed anxiety and worry. Slowly, Slade unwound the sordid chain of events. When he finished, Kai grimaced.

"I'm sorry, Slade. I didn't mean to mention your mine to Cat. I had just assumed that you had already discussed the possibility of her working with you." She reached over, apologetically squeezing his arm.

"It's not your fault, Kai. Cat thought I had brought her to the ranch just to use her professional talents."

"Does she still?"

"I took her on a picnic earlier today and we got that issue straightened out." Slade shook his head. "And then I really blew it. I tried playing amateur psychologist by making her think she could repay me for saving her life by building the mine. How could I have been so stupid? Words were just pouring out of me. I was in such a panic, afraid that I was going to lose her. I didn't want to, Kai, I spoke without thinking. It had a devastating effect on Cat. She's probably still crying…"

With a sigh, Kai got up and went to the cabinet, pouring each of them a bit of brandy. She handed one snifter to Slade and sat back down. "Drink up, you need it."

Sorrowfully, Slade downed the stinging brandy. He sucked air between his clenched teeth, holding the delicate crystal in his hands. Slowly, the knots began to dissolve in his gut as he sat with her in the intervening silence.

"She's probably going to run," he muttered.

"You mean, leave Mourning Dove?"

"Sure, wouldn't you? Put yourself in Cat's place. I'm barely able to get her to believe that I didn't bring her to the ranch under false pretenses. And then I tell her she owes me." Slade suddenly stood up, unable to stand the anger he was aiming at himself.

Kai watched him pace for several minutes. "What will you lose, Slade?"

He halted. "Cat."

"You love her?"

"I didn't realize that I did until a half hour ago. I had all these feelings about her, Kai. I never thought there was a woman who could tolerate my life-style, but I know she can. Cat's just like me in many ways."

"And does she love you, Slade?"

He ran his fingers through his hair in aggravation. "Who the hell knows?"

"I think she does," Kai provided softly. "Slade, stop pacing for a minute and come and sit down."

Slade sat, staring at Kai. "Sometimes, I see longing in her eyes and I hear the emotion in her voice, Kai. Every time we're together, it's so damned special."

With a smile, Kai said, "I've been privileged to share a great deal with Cat since she's been here, Slade. I know you're very special to her, too."

"Well, I just destroyed whatever was there."

"Maybe, maybe not. Why don't you go home and talk with her? Iron this out and tell her how you feel. Let her know that you really didn't mean to make her feel guilty

or hold her to building your mine. Tell her you were trying to make her address her fear."

"I just thought that she'd want to face up to it. I saw it
as a perfect solution to all of Cat's problems."

Gently, Kai reached over and patted his sloping shoulder. "That's how you would have done it, Slade, if you'd
been in her shoes. Let Cat tell you how she wants to handle her own healing process. Go on…go home and talk
with her. I know it will do some good."

Slade caught Kai's hand, giving it a grateful squeeze.
"We'll have that talk," he promised. "I've been wanting
to make Cat a gift, anyway. Maybe, if I can persuade her
to stay, I can get it done for her."

Kai's eyes twinkled. "Knowing how talented you are
at making jewelry, I'm sure she'll be pleased."

"Better yet," Slade said, hope in his voice as he rose,
"let's the four of us go to Houston in a couple of weeks.
I can give it to Cat then. A sort of peace token for the
way I've behaved."

Walking with Slade to the porch, Kai waved to him
as he left. "Houston sounds like a good idea. And don't
worry, your heart was in the right place, Slade. The words
just came out wrong. Cat will forgive you."

Throwing his leg over his horse, Slade managed a thin
smile. "I hope you're right, Kai. I'll let you know. Think
good thoughts for us, will you?"

"Always."

Chapter 8

Cat tried to repair the damage that her crying jag had done to her face. Slade had knocked at her door earlier, but she had refused to answer. She had to get a hold on herself before she faced him. She put color into her pale cheeks with a brush, and a rose-colored lipstick actually made her look almost normal. She winced, avoiding the look in her eyes as she combed her hair. She had taken a warm, cleansing shower and changed into some of her more practical clothes: a peach shell and a pair of no-nonsense khaki pants. Now, she looked more like her old self, before the trauma of the cave-in. The only thing different was that her hair was longer, making her look more feminine. Cat didn't want to cut her hair even though she knew she was going into the jungle again.

No, I want it to grow. I don't care. And she didn't question why she violently fought the idea of a haircut.

Wasn't that what Slade wanted? A mining engineer, not a feminine-looking woman? He'd made that very clear earlier. A life for a life. Okay, she owed him, and she'd pay up. Kincaids recognized that some things in life were sacred; you save a man's life, he owes you. It was that simple. She shut her eyes, allowing the brush to lie on the vanity for long moments.

Cat tried to ignore the ache in her heart. Was she so mixed up after the trauma of the cave-in that she hadn't read Slade accurately? She had thought she had seen and felt something special with him, but it had all been an act to maneuver her into going to Colombia with him. When she opened her eyes and warily stared at herself in the mirror, Cat could barely stand to look at the image that stood before her. There was hurt and pain in the depths of her emerald eyes, and anger. Yes, anger at being betrayed by Slade. He had deftly used her to get what he wanted— and he wanted a tough-minded mining engineer. Okay, he'd get it his way. She firmly placed the brush on the vanity, girding herself for the coming confrontation.

Cat allowed all the anger and hurt Slade had caused to rise and protect her. It gave her strength when she had none of her own to call on. Opening the door to her bedroom, Cat walked purposefully down the cedar hall to find Slade.

Slade heard a knock at his office door and he made a half turn in his chair. Cat was standing outside the sliding-glass door, and immediately he was on his feet.

"Come in," he said, opening the door for her.

The coolness of air-conditioning hit Cat as she stepped through the entrance. She saw hope in Slade's eyes, and his exhaustion, and tried to steel herself against feeling anything remotely human toward him. As he slid the door closed and turned toward her, she said, "I'll pay off the debt between us, Slade. I've got another two weeks before I'm freed by the doctor to resume my normal activities. In the meantime, I want all the core-sampling reports, maps and any other geological items you can supply me so I can begin studying the mining situation in Silla de Montar Valley."

Slade's face softened and he took a step toward her. "Cat—"

She stepped away, arms rigid at her sides, her chin raised, eyes defiant. "No."

Slade froze, all hope shattering like an emerald struck by a pickax. When he finally spoke, his voice was charged with feeling. "I have a spare office in the west wing of the house. I can have all those things brought to you."

"Fine."

"Look, you don't have to jump into this with both feet. Kai said you still needed rest. I don't want you working eight hours a day—"

"My life for your mine. That's the way you wanted it, wasn't it?" Cat's jaw tightened. "I'll work however long I want. Don't try and set how many hours a day I can work even if I'm still mending." Her chin quivered. "I'm surprised you waited this long. It was probably killing you to wait six weeks—six weeks that could have been spent down in Colombia instead."

Slade's eyes narrowed with barely contained fury. "That's unfair, Cat. We need to talk."

She smiled wearily, some of her anger dissipating. "Nothing's fair in life, is it? You were raised with rocks. Well, so was I. I'll be just as tough as the situation demands. If you've got all the core and mining information I need, you'll have a rough blueprint for a mine in two weeks."

Slade opened his hands. "Cat, I didn't mean to make it sound as if you owed me. What I said was a mistake."

Her smile was brittle, her eyes dangerously bright with unshed tears. "We all make mistakes, Donovan. My mistake was in trusting you and your intentions. You've made it clear what you want and I'm prepared to give it to you. Your mine for my life. Okay, you've got a deal."

"Damn it, will you give me a chance to explain, Cat?"

"No!"

Slade wanted to strangle her. He also wanted to take Cat into his arms and erase the anguish he saw so clearly in her haunted expression. Her act was all a bluff on her part, and he knew it. And so did she. She was like brittle glass ready to explode right in front of him. But he didn't dare call her hand, or she might run away. No, he'd have to play by her rules, allow her to retreat and hold him at arm's length and maybe, just maybe, she'd gradually lower that shield she had in place and allow him a second chance. "All right," he rasped, "you've got a deal."

Cat swayed slightly, feeling light-headed. She took a step away, covering up her reaction by walking to the door. "Fine. Get me what I need to figure out a construction blueprint for you."

He followed her out to the patio. "Come with me," he said, trying to keep his voice steady.

Cat nodded and walked a few paces behind him as they crossed to the western wing of the ranch house. She tried to contain her surprise when he opened the door to a spacious office replete with several personal computers, calculators and drafting board. Everything she might need to formulate the kind of mine required was present.

Slade made a slight motion toward the office. "This will be yours. The IBM PC is hooked up to the data bank at Texas A & M in Houston, by phone modem, should you need more mining information."

She wondered if Slade had built this with her in mind, but bit back the question, not wishing to fight any more than necessary with him. Her strength had to be focused on the project at hand, not wasted on him. There was a cot in the corner complete with blankets and a pillow. Fine, she'd live, eat and sleep there. In two weeks, she ought to be able to come up with a decent preliminary blueprint to begin digging a mine.

"Thank you." She stepped past him, deliberately avoiding touching him.

Slade went to the drafting board, pointing to a black buzzer on the phone beside it. "If you need anything, you can ring me in my other office." He turned, pointing to a wall of cabinets opposite them. "Every core and drilling-sample spec I took on the mine is here. There are topographical maps of the valley, overburden, ore and basement-complex sample reports. I don't think you'll need anything else, but if you do, call me."

Cat refused to look at Slade and went to the cabinet. Everything had been carefully labeled, numbered and categorized. Her assessment of Slade's abilities grudgingly rose. She pulled out a roll of specs from the first cubbyhole. "I think I've got enough to keep me busy," she murmured.

Slade nodded and retreated. "Dinner's in two hours."

She went to the drafting desk, unrolling the specs and studying them intently. "Have Pilar bring it in here, please."

Well, what did he expect—for Cat to forgive and forget? Slade shut the door quietly behind him, a bitter taste in his mouth. This was a new side of Cat Kincaid: the brilliant, tenacious mining engineer who had carved out a name for herself in one of the toughest businesses in the world. He'd have to keep reminding himself of her steel determination, because she was certainly wearing it like armor now. And he'd forced her into donning it. Damn it, anyway!

Night melded with day and day with night. Cat immersed herself in the exploration of details that would help her determine what kind of mine shaft would be best suited for the Verde Mine. Slade had named the mine at the top of all the specs. "Green Mine"—that fit, she thought. Verde to her meant growth, as did anything green. Rubbing her eyes tiredly, she pushed aside the computer keyboard and placed her pencil on the pad. What day was it? They all blended together when she attacked Verde's challenge. Looking at her Rolex, now scratched from the cave-in, she saw that ten days had passed. A slight smile cut across her lips as she slowly rose. Dawn was crawling onto the horizon as seen from the wall of windows that faced east.

Sleep.... She took snatches of three or four hours at a time. Lying down with a groan, Cat closed her eyes. When she awoke, she would go back to her room, shower and get a fresh change of clothes. As she sank deeper into the embrace of sleep, Slade crossed her mind. To her chagrin, Cat had found that if she wasn't actively pursuing her job, he would slip into her thoughts, catching her unawares. And every time that occurred, her pounding heart would underscore the wild, unnamed feelings that came on its heels. As much as Cat wanted to hate him, she could not. She was angry with him, and disappointed, and she would never trust him again…not ever.

Slade tried to contain his surprise when Cat came up to the sliding-glass door of his office on the tenth day. She had successfully avoided seeing him for nearly two weeks. Only Pilar's insistence that Cat was in the other office and appeared well had kept him from seeing for himself. Slade knew he didn't dare push Cat too far by showing up on her doorstep. He rose to open the door, but she beat him to it.

"Come in," he invited, pulling up a stool.

Cat felt the heat rush to her face. Why did she have to blush? She stood just inside the office, holding his anxious stare. Slade looked as tired as she felt. There were shadows beneath his eyes, as if he'd slept little. His clothes were rumpled, which wasn't like him. He always wore a crisp cotton shirt and dark blue jeans that outlined his beautifully narrow hips and well-formed legs. He was beautiful, Cat admitted weakly, her pulse pounding unevenly. As much of a bastard as he was, Slade still affected her physically, and she couldn't ignore the sensations racing through her even now.

"I've finished the rough calculations. I need to sit down and discuss them with you. Do you have a couple of hours to spare?"

Slade heard the strain in Cat's voice. How he had missed her! Ten days without Cat had been a prison sentence for him. He had longed for her voice, her effusive laughter, her quiet, steady presence. Hungrily, he now drank her in as she stood like a wary doe ready to flee at the first sign of danger. She was pale, he realized with a pang, and she wore no makeup to hide it. She wore a light blue short-sleeved chambray shirt, jeans and sensible brown shoes. It looked almost as if she were dressed for field work, except for the mandatory hard hat and rough boots. Her outfit didn't diminish her femininity in his eyes, though. The fullness of her parted lips sent an ache throbbing through him. Slade had often remembered kissing those lips.

"Sure, I've got the time." He sounded like an eager schoolboy on shaky ground. Well, wasn't he?

Cat turned without preamble and began the walk back to her office. Her hands were damp and she longed to rub them on her thighs to dry them off, but Slade would notice, and she didn't want to broadcast her nervousness. She almost smiled in spite of herself, though. Slade's harsh face had softened the moment he saw her. Was that an act on his part? Was it real? Cat groaned inwardly; why did she even care? Hadn't he shown his real character already?

Slade entered her office and saw two chairs sitting side by side at the drafting desk. Cat sat down, waiting for him. He wiped his sweaty hands on his jeans and then sat beside her.

"What did you come up with?" he asked. *Great, Donovan, you sound like a twelve-year-old boy whose voice is changing.*

Cat drew the first sheaf of papers between them, keenly aware of Slade's closeness. She tried valiantly to cap her own escaping feelings and cleared her throat. "I've made a study of the Chivor and Muzo mine operations before deciding what ours would be. Muzo's emerald fields are found in a loose, black shale that quite literally is on the surface. All they've had to do is clear out the jungle and go to work to reclaim the gems." She scowled, placing a paper in front of him. "Their mining operations are antiquated and, to say the least, environmentally damaging. As you can see in this color photo, they're using strip-mining techniques. They blast with dynamite and then go in with huge bulldozers, shoveling the black shale into vast washing and screening areas. Water is used to wash away the debris and leave the emeralds. What can't be bulldozed after a blast is jackhammered by miners and then pushed into the gullies." Cat glanced at him and lost her train of thought. She loved his mouth despite herself. It had ravished hers until she had melted into an oblivion of wildly boiling heat and desire. His nearness was devastating to her, and her voice faltered as she tried to pick up the reins of her conversation. "The gangue, or waste rock, is pushed into the Rio Itoco below. There the guaqueros sift through the tailings during the day, hoping to find a stray emerald."

Slade nodded, resting his chin on one of his hands. He saw her hand tremble as she turned the page of her assessment. Automatically, he wanted to reach out, take her hand and tell her everything would be all right. Miserably, he knew that wasn't true. If only he could make things right between them. With a monumental effort, he addressed her comments. "The people pan the waters of the river during the day and become tunnel rats at night. They try to either break into the terraces, which are heavily guarded by the Colombian police, or dig into the shallow mines."

"Right." Cat brought out another paper, swallowing hard. She had seen the tenderness in Slade's eyes as he locked and held her gaze. Despite everything, he did lay claim to her heart, Cat realized in anguish. She wanted to reach out and caress his cheek, to take away some of the pain that lay at the downturned corners of his mouth. Yes, they were both suffering. "Muzo's methods are outdated. Not only that, but indiscriminate blasting with dynamite is going to certainly destroy some of the emeralds."

Slade snorted. "That's already happened. At Chivor they blast cautiously and with low charges and only when necessary." Why did she have to look waiflike? It devastated him to think that he had caused Cat to appear almost a ghost of her former self. No longer was her skin that golden color, her eyes that glorious velvet green sparkling with life. When she stared at him, all he saw was fear and...was it longing? Was that possible? He clung to that possibility, barely hearing her speak about the assessment. Each word she formed with her full lips created a widening ache through him. He loved her.

Cat couldn't relax beneath Slade's intense stare and she retreated deep into her mining-engineer mode. "Your mine, on the other hand, will be a mixture of open-pit mining methods involving the terracing of the surrounding hillside, plus sinking a shaft." She cleared her throat and traced one line of figures on a core-sample readout. "My educated guess, based upon your channel samplings, is that the calcite-limestone vein surfaces here on the hill and slowly moves back down into the earth over here." Cat drew him a quick picture, showing the stratum that might hold emeralds between its thinly wafered sheets.

"What's your opinion? Are we in business or not?" he asked.

Cat straightened up, running fingers through her hair. She expelled a breath of air, taking another paper and handing it to him. "If my calculations stand up and if your channel samples were spaced properly, the Verde should yield one emerald for every twenty million particles of surrounding overburden. You're in business, all right."

Slade stared down at Cat's figures. Her numbers, all in dark leaded pencil, were agonizingly neat and precise. A slight smile hovered around the corners of his mouth. "This is even better than I had roughly figured."

"You'll have everything you want, Slade." The words had come out flat and emotionless as Cat stared at him.

Slade ground his teeth together, bristling over her unspoken accusation. Her eyes were a cool green. He tried to tell himself he deserved that from Cat because of what he'd done to her. Damn it, it hurt! And he was angry at her for prodding that festering wound that now stood between them. "Why don't you give me your mine evaluation?" he asked.

Cat slipped back into her professional mode easily, like a horse into a familiar, comfortable harness. She went over the determination factors: an estimate of future operations, a suitable production schedule, the grade, market and selling price of the product and the production life of the mine. She went into the size, shape, attitude and quality of the emerald deposit, which was determined by geologic studies and maps. She missed nothing in her smooth, methodical presentation. At the end of the second hour, with a large flowchart concluding the final presentation, Cat wrapped it up.

"The mine itself will be tricky. Transportation of certain types of timber is going to be a problem. I'm going to need heavy equipment to get that lumber out of the jungle. And you'll need to build a good road that won't wash out in the tropical rains of winter." She shrugged and gestured toward the plans on the drafting board. "All of this is detailed and you can read it at your leisure."

Slade nodded thoughtfully, watching as Cat shoved her hands into the pockets of her jeans and walked over to the wall of windows. The sun was slanting through the glass, making her sable hair come alive with threads of gold. He had sponged in her presence in the past two hours, as if starved. God, how he had missed her.

"You've done a thorough job on this, Cat. A damn good job." His voice shook with gratitude and pride in her abilities. Slade managed a tight smile, holding her thawing emerald gaze, realizing he had reached inside those defensive walls and touched her, the woman. "Now I see why you've got one hell of a name for yourself in our industry. It would take most people a good month just to put a preliminary study like this together. You did it in two weeks."

"You had everything I needed here," Cat countered, feeling warm and good as his praise flowed through her. "Part of the time factor is based on how much an engineer has to run around collecting all the pieces of various data that are needed to put a show like this together. You're good at your job, too, Slade."

He arched like a cat beneath her flattery, and his mouth stretched into a smile. "What do you say we celebrate? Matt and Kai want me to fly us to Houston for dinner tonight. We'll go to a nice restaurant and relax. We both need that."

Cat stiffened. At first, she was going to say no. But Kai had been a godsend the first two weeks of her stay at the ranch, and she owed her thanks. More importantly, Kai had become her friend. But every minute spent with Slade weakened her resolve, her past hurt over his actions. Cat anguished over the decision.

"Come on, say yes," Slade coaxed. "Kai's called over

here three times in the last ten days wanting to see you. She's been craving some female company. What do you say?"

Cat gnawed on her lower lip and stared down at her shoes. "Okay." There was a razor-honed edge to her voice.

"I'll keep my distance from you," Slade said, sensing she wanted to hear some sort of verbal promise from him.

"Fine." She lifted her head. "I think it's best if it's business all the way between us."

"I haven't forgotten."

Cat eyed him. At first, she had been angry with Slade for tricking her. Then, she felt childish after leveling a barrage at him—although she had gotten it cleaned out of her system once and for all. But ten days had modified her initial anger. The past week had made her aware of just how much she liked Slade, regardless of what had happened to damage their relationship. Cat was afraid of her own feelings toward Slade. The less she saw of him, the more she was able to control them. "Good. I'll see you later, then."

Slade rose. "They'll be here at six tonight."

"Is this formal?"

"Yes."

That meant a dress. And judging from the look of longing in Slade's eyes, Cat knew she was in trouble. She had tried her best for the past two weeks to dress for business, not pleasure. She didn't want any more of Slade's mesmerizing advances weakening her resolve. Wearing a dress would invite his advances, and she knew it. How did she get herself painted into corners like this? If she hadn't been angry with Slade, it would be funny. Normally, her sense of humor rescued her; this time it didn't.

"I'll be ready about five-thirty or so," she promised.

"What color dress will you be wearing?"

"Turquoise."

Slade smiled enigmatically. "Perfect," he murmured. "I'll come for you at five-thirty."

Why am I taking so many extra pains to look pretty? Cat gave herself a disgruntled look in the floor-length mirror. She wore a designer dress, a stunning turquoise creation made of rich georgette and luminous satin. Together, the materials created an elegant dress for any special occasion. The deep-draped neckline was graced with a satin camisole inset. The satin sash with a rosette emphasized her narrow waist, while the full-circle skirt flowed with breathtaking grace each time she moved. The sleeves were full and cuffed at her wrists, adding to the overall frothy look. This was a dress to dance in, no matter how poor a dancer she was. Cat sighed, running her fingers across the beautiful, wispy fabric. That was how she felt around Slade despite everything he had done—feminine and…loved.

Cat chose pearl earrings set in a circle of thin gold, but realized something was missing. She needed some kind of necklace to set off the dress. Oh, well, such was life, she admitted regretfully. Taking one more look at herself in the mirror, she decided she looked unusually attractive. Was it the soft sweep of her recently washed hair? The dress? Glumly, Cat knew that despite everything, she wanted to be beautiful for Slade. Damn his hold over her!

When the knock came at her door, Cat turned on her turquoise sandals and opened it. She was completely unprepared for what she saw. Slade was darkly handsome in a black tuxedo, white shirt and black tie. He had shaved, erasing the five o'clock shadow he grew daily, and his hair was still damp and neatly combed into place. Her lips parted as she stared helplessly up into the warmth of his blue eyes.

"You look beautiful," he said huskily, holding out his hand toward her. His heart started violently as he absorbed Cat's unparalleled beauty. The fragrance of her perfume drugged him and his nostrils eagerly drank in her scent. The design of the turquoise dress enhanced the delicious, exotic tilt of her green eyes. Never had he seen her look so desirable. She was all curves and softness and Slade fought the urge to take Cat into his arms, crushing her against him. Holding himself in check, he shared an unsure smile with her. Cat was just as nervous as he was, he discovered to his relief. Her fingers were damp as she lightly placed her hand in his.

"Thank you," Cat said a little breathlessly, walking slowly toward the living room with him.

"Kai and Matt are already here. We've got time for a drink before we go." Slade accompanied her into the living room, where Kai and her husband, Matt, were sitting on one sofa, drinks in hand. "About an hour from now I'm flying us all to Houston and we're going to have dinner at the Brownstone."

"The Brownstone?" Cat stared up at him in disbelief. That particular restaurant was the best in the city. Slade had made it sound as if the night's excursion was going to be less posh, less intimate. "But—I thought—"

Slade grinned rakishly, guiding her to the couch opposite the Travis's. "You need a break. We both do," he explained in his dark, honeyed voice, his mouth close to her ear. "Want your usual? A margarita?"

Cat stared up at him, nonplussed. She saw the glint of

mischief in his eyes. If she read accurately between the lines, Slade had deliberately set up this plan and put it into motion. "No. Give me a double Scotch on the rocks," she said, at a loss to stay ahead of his surprises. It was supposed to be business only between them, not pleasure. She was frightened of her own emotional reactions to him. Ten days had not assuaged her feelings for Slade. How could she control them for an entire evening in one of the most romantic restaurants in Houston?

Slade stood there uncertainly. "A double?" he voiced.

"I'm not the one flying, Slade. You are. I want a double Scotch on the rocks."

"Twist of lemon?"

Cat gripped her clutch purse tightly, trying to look cool and collected in front of their guests. "Yes." *Donovan, I'm going to murder you when we get back. I swear I will...*

"This was a wonderful idea," Kai spoke up. She wore a white chemise that brought out the highlights of her shoulder-length auburn hair. The gold earrings and slender necklace at her throat matched the sparkle in her eyes. "Frankly, when Slade called over, we were ready to go to the city, but didn't plan on the Brownstone." She laughed delightedly. "I love the restaurant! It's so Victorian and so thoroughly romantic."

One confirmation, Cat thought. She shot Slade a withering look as he ambled back over with her drink.

"Yes, he's always cooking up something, isn't he?" Cat said, taking the drink. When Slade sat down and hooked his long arm around her, Cat fairly sizzled. No matter how black her look, Slade smiled, enjoying her predicament. He knew her well enough to know that she wouldn't embarrass herself or him in front of company.

Matt Travis was equally handsome in a white tuxedo

trimmed in black. It brought out his dark attractiveness, Cat thought. And both Kai and Matt looked so happy together. She envied them their loving relationship.

"That's one of the many things this lady likes about me," Slade drawled, giving Cat a wide smile.

Cat clamped her mouth shut after she swallowed a healthy gulp of Scotch, silencing her urge to protest the game he was playing with her.

Kai leaned forward, her eyes fairly sparkling. "Slade was telling us he had a surprise for you, Cat. I can hardly wait for you to see what he's done."

"He's done enough already," Cat said, choking on the words that sounded almost sweet coming from her.

Kai shared a knowing glance with her husband. "Slade, why not give it to Cat now? We saw what he's made for you and I'm just dying to see the look on your face when you get it. Slade? Please?"

Slade groaned. "Kai, when you give me that pleading look of yours, how can I say no?" He got up, setting his drink on the coffee table.

Matt grinned, putting his arm around his wife, giving her a warm embrace. "See why I fell under her spell, Slade? I told you before, you can't resist those beautiful eyes of hers."

Slade tilted his head, meeting and holding Cat's gaze. "I don't want to take anything away from Kai, but this exotic beauty over here has the most beautiful emerald eyes I've ever seen."

Cat felt heat rise in her face as his compliment reached through her like a caress.

"Agreed!" Kai said, smiling.

"Exotic's the right word," Matt said thoughtfully, studying Cat.

"Well, wait here, gang. Since Kai can't stand the suspense, I guess I'll have to give Cat her present now, rather than after dinner."

Cat nervously cleared her throat as Slade left the room. She looked at them. "What's he talking about, Kai? What's going on?"

She smiled warmly. "Oh, Cat, don't you know?"

Cat wished she did. Trying to hide her desire to escape, she shook her head. "No, I don't."

Matt patted his wife's hand. "Slade's sort of like a brother to us, Cat. Ever since he brought you here, we've seen a tremendous change in him—a good, positive change. We've watched him settle down and relax, for once. He's pretty happy with you around, you know."

"And Slade is the type of man who loves to give people gifts," Kai said, a wistful look on her face. "He's given us so much over the years we've been here."

"And to our son, Josh," Matt added warmly.

"Sometimes, I think Slade collects all his strays and turns them into an extended family of sorts." Kai lowered her voice to a conspiratorial whisper. "I told Matt all along, Slade is made for marriage. Until you came he was restless, Cat. You could see it in his walk, his eyes and the way he ran his life. Now, this past month and a half, he's been so incredibly content, it's blown us away." Her voice grew husky. "I don't know what your relationship with Slade is, Cat, but he thinks an awful lot of you." And then Kai traded a merry look with Matt. "We're keeping our fingers crossed for the two of you!"

"Now what's all this whispering about?" Slade entered the room, carrying a dove-gray velvet jewelry case.

Cat nearly dropped her drink. "Uh, nothing, just girl talk," she stammered. "You know…"

Matt and Kai chuckled like indulgent parents as Slade came and sat down next to Cat.

"Girl talk, hmm?" Slade's blue eyes glimmered with mirth. "If I know Kai, she's up to no good again."

"That's not fair, Slade!" Kai protested laughingly. She got to her feet and so did Matt, coming to stand near Slade. "Go on, show her!"

Cat gripped the tumbler as if it were her last hold on life. Slade set the gray velvet box on the couch between them.

"I will. Patience, pretty lady." Slade devoted a hundred percent of his attention to Cat, his smile waning. He soberly held her nervous gaze. "Ten days ago I started a project in my hobby shop. I wanted to make you something that would somehow tell you how I felt about you. I wanted a gem that would show you what I saw in you, Cat." Slade reached over, gently unclipping her pearl earrings. "You won't be needing these tonight," he told her.

Cat swallowed hard, swayed by the huskiness in Slade's tone. She heard the unsureness in his voice and saw it in his cobalt eyes. And suddenly, Cat wanted to reassure him that she would not reject him or make him feel embarrassed. Ever. "Ten days ago?" she whispered, an ache in her voice.

Slade's mouth twisted into a grimace. "Yes." He glanced up at Kai and Matt. "We had a big fight then," he explained to them, leaving out the details. He pried open the spring-latched lid.

Cat gasped, her hand flying to her breast. There, nestled on a deep-blue velvet cushion, was a set of opal earrings, a pear-shaped necklace on a delicate gold chain and a cocktail ring. The silence was eloquent as Slade, whose fingers were scarred and huge in comparison, gently took the necklace from its placement on the velvet.

"People remind me of gems," Slade told Cat in a low voice fraught with emotion. "To me, the opal is the most complex of all gems, like you." He settled the stone around her neck, easing the clasp closed. The huge pear-shaped opal, almost the size of a nickel in diameter, nestled into the hollow of her throat. Then Slade dared to meet Cat's eyes for the first time, afraid of what he might see and praying for the opposite. The words died on his lips as he drowned in the shimmering emerald of Cat's eyes, now filled with huge, luminous tears. In their depths he saw her incredible fire and warmth toward him. He didn't deserve this kind of a reaction from Cat after all the blundering mistakes he'd made with her thus far.

Suddenly, Slade wished Kai and Matt weren't there. The open invitation in Cat's gestures made him want to lift her up into his arms and carry her off to his bedroom to seal their fate. He wanted to make her his own, to drink her into his thirsty, starving soul. Cat could give him the serenity he sought. She was peace, he realized, as he gently cradled her hands. There was so much he wanted to blurt out to her, to apologize for. He longed to ask forgiveness. But now was not the time. If the compassionate look in Cat's eyes was any kind of a promise, she would yield despite the pain he'd put her through, and allow him to explain…to forgive him and start over with a clean slate.

As Slade clipped each of the opals to her earlobes, the iridescent layers of the precious gems gleamed with the fires of emeralds, rubies, topaz, and sapphires. The colors brought out the natural beauty of her eyes and he silently thanked God and Cat for giving him a second chance he didn't deserve.

Slipping the ring on the fourth finger of her right hand, Slade said quietly, "There's a matchlessness to opal, Cat. The layers of color change as you turn your hand one way or another. You're like that—you have so many brilliant facets that change, depending on your mood. You keep me enthralled to the point where nothing else exists for me." He held her gaze, his hands tightening slightly on hers. "You've become my day, my night, sweetheart. Nothing else comes close to you in importance. You've got to believe that. Richness from the heart outstrips monetary concerns. The color of your eyes when you look at me gives me a wealth of feelings and emotions that no emerald mine or money could ever give me. Do you understand?"

Shyly, Cat touched the opal at her throat, all of her disappointment and hurt melting away beneath Slade's beautiful words. He meant them with every fiber of his being, she realized, completely dissolved by his admittance. Placing her fingers in his hand, she gravely met his anxious look. Her voice came out in a husky, quivering whisper. "Yes… I understand, Slade."

He squeezed her fingers gently, a powerful wave of relief smashing through him. And when he dared to look into her green eyes, bright with tenderness and awash with tears, he knew she did.

Chapter 9

"Are you enjoying yourself, Cat?"

Slade's words, whispered lightly against her temple, caused Cat to tremble. He held her close as the quiet music fell over them on the dance floor. "I shouldn't be, but I am."

His chuckle was a deep, pleased sound. Slade held her a little more tightly, aware of how her soft pliant curves fitted against his harder, unyielding body. "I took a big risk," he admitted, pressing a kiss to her hair.

"I'm still upset with you, Slade."

One eyebrow cocked and he looked down at her. If that was true, he didn't see anger in Cat's eyes. Instead, he saw the molten gold desire in her dark green gaze. "For what? Arranging this weekend in Houston with Matt and Kai?" he asked innocently.

She laughed and shook her head. "You're such a ras-

cal, do you know that? One minute you're Peck's Bad
Boy. The next, you've made up for what you caused by
giving me the most beautiful gift I've ever gotten. And
then you have Pilar pack a suitcase for me and hide it on
the plane. If Kai hadn't told me on the way to Houston
that you were planning a weekend here and not just the
evening, I'd probably have dropped my soupspoon when
you blithely announced it at dinner."

He grinned engagingly, whirling her around, the airy
folds of her dress moving like the wind around her tall,
graceful body. The night was turning into magic, Slade
thought, unable to contain his joy. "You'd never drop a
soupspoon in front of anyone," he drawled. "You're too
cool to do that."

"Being around you is like running a big risk without
insurance, Slade."

He smiled. "Thank you."

"That wasn't a compliment."

"Am I a risk?"

"You know you are, Slade Donovan. So quit giving
me that engaging little-boy look. It won't work."

"It's worked so far…"

Admittedly, he was right, Cat thought, unable to resist
his smile. "What else do you have planned?"

He looked above her head, noticing Kai and Matt
dancing nearby on the crowded dance floor. "Actually,
Kai begged me to fly her to Houston to shop. I got to
thinking about it and called her back and asked her if she
and Matt would like to make it a weekend with the four
of us. She thought it was a great idea. I've made reserva-
tions at the Westin Hotel over at the Galleria. Saturday
morning, if you want, you and Kai can go shopping. Matt
and I are going to do a little golfing. That evening, we'll

go to an excellent French restaurant." He looked down at Cat, devilry in his eyes. "Then, we'll go to an amusement park nearby. They have one of the best bumper-car rides around."

Cat gasped. "An amusement park?"

"Sure. Kai wanted to do something different. I figure it's been at least twenty years since any of us went on a merry-go-round or tried to win a stuffed toy. It ought to make for a fun night."

Cat laughed delightedly. "It sounds wonderful. What else?"

"Brunch on Sunday morning. I figure we'll get up late and then reward ourselves by crawling into the hot tub in my suite. We'll sip champagne, have eggs Benedict and generally pry our eyes open. Then, around one-ish, we'll head back out to Del Rio. How does the game plan sound?"

Cat tried to hide her enjoyment and didn't succeed. "It sounds great and you know it."

"Remember, this was Kai's idea, originally."

"Slade, one of these days your cleverness is going to catch up with you."

He sobered. "Yeah, I know. Contrary to what you might think, I got two rooms at the Westin for us. They're both suites and are joined by a door."

Relief flooded Cat. "Thank you, Slade..."

"I didn't want to," he admitted softly, trailing a slow series of kisses along her hairline, "but I did."

"It probably killed you," she said wryly, her knees weakening as each of his kisses melted her a little more.

Slade had the good grace to chuckle. "Yeah, I really fence-sat on that one." He eased Cat away from him,

staring darkly down at her. "Look, after dancing when
we get over to the hotel, we need to sit down and talk."

"Yes, about a lot of things."

"I've been a real bastard, Cat. I'm sorry. I didn't mean
to hurt you like I have." Slade drew in a breath and forced
a slight smile. "Tonight, come to my suite when you're
ready."

Cat lifted her chin, lost in the warming cobalt of his
gaze, her pulse unsteady. "I will."

Pilar had packed with great care, Cat discovered as she
opened her luggage. The peach silk nightgown and ac-
companying robe had been carefully folded on top of everything else. She held up the shimmering gown. Should
she wear that over to Slade's suite? Or should she go over
dressed as she was? Indecision warred with what her
heart desired. "Oh, to hell with it," Cat muttered, heading to the shower.

Slade was standing by the window overlooking the
scintillating lights of Houston at one o'clock in the morning. He had gotten rid of his tie and opened the throat of
the shirt. The jacket had been shed on a silk settee and
he'd eased out of his shoes. In a spasm of nervousness,
he'd poured himself a snifter of brandy. He held the glass
in his left hand as he stared out at the sleeping city. He
and Cat had sobered as the evening wore on, realizing the
coming confrontation between them. Slade expected to
be justly brought to task by Cat. What he wanted was to
make love with her, to apologize that way, instead. But
that wasn't a reasonable solution to everything. No, this
talk had been long overdue between them, and he was
willing to endure it if it would give him hope of a future
with Cat. Any future was better than none.

A faint knock at the adjoining door made him turn. Slade's eyes widened appreciatively as Cat silently walked into the room. A flood of heat uncoiled deep within him as he stared at the huge fuzzy white hotel robe she wore. Her hair was damp at the ends, indicating she'd just taken a shower.

"Come in," he said, motioning for her to sit on the pale blue Oriental couch nearby. He saw the high color in Cat's cheeks and her unsureness. She was just as scared as he was. A load slid off his shoulders when he realized that, and Slade poured her some brandy, handing her the crystal snifter after she had sat down. Cat curled up, her long, coltish legs tucked beneath her body. Her hair was newly brushed and he could smell her showered freshness.

"Thank you," Cat murmured, lifting the snifter to her lips. The apricot scent flowed across her tongue, warming her mouth and going down smoothly, relaxing her in its wake. Cat watched as Slade sat down, his hip only inches from her knees. A hesitant smile touched her lips. "I think we both needed this."

"Yeah," Slade agreed. He noticed that Cat still wore the opal ring and that gave him hope. "You're wearing the ring."

Cat smiled gently, lifting her hand to study the iridescent colors of the oval gem. "How could I not wear it?" She held Slade's gaze. "You didn't have to make all this jewelry for me."

"Why do you think I did it?"

The silence wove between them as Cat considered his quietly asked question. She struggled to answer. "I honestly don't know, Slade."

"Guess."

She grimaced. "I'm not very good at guessing games. Why don't you just tell me why you did it?"

"Because I want to know what you thought my intentions were toward you."

Cat closed her eyes, pain in her voice. "Slade, you don't make this easy on me. The worst possible reason you might have done it was to buy my forgiveness for tricking me into doing something you wanted from me." She opened her eyes, meeting his opaque stare. "You know that, if nothing else, I try to be an honorable person. My word is my bond. You knew that by saving my life I would owe you. And you used that knowledge in a way that I'd never have expected."

He turned the snifter slowly around between his large hands. "All right, that's the worst scenario. Any others?"

"That the gift was a way of apologizing to me?"

"Possibly. What else?"

Cat heard the strain in his voice. "No. None that I can see. Is there another, Slade?"

He nodded. "Yeah. All my life I'd been bitten by green fire, the dream of finding an emerald mine. There's just something about the gem that fascinates me. I'd set up my entire life-style and reason for being a geologist to make the big find." Slade pinned her with his gaze. "It wasn't for the money, but just for the sheer challenge of finding such a rare gemstone. I got close in Brazil when I discovered the tourmaline deposits at El Camino. That just made me that much more determined and thirsty to find green fire. I knew it was close; I could feel it in my bones like a gold prospector can feel when he's approaching a vein. I could taste it. And then, it happened: that poker game in Bogotá changed my life. Or I thought it had," he added wryly.

Slade held her unwavering gaze. "I then went in search of the very best mining engineer I could find. I sought you out. When I first saw you in that shack, Cat, I didn't know what to expect. I never realized how beautiful you were, besides being accomplished and an expert in your field. The magazine photos didn't do you justice. Anyway, when that cave-in occurred, I was worried for you. And those next three days of staying in contact with you on the radio slowly began to change me. It was subtle at first, and I can't exactly find words to tell you how you began to affect me and my objectives. And then I found myself wanting you to myself for more than just professional reasons."

Slade placed the snifter on the coffee table in front of them and stood up, thrusting his hands deep into the pockets of his trousers. His face was etched harshly with conflicting emotions as he turned and continued in a low timbre. "For eight weeks, you lived with me. Until the day of our argument and my blunder trying to play amateur psychologist with you, I never realized just how much you had come to mean to me." He ran his fingers through his hair. "I guess I had given up finding a woman to share my world. It took something like this to make me discover it, Cat.

"When I came back to the ranch, I went to my office and searched through every gemstone I'd collected over the years. I wanted to find something that would reflect to you just what you had become to me in this past month." The tension in Slade's face dissolved. "I didn't make the opals as an apology or to buy anything from you, Cat. I was hoping they would show you what I hadn't been able to do with any success, to tell you that you mean far more to me than green fire…"

Cat touched the warm, fiery-colored opal, tears blurring her vision. "I'm sorry I thought the worst, Slade. I didn't know…"

He shrugged almost painfully and sat down next to her. "I haven't exactly been good at expressing myself, either, Cat. And for that, I also apologize." He reached out, capturing her right hand, holding her luminous gaze. "You were hurting so much inside from the trauma and the mine accident that I wanted to help you, and I blurted out the first half-baked idea that came to mind. I figured that if I could set you up under a condition where you'd be forced to face your fear, it would work out fine. I could see my idea wasn't having a positive effect on you. I got panicky." His words came out low and tortured. "The last thing I wanted from you was a payment of your life for the mine. My good intentions to get you to conquer your fear backfired. Sometimes, my mouth gets ahead of my thoughts. Or, at least, dealing with you it does."

Cat murmured his name softly, sliding her hand along his sandpapery cheek. "I shouldn't believe you, Slade, but I do. There's something that keeps drawing us back to each other no matter how much we've hurt each other. What is it about you that makes me believe you? What?"

Slade closed his eyes, feeling the warm caress of her hand across his flesh. He brought Cat into his arms and she sank against him, trusting him once again. Nuzzling her neck and shoulders with a flurry of moist kisses, he inhaled her feminine fragrance. "I don't know, sweetheart, I don't know." He felt Cat stiffen as he pressed a kiss between the cleavage of her taut, firm breasts before he raised his head. Reading her tender expression, he saw her eyes were lustrous and warm, with invitation in their green, sultry depths.

"The past ten days have been hell on both of us," Slade told her thickly. "You're under no obligation to me for saving your life, Cat. I would do it a hundred times over. This mine down in Colombia has no strings attached to you or me. I don't want you captive to me out of guilt. If you choose to become involved with it, it's because you want to. I'm going to fly to Colombia Monday morning. If you want to fly down with me, fine. If you don't, I'll understand." Slade stared down at her widening eyes. "No more pressure on you, Cat. Kai made me realize that no one has the right to tell you how to live your life. If you're afraid to go back down in a mine, that's something you have to deal with in your own way and time. I can't force you back into a shaft before you're ready. As much as I wish your life was in my hands, it's not." He feathered a kiss across her parting lips, tasting the apricot brandy on them.

"Wait…" she pleaded breathlessly, palms flat against his powerful chest. "Slade…who would you get to put that mine shaft in for you, then?"

"I don't know yet. It doesn't matter."

"But it does matter!"

Slade's mouth curved upward and he slid his hands up the sleeves of her arms. "Not right now, it doesn't."

Cat licked her lips, trying to pull from the heated cocoon spinning around both of them. "Slade, listen to me. We're not done talking."

He released her, sensing her concern. "All right, go ahead."

"You're really serious about this, getting another engineer?"

"Yes."

Cat muttered something under her breath, searching

Slade's features. "Look, that mine is going to be tricky to build. You've got very movable layers of shale and limestone that can quiver like a dog's back if there's even a slight earthquake tremor. Not every mining engineer has the experience that I have in building one to withstand that kind of unexpected stress."

Slade wanted to embrace her, realizing she was putting his safety above her own fear. "I'm aware of that. And I'll find someone who can do it."

Getting up, Cat paced the suite for several minutes. Finally, she turned to him, her face set. "Slade, I care what happens to you. I've just spent ten days preparing blueprints for the Verde. And frankly, there isn't anyone who can build that mine more safely than I can."

"I believe you, Cat. But you don't have to go. I don't want you down there unless you're sure you're ready to tackle mine entry."

She gave him a frustrated look. "Damn it, Slade, if I didn't know any better, I'd say you were using reverse psychology on me to get me to go down there with you!" She stamped her bare foot to underscore the depth of her feeling. "Not only that, you make me feel like a child! And no one has ever brought out those feelings in me like you have." She knotted her fists. "I can't live with you. I can't live without you. On the other hand, I'm so damned scared of having to go into a mine that I turn icy cold all over."

He rose, barely aware of most of what she'd said. "You can't live without me?" Slade asked, coming up and placing his hands on her shoulders.

Petulantly, Cat shot him a withering look. "I said it, didn't I?"

"Really? You kinda like being around me despite everything that's happened?"

"I can't live with you either, Slade. You drive me nuts. I used to be a stable, steady, sane person until you dropped into my life. I don't know which way is up anymore. Or down. Or sideways. When I get around you, everything else just kind of fades and there's only you..."

His smile increased like the radiance of the sun rising as he brought her to him. "There's you and me, Cat. Just you and me," he whispered, molding his mouth against those provocative lips that were just begging to be tamed. "That's all that matters..."

A soft moan slid up her throat as Cat melted a little more beneath Slade's caressing kiss. So much was happening at once. She could barely think coherently beneath his fiery, coaxing touch. A shiver of need jolted through her as his tongue stroked each corner of her mouth, a tantalizing promise of more to come if she wanted him. An ache grew deep within her and Cat realized that only Slade had the magic to bring her to surrender. He was barely caressing her and she could feel him controlling himself for her sake.

Breathlessly, Cat eased away, seeing how his hooded eyes smoldered with a vibrant blue fire of their own. A delicious warmth flowed down through her as Slade lifted her into his arms. Cat sighed, resting her head against his, closing her eyes. "You're not an easy man to understand," she murmured.

Slade looked down at Cat as he carried her into the darkness of his bedroom. "I know that, sweetheart. Let's heal some of the wounds that still stand between us. When the sun rises tomorrow, we'll both be the better for it."

Cat smiled as he gently laid her down on the quilted satin surface of the huge king-size bed. As she awaited him, he slowly undressed. Like the mountains carved out of the enduring earth, he was beautiful to behold. Every angle of his darkly bronzed body slipped like a well-fitted plane into the next. Slade's chest was covered with a mat of dark, fine hair. His shoulders were broad, thrown back naturally, shouting of his rugged heritage. A sleek torso flowed smoothly into narrowed hips and long, muscular thighs to lean but finely sculpted calves. As Slade moved to her side, Cat whispered, "You're beautiful..."

She ran her fingers lightly across his shoulders, feeling his silent, coiled strength. Slade's hands settled around her, moving slowly and sending a sheet of prickling fire outward toward her tightening belly.

A growl reverberated in Slade's throat as she slid her hand across his chest, following the wiry carpet of hair down across the slab hardness of his stomach to—

"Cat," Slade growled savagely, pulling her tight against him. He gasped, unprepared for the caress of her warm fingers around him. As he crushed her hard against him, he branded her lips with a fiery kiss, stealing the breath from her. The pebbled hardness of her nipples pleasantly chafed the wall of his chest, taunting him. In one motion, he slid his hand beneath the terry-cloth robe revealing first one breast and then the other. Slade gave her no chance to protest, smothering her full, glistening lips with another kiss. His long, teasing kiss demanded that she submit fully beneath his onslaught. Tonight, he wanted to please Cat as he had no other woman. Tonight was for her; tonight was for healing...

Dizziness sang through Cat as she lay helplessly in the path of Slade's ravishment. His lips created a trail of blazing fire from her earlobe, down her neck, across her collarbones and then... A gasp tore from her as his mouth settled over the first nipple. Reflexively, Cat's fingers dug into his bunched shoulder muscles, and she arched her entire body against him. Fire rippled outward, as if a stone had been tossed into the quiet surface of a deep pond, until a powerful, aching sensation gripped her loins. Each sucking motion drove her farther and farther from rational thought. She was flung into a universe where only emotion ruled.

Slade felt Cat's surrender to him, the discovery filling him with potency. She trusted him entirely. He lay on his back and pulled her gently on top of him. The instant her hip brushed his aching body, a hiss of air came from between his clenched teeth. Her eyes were barely open, her lips wet with further invitation as he settled her above him. Slade saw vague confusion register in her desire-clouded emerald eyes. He kept his hands on each of her arms to prevent her from falling.

"Your ribs," he explained thickly. "If I lie on you, I could hurt you. And I don't want to do that. For now, this is best." Slade smiled up into the shadowy planes of her radiant face and placed his hands on her hips, helping to guide her. "Come to me, sweet Cat, woman of the earth, my woman..."

A cry of pleasure tore from her as she settled down on him, her fingers digging into his arms. The fire that had simmered so long within her finally burst into brilliant life. One twist of his hips sent such a powerful tidal wave of pleasure that Cat sobbed. Together they were fused like molten, volcanic lava, each stroke, each movement a little deeper, more giving, taking and melding than the last. He whispered her name like a prayer given those who hold the earth in reverence. She felt him return all she meant to him in those shattering moments that tore a cry from within her. Cat went spinning off in a directionless universe of splintered sunlight. And then, precious moments later, Slade stiffened, groaned and clung to her as if to life itself. As she leaned down on him, her cheek against his warm, damp chest, she knew they had given each other the most precious gift of all.

Slade absently ran his fingers over her drying back, marveling at her natural beauty. Cat lay beside him, one hand across his chest, one leg across his. He smiled into the darkness. "Has anyone ever told you how giving and loving you are?"

A quiver of pleasure spun through Cat as she languished in the timbre of his voice. "Not like you have," she whispered, incredibly satiated and fulfilled.

"Every time I hold a handful of warm earth in my hands, I can feel the life in it." Slade splayed his hand across her shoulder, pressing Cat gently to him, kissing her damp temple. "I like you; you're the earth. You're warm, yielding, fertile and incredibly alive."

A soft smile played on her lips as she weakly ran her hand across the drying hair of his chest. "Then you're the ocean: quixotic, mysterious and powerfully emotional."

Slade turned thoughtful as he eased to his side so that he could see her. He cupped Cat's cheek, watching as her eyes barely opened and focused on him. "Believe me when I tell you that I've never made such incredible love with a woman as I have with you."

Cat felt euphoric. "Do you always have the right words?" she asked in a wispy voice, content to close her eyes and simply drink in his touch, his honeyed tone and male essence.

Slade's chuckle was derisive. "No. You know that better than anyone. I've blundered and tripped all over myself with you. And like the earth, you've forgiven me." He reached down, pulling up a sheet to cover them. He drew Cat into his arms, holding her gently for fear of putting too much pressure on her recently healed ribs. "My beautiful earth mother," he teased her huskily. "Let me hold you close to my heart."

Cat nuzzled beneath Slade's jaw, content as never before. For once, she was washed free of all her anxieties and fears. Slade had cleansed her; he had filled her with himself and given back to her. The last words she spoke before everything receded were, "You're healing me, Slade…"

The sun had barely edged along the horizon when Cat slowly awoke around six o'clock, unsure why she had left the cradling embrace of her euphoric dreams. She lay quietly in Slade's arms, a soft smile touching her mouth as he occasionally snored. One lock of dark hair had dropped across his smooth brow and she gently coaxed it back into place. For no reason, Cat was glad she was awake and Slade was still asleep. It gave her a chance to study him in the morning light.

Where are we going with one another? she wondered as she lay in his arms. *We have such a roller-coaster relationship. You lift me up higher than I've ever been and yet, like the restless ocean you are, you have the capacity to hurl me deeper into a morass than anyone ever has.* Cat studied Slade intently, trying to find the answers she sought. Last night, when he'd told her she didn't have to build that mine, she had felt a deep sense of relief. Slade had no ulterior motives where she was concerned, and he had proved it by releasing her from any obligation to him. She didn't want anything to happen to Slade. And yet, until that moment, Cat hadn't realized just how much he meant to her.

What was that saying? You must love someone enough to let them go, and if they come back to you it's from love. But if they leave and don't return, perhaps love was never there, anyway. Cat's eyes darkened as she focused on Slade's features. *Do I love you? I don't know. I'm not sure.* And then she almost laughed aloud because Slade had admitted as much to her last night: that she had somehow become more important to him than anything else in his life. Did he love her? He hadn't said so. And she was old enough to know that if Slade did, he'd tell her in time. Yes, time…time would yield what was and was not between them.

Cat found herself wanting a chance to find out where life would lead them. They'd had a rocky start with one another, and she knew it would become rockier because they had another equally powerful test before them: entering a mine. Now, however, Cat no longer struggled with the fear because she knew that when the time came, Slade would be there to help her.

Suddenly shaky at the thought, Cat grew uncomfortable. Slade would receive nothing from her, while she would be taking from him. Well, she must trust Slade on this point, let him guide and help her. All she had to do was communicate when she was in trouble. Somehow, Slade made her feel relaxed, almost eager to work with him, no matter what dangers the mine posed to either of them.

* * *

"Are you ready?"

Slade's tone was filled with amusement as he held Cat with one arm, his other hand wrapped around the pole of the carousel horse they sat upon.

A peal of laughter burst from Cat as she felt the merry-go-round gently start to move. She cast a look over at Kai and Matt, sitting haphazardly on another horse ahead of them. "Ready," she promised. Rich, warm feelings flowed through Cat as the memory of their night and day together came back to her.

Slade grinned happily. "After this, how about a round of bumper cars?" He kept a firm grip on Cat so she wouldn't fall as the horse moved up and down in time with the music. "Where's that sense of challenge you always like to grab by the horns, Kincaid?"

"Challenges, not death-defying feats, Donovan! Agh!" She nearly lost her balance when Slade moved around on the rear of the horse. Cat clung to the pole, but the carousel horse simply wasn't big enough for both of them. Still, she enjoyed Slade's closeness. She leaned back, catching his dancing sapphire gaze. "No bumper cars. Do you want me to crack my ribs again?"

Slade looked crestfallen. "Oh, sorry. I forgot." He brightened. "The Ferris wheel, then?"

With a moan, Cat said, "I'll think about it."

"I'll buy you cotton candy as a bribe. No Ferris wheel, no cotton candy," he teased, nibbling gently on her exposed earlobe.

With a laugh, Cat dodged his moist, tantalizing tongue. "You're such a rogue, Slade Donovan! You and Matt go on the Ferris wheel. Kai and I will find something tamer to ride.

"Come on, Kai," Cat said, as they walked out the exit. She pointed toward the merry-go-round again. "I think we girls ought to stick together. Men can take all the wild rides they want, just like how they drove cars when they were eighteen: without us."

Kai giggled and followed Cat after the men were safely aboard the huge Ferris wheel. "I think we ought to have liability insurance around Slade and Matt," Kai said good-naturedly.

Cat couldn't stop laughing as they made their way back up to the brightly painted horses. The men had bought them each cotton candy and they sat aboard their chargers waiting for the music and movement to begin.

Kai's eyes gleamed with humor. "It feels strange to be at an amusement park again. I haven't done this since I was a kid of fourteen."

"I suspect Slade never grew up," Cat pointed out dryly, watching the Ferris wheel slowly start rotating in the distance.

"Ever since Slade bought the ranch, things haven't been the same out in Del Rio, either." Kai chortled. Slowly, the horses began to rise and fall beneath them, the music lilting and infectious.

"I can imagine. Slade constantly catches me by surprise," Cat agreed.

"Welcome to the club!" Kai's smile was warm. "Matt and I have been hoping for such a long time that Slade would find someone like you, Cat." She reached out, squeezing her hand for a moment. "We can tell Slade loves you."

Shock almost made her fall off her horse. Cat stared at Kai. "Slade loves me?"

"You know that misunderstanding you two had two weeks ago?"

"Yes?"

"Slade came over that day, Cat. He wanted to talk so I dragged him into the living room to tell me why he was so moon-eyed."

"Moon-eyed?"

Kai grinned. "A Texas expression. It means sad."

"I see."

"I pulled everything out of Slade, piece by piece," Kai went on. She flashed Cat an understanding look. "He felt terrible about what he said to you. I don't want to seem like a nosy neighbor or anything, and I know it's none of our business, but Slade sometimes, in his haste to make something right that's going wrong, digs himself a deeper hole."

Cat nodded. "He did, Kai. But he apologized, too."

"Then things are better between you?"

Better? Cat thought, a rush of heat suffusing her. "Yes, much better," she reassured Kai.

"Oh, wonderful!"

Fifteen minutes later, Slade and Matt swooped up from behind them, each grabbing his respective woman.

"Gotcha!" Slade growled, whisking Cat off the horse and into his arms.

Her eyes widened considerably as they wobbled off balance for a second before righting themselves. "You're going to kill me, Slade Donovan!"

He chuckled and gently lowered her to the ground. "Have I yet?" he demanded archly.

"It's just a matter of where and when," Cat muttered as his large hands spanned her waist and he slipped behind her.

"Trust me," he coaxed near her ear, kissing her quickly.

Cat smiled, melting all over again at his nearness. "I do and you know it."

"Mmm, do you ever."

For the next three hours, Cat felt like a teenager again. The fact that they were one of the few older couples at the amusement park that Saturday night didn't bother them. She and Kai watched the men ride the bumper cars, Slade trying to show off for her by outmaneuvering Matt on the slick steel surface of the arena. The safety of the rail was comforting as Slade missed Matt and collided with two ten-year-olds because he couldn't control the direction of his car. Cat howled with laughter until her ribs started to hurt. But it was worth it just to laugh freely again. The ten-year-olds quickly disengaged themselves from Slade's plodding car and he waved to her. Only his pride had been impaired in the melee. Matt hustled his bumper car through an opening and smashed Slade's car from the other side of the enclosure. Slade spent the remainder of the ride backing out of the corner, only to be hit and driven back into it by every gleeful kid around. The entire rink broke into cheers as Slade drew a white handkerchief from his back pocket and waved it above his head in surrender, bowing to his ill-begotten fate.

Afterward, they drove to a nearby A & W. Cat had to laugh. Somehow a silver Mercedes-Benz just didn't look at home among all the souped-up pickups and gussied-up vans that jammed the place. But Slade was oblivious; he was having too much fun ordering from the machine. Soon a waitress on roller skates came out with a tray loaded with hamburgers, icy glasses of root beer and hot french fries for their late-evening snack. The car rang with nonstop laughter, and most of the time, Cat was laughing so hard that tears came to her eyes.

"Honestly," Cat told everyone, "I can't ever remember having had a better time."

Slade was pleased and fed Cat some more french fries.

"My stomach aches from laughing so much," Kai confided.

"My rear is bruised," Matt added dolefully, giving Slade an accusing look.

"My ribs hurt," Cat said, smiling at Slade, "but it was worth it."

Kai prodded Slade. "Come on, big guy, something has to hurt on you, too. After all, you were the one who thought he was a kamikaze pilot dive-bombing all those poor, defenseless kids out there in the bumper-car ring."

Slade's laughter was deep and rolling. He threw up both his hands in a gesture of peace. "Hey, what can I say? I'm just a kid trapped in a thirty-five-year-old body." He showed them a scraped elbow. "See? Do I get a Purple Heart for all my efforts?"

The car rocked with more laughter. An intense feeling of warmth encircled Cat as she met Slade's cobalt eyes and his roguish smile. So much was happening so quickly. One night in his arms had deeply changed her, for Slade made her feel good about herself, despite everything.

"Happy?" Slade asked later, pulling her into his arms.

Cat contentedly fitted herself beside him, the satin of her apricot silk gown molding against his heated, hard body. She sighed, glad to be in his arms, his breath moist across her cheek.

"Happy?" she murmured throatily, sliding her arms around his neck. "I'm floating."

He chuckled, kissing her cheek, eyes and nose, and then rested his mouth against her smiling, lush lips that parted to his advance. "Even with that bruise I found on your pretty derriere? What did you do, fall off the carousel horse?"

Cat leaned up, molding her lips to his strong, male mouth, lost in the heat of their tender exchange. His jaw was rough against her cheek, his skin smelled of soap and his hair was damp beneath her gentle fingers. "You know I got it when you dragged me off the horse," she teased. Slade's lips caught hers in a devouring kiss, and she melted as his knowing touch set her on fire again. "Oh, Slade, somehow you take the hurt away from me…" Cat rested against him, staring up into his smoldering blue eyes as he lay above her.

"Don't sound so surprised, sweetheart. Occasionally, people can do good things for one another."

"You make me feel magical," Cat said, cupping his stubborn jaw. Then with a tremulous sigh, she whispered, "I don't know when I've ever felt happier, or laughed so much. You're good for me."

"We're good for each other; it's not a one-way street, Cat." Slade tunneled his fingers through her silky hair, his voice deep with emotion. "We've had a rough and, if you'll pardon the pun, rocky start." He grimaced. "And it can get rockier."

She frowned, hearing the worry in his voice. "What do you mean?"

"Are you planning on going down to Bogotá with me on Monday?"

"Yes."

Slade rested his hand against her back and hip. "Look, I meant what I said about your not going. You could stay at the ranch, if you want or—go to another job assignment." It hurt to say the last of that sentence. "I think too much of you, Cat, and what might be, to have you go down to Bogotá unless you're very clear as to why you're going. I don't want you to go out of guilt. The slate is clean between us."

The troubled look in Slade's eyes made her heart wrench, and Cat offered him a slight smile. "I'm very clear about why I'm going down there with you, Slade. It's not out of guilt."

He accepted her explanation. Cat and their relationship were more important to him than the mine. The softness of her skin as he stroked her cheek sent another wave of exquisite longing through him. "It's going to be dangerous, Cat."

"What mine isn't?"

"I mean outside the mine. You'll have to wear a pistol at all times, and we'll be followed and watched. You'll have to have eyes in the back of your head."

"I've been in some pretty tense situations before, Slade. I'm no stranger to carrying a pistol when I have to. My dad taught me how to hit what I aimed at."

"Those guaqueros are tough and dangerous. They've been bred and raised in the back alleys of Bogotá's slums. If they think you're carrying an emerald on you, they'll slit your throat to get it."

Cat gave an exasperated sigh. "Slade, why, all of a sudden, are you trying to scare me out of going?"

"Because," he said thickly, leaning down to capture her lips, "your life means more to me than green fire."

Chapter 10

Pools of sweat had darkened the color of Slade's khaki short-sleeved shirt, and Cat wiped her brow with the back of her hand, grimacing. For seventy-five miles, they had bumped along in a ten-year-old Jeep on the only rutted dirt road leading from Bogotá to the emerald fields of the Muzo Valley. They passed several motley-looking groups of men, all stripped to the waist, their coffee-colored skin glistening from the harsh sun overhead and the humidity of the surrounding tropical forest. When they were near the guaqueros, Cat placed her hand over the handle of her revolver. The guaqueros glared, their dark, narrowed eyes quickly appraising Cat and Slade, trying to determine whether they were carrying emeralds.

Cat glanced over at Slade. All his attention was focused on keeping the Jeep on the miserable excuse for a road they were on. It had been washed out due to an unexpected thunderstorm the day before. Mud was everywhere. The guaqueros were covered with mud; only the whites of their wary eyes were visible. Despite the hardships, however, Cat was happy. She was back in the field once again, braving the inhospitable elements that seemed to come with sinking a shaft in some remote part of the world. Only when she thought about having to go in and inspect the mine shaft soon to be under construction did the black fear envelop her.

They crossed the brackish Rio Itoco on their way past Muzo Valley. The river's once-clear waters had turned black with gritty shale washed down into it by the heartless bulldozers. Cat saw hundreds of guaqueros in the river at the V of the valley, backs bent as they sluiced through the river's lifeblood. They sought the one precious pebble that would bring them a better life. Slade had told her that if a guaquero found one emerald a year he was lucky. In the same breath, he'd said: "The instant the emerald is found, the smart guaquero will hide it. If others have seen him discover it, they'll ambush him on the only road to Bogotá. If he's smart, he'll sell it to one of the esmeralderos who wait on the banks of the Rio Itoco."

Her heart went out to the treasure seekers. Cat saw not only men, but women and children amongst those who crowded in the Rio Itoco's shallow waters.

"You never said there were women and children out here, Slade."

It was his turn to grimace. He took off the baseball cap he wore to protect himself from the overhead sun. Blinding shafts stole in between the straight *pao d'arco* trees swathed in reptilian-looking vines. "Didn't want to depress you, Cat. It's a sad state of affairs down here. The women and even the children dig tunnels into

Muzo's shale mountains at night. Sometimes they suffocate because of lack of oxygen in the longer tunnels. Sometimes they die in cave-ins." He glanced at her, seeing the anguish register on her features. That was one more thing he liked about Cat: she was incapable of hiding her reactions. He gripped her hand momentarily, giving it a squeeze. "It's a perilous life at best, looking for green fire," he said.

The jungle closed around them once again and the frequent foot traffic of guaqueros in the Rio Itoco area shrank as the miles fell away. Humic acids of decayed vegetation surrounded them and Cat spotted a white monkey above them on one of the cable-strong vines before he went into hiding. The macaws' brilliant reds, blues and yellows made the dark, almost forbidding jungle come alive. Ferns, some as high as a man, cluttered the jungle floor, as did ringworm cassia and angel's trumpet shrubs. Perhaps most beautiful of all were the multicolored orchids, peeking out in breathtaking splendor to relieve the green walls on either side of the thin ribbon of a dirt road.

The odors of life and death clung to Cat's nostrils as Slade swung the Jeep up and out of the Muzo valley. The air was fresher and less humid as they traversed a shrinking road across the ridge, heading for Gato Valley. Compared to Muzo, Gato was spared man's plundering. No human beings were in sight. Gato, named after the jaguars that ruled the valley, seethed with wildlife and birds. Cat began to relax and let go of her pistol. Slade had given her stern warning that if a guaquero made any kind of move toward them, she was to draw the gun and ask questions later.

By the time they reached the third and final valley, Silla de Montar, the sun was a red orb hanging low on

the horizon. Cat was bruised and banged from the tor-
tuous ride. From the rim of the valley, she saw the two
peaks that created the saddle for which the valley had
been named. On the left was Caballo Mountain, where
Slade and Alvin owned the Verde mine land. Clothed
in the green raiment of jungle, Caballo gave no hint of
what lay beneath its verdant mantle. Cat smiled, thinking
how skillfully the earth hid her treasure from passersby.
Only Slade's patient, methodical channel samplings had
hinted of the wealth that lay on Caballo and down into
the mountain's heart of limestone and shale.

"It's beautiful here," she told him, meaning it.

"The air's a little less humid over here than at Muzo,"
Slade commented, aiming the nose of the sturdy Jeep
down a steep incline toward the valley floor. "I think it's
because of the higher elevation." He flashed her a tired
smile. "We'll be working up on Caballo and not down in
the valley. That's a plus, believe me."

"More like Chivor's mines," Cat agreed. Her short-
sleeved cotton shirt gave her some relief from the static
heat and sweltering humidity. She took the red necker-
chief she always wore out in the field and wiped the latest layer of grit and sweat off her face. In the distance,
she could see the faint outline of two tented camps. Halfway up Caballo sat a smaller camp with three olive-drab
tents and one fire. About a quarter of a mile below that
was a small city of tents, bustling with men and activity.
Construction machinery sat behind the main camp, steel
chargers that looked dark and forbidding in the jungle
twilight. In the valley, Cat could barely make out huge,
neat piles of posts and stulls to be used in the creation
of the mine shaft. Electricity was provided by a number
of diesel generators, now heard faintly in the distance.

All the comforts of home, Cat decided with satisfaction. Suddenly excited, she looked forward to meeting Alvin Moody, Slade's partner.

Cat couldn't resist a smile when she saw Alvin. He was stooped over a fire, stirring the contents of a black kettle, when he saw them. Slade hadn't exaggerated the facts, she saw as Alvin rose to his full height. He looked like an honest-to-God Texas legend come to life: a ten-gallon straw hat was angled low on his silver hair and a caterpillar mustache sat above his lean mouth. A long, brown, chewed-up cigar was clamped between his teeth. Cat turned to Slade as he braked the Jeep to a halt.

"Alvin looks like a page torn out of the 1860s," she said.

Slade grinned, shutting the Jeep off. "That's Alvin, all right."

"He's dressed like a marshall from Dodge City— leather vest and two six-shooters low on his hips," she pointed out gleefully.

"This is Dodge City and he is the sheriff, for all intents and purposes of this camp," Slade growled. "Those two pearl-handled Colts he carries are the real thing. He's used them a time or two, believe me."

Cat gratefully slid out of the Jeep, her muscles protesting as she stretched to unknot all the kinks in her back and rear. "Where's his badge?"

"Those Colts are his badge and they do all the necessary talking for him." Slade came around the Jeep, sliding his hand beneath her left elbow. "Come on, he's been waiting to meet you."

She laughed. "The big question is, am I ready to meet him! My God, he's a giant of a man!"

"Texas born and bred, sweetheart. In that state, they don't do anything on a small scale."

Cat agreed. As they drew up to Alvin, who stood with his large hands resting comfortably on the handles of his low-slung Colts, he grinned.

"Say," he crowed, sweeping off his hat in a courtly gesture, "you ugly-lookin' rock hound, you never said how purty this little filly was."

"Hi, Alvin. The name's Cat, Cat Kincaid." She extended her hand, grinning broadly.

Alvin gripped her hand, refusing to relinquish it as Slade stood nearby.

"If I'd told you how pretty she was, Alvin, you'd have left this pit and come back to Texas," Slade said, slapping him on the back.

"That's for sure, Slade. Miss Cat, welcome to the Verde mine," he told her, sweeping his arm toward Caballo Mountain just above them. His pale blue eyes twinkled. "We're right glad you're here to help us."

"Thanks, Alvin." Cat cast a glance over at Slade. "Your partner had to do a lot of talking to get me out here."

Alvin chortled and finally released her hand. He settled the huge hat back on his head. "This Texan's got more ways to twist a cat's tail than even I do. I figured if anyone could talk you into consulting for us instead of that kangaroo outfit in Australia, Slade could do it. By Gawd, I was right. You're here and that's all that matters."

Slade looked around, taking off his cap and stuffing it in the back pocket of his jeans. "What's cooking, Alvin?"

Alvin gave him a hint of a smile from beneath his mustache. "In my kettle or around Caballo?"

Hunkering down over the kettle, Slade stirred it briefly. "Both."

Alvin motioned for Cat to sit down on a log near the fire. "We got us some sidewinders prowlin' around, Slade." He patted his Colts affectionately. "Nothing I can't take care of."

"How many?"

"About half a dozen guaqueros have been hoverin' around since the mining equipment and workers was brought in." He pointed to the left, toward the shadowy mountain. "Everything you ordered is here—bulldozers, backhoes, shaft equipment. The whole kit and caboodle. That pack of guaqueros came with it." He squinted to the east of them. "As far as I can tell, they're makin' camp up there on Lazo Mountain and waitin'."

Cat glanced at Slade, watching the frown on his face deepen. "Waiting for what, Alvin?" she asked quietly, almost afraid to hear the answer.

The Texan joined them, pulling three tin plates from a nearby wooden trunk that had seen better days. "They smell green fire, Miss Cat. This bunch has a nose for emeralds like a starvin' coyote does for meat on the hoof. Right now, they're being real patient and checkin' us out." Alvin cocked his head in Slade's direction. "El Tigre is headin' up that bunch of no goods."

Slade scowled. "Him?"

"Who's El Tigre?" Cat asked, suddenly interested.

Alvin heaped a tin plate with the vittles. "One of the meanest two-eyed snakes in the business of being a guaquero. He's a puny little bastard. Lean as a whippet, with eyes like a viper. He got his nickname over at Muzo because of his reputation of jumpin' other guaqueros after they've found green fire."

With a muttered curse, Slade stood and came over to where Alvin was doling out the food. "He's been accused of kidnapping, raping and thievery. Not necessarily in that order."

Her eyes widened. "Raping?"

"Sure," Alvin snorted, handing her a plate. "Men ain't the only ones to hunt for green fire. We got some tough women who pan right alongside the other guaqueros. El Tigre doesn't care if it's a male or female who has the emerald on them. He treats both sexes equally. If they don't give 'em the green fire, he'll do whatever's necessary to get it. That can be anything from torture to murder. If the guaquero's smart, he or she will hand over the loot and thank God for getting away alive. Sometimes, just for the hell of it, El Tigre will butcher his victim anyway as a warning to other guaqueros. There's a hundred-thousand-peso warrant out for his arrest by the owners of the Muzo mines." Alvin snorted. "El Tigre was born and raised in these mountains. Ain't no one gonna catch that oily weasel alive." He patted one Colt. "That's why you wear these at all times, Miss Cat. You eat, live and sleep with 'em."

Cat took the tin plate, now covered with beans and something with a red sauce on it. She sniffed it cautiously.

"That's rum beans for a main course," Alvin explained, "and sourdough bread and the tomatoes with biscuits is called pooch. It'll stick to your ribs."

Cat grinned. "As long as it doesn't grow hair on my chest, Alvin."

Alvin slapped his thigh, his laughter sounding like the rumble of thunder in his large chest. "Spunky little filly, ain't she? I like her, Slade. She's got a down-home sense of humor."

With a grin, Alvin served up a heaping plate for Slade and himself. The Texan sat across from them at the fire, wolfing down his portion of the food. "All I cook is cowboy food served on the open ranges of Texas. Rum beans has some bacon, molasses, mustard and a half a cup of good hundred-and-eighty-proof rum in it. Pooch is an old cowboy dessert."

The beans were tasty, maybe because she was starved. Alvin was a fine cook, Cat admitted. She smiled at him. "Well, I know you aren't going to try and poison me with your cooking, Alvin. This stuff is pretty good."

Alvin gave her an effusive grin, pleased by her praise. "I'll make you a real 'welcome to the Verde mine meal' tomorrow night, Miss Cat. I'll even throw in the horse-thief special for dessert. Hell, there ain't a cowboy alive who wouldn't ride hard like a horse thief to get a bowl of it." He winked conspiratorially at Slade. "We'll have her puttin' a few pounds on that skinny frame of hers in no time."

"Alvin, I'm not a heifer to be fattened up," Cat warned. "I like being thin."

"I like her that way, too," Slade agreed, laughing.

Alvin looked at them and said nothing, a knowing gleam in his eyes. "I'll only make half the amount of horse-thief special, then."

"No, make all you want," Slade countered quickly. "I'll eat the leftovers."

"See what I mean, Miss Cat? Men will do anything to get that dessert."

"I can hardly wait until tomorrow night," she promised him.

Conversation gradually drifted to the equipment, the work timetable and a long business discussion. The sun dropped behind the saddle formed by the two mountains, and the surrounding jungle suddenly came alive with the songs of insects. The mosquitoes had been pesky earlier; now they were vicious. The trio saturated themselves with insect repellent so they could sit around the fire without being attacked by the bloodthirsty insects.

By eleven o'clock, Cat was barely able to keep her eyes open, despite the interesting conversation. She got up, brushing off the seat of her pants.

"Which way is my cot, Alvin?"

Both men stood. "You and Slade share that larger tent on the left. The smaller one on the right is mine. Slade says you know how to live in jungles."

She smiled. "As long as you've got a mosquito net over the cot, that's all I'll need."

"You got it, Miss Cat."

"Are the guards set?" Slade asked.

"Yeah."

"Can they be trusted?"

Alvin grinned tightly beneath his silvery mustache. "Didn't I tell you? I brought some of my boys down from one of my Texas ranches."

"How'd you get them to come?" Slade asked admiringly.

"I'm payin' them double what they'd get to sit on a cow pony back home. They don't mind totin' around a rifle and standin' watches to make sure we don't get our throats slit."

Cat shivered as unpleasant reality settled over her. Seeing her shiver and rub her arms, Slade came over, placing an arm around her waist.

"We'll see you in the morning, Alvin."

"G'night, you two."

"Good night," Cat responded, casting a worried look up at Slade. Even so, she felt safe with him near. He guided her over to their tent, which was illuminated by a lantern hung inside.

"I told you this was going to be a rough place," Slade warned her in a low voice. "You can still back out, Cat."

She shook her head. "A Kincaid never backs out. We only know one direction, Slade: forward."

He opened the flap for her and ducked in after she entered. The floor was made of plywood in an effort to keep most of the insects, snakes and rodents out. A cot sat on either side and Cat tested the sturdiness of one of them, then sat down, unlacing her boots. A porcelain basin filled with warm water sat between the cots.

"I hadn't counted on El Tigre being here," Slade muttered, stripping off his damp, sweaty shirt. His chest gleamed with perspiration as he quickly washed up.

"Can't you call in the Colombian police to capture him?"

Cat sat there watching Slade, realizing once again how beautiful a man he was. Then she smiled, because Slade didn't like that term applied to him. Nudging off her boots, she peeled off the heavy white cotton socks, waiting until Slade had finished with his spit bath.

Slade scrubbed his face vigorously, the cooling water a blessing against the humid heat. "Alvin and I are going to try and operate Verde like Chivor: a private mine with no state influence." Drying his face and arms, Slade threw the water out the door and refilled the basin from a five-gallon plastic jug that sat beneath the rickety table. He motioned that it was her turn to wash up.

"We haven't even begun mining operations, so what

is El Tigre going to do?" she wondered, sending a worried look to Slade.

But Slade's mind was on other things. Taking off his khaki trousers, he dropped them at the end of his cot. Cat had shed her blouse, revealing her golden tan now deepened by the kerosene lamp above them. His body hardened for her all over again. Their living quarters might be spare, but that wasn't going to stop him from loving her. He'd like to time a trip to Bogotá after the mine was under construction, taking Cat back to civilization every once in a while. That way they could spend a night in a real bed with sheets, a hot shower and air-conditioning. Now, all that seemed like real luxury. Slade smiled, watching as she washed her arms and shoulders. His gaze moved slowly up and then down her tall, graceful body, and the stirring heat in his lower body became an aching reality. Slade was amused at himself. Cat made him hungry no matter what she was or wasn't wearing.

"El Tigre will watch, catalog and send his spies down to talk with our newly hired miners," Slade said, sitting down on his cot. "He's going to see who's the boss and who might know where the emeralds are located."

Cat toweled off, standing on the wooden floor in only her lingerie. She saw the cobalt flare in Slade's eyes and swallowed hard. How was it possible that only one smoldering look from him set her on fire? No man had ever made her feel her feminine power as he did. No man had ever made her feel so cherished. Shakily, Cat placed the folded cotton towel near the basin. Before she could turn, Slade had captured her hand, pulling her over to him. He guided Cat to his lap and she smiled languidly, placing her arms around his neck.

"Let's forget about the bandits, sweetheart," he told her thickly. "This is more important…"

As his hand slid lightly up her rib cage to cup her breast, Cat gasped, dissolving into his arms. Desire coursed through her as his thumb caressed her nipple, and she was lost to his warm, knowing mouth. Cat hungrily matched Slade's mounting desire with her own.

With a groan, Slade eased his lips from hers. Cat's languorous smile went straight to his heart as she rested weakly in his arms. "I want you," he growled.

"I know…" With a sigh, Cat sat up, running her fingers through his unruly hair.

Slade patted her nicely rounded rear, the silk of her panties driving him closer to total loss of control. He saw the exhaustion in her eyes and admitted he was equally fatigued by the long trip. As much as his heart and mind were willing to carry Cat over that delicious edge and love her, Slade put a check on his desires. He didn't want to take her to his bed when he was this groggy. No, he wanted both of them awake and eager. Right now, they were both ready to keel over. He contented himself with holding and sharing this precious time with Cat instead. Moments later, he whispered, "Come tomorrow morning, we're going to be putting in twelve-to sixteen-hour days. I may not be able to hold or kiss you out there, but remember how I feel about you. We'll make up for it here in the tent every night. Deal?"

With a small laugh, Cat embraced him. "Deal. But by the time we drag ourselves into the tent to sleep, we might be too tired to do anything."

"No, we won't," Slade promised, trailing a series of moist kisses from her throat to the provocative swell of her firm breasts. "Even when I'm eighty, you'll still turn me on. Come on, let's get some sleep. We're going to need it."

Reluctantly, Cat knew he was right. Slade's words filled her heart with unexpected joy. "I'll see you in the morning, Slade," she said, rising from his cot to return to hers.

After getting the mosquito netting in position, Cat settled down to sleep. Slade turned off the lantern, and a consuming blackness quickly descended on them. The sounds of insects mingling with the howl of monkeys provided a strange symphony. Cat barely heard them, since her head and heart centered on Slade's last comment. They were growing closer to one another, and Slade was becoming her friend as well as her lover. As her eyes closed, Cat recognized that theirs was an ideal combination. She had known men in the past who only wanted her as a lover. Others she had liked well enough to call friend, but they hadn't stirred the embers of her heart or body to vibrant life. Slade did both. She felt a never-ending thirst to satiate herself with him in every way possible. As Cat sank into the oblivion of sleep, she found herself glad, despite her own personal fears about entering a mine, that she had come to Colombia.

Cat silently asked the earth to forgive their invasion as the first bulldozers roared to life. They would clear away the jungle over the site of the open pit location for the Verde mine. She stood on a small rise, white hard hat in place, watching as the powerful, growling noise of the huge machines reverberated through the surrounding jungle. Slade was down there with the dozer operators, making sure each man knew what he was doing. Alvin was coordinating other activities with the hired miners. As soon as the earth had her green mantle scraped free, the miners would carefully go over the newly shorn earth and walk it, an inch at a time. They would be looking for emeralds before another foot of overburden was scraped away.

Cat turned and went back to the newly erected shack, which would serve as her headquarters during the entire venture. The Indians had built her a small building composed of *pao d'arco*, or trumpet tree. The wood from the sometimes-two-hundred-foot giant would be the prime source for shoring beams in the mine. As Cat spread out her next blueprint on the roughened drafting-board surface, she smiled. Some of her fear left as she focused on the complexities of starting up such a project. With the throaty sound of bulldozers in the background, Cat took off her hard hat and sat down on the stool. Her final calculations would prepare for the excavation that would eventually become the mouth of the Verde mine shaft.

Night did not fall until after nine o'clock. Cat was still in her office on the hill, struggling with figures on her calculator, when the door opened. Thinking it was Slade, she turned, squinting from the light of the lantern that hung on the wall in front of her. She froze, her hand automatically moving to the Colt she carried on her hip.

"Do you want to die, *señorita*?"

Cat's mouth went dry as she stared at a dark-skinned man barely her height. He was dressed in black-and-gray military fatigues. Two bandoliers of ammunition crisscrossed his thin chest and an array of knives, grenades and other military hardware were held in web belts. Two more men, less well equipped, slipped inside, shutting the door quietly behind them. Her gaze moved back to the leader.

"What's going on?" she forced out. Her pulse was racing, her throat growing dry. The look on the leader's oblong face was anything but friendly.

He smiled, showing his crooked yellow teeth. Motioning to the maps, he said in halting English, "These are the maps where the emeralds are?"

Cat's fingers closed over the handle of the Colt, but she knew she would be foolish to try anything. All three soldiers carried weapons.

"No," she lied, "I'm an engineer. I build mines. These are construction blueprints."

His smile remained fixed as he slowly approached her. "I'm El Tigre, *señorita*. You have heard of me, no?" He twisted one drooping end of his greasy mustache, which hung down over his mouth.

Cat nodded carefully. "Yeah, I've heard of you."

"Then you know enough not to lie." He let his hand fall on an eight-inch sheathed blade in a black leather belt at his waist.

"I'm not lying."

El Tigre's brown, feral eyes glittered and he ruthlessly assessed her in the thick, mounting silence. "No? Then who knows where the emeralds are to be found?"

Cat slowly turned, letting her hand move away from her pistol. "Listen, the owners don't even know if there are emeralds here, Señor Tigre."

He laughed; it was a curt, harsh sound. "No one gathers this kind of equipment and men if there aren't emeralds, *señorita*. Don't think me stupid!"

There was no way to escape; only one door had been built into the shack. The portable radio was set on the drafting board, but she couldn't signal Slade or Alvin that she needed help. Cat had the feeling if she made even the slightest move to escape, the Colombian guaquero would turn violent, like a rabid dog.

"I've been hired to build, that's all. I'm not a geologist."

El Tigre stepped up to her. "Then who is?"

Cat winced, assailed by the sour, unwashed smell of his body. "The geologist is still up in the States."

"Maybe, maybe not…" He reached out to touch her cheek.

Cat reacted out of instinct. The sound of the slap she delivered to the man shot through the shack. She scrambled out of the chair, her back against the wall, braced for whatever retribution might come.

El Tigre cursed, holding his injured jaw, glaring at her. "You," he snarled softly, "will live to regret this. I'm not done with you, *señorita*." He grabbed several sets of blueprints, turned and snapped orders to his men. They opened the door, disappearing into the gathering night. Before he left, El Tigre lifted his finger, waving it at her threateningly. "No one touches me, especially a gringo woman. Sleep lightly, *señorita*, for I'll be back. And next time, have the information I want or your pretty face will look like this." He jerked the knife from its scabbard and stabbed it into the drafting board, tearing long, deep scars through the remaining maps and wood.

Slade had noticed three men go up to the construction shack on the hill. He had climbed down from the bulldozer he'd been manning to give the driver a break. By the time he had gotten to the Jeep and driven up the rutted excuse of a road, they were gone. He walked in the open door and immediately saw Cat slumped against the drawing board, her head resting in one hand. And then he saw the destroyed blueprints beneath her elbow and the damage made by the knife.

"Cat? What happened?"

She looked up, giving Slade a wobbly smile meant to neutralize the concern in his voice.

"El Tigre and two of his men dropped in for a chat— of sorts."

Slade was instantly at her side, anxiously turning her toward him. "Did he hurt you?"

"Scared the hell out of me, but no, he didn't hurt me." She leaned against Slade's powerful chest, sinking into his arms. Only then did Cat release a shaky sigh, showing just how scared she had been.

"Tell me everything," he ordered harshly.

Afterward, Slade gathered up the rest of the blueprints, rolled them and stored them in the Jeep. The scowl on his brow had deepened as Cat had relayed the sequence of events. As they bumped on down the road toward base camp, he muttered, "I didn't think he'd jump us this soon."

"We should probably thank him, Slade."

"Why?"

"If he's got that good a nose for green fire, then your mine is a success even before we get a chance to start looking for the calcite matrix."

With a snort, Slade agreed. He gripped the steering wheel hard, his knuckles whitening. "You think on your feet pretty good. Telling him the geologist was in the States was an excellent idea."

Cat traded a glance with him. "Only if he believes it." She tried to quell her own fear that if El Tigre knew Slade was the geologist, his life, too, was in very real danger. She tried to shove back the nightmare played out by her overactive imagination. El Tigre would torture the information out of Slade, and she knew it. After having met the bandit, there was no doubt in her mind that he'd kill Slade after he got the information. An icy shiver moved up her spine.

"There's no safe place, is there?" she asked hollowly.

Slade brought the Jeep to a halt near their tent. He reached over and covered her hand, now clenched against her thigh. "No, there isn't. Come on, let's tell Alvin what happened. We'll figure something out."

The next week went by without incident. Two of Alvin's cowboys guarded Cat at all times while she worked at the shack. The jungle was removed, leaving the black overburden of soil. Almost immediately, a thin white vein of exposed limestone was discovered by the miners. Cat had watched in fascination as Alvin and Slade went down with the miners, gently breaking up the soft limestone with crowbars, prying it apart to see if they could find the telltale white calcite. And all the time, her gaze moved restlessly across the wall of jungle surrounding them. Somewhere in there were El Tigre and his cutthroat band.

The five or six hours Cat slept, with Slade nearby, became important. She rarely saw him during the day, although he would drop in unexpectedly to see her. The stolen kisses, unseen by anyone in the privacy of the shack, became her sustenance. At night in the privacy of their tent Slade's hands would slide knowingly down her damp body, filling her with the fire of their longing and erasing her fears. The mine became secondary to the threat El Tigre presented. Cat lived with the terror that the guaqueros would capture Slade.

Going back into the shack after dinner one night, Cat focused on her next project: getting the hardwood tree, *pao d'arco*, cut and brought down from the hillsides of Caballo so the beams could be cut and measured for use. The numbers before her blurred and Cat squeezed her eyes shut. You're tired, her mind screamed. Yes, she was tired. Sleep came grudgingly, if at all. She tossed and turned on her cot, El Tigre's viperlike eyes haunting her. *If nothing else,* Cat thought as she opened her eyes, pulling the hand calculator toward her, *it's made me own up to the fact that I'm in love with Slade.*

One week later, it happened.

"Pay dirt!" Slade breathed. The three of them crouched on the ground over a partially exposed limestone vein halfway up Caballo's western flank. A miner had discovered the white, flaky calcite matrix in the oppressive afternoon heat. Slade had called Alvin and Cat on their radios. They stood nearby while he patiently pried the matrix, as large as his hand, out of the embrace of the limestone. Pleasure wreathed Slade's features as he held the matrix up for them to see.

Cat gasped. Alvin gave a pleased chortle. Slade grinned rakishly, holding the white calcite in his palm. There, in its center, were four hexagonal green crystals varying in height from one inch to six inches. None of them was less than a quarter of an inch in diameter. Stunned, Cat watched as the rays of the sun glinted through the emerald crystals, showing their clarity.

"Green fire," Slade said hoarsely, holding the crystals up toward the sun. The molten emeralds gleamed like living beings, catching and refracting the light.

"My gawd," Alvin whispered, "look how clear they are."

Slade's face glistened with sweat, his teeth white against his darkly tanned flesh. "Muzo's deep color and Chivor's clarity. This is what I had been hoping for…"

Word of the find spread through the miners like a ripple of wind through a field of wheat. Cat stood back, watching the spectacle unfold. For a week, they had carefully poked and prodded through the limestone vein without success. A six-foot-high cyclone fence topped with barbed wire had been erected around the pit. As she stood watching the hope suddenly come alive in the Indians' faces, Cat felt frightened. El Tigre was out there, watching them—she could feel his eyes. She turned away, heading back to her shack on the hill. By four o'clock, the first of the dynamite that had been drilled into the limestone face would be triggered and an opening would be made. The mine—her mine—would begin taking shape, and soon she would have to go back inside the earth.

Despite the hundred-degree heat and ninety-percent humidity, Cat was cold. She took off her white construction hat, wiping the sweat from her brow with the back of her hand. The day she had been dreading had come. Part of her was happy about the emerald find, and Cat was sure there were more stones to be discovered. Taking a breath to support her deteriorating courage, she plunged ahead with her plans. A dynamite expert from the U.S., Tony Alvarez, was standing at the door to her shack when she arrived.

"We're ready when you are, Cat."

Cat forced a slight smile, then went inside to grab her portable radio and hook it on her web belt.

"What have we got?" she asked, getting into the Jeep.

Tony hopped in. "I prepped the area after I got rid of the overburden." He used his long, expressive hands. "The shot holes are drilled and loaded with dynamite. The blasting caps are in place and my crew has just collared each of the holes with clay."

Cat glanced at him as she drove the Jeep down the dusty road toward the valley. "Are you going to use millisecond delays between detonations to produce maximum fragmentation of the rock?"

"Sure am, boss. I'm using a four-hole, pyramid-cut pattern. It will give us a seven-by-seven-foot entrance and blow out rock seven feet behind it. We're using low charges so we won't destroy any emeralds that get in the way of our creating an opening into Mother Earth."

"Good," Cat said. She parked the Jeep a good distance from where the series of blasts would take place in the hill. All jungle growth and soil had been removed, exposing the pale green limestone. From her vantage point, using binoculars, Cat could see that Tony had set up the wall for detonation. She signaled Tony to set off the siren. The high-pitched wail shrieked over the area of the Verde, alerting everyone that blasting was going to take place. Tony raised his arm, alerting his two men who stood by the plunger.

Her mouth was dry as she lowered the binoculars. "All right, Tony, give them the signal."

The plunger was shoved down, making electrical contact with the pattern Tony had drilled into the limestone face. Ten explosions rocked Caballo, each seconds apart. Limestone spewed outward in fragments, and a huge, roiling white cloud of dust rose in the wake of the detonations. Cat's ears ached from the puncturing, thunderous roll that each one had caused. The air was pregnant with humidity and swallowed up the sound. Ears ringing, Cat lifted the glasses to her eyes. The dust slowly cleared and, as it did, she got the first look at the opening.

"Looks good, Tony," Cat praised. She had chosen a slope mine, using a slanting entry to follow the vein of limestone that carried the calcite and emerald. The dynamite had done its job, creating the entry, or adit, into the hillside. Now excavation of the debris would begin and the first of the *pao d'arco* beams would begin to be shored into place. The Verde mine had just been born.

Chapter 11

"Come on, I'll go in with you." Slade rested his hand on Cat's shoulder, feeling her tension. He saw the distraught look in her eyes and smiled. "What's this? Did you think I wouldn't escort you into the Verde mine?"

Cat relaxed beneath the massaging power of Slade's fingers on her shoulder. She had stayed away from actually entering the new mine shaft as long as she could. The last time she had seen Slade, he had been far above them in the pit, working side by side with the miners, looking for another calcite nest. A good, warm feeling flowed through her as Slade matched her slow walk toward the maw.

"I thought you were busy elsewhere," she said, knowing her voice sounded strained.

"Remember?" Slade said, becoming serious, settling his hard hat on his head. "I told you that you were more important than green fire."

A tremulous smile fled across Cat's mouth. "Judging from the look on your face earlier when you held that calcite bearing the emerald, I wondered, Slade."

His smile was devastating. "Don't. I promised you I'd be here when you needed me."

The shadow of the hill enveloped them, and Cat slowed to a stop a few feet from the shaft entrance. Already, wooden forms were being erected to create a permanent opening to the Verde. Once the forms were in place, concrete would be poured into them. Thick, rectangular beams of *pao d'arco* lay in huge, neat piles nearby. Some were already being hauled over to the mouth of the shaft.

Cat felt her stomach shrink into a knot. Her lips felt dry. She didn't dare hesitate in front of the miners who covertly watched her. The limestone was jagged from the explosions and would have to be knocked off the walls to prevent injury. She stepped into the mouth, vaguely aware of a minimal temperature drop. Slade remained at her side as they walked back the first seven feet. They stood in the center of the footwall where the rubble had been removed, both looking overhead, studying the manging wall.

Slade glanced down at her. Even in the shadowy grayness of the mine, he could see how pale Cat had become. Small beads of sweat stood out on her wrinkled brow as she assessed the ceiling with a critical eye. A fierce wave of pride overwhelmed him. Despite Cat's fear, she was holding her ground.

"We're going to need rock bolts," she said, pointing to the spiderweb pattern on the ceiling where the rock had been fractured.

Slade nodded in agreement. Often, the systematic use of rock bolts reinforced roofs of mines that might cave in, or they strengthened existing walls in case of earthquake. "We've got an ample supply," he said.

Suddenly, Cat wanted to run. She wanted to scream. Swallowing hard, she forced herself to measure off the distance to where the first post and stulls would be set. The activity helped keep her fear contained, and as she talked with the Indian foreman in Spanish, a little more of the fear receded.

"I want those rock bolts under high tension, Pablo."

The foreman, a man close to fifty with graying hair beneath his red hard hat, nodded. *"Si, Patrona."*

"I'll be testing them," she warned him.

Slade smiled to himself. Cat would, too. That would mean she'd be spending a hell of a lot of time in the mine measuring them with a torque meter. Much later, Slade followed Cat out of the mine. He traded a knowing glance with her as she took off her hard hat, wiping her sweaty features.

"Congratulations," he told her in a low voice, "you did it. First time's always the toughest."

With a weary smile, Cat threw the hat back on her head. She watched the beams being hauled to the entrance. From here on, the building of the mine would continue for twenty-four hours a day with three crew shifts working. She would be up sixteen of those hours to keep pace with the rapid expansion of the mine until they hit a vein with calcite in it. Then, work would slow accordingly to open up the vein and hunt for the emeralds.

"I'm so shaky, my knees are knocking, Slade."

"How about if I hold you tonight?"

The gritty warmth of his lowered voice washed through her and Cat shared a soft smile with him. The words *I love you* were almost torn from her. "Sounds wonderful, fella."

"Hey, this evening, Alvin's celebrating the mine start-up by making a special dinner for us."

Alvin was a fine cook and Cat eagerly looked forward to most of his cowboy meals. "What's on the menu?"

Slade chuckled. "Texican beef, hunkydummy, potato dumplin's and apple pan dowdy. A meal fit for a king and queen, believe me. My mouth's watering already."

Cat's wasn't. "Hunkydummy? What's that?" Alvin had a couple of other cowboy recipes she'd just as soon forget about. Every night when they settled around their campfire where Alvin was fixing the vittles, Cat went over every item he was cooking before she ate it.

"It's a kind of bread with raisins and cinnamon sprinkled over the top of it."

"Oh, that sounds pretty good."

Slade laughed. "You're such a sissy," he chided.

"I'm from Colorado, Slade, not Texas. Some of the wild food Alvin whips up could only be consumed by a Texas cowhand. Give me a break!"

Back at the shack, Cat sat down at her drafting board. Her hand shook as she picked up a blue pencil. Closing her eyes, she dropped the pencil and sat there, allowing the cold wash of fear to drench her. After a few minutes, she lifted her head, a wry smile on her lips. How could she have lived so long and not known real fear?

Absently, she picked up the pencil, going through the motions of making notations on the blueprint. The fear wasn't all negative, she mused, nearly awed by that realization. No, it had shown her that another person could give her the necessary strength to press forward.

Had Slade's love given her that support? Cat hesitated over the blueprint as she centered on that question. He had never said he loved her, nor had she told him. Nevertheless, she felt whole as never before, regardless of the fear that stalked her about mine entry. With a soft laugh, Cat shook her head. So, was this real love, this feeling of completeness that Slade automatically gave to her? Cat couldn't imagine life without Slade's presence. He made each minute, each hour important. And they were, with him.

Eventually, Cat returned to the demanding work in front of her. But numbers, formulas and figures couldn't compete with the powerful sensations in her heart. Cat allowed the full gamut of her emotions to surface and be felt. She could barely breathe for the sheer joy of being alive in every sense of the word.

Near four o'clock, Slade knocked on the door and entered. He saw Cat bent over her drafting board, hard at work. A swell of pride and love overwhelmed him as he stood in the open doorway, watching her. As she turned, he saw the sudden happiness in her green eyes because he was there. Slade was deeply moved. With a smile, he held his hand out toward her.

"Come on, I'm taking you someplace special."

Cat stared at his large, powerful fingers; they were dirt-stained and his nails worn to nothing from prying calcite apart, looking for green fire. Without a word, she slipped her hand into his.

"Where?" Her voice was breathless with anticipation.

"While El Tigre is busy watching Alvin and his men digging for green fire, you and I are going to slip off to share some well-deserved time together. What do you think? Are you ready to be carried off by your knight on his white charger?"

Gladly, Cat put down her hard hat and followed Slade out the door. "More than ready, my lord. Lead the way."

Slade gave the Jeep an apologetic look as they climbed in. "Not exactly a white charger, but it'll have to do. Still game?"

"You bet. Is this a surprise or can you tell me where we're going?"

He wanted to ruffle her hair, run his fingers through it and feel the silk of her skin beneath his hands. His voice husky, he traded a tender look with Cat. "I want it to be a surprise. I've been planning this a long time before we came down here. Just sit back and enjoy the ride, my lady."

With a sigh, Cat nodded and leaned back. The movement of the Jeep as it took them up and out of the mining area cooled her sweaty skin. She felt Slade's hand cover her own and she squeezed it. "I love you," she almost whispered. Cat had trouble not saying it out loud to Slade. The adoration in his dark sapphire eyes made her tremble with need.

As they crossed the only road up and out of the valley, Slade turned off, heading down a little-used path. The foliage and low-hanging vines swatted at them and the Jeep cautiously crept forward. Brightly colored macaws ranging from blue and yellow to a garish crimson and purple cawed raucously, their late-afternoon siesta disturbed by the noise of the vehicle. Cat filled her senses with the heavy, intoxicating smell of orchids hanging in patches of brilliant color against the jade jungle.

"If I didn't know better," she confided to Slade, "I'd say this was a slice of heaven tucked away by Mother Earth."

"It is. All right, close your eyes before we go around this bend in the path. I'll tell you when to open them."

Heartbeat escalating, Cat heard a distinctly different sound ahead and to the right of them as they rounded the corner. The Jeep came to a halt and she felt Slade's arm around her shoulder, drawing her close. His voice was low and dark next to her ear.

"Now you can open them. Welcome to our heaven, Cat."

A gasp of pleasure escaped from her as she stared at a small waterfall sitting thirty feet above them. Slade had brought the Jeep to a halt at its base in a small grassy clearing, complete with brilliantly colored flowers of all varieties. A circular pool of an inviting aquamarine color held tiny white suds floating at the foot of the waterfall. Deep green moss hugged small gray boulders along the bank. At the quietest point were several pink-and-white water lilies floating like crown jewels on the surface.

"Slade...this is incredible!" Cat whispered, struck by the beauty surrounding them.

He got out, pleased. "It's all ours. And," he emphasized, helping Cat from the Jeep, "private." He halted near the lip of the bank and turned, placing his hands on her shoulders. As she lifted her chin, her emerald eyes lustrous, Slade groaned softly, capturing her. He claimed her pliant, welcoming lips beneath his, reveling in the scent of her hair and damp skin. Fire tore wildly through him as she melted willingly against him, her arms coming around his shoulders. Slade couldn't get enough of her, ever.

Tearing his mouth from her lips, he rasped, "Today... out there at the mine, Cat..."

Dizzy with the scent of his virility, Cat forced her eyes open. "Yes?" She clung to him, wanting nothing more.

Slade framed her darkly tanned face between his hands, absorbing Cat's sultry look. "I wanted to kiss you, to tell you how damned courageous you were. It's one thing to live through a cave-in. It's another to walk back inside again. You did it, and I'm so damned proud of you."

She managed a tremulous smile, sliding her fingertips across his shoulders. "Be proud of us. I was glad you were there, believe me."

"You were going in whether I was there or not. That's what counted." He leaned down, capturing her mouth again, drowning in the only taste and texture that could satisfy his yearning.

Gradually, Cat broke away, heart racing wildly, her breasts swollen and nipples taut. She wanted Slade's touch so badly, it had become a craving. Barely able to think after his exquisite assault upon her senses, Cat whispered, "I'm discovering I can't live without you, Slade."

He grinned, kissing her lashes, nose and mouth. "Nothing wrong with that, my proud beauty."

She smiled as his tongue lazily traced her lips, sweetly sipping from each corner until crazy tingling sensations shot through her, intensifying her ache for him. "I didn't realize how lonely I was until you came into my life," she admitted softly.

Raising his head, Slade melted beneath the tender flame deep within her eyes. His fingers trembled as he sifted strands of her hair through his hands. "I've been looking for you a whole lifetime, Cat. Come on, let's take a well-earned bath. I want to love you afterward..."

Everything else ceased to exist as Cat allowed Slade to unbutton and peel off her damp cotton shirt. Drowning in the love she saw in his blue gaze, she then helped Slade undress. No longer was she aware of the grit or dirt as he led her into the cool embrace of the waist-deep water. She watched as Slade took a handful of moss from the bank. It had a soft, slightly abrasive texture as he sluiced water over her shoulders and across her breasts and gently began to wash her. For the next ten minutes, he did not speak. Instead, each touch became his focus. Then Cat took the damp moss and washed him.

"I found this place a week after we came up here to the Verde the first time," Slade explained as he took the moss and allowed it to float away from them. His hands stilled on her glistening shoulders as he looked around them. "This is a place out of time, Cat. It's special. You can feel it."

Placing her palm against the matted hair on his broad chest, she murmured, "There are some places on the earth that have their own unique vibration." She leaned forward, slowly placing kiss after kiss along the hard, uncompromising line of his jaw. "Just like the vibration beneath my hand is special." She ran her tongue across his mouth, tasting the salt of his sweat and his male earthiness. "You are one of a kind, Slade," she whispered, claiming his mouth with all the fire she possessed.

A tremor shook him as her slick, warm breasts pressed against his chest. The sweet demand of her hips against his own powerful hardness sent a tumult of raw desire coursing through him. Cat was willing, pliant and so much woman that it brought tears to his eyes as he swept her against him, holding her forever. Hungrily, he claimed her mouth, lost in the primal senses that she stirred within him. As her thighs joined his beneath the water, his control was shattered.

Cat swam in the molten heat of their desire, barely aware that Slade had slipped his arm beneath her. Then he lifted her, carrying her from the pool to a carpet of grass. Cat relaxed into the verdant expanse and welcomed him back into her arms. Never had she wanted a man more.

Never had Cat wanted to share the unleashed love that throbbed through her. She felt Slade's hand slide across her hip, gently parting her thighs. The mere touch of him against her damp, waiting core brought a gasp from her. Arching, she pulled Slade down upon her, welcoming him.

Patches of sunlight laced and danced through the heavy jungle canopy overhead. The ripeness of the grass aroused her, as did Slade's masculine scent. Nostrils flared, she met each of his powerful thrusts, responding wildly to his primal demands. Sunlight and darkness, day and night, loneliness and love. All those feelings, words and sensations spun through the hallways of Cat's emotions as Slade carried her beyond any pleasure she had ever experienced. White-hot fusion exploded violently within her and she cried out, sinking her fingers deeply into his taut shoulder muscles.

"Yes…" Slade cried hoarsely, gripping her tightly, twisting his hips to give her every bit of pleasure. "Feel me, Cat. Feel how much you mean to me…" Unable to stop his own need to claim her, he gripped her hard and buried his head next to hers. Explosion after explosion tore through him, ripping him apart and putting him back together again. The French called it *la petite mort*, "the little death." He called it love. With Cat, the meeting of their bodies was an overwhelming symbol of the love he felt for her. He didn't die that small death the French referred to. No, he never felt more alive, more joyous or more sure of his destiny as when he was buried within the yielding core of Cat's body.

With a sigh, Cat sank back into Slade's embrace, floating on a wave of sensations within her. A slight, tremulous smile pulled at her well-kissed lips. She ran her fingers through his dark hair, reveling in the cobalt fire banked in his eyes.

"You take my breath away..." she murmured.

Slade laid his head on her breast, holding her, listening to the ragged pound of her loving heart. "You make me feel so deeply that I can barely breathe...or think..." He laughed softly. "You make me feel whole, Cat."

She continued to smolder beneath his husky compliments, content to lie there with him forever. "I've never flown like this," she admitted, her voice throaty. "You free me, Slade. I didn't know how chained I was until you came and unlocked so many secret places within me..." Gently, Cat ran her hand across his drying flesh, reveling in both his power and his tenderness for her.

Barely opening his eyes, Slade moved his hand down her hip and across her finely curved thigh. "Love has a way of releasing the best in all of us," he murmured.

Cat turned, meeting his eyes as he raised his head to look down at her. "You've taught me so much in such a short amount of time, Slade. You made me aware of how alone I've been. You've made me hungry for you in a way I've never experienced." She cupped his sandpapery cheek. "You've got the keys to my heart. You know that, don't you?"

Gravely, he turned, kissing her palm as if she were fragile glass. "No one's more aware of that than me, sweetheart." He watched as a cloud marred the joy in her eyes. "What is it?" he coaxed. "Are you frightened?"

"Y-yes."

"Me, too. Let's be scared together, okay? Misery loves company and no one cares for you more than I do..."

With a muffled laugh, Cat embraced him. "You crazy Texan! What did I ever do before you crashed into my life?"

Matching her effusive laughter, Slade rolled over on his back, bringing Cat on top of him. She fitted against him perfectly and he absorbed the happiness that had returned to her face. God, how fiercely he loved her. *Soon, he promised Cat silently, you and I are going to show our hands; we're going to admit that we love one another.*

"I can say one thing," he stated out loud.

Cat leaned down, kissing the tip of his nose, euphoria making her feel giddy with joy. "What?"

"Life hasn't been dull since we met."

"That's an understatement, Slade Donovan!"

"Well," he said in a pleased tone, "when you consider we met at a cave-in, that's pretty symbolic."

She nipped playfully at the cords of his neck, inhaling his wonderful scent. "In what way?"

"I've always believed life speaks to us in symbolic terms. For instance, a bird can mean news."

"How do you interpret a cave-in?" Cat wondered, planting her hands on his chest and smiling into his warm blue eyes.

"What's a cave-in do?"

She wrinkled her nose in distaste. "Changed my life, that's for sure."

Slade grinned. "Exactly. It symbolized that each of us would have a devastating effect on each other. It was also an opportunity for a new beginning, together."

Cat grew thoughtful, then met his warming smile. "I like the way you see life, Slade. I've never thought of it in those terms, but it's provocative."

Running his hands suggestively up across her hips and back, he murmured, "And so are you."

Chapter 12

Cat walked down into the Verde mine. After three weeks of blasting and setting up posts and stulls, the tunnel now stretched almost a third of a mile into Caballo mountain. Rock bolts screwed into the limestone ceiling hung like silent baubles above her head every few feet. The chut-chut-chut of several portable generators hammered through the tunnel, providing electric light for the miners removing rubble and those shoring up the beams. The fear was still with her, but less a monster than before. The first week, Slade had miraculously appeared at her side every time she had to go in. Cat didn't know how he knew when she would go into the mine, but she was grateful for his unexplained presence.

As she walked along the adit, a coolness enveloped her. Her main concern was installing proper ventilation through the roof of the mine to the air outside. Exhaust from the generators fouled the air with colorless and odorless carbon monoxide. If it wasn't properly managed, it could eventually kill an unsuspecting miner. The footwall beneath her feet was swept free of all debris, something she had demanded. Dust in any form in a mine ate away at everyone's delicate lung tissue. At first, the workers begrudged the amount of cleanliness she wanted in the adit. Cat stood her ground with them and they finally did as they were ordered.

Gangue, or worthless material, was now being pried off the walls at the end of the tunnel. Cat had discovered a limestone vein bearing calcite yesterday and everyone's hopes had risen to almost a fever pitch. Every shift worker who entered the mine worked in silent tension as he walked the distance of the adit to where the vein was located. There was little talking as sweating men, stripped to their waists, worked. Crowbars in gloved hands, they carefully began to chip away at the vein, searching for green fire.

Cat felt excitement thrumming through the Verde as she checked the next set of posts, stulls and rock bolts. She slid her fingers across the limestone surface of the manging wall. From all appearances, as they went deeper, following the vein, the walls would strengthen, because the rock was more compact. That was good, since they needed all the help they could get from possible earth tremors.

It was nearly 1:00 a.m. when Cat left her shack and drove back down to base camp to call it a night. Everywhere she looked, the garish flood lamps lit up the blackness. Diesel-fueled generators ceaselessly supplied the necessary light so the graveyard shift could work throughout the night, hunting for emeralds in the open-pit area. Cat dropped off her two guards at their camp and swung the Jeep down the rutted road to their private camp that stood an eighth of a mile away.

Slade was standing by the fire beside Alvin while he stirred one of many kettles. He saw Cat's Jeep approaching when suddenly, out of the jungle, four shadowy shapes emerged behind the Jeep. Cold terror raced through him and he raised his hand to warn Cat. Too late! He saw the guaqueros leap into the rear of the vehicle. The first held the blade of a knife against her ribs. Slade took two steps forward, his hand moving to his pistol.

"Now," El Tigre breathed close to Cat's left ear, "you will continue toward the encampment." He took her pistol and handed it to one of his other men. With an icy smile, he pressed the point of the blade a little more firmly against her ribs. *"Comprende?"*

Cat kept her booted feet down on the brake and clutch. *"Si..."*

"Bueno. Drive slowly, now."

Cat nearly gagged on the sour smell that assailed her nostrils as El Tigre leaned over the seat, his body pressed against her back and left shoulder. Her heart pounded heavily and she wondered who he wanted. Slade? Alvin? All of them? Cat saw several guards running down toward the camp and Slade's tall figure silhouetted against the fire. As they drove within twenty feet of the camp, El Tigre hissed, "Halt!"

Slade saw the guaquero take the black-bladed knife and press it to Cat's slender throat. The vicious blade looked stark against the whiteness of her flesh. His fingers wrapped around the pistol's handle.

"Whatever you want, you can have," Slade shouted to them in Spanish, "just let her go."

"*Señor!* I am El Tigre. Your woman here has met me before. Come!"

Slade's eyes narrowed and he barely turned his head to Alvin, who was standing there scowling.

"Follow us, if you can," Slade growled over his shoulder and then walked quickly toward the Jeep. He saw Cat's eyes widen as she sat frozen in the Jeep. Anger coursed through Slade as he saw El Tigre press the blade even more against her flesh.

"Stop there, *señor*," El Tigre commanded. He grinned tightly. "You are the geologist, *si*?"

"*Si.*"

With a chuckle, El Tigre glanced down at Cat. "Your woman led us to believe you were in Texas. She is wily like a jaguar. But we wait and we watch. We see you out in the pit every day. If there is an emerald find, you are always called. Not her, not the gringo with the white hair. But you."

Slade held Cat's frightened gaze. "What do you want?" he ground out.

"Both of you. Come, sit here in the jeep." El Tigre's eyes glittered. "One wrong move and she is dead, *señor*. Watch."

Cat felt the razor-edged blade sink into her flesh. Her eyes bulged and her breath lodged in her throat as she felt the trickling warmth of blood running down her neck, soaking into her shirt. She closed her eyes, fighting off sudden faintness. Slade's savage curse startled her.

"That's enough!"

El Tigre smiled mirthlessly, easing the pressure on the knife. "Enough for now, *señor*. This blade has killed many. It doesn't care whether it's a man or woman. Nor do I. Now, drop your holster and pistol at your feet, then join us. And warn your men that if they try to shoot at us when we leave or try to follow, your woman will breathe her last gulp of air through her windpipe."

Slade slowly unbuckled the holster, letting it drop around his feet. He turned toward Alvin, telling him of El Tigre's orders. Immediately, all the guards lowered their rifles. Slade made his way to the Jeep and halted in front of it.

"Why don't you put that blade on me instead of her?"

"I think not, *señor*. No more talk! Get in!"

The moment Slade slid into the passenger seat, one of the guaqueros came forward. He immediately bound Slade's wrists with hemp rope. Satisfied, El Tigre eased the knife from Cat's throat.

"Drive, *señorita*. Turn around and take the road leading back toward Muzo."

Cat's mind spun with options and possibilities. She jammed the Jeep into gear and they headed out of the well-lit area, swallowed up by the shadowy jungle on both sides of the narrow, bumpy road. As soon as they were out of sight of the Verde, El Tigre relaxed, laughing.

"*Aiyeee, compadres!* I told you how easy it would be to capture them."

Thomas, his second-in-command, whose weapon was trained on Slade's back, nodded, a half smile on his mouth. The other two men cheered in unison, waving their weapons above their heads.

El Tigre rubbed Cat's right shoulder in a provocative motion, his dirty fingers trailing down her arm to the elbow. Cat jerked her arm away.

"Leave me alone!"

"This one has claws," the leader crowed.

Slade turned, his eyes a deadly black color, settling

on the bandit. "You lay another hand on her, and you'll answer to me."

El Tigre smiled slowly. "You'll talk to me anyway, señor. You will tell us where you keep all those emeralds you're finding. If they are in a safe, you will give me the combination."

"Over my dead body."

With a chuckle, El Tigre pointed to Cat. "No, señor, over her dead body. She is how you say it, insurance? If you do not talk, she will die an inch at time."

Cat's skin crawled over the frigid tone in El Tigre's voice. He meant business. The twin beams of light from the Jeep stabbed through the darkness. There was no moon as they drove on, mile after mile, the blackness embracing them until Cat thought she was back in a caved-in mine once again. They had to escape! If El Tigre got them to his camp, they were as good as dead. She didn't dare look at Slade or the guaqueros might suspect something. Her mind raced to remember the road back to Muzo. Right now, they were climbing steadily out of the valley. Soon, they would be following the nose line of several ridges before dropping into the Gato Valley. Slade's hands were tied in front of him. Grimly, Cat wiped the sweat stinging her eyes.

Slade braced himself as Cat pressed down the accelerator once they had bridged the hill. The road was rocky and rutted. What the hell was she doing speeding up like this at this time of night? Didn't she know there was a series of sharp S-turns up ahead? The gravelly surface of the road would make the Jeep slide if she took them too fast. Slade glanced at Cat. Her face was grim and barely outlined by the dashboard lights. Then, realizing what she was going to do, he almost smiled. In those split seconds before they raced down on the first set of curves, Slade promised himself that if they escaped this with their lives, he'd tell Cat how much he loved her.

"Slow down!" El Tigre shrieked in her ear, pounding her right shoulder sharply with his fist.

Cat winced as his knotted fist struck her twice with hard, well-aimed blows. The lights from the vehicle outlined the first turn. She jammed her boot down on the accelerator. The Jeep lurched forward, careening toward the first curve. El Tigre cursed and was thrown backward. He fell into the two men who sat squeezed in the back, and Cat wrenched the nose of the Jeep toward the cliff. One man tumbled over the side, the gun flying out of his hand. Another fell off with a scream. For terrifying seconds, the Jeep slid sideways and then, as Cat wrenched the wheel back to the left, the heavily treaded tires screamed in protest.

"Jump, Slade!"

Everything was a blur as Slade threw himself out of the Jeep. He struck the road with his left shoulder, rolling instinctively into a ball to lessen the shocking impact. Flesh was torn from him, but he felt little pain. He heard the vehicle roar off the road, sudden silence, and then a crash as the Jeep smashed and tumbled down the steep cliff. Cat! Where was Cat?

Drunkenly, Slade got to his feet, searching the choking dust and darkness. He stumbled across unconscious guaqueros. Nearby was a rifle. He picked it up. Had everyone else gone over with the Jeep? Where was she—

"Slade!"

He jerked to the left, crouching. Cat was running toward him, her face smudged with dirt, her blouse ripped and bloodied. Both had paid dearly for landing in the gravel. Her fingers closed around his arm.

"Come on!" she gasped.

"Where are the—"

"Two went over the cliff with the Jeep," she sobbed. "Come on, we've got to get away! Give me the rifle."

There was no time to stop and untie his wrists. Slade nodded and they took off at a dead run down the road, heading back for the Verde camp they had left at least ten miles behind. Every once in a while, Cat would look back. The rifle's safety was off and she held it close, ready to fire if necessary. After running a mile they were both gasping and gulping for air. Slade angled them off the road and into the foliage of the jungle.

"Come here," he panted, holding out his hands toward her. "Get these ropes off me."

Cat came and crouched at his side. She set the rifle nearby and shakily began to untie the knots. "I—I think we're safe."

"Don't count on it," Slade said grimly, sweat streaking down his dirty, bloody face. "Those bastards have nine lives."

She grinned tightly, the adrenaline high, keeping her mind sharp as a steel trap. "So do we. There."

Slade rubbed his raw wrists tenderly. Then he turned his attention to Cat. "How are you?"

"Cuts, bruises...nothing that won't heal. I'm just scared spitless."

His grin was wobbly. "Makes two of us. All right, come on. Those four guaqueros, or whoever is left, won't let us go easily. We've got to make it back to camp or—"

Cat stood, nervously watching the dark road, expecting to see shadowy shapes emerge from it at any moment. "I know. Here, you take the rifle. I'm not sure I could shoot straight if I had to. My hands are shaking like leaves."

With a nod, Slade guided her over the bank of the road. "You run in front of me. Keep your eyes peeled and ears open. If you hear anything, signal me. Don't talk. We can't afford to make any more noise than necessary."

The construction boots felt like lead on Cat's feet. She wasn't in the world's greatest shape, but not the worst, either. After jogging another two miles, she had to ask Slade to halt. Her throat was burning and her lungs felt ready to burst. They found sanctuary in a banana-tree grove, the huge, long fronds covering them so they couldn't be seen from the road. Slade knelt near her, his concentration aimed behind them. Cat felt safe, falling back against the trunk of a tree, taking huge gulps of air.

"You—never told me about this, Donovan."

Slade wiped his face, glancing over at Cat. "I told you it would be rough. This is the Dodge City of the eighties. It's wide open, and the only law is the gun you carry. You let it do the talking for you."

"I'm demanding hazardous-duty pay," she whispered, finally sitting up.

Slade reached out and gripped her hand, squeezing it gently. "If you've accidentally killed El Tigre, you've got a hundred-thousand-peso reward coming from the Muzo mine. Is that enough?"

Cat shivered, suddenly cold. The adrenaline that had given her the courage to deliberately wreck the Jeep and leap from it deserted her. Miserably, she shook her head. "I hope I didn't kill him…"

A flat snort came from Slade. "I do. That bastard was going to kill us."

She believed him, but it still didn't make her feel any better that she had possibly killed one or more men. Slade got up, bringing her to her feet. Cat felt dizzy and leaned against him.

"All right?" Slade asked huskily, pressing a kiss to her dusty hair.

"Yes… I'm whipped."

"Adrenaline letdown. We'll jog, walk, jog. We can't afford to dally."

The fifteen-minute rest hadn't been a good idea after all, Cat discovered. Every bone and socket in her body was beginning to ache in earnest. The scrapes on her arms and shoulders smarted. The boots she wore felt like twenty-pound weights on each foot. Lift them up, put them down, she instructed herself.

Five miles had fallen away under their jog-and-walk routine. Slade kept looking back, never dropping his guard. Cat kept angling toward the center of the road, where it was less rutted. He kept pulling her back, forcing her to walk on the side where it was hard to maintain a balance. If they had to dive for cover, Slade wanted to get into the jungle with one leap. He didn't try to explain to her, realizing Cat was close to exhaustion.

The bark of a rifle silenced the jungle sounds around them. Slade cursed, throwing his full weight forward, landing on top of Cat. They hit the ground hard and he rolled them into the foliage. More bullets spit up geysers where they had stood seconds before. Slade threw Cat off him, scrambled to his knees and hid behind a trumpet tree, both hands on the rifle. There! He saw the figures of two men weaving steadily toward them.

"Son of a bitch," he muttered. He jerked around to look at Cat. She was lying nearby, the breath knocked out of her. "Cat!" he hissed between clenched teeth. "Get up! Hurry!"

With a groan, Cat blindly scrambled to her knees and dove into the brush.

Slade aimed, drew a bead on the lead guaquero and fired twice. The second shot felled one bandit. Then, he had to duck as a spate of savage automatic-rifle fire spewed into his position. Bark exploded and splintered in all directions. Slade lunged for the earth, crawling away from the tree. He got to his knees, scuttling forward in the same direction Cat had gone.

The damp humid jungle floor smelled like so much rotted flesh to Cat. She fell and tripped numerous times over unseen tree roots or vines that snaked across her path. She had heard the gunfire, and adrenaline shot through her, giving her the second wind she needed to escape. Slade! Where was Slade? Had he been wounded? Cat turned, almost running into him. Slade gripped her tightly, his breath hot against her face.

"I got one of them. The other will trail us."

With a groan, Cat clung momentarily to him. "Wh-what can we do?"

He gripped Cat's shoulder firmly. "Listen to me, Cat. Aim yourself east, toward the camp."

She looked up at him, her face blank. "What about you?"

"I'm going to lie here in wait for him. That's the only way we're going to get out of this alive."

"But—"

"Go on and don't argue."

"No, damn it! I'm staying. I can't go into the jungle at night, Slade. I'll get lost!"

His face was glistening with sweat, eyes narrowed

dangerously in the direction from which the guaquero would be sure to come. "At least you'll be alive in case that bastard gets me first. Now, go on. And stop arguing with me."

Cat stood her ground, her jaw set. "I'm staying, Slade."

With a curse, he jerked her to a trumpet tree, forcing her to sit down behind it. "You stay here and don't breathe. You understand me?"

She nodded, her eyes growing large. He started to turn away and she gripped his hand. "Slade?"

Impatiently, he twisted his head in her direction. "What?"

"I love you—"

The harshness on his face melted for a split second. "I know you do. Now just lie low and stay still."

Cat nodded and scrunched herself behind the girth of the tree. How long she sat there, frozen like a fawn while a predator stalked nearby, Cat did not know. She muffled her breathing, hand over her mouth, eyes and ears focused on the path they had made coming into the jungle. Cat quickly lost sight of Slade, who had moved out into the darkness. Time drew to an excruciating halt as the noises of insects covered all other sounds. Who was left? El Tigre? Thomas? Cat shivered. The guaqueros would be excellent trackers and hunters, having been raised in these jungles.

And then Cat's hunting instincts came back to her. She remembered her father teaching her and Rafe how to hunt and stalk food. Cat grew very still, breathed shallowly and listened carefully. There! She detected a faint, perceptible change in the number of insects singing. Cat gripped the tree trunk. Was it because Slade was still moving around, or was it a guaquero? In the minutes that followed, Cat had no doubt someone was coming in her direction.

Her heart beginning to pound in dread, Cat pressed one hand against her breast, wondering if everyone else could hear it pumping as loudly as she could. Could a heartbeat give her away? A soft crunching sound to her right made her jump. She froze, her nostrils flaring. A sour smell reached her. El Tigre! She'd recognize the odor anywhere. Oh, no! His shape melted out of the surrounding foliage, no more than ten feet from where she crouched. Where was Slade? Was he even aware of El Tigre's presence? The guaquero turned, the automatic weapon ready to fire in his hands, walking toward Cat.

A scream welled up from deep within her. Cat felt a trickle of sweat run down her temples. Her fingers dug convulsively into the tree trunk and she leaned down, face and body pressed against the rough bark, willing herself to become part of the tree. He was only five feet away. Did he see her? If he caught her, he would show no mercy. Cat's eyes grew huge as he took another careful step in her direction, the ugly muzzle of his military weapon pointed right at her.

Suddenly, the night exploded around her as Slade's dark shape lunged from the left. Both men fell heavily, grunting and groaning. Cat leaped to her feet the instant El Tigre's weapon flew out of his hands, and she scrambled for the weapon as the men wrestled on the jungle floor. The sickening sound of bone breaking beneath the power of a fist tore into her shock. Cat lurched to her feet, screaming at them. She shoved the muzzle of the gun down into El Tigre's heaving chest and Slade got off him.

"Don't move," she warned the guaquero harshly. "Slade?"

"I'm all right," he rasped, coming to her side. "Get up!" he ordered El Tigre.

The man glared at Cat, his eyes feral with hatred as he held his injured jaw. Cat slowly removed the muzzle from his chest and handed the gun to Slade. The roar of vehicles shattered the jungle. Cat looked toward the road.

"Alvin?" she asked.

"Yeah. Get up there and flag them down. I'll bring our friend here in tow."

Cat crashed through the thick barrier of leaves, vines and roots. She finally made it to the road as the first Jeep passed by her. Waving her arms, she managed to flag down the second one. It was loaded with armed guards from the Verde mine. Tony Alvarez was driving.

"Man, you're a sight for sore eyes!" he said, getting out. "Where's Slade?"

Cat gave him a weary smile. "Coming with El Tigre."

"You two gave that snake a run for his money, eh?"

"I guess we did. There's Slade."

The next hour became a blur for Cat. The guards were enthusiastic that El Tigre had been captured alive. Slade sat behind her on the way back to their camp, his hand resting protectively on her shoulder. Alvin was like a mother hen, insisting on scrubbing their cuts and bruises with soap and water plus a healthy dose of iodine. Tears had watered in Cat's eyes when he had plastered her injuries with the yellow tincture, and she wasn't sure if the tears came because of the pain or the fear of what might have happened if El Tigre had made good his escape with them.

Slade watched Cat out of the corner of his eye as she slowly began to undress in their tent. She sat wearily on her cot, her fingers trembling as she tried to unlace her boots.

"Here," he said, crouching down in front of her and removing her hands, "let me do that."

Cat straightened up. Her shirt was unbuttoned, revealing the lace and silk of her lingerie. "Thanks. I think I'm falling apart now that it's over."

"I know you are. Just sit and relax, the worst is over."

"Why aren't your hands shaking? Aren't you feeling torn up inside?"

Slade grimaced, gently removing the first boot and tackling the second. "This isn't the first time something like this has happened to me, Cat. Maybe I'm more used to violence than you are. It comes with the territory when you get into gem mining."

"I've never seen it this bad, Slade." Cat swallowed a lump in her throat. "You can taste the violence in the air." She shivered as he pulled the second boot off.

Slade slid his hands up her curved thighs and looked at her in the flickering light shed by the lantern. Her left cheek had a cut on it and was slightly puffy. He knew she had landed on her left side, and luckily her shoulder, upper arm and elbow had received the brunt of the punishment.

He tenderly framed her face and said, "The next few days are going to be hectic. I'm going to take El Tigre over to Muzo. From there, I'm sure the Colombian police will be more than happy to take him into custody."

A tremulous sigh broke from her lips. "But that doesn't promise an end to the violence, does it?"

Slade sadly shook his head. "No. As long as there's green fire, you've got men who will do anything to get it, legally or otherwise." He brushed away the first tear that rolled down her cheek. Cat was having a natural letdown after their narrow escape, and he leaned forward, molding his mouth lightly against her lips. He felt her tremble, her arms moving around his shoulders to draw him nearer.

"God," he groaned against her soft, yielding mouth, "you taste so good…"

"Hold me, Slade. Just hold me, please…"

In one motion, he got to his feet and joined her on the cot. Cat blindly found his arms as the first sob wrenched from her. Slade murmured her name brokenly, burying his head beside hers as she cried. He rocked her gently, whispering words of comfort.

"We're good for each other, sweetheart," he told her comfortingly. "Sometimes I'm weak and you're strong. Sometimes I'm strong and you're weak. Like tonight; you took one hell of a risk on that curve. You could have turned the wheels too sharply and that Jeep would have rolled over instead of sliding off the cliff. You knew what you were doing."

Cat sniffed, trying to wipe her nose. "It was pure luck, Slade," she said, hiccuping through her tears. "I'm not a racing-car driver." She looked up at him, taking the clean handkerchief he tucked into her hands. "I never even thought about the Jeep flipping over."

He grinned, running his fingers through her freshly washed hair. "What matters is the outcome, Cat. You made a perfect skid, giving both of us the time we needed to jump clear. In my eyes, you're the female equivalent of Parnelli Jones."

Cat laughed, but it came out as a hiccup instead. "I was scared to death, Slade. I-I didn't know if you'd caught on to what I was going to do. I didn't dare look at you…"

He held her lightly against him, allowing Cat to bury

her head beneath his chin. "Must have been mental telepathy. One look at the set of your jaw and I knew you weren't going to go down without a fight." Slade pressed a kiss to her clean-smelling hair. "More important, this has taught me a lesson, Cat."

She closed her eyes, reveling in Slade's protective arms around her. Now she felt secure and safe. "What?" His heartbeat was slow and strong beneath her ear, soothing away the remnants of her emotional storm.

"You remember out in the jungle, when you told me you loved me?"

Cat was afraid to nod her head, but she did. Automatically she rested her hand against Slade's chest, as if to steel herself against what he might say. "I didn't know if we'd live or die, Slade," she began in a hoarse tone. "I know you may not feel the same, but that doesn't matter to me anymore."

"How long have you loved me?"

Cat closed her eyes. "I don't know. You just kind of grow on a person, Slade."

"Like mold?"

She laughed, her hand slowly unclenching. "You make loving another person sound like a virus."

"Isn't it?" And then he chuckled, pressing a kiss to her hair.

"No."

Slade closed his eyes, relief washing through him. "What I feel for you, Cat, I've never felt with another woman."

She pulled away from him and sat up, looking deep into his eyes. "Think we've got the same virus?"

A grin tugged at his mouth. "I don't know. Maybe we ought to compare symptoms. What do you think?"

Cat couldn't help but match his widening smile. The warmth and tenderness in Slade's eyes made her feel cherished. "This is a hell of a way to find out we love one another."

With a shrug, Slade picked up her bruised right hand, cradling it in his own. "People like us have to be hit over the head with a sixteen-pound sledgehammer, sweetheart."

"You made me aware of how lonely I'd been, Slade. And despite our shaky beginning, I really enjoyed your company those two months I spent at your ranch. I liked talking to you."

"And I liked just looking at you." Slade grazed her cheek with his. "Do you realize how beautiful you are to me? Every day, I'd count the hours between breakfast and lunch until I could see you again. And then I'd count them between lunch and dinner."

"You didn't have to hole up in that office of yours, Slade."

"At the time, Alvin and I were coordinating all equipment details being moved from the U.S. to Colombia. I was getting men from his ranch and working with the State Department on visas and passports. It was a couple of busy months for me."

She gave him an accusing look. "If you weren't in your office, then you were in your hobby shop grinding those gems."

He held up both hands, laughing. "Guilty as charged. I wanted to spend more time with you, but I felt if I did, you'd interpret it as me wanting something from you. Your health came first, not the project I had wanted to discuss with you."

"Touché," Cat murmured, realizing Slade was right.

"Still," Slade murmured, cupping her chin to make her look up at him, "I fell in love with you anyway."

"Because of my looks?"

"Other things, too," he said patiently. "I like the way your mind works. I was as starved as you were for those times when we could sit and simply share time and space with one another, Cat." Slade leaned over, his mouth caressing her parted lips. "And more than anything, I like you, Cat Kincaid. You make no apology for being yourself."

Cat quivered. "A lot of men are threatened by me."

"That's their problem, sweetheart. If they can't deal with an intelligent woman, let them turn and tuck their tails between their legs and run."

Laughter bubbled up in her throat and Cat rested her head tiredly on his broad shoulder. "I love you, Slade Donovan. For better or worse."

"It's gotten worse lately, hasn't it?"

She nodded, exhaustion flooding her as Slade held her. "I thought my fear of the mine was my worst enemy. Now I know there's something worse—guaqueros."

"Things will settle down now, Cat," he promised her. Slade gently positioned her on the cot and he lay down beside her. Pulling the protective mosquito netting over them, he murmured, "Just keep Bogotá in mind. If we're lucky, we'll get there in less than a week."

"What's in Bogotá?" Cat asked, her voice slurred with exhaustion.

"A surprise for you. It's something I've been planning all along…"

Chapter 13

Cat stood out in the burning sun. It melted the knot of fear that insisted on staying inside her every time she had to step into the Verde. In her hand was the torque meter, ready to test rock bolts recently secured in the newest section of the mine. It was a crosscut sheering off to the left that would follow the vein. Yet something was nagging Cat and she tried to pinpoint the unsettling feeling. The sky was an unusual pale yellow, something she'd not seen before over the Colombian jungle. Then she smiled to herself: Colombia had taught her a lot of new things.

As she walked into the shadow of the busy mine, Cat centered on its positives. Slade had promised her a weekend in Bogotá more than a month ago. That hadn't materialized because he'd ended up having to take El Tigre to the capital and file charges against him. Slade had returned a week later, after they had finished dynamiting into the crosscut to follow the abrupt turn of the vein. They had dug almost three-quarters of a mile into Caballo when the vein suddenly plunged down and to the left. Up to that point, very little emerald-bearing calcite had been found. Verde was looking like a lost cause. The open pit, on the other hand, was rich with emeralds. The mine was not.

Cat nodded to a group of sweaty, dirty miners as they trudged out toward the entrance. It was noon, and time to eat. Her stomach growled, but she ignored the signal. Testing the rock-bolt tension was more important, and with the miners out of the way, she could do it more quickly. The darkness between the electric lights strung on each side of the adit always reminded her of the fear. At times claustrophobia nearly overwhelmed her, but she fought it. Her fingers tightened around the torque meter, and Cat moved her gaze up and down, automatically checking posts and stulls.

The crosscut came into view and she slowed. Standing at the Y, she was reminded of the mine in Maine that had nearly claimed her life. Lips compressed, she began to check each one of the newly placed rock bolts on the manging wall, concentrating on her job with one part of her mind, and thinking of Slade with another. He would be back today! He had been gone for three days, testifying once again in El Tigre's case in Bogotá. Cat smiled, remembering Slade's disgruntled comments that if he'd known about all the governmental red tape awaiting him, he'd have let the guaquero go. *Soon,* Cat promised herself, stretching up to place the torque meter on the next bolt, *soon we'll have that weekend together.*

Their relationship had subtly changed since the night they had admitted their love for one another, Cat thought.

They had grown closer, establishing a friendship so powerful that she was sometimes awed by what they had created. It was a good feeling, Cat admitted, hearing the telling click, and checking the meter to read it. Making a note on the pad she always carried with her, she moved on to the next bolt. How she ached with love for Slade. Stolen kisses and passion shared late at night, bone-weary with exhaustion, was their only consolation. Soon...

"Cat?" Slade's voice echoed off the light green walls of the shadowy Verde.

Cat gasped and spun around. He was back! Before she could leave the crosscut, she saw him appear far above her at its lip. Despite the shadows, she saw his mouth turn up in a devastating smile of welcome. Her heart wrenched powerfully in her breast and she set the torque meter down as he approached.

Taking off his hard hat, Slade lifted Cat into his arms, crushing her against him.

"Mmm, sweetheart, you not only smell good, you feel good," he growled.

Her laughter was silvery as she threw her arms around him. "Slade! You're back early."

He sought and found her ripe mouth, then allowed Cat to slide down across his body. "I missed you," he said thickly, claiming her.

Slade's breath was moist against her cheek and she returned his hunger with hers. "I need you," Cat whispered huskily, holding him tightly.

With a groan, Slade held her. "No more than I need you, my beautiful lady."

Alone in the silence of the shaft, Cat languished in his arms, smothered with his volcanic desire, wildly aware of his hardened body against her own. Just the salty taste of his skin and the odor that was uniquely his overwhelmed her senses until she was dizzy with need.

Shuddering with a primal urge, Slade gently eased Cat from him. His eyes were burning with undisguised hunger as he stared down at her. "We're going to take off for Bogotá tomorrow morning. How does that sound?"

With a cry of elation, Cat hugged him. "Wonderful! Then this court business with El Tigre is wrapped up?"

Slade grinned. "Finally. He's getting twenty-five years at hard labor."

"Good."

"How's the crosscut looking?" Slade wanted to know, reluctantly releasing her.

"No better than the rest of the vein, so far," Cat admitted, motioning him to follow her to its end.

Slade scratched his head, then settled the white hard hat back on as he listened to her explanation of the recent dynamiting. The Verde itself was a major disappointment. Millions of dollars had already been sunk into securing the mine. He watched as Cat ran her fingers over the vein, which disappeared into the seven-foot-wide limestone wall that signaled an end to the crosscut until they could do more blasting.

"I'm having the miners on the second shift come down here with picks and crowbars to try and find some calcite." She motioned to the pile of tools and the five safety lamps placed there earlier that day.

Slade ran his hand over the vein, shaking his head. "I just don't understand this, Cat. I did extra channel sampling over this area to determine its feasibility." He glanced at her, his brows knitted. "Those small emeralds I showed you from the pouch were from this vein.

It doesn't make sense that we haven't run into the calcite again."

"Listen," Cat explained reasonably, "you know gem mining isn't a very safe bet. Maybe your Texas luck held and you tapped into the only nest of calcite and emerald the vein carried when you made your channel sample. That's happened before."

He grimaced, his face glistening with sweat. "Ouch. Don't even say it."

"Well, if this crosscut doesn't yield something soon, I'm going to recommend shutting this portion of the mine down, Slade. You can't keep funneling money into a worthless operation. We both know that."

Slade stared at the limestone wall in front of them, his mouth twisted. "Yeah, I know it. Damn! I've just got a sixth sense about this vein. I know there's emeralds somewhere in this thing. I can almost taste it."

With a gentle smile, Cat reached over and touched his sun-darkened arm. "You've got green-fire fever, Slade. That's all."

"We're doing so well out in the pit. Matter of fact, what we're finding out there is keeping us from going into the red with the mine."

Cat gave him a sympathetic smile. "Count your blessings, Slade. At least the pit is yielding. One out of two isn't bad. You could have gone bust on both, you know."

He smiled and took Cat into his arms, kissing her long and tenderly. "You're my blessing, sweetheart," he told her thickly. "Green fire is one thing, but you're far more important to me—"

Slade's head snapped up, his arms tightening protectively around her. Cat felt the earth quiver once. A sound like a freight train started deep in the bowels of the earth, rolling toward them with frightening speed. Cat's eyes widened.

"Slade—"

"Son of a bitch!"

The earthquake struck with lightning fury. In seconds they were both knocked off their feet as the earth buckled and groaned. Cat struck her head on the footwall and was knocked semiconscious. Slade was hurled over her as the second wave of the quake shuddered through the mine. Rock began to fall from the manging wall as rock bolts snapped in half like guns being fired at close range. Dust spewed through the crosscut behind the avalanche of rock that fell to the footwall.

After the last of the tremors, Slade got to his knees, cursing and coughing violently. He reached out to find Cat, panic eating at him.

"Cat?"

"I-I'm okay," she said, and she struggled to her knees, wiping blood from her mouth. The dust was suffocating and Slade fumbled with the handkerchief she had around her neck.

"Lie down," he gasped.

Cat lay on the pebbled hardness of the footwall, the cotton handkerchief folded across her nostrils and mouth to act as a filter against the deadly dust. Slade joined her, his body against hers, to protect her from further injury. She hugged the wall, trying to stop hyperventilating. Trapped! They had been trapped by an unexpected earthquake! The grayish light on her hard hat was the only source of illumination in the chamber.

"I wonder how much rock fell?" Slade muttered, all the while listening for other sounds. It had been a sharp quake, and there were bound to be aftershocks.

"Not much, I hope. Are you okay?"

He heard the terror in Cat's voice, and kept his arm wrapped tightly around her. "Yeah. Hurt feelings more than anything else. You?"

"Bump on the head, nothing more."

"You've got a hard head."

"Yeah." She snorted. "Slade?"

"What?"

"How much rock do you think fell behind us?"

He tried to keep his voice cool and free of his own fear. "Probably not much. If we're lucky, most of those rock bolts held. Don't worry, Alvin will have us out of here pronto." He forced a laugh for her benefit. "He doesn't want to lose his chief geologist and the best mining engineer in the world."

"No, he'll come and dig us out because we appreciate his cowboy cooking so much," Cat rallied.

Slade chuckled. "Lady, I love the hell out of you."

Tears tracked through the dust on her face, but Cat didn't want Slade to know she was crying. When she spoke, the words came out staccato. "I love you too."

"We'll get out of this, Cat, I promise you." Slade slowly got into a kneeling position, keeping a hand on her shoulder. He located his hard hat, plugged the jack into the battery pack he carried around his waist and turned on the light. "Stay here by this post. We're bound to get aftershocks. I want to see just how far up the crosscut that cave-in occurred. Do you have a portable radio with you?"

Cat automatically patted her side. "Yes. I'll try and contact Alvin while you check out the wall." The gloomy darkness swallowed up Slade's tall figure. Cat licked her lips, realizing that this time there was no water to slake her thirst. She pulled the dusty radio out of its protective leather case at her side. Her heart sank as she switched it to the On position. The red light did not blink to indicate it was working properly. Then she remembered hitting the footwall first with her hip and then her head. The radio, when she held it directly up into the light from her hard hat, had a large crack running vertically through the tough plastic casing. Alvin wouldn't know if they were alive or dead...

She pushed trembling fingers through her dust-laden hair and returned the useless radio to its case. Cat rose to her feet. Oddly, she was calmer than she would have thought. As she turned to examine the damage to the end of the crosscut, a gasp tore from her.

"Slade! Slade, come here! Quick!"

He came on the run. "What?"

Cat grabbed him by the arm and dragged him over to the wall. "Look. My God, look at this, Slade." She pointed toward the vein.

Slade's breath jammed in his throat as he lifted his head and settled the light on the area she was pointing out. The quake had opened up the vein, exposing what appeared to be an endless green crystalline structure more than two feet long, which disappeared into the wall where blasting hadn't yet taken place.

"Green fire," he whispered hoarsely, reaching out and tentatively touching the nearest emerald crystals.

Cat's laugh echoed in the chamber. "There must be millions of dollars' worth in this one vein alone."

"Look at their color," Slade breathed. "Dark green and clear. Look at this!" He took off his helmet, casting the light directly on the emeralds that glittered fiercely back at them. "They're so clear, Cat. I've never seen anything like this…"

She shook her head in disbelief. It was as if the earth had opened up her most precious treasure chest and allowed them to see her finest gems. Reverently, Cat touched one of the crystals. "They're magnificent."

"You're right, they'll be worth millions," Slade confirmed, his voice hushed. "And I'll stake my life on the fact that the emeralds here are of better quality than those of any other mine in the world. I don't believe it… This is a miracle, a miracle…"

Nodding mutely, Cat agreed. Oh, she'd seen gems in calcite matrix before, but they'd been in single nests once every hundreds of thousands of tons of earth. She'd never seen a long, continuous vein like this. No, this was one of a kind, just like Slade, and his belief that something special—green fire—lived here in the earth.

As if shaking his head from a dream, Slade turned to her. "They're the color of your eyes," he said huskily. "Clear and beautiful and exotic."

Cat walked over and threw her arms around him. Words were useless compared to what she was feeling for Slade. "I'm happy for you, Slade. Your dream has come true. It's paid off."

He managed a soft laugh as he slowly released her. "Sweetheart, when I met you, my most important dream came true." He looked at the emerald vein. "I have you, and we have a mine that's going to yield the world's highest-quality emeralds ever seen by man."

Cat smiled grimly, looking toward the dust-laden crosscut. "Only if we get out of here, Slade. I don't want to be a wet blanket, but—"

"I know. Come on, pick up a crowbar. I'm getting a pickax."

She followed Slade to where the manging wall had fallen. The snapped rock bolts were scattered around like so many toothpicks, shattered by the force of the quake. Slade pointed up at the manging wall and shrugged out of his shirt.

"If you hadn't spaced those rock bolts so closely together, even more would have come down, burying us."

Cat shuddered. "We're not out of this yet, Slade."

"Wet blanket," he teased, handing her his shirt and hard hat. In the semigloom his massive chest and shoulders gleamed with sweat as he hefted the ax in his large hands. "What I want you to do is focus both hard-hat lights here. I'm going to start digging. We can't wait for Alvin to start because we've only got so much oxygen left."

Cat nodded, standing out of the way. "Slade, I can take a crowbar and—"

"Not yet. Let me work at this wall, then I'll let you clear away the gangue and I'll go back to work."

Biting her lower lip, Cat nodded. No holes were visible through the rubble blocking their escape and Cat didn't know how thick the wall was. If too much had fallen down, they could suffocate before getting rescued. As Slade began to swing the head of the pickax into the limestone, she prayed that the rock bolts had prevented a massive cave-in. Each rhythmic swing of the ax echoed throughout the chamber. The limestone crushed easily, powdering beneath Slade's swings. His body looked like burnished metal beneath the light. Sweat ran off the bunched muscles of his back and shoulders, and his dark hair clung to his head as he heaved the pick savagely into the wall over and over again.

How long Slade worked, Cat did not know. Minutes grew into hours, and his facial expression never altered. His jaw was set, lips pulled away from his clenched teeth, eyes narrowed as he glared at the wall that prevented their escape. Cat saw his rugged jeans darken with sweat and cling to his long, firm thighs as he began to make progress into the wall. The limestone was no match for steel and brawn. Each precise swing exploded into the wall, loosening a little more debris, moving them inches closer to freedom. Finally, Slade stopped. He wiped his wet brow with the back of his arm. Dust caked his massive chest, his hair and face.

Cat gave him the shirt so he could wipe his face. She set the lights down, and went to work with the crowbar to clear the gangue out of the way. Slade's incredible strength gave her strength. She knew she could not match his physical power, but she doggedly labored at clearing a space for him to work in. Her shirt clung damply to her body as she lifted some of the larger rocks, throwing them behind her. Sweat stung her eyes and she shook her head to clear them. After half an hour, most of the debris had been moved aside so that Slade could take over.

"You did a good job," he told her, coming up and sliding his arm around her shoulders.

Cat leaned against him and slid her hand across his chest, feeling the mat of wiry hair beneath her fingertips. "Aren't you tired?"

"Not when I consider the alternative," he told her, wrapping his long, callused fingers around the wooden handle of the pick. Leaning over, Slade kissed her cheek, then sought her lips. A satisfied growl rumbled from him as he kissed her quickly and hard. Reluctantly he released her and went back to work.

Glumly, Cat thought about what he'd implied: the air was growing more sparse as time went on. Each breath lessened the oxygen content. Each breath brought them closer to death's embrace. She shifted her attention back to Slade, who had resumed his rhythmic attack against the wall. If possible, he seemed to be exerting even more energy and concentrated power against their foe, death. Huge chunks of limestone flew around him, and sparks flashed as steel bit into rock. The chamber echoed with the tortured crack of rock pulverized beneath his Herculean strength. With each swing of the pick, Cat held her breath. How long could Slade sustain his backbreaking pace? His muscles bunched and released, bunched and released. Looking at his set features, Cat knew she needn't give up hope. Ever.

Five hours had passed and they sat huddled together in the pitch blackness. They had to save the battery-powered light for Slade to work by. The safety lamps required oxygen to remain lit and Slade didn't want their precious supply to be eaten up. The electrical lamps on their hard hats would have to suffice. Cat wiped Slade's shoulders and back with the wet shirt. She splayed her hands on his flesh, feeling an almost imperceptible tremor beneath her palm. He was close to exhaustion. Any other man would have quit hours before, physically unable to go on as long as he had.

"Let me massage you," she whispered, positioning herself behind him. "You're going to get cramps if I don't."

Slade nodded wearily and rested his brow on his arms, which hugged his drawn-up knees. "Thanks," he murmured hoarsely. God, what he'd do for a glass of water right now. He said nothing, realizing Cat had to be as close to dehydration as he was. Her clothes were wet and clung to her like a second skin. He groaned as her fingers worked over his weary, protesting back muscles, helping them relax from the brutal workout he had given them. For almost fifteen minutes, Cat worked out the kinks and knots.

"Thanks, sweetheart," he muttered, patting her thigh.

Cat laid her head on his back momentarily, shutting her eyes. "I love you, Slade. You're incredible."

He snorted softly, rubbing his hand up and down the length of her thigh. "I love you, too. But incredible? Hardly."

"Your strength is unbelievable."

"It's called fear of dying. That's what keeps me going right now."

Cat wrapped her arms around him, feeling the ragged pound of his heart beneath her palms. "You must have moved a ton of gangue from that wall. That's a lot."

Slade knew what she had left unspoken: it was looking more and more as if a huge section of the manging wall had fallen. They were going to be trapped for a long time. Maybe longer than they had oxygen to last them. He wiped the accumulated sweat off his face.

"Come around here. Sit between my legs."

Cat moved carefully in the darkness. She nestled between his thighs, one arm around his waist, and her head resting against his hard, flat stomach. "At least you're with me this time," she uttered tiredly. "Sharing a mine cave-in takes away some of the fear."

Slade curved his palm against her cheek, savoring her warmth and softness. "Not as scared as before?"

"No." Cat managed a choked laugh. "Maybe I'm getting used to them, Slade. I don't feel that overwhelming fear."

He glanced around, unable to see anything. "Yeah, this is my fourth one. They get to be pretty routine after a while. Only one thing occupies your mind, and that's how much oxygen you have left."

Cat pressed a kiss to his slick flesh. "That and water. What I'd do for some water for both of us."

"I'd trade that vein of emeralds for a glass for both of us right now."

She laughed with him. "Amazing how some events in life can put everything into very sharp focus, isn't it, Slade?"

"Yes." Silence settled over them. "Cat?"

She closed her eyes, her arm tightening around his waist, hearing an unexpected tremor in his deep voice. "What is it?" Was he going to tell her that they didn't stand a chance? That most likely, they would die in here together? A fierce love for Slade welled up through Cat like a fist, taking her breath away as she prepared herself to hear those words.

"Marry me."

"What?"

"I know it's a little soon and we haven't talked about it before this, but I want you to marry me." Slade's hand came to rest on her hair. "I can't imagine life without you, lady." There was a long silence and then he felt the wetness of her tears beneath his fingertips. He leaned over, holding her tightly, anguish soaring through him. His voice cracked as he brought her up against him.

"Damn it, I know life isn't fair, but when I've finally found you, it could be too late."

Cat stubbornly shook her head, burying her face next to his and trying to stop her tears. "No, it's never too late—never!"

"I love you, Cat."

"I'll marry you, Slade…"

"You will?"

She managed a half sob and half laugh. "Of course I will!" Cat traced trembling fingers through his sweat-soaked hair, kissing his brow, eyes and finally his mouth.

Savoring her flurry of kisses, Slade held her even closer to him. "It'll be a hell of a marriage."

Cat groaned. "Tell me about it!"

"I'll have your Kincaid stubbornness to contend with."

"You're not exactly a willow in the wind, Slade Donovan," she pointed out archly.

He chuckled, the rumble moving up through his chest. "But we both have a good sense of humor. We know how to take a joke."

"Only because I'm the straight person and you're the comic of our team."

Slade nuzzled his face between her breasts, absorbing her scent. "I need you, Cat," he whispered thickly. "Now, forever. Living with you those months made me realize just how much I liked having you underfoot."

A smile touched her tear-wet lips and Cat closed her eyes, realizing the futility of their situation. "What made you suddenly ask to marry me, Slade?"

He caressed her waist, then settled his hand on her hip. "Sweetheart—" he paused and swallowed "—if I can't break through that wall, I wanted you to know just how damn much you mean to me."

How long they held one another, Cat didn't know. It no longer mattered. The chamber was stiflingly hot and stuffy; the ripe smell of their sweat assailed her nostrils along with the chalky limestone dust that still hung in the air and caked their mouths. Just as Slade took up the pickax and walked to the wall, she heard a distinct drilling noise from the other side.

"Slade!"

He turned, relief etched on his exhausted features. "I hear it..."

Cat clutched the hard hat, the light trained on the wall. "Alvin...he's coming through. That's an auger bit!"

A grin creased Slade's face as he stepped back and joined Cat against the far wall. He slid his arm around her shoulders and pulled her to him. Leaning down, he kissed her hard and long. Releasing her, he murmured, "Well, gal, it looks like you have to make good on that promise to marry me now."

She laughed, sinking against Slade, dizzy from joy that they were going to be rescued. "You mean asking me to marry you wasn't a sham, Slade Donovan? Some last-minute admission before you said hello to your maker?"

His grin widened against his stained face. "Come to Bogotá with me and find out," he challenged.

When they entered the Bogotá Hilton together, nearly every patron sitting in the lobby turned and gawked at them. Slade grinned at Cat as they came to a halt at the desk.

"I think we're a sight for sore eyes."

Cat grimaced, looking down at her disheveled appearance. "I think we're a sight, Slade." Although they'd washed and changed after they'd been rescued, they had come straight to Bogotá afterward, leaving the clean-up and newly discovered emeralds in Alvin's capable hands.

Slade's eyes sparkled as he took the registration card and signed them in. "We'll buy any clothes we need," Slade said, pulling out his wallet. He gave the clerk his credit card. Within minutes, Slade had the key to their room. "Come on, Cat. You and I are going to take a very long, hot shower. Together..."

From the balcony of their air-conditioned room, a flaming orange sunset bid them good-evening. Cat had groggily awakened from a much-needed sleep and gotten up, wrapping the thick white hotel robe around her. She looked over her shoulder; Slade was still sleeping soundly. A tender smile pulled at her lips as she sat down in the ivory satin settee facing the king-size bed where he lay.

Tucking her legs beneath her, Cat was content to simply watch Slade. She smiled softly. Once they had gotten beneath the hot, pummeling streams of water, their hunger for one another had been tempered. Pure exhaustion combined with the relaxing massage of the water had made them both too drowsy to think of anything else but sleep.

They had curled up in bed on the white cotton sheets, their bodies hot and moist against its cool, crisp texture. Nothing had ever felt so good, and Cat vaguely remembered curving into Slade's waiting arms and promptly falling asleep. Now she looked at her watch; it was almost nine o'clock. They'd slept a long time. Her stomach growled, reminding Cat that she hadn't eaten all day. Quietly, she rose and went to the phone to order dinner.

Slade awoke to the mouth-watering smell of beefsteak. He groaned and rolled onto his back, the sheet covering him from the waist down in twisted disarray.

"Slade?" Cat walked to the bed and smiled down at him, thinking how boyish he looked. She sat on the edge of the mattress, one arm across him, watching him awake. "Come on, time to rise and shine."

Groaning, Slade dragged an arm across his eyes. "What time is it?" he asked thickly.

Cat leaned down and kissed his petulant mouth. "Ten o'clock. Time to get up and eat."

Slade slid his hand up her long, robed thigh. "You have great legs. Did I ever tell you that?"

"I thought all such admissions were given in the cross-cut."

A grin tugged at his mouth and Slade moved his arm and opened his eyes. Cat's hair was long, nearly touching her shoulders, and was shot through with gold from the light above. She looked like a ragamuffin in the oversize robe. "Spunky gal, aren't you?" he challenged, sitting up and leaning against the headboard. The sheet pulled away, leaving him nearly naked, but he didn't care. All of his attention was centered on Cat's shining green eyes. Her smile made him go hard and hot inside.

"You wouldn't want me any other way." Cat patted his flat, hard stomach. "Come on, I ordered us a Texas-size meal. I'm starved."

Slade glanced past her at the sumptuous meal over-flowing from the cart behind them. "What? No spotted horse thief? Where's my stewed kidneys? My johnny-cake?"

Giving him a playful pat on the hip, Cat rose, laughing. "If you're expecting Alvin's cooking, forget it." She went to the cart and drew up two chairs.

Slade got up and padded to the bathroom to retrieve his robe. He had an odd look on his face as he came back out with it. "Let's trade robes, Cat. You've got mine and I'm sure as hell not going to be able to fit into this one."

Nonplussed, her silverware poised above her thick, medium-rare steak, Cat grimaced. "Oh...sorry. I thought they were all the same size." She got up and came around the table, struggling out of the robe, revealing her nakedness.

"I lied." Slade grabbed her and carried her to the bed.

Cat laughed, throwing her arms around Slade as he settled down beside her. "You're such a joker, Slade Donovan."

Slade's smile grew wide as he leaned over and kissed her laughter-touched lips. "But you love me anyway?" he coaxed thickly, tasting her sweetness.

With a tremulous sigh, Cat slid her fingers across his shoulders. "Yes...yes, I love you anyway."

"Enough to marry me tomorrow morning?" He trailed a path of nibbling, moist kisses from her earlobe down the length of her neck, feeling her pulse flutter wildly at the base of her throat. Her fingers were wreaking havoc on him, too, as she followed the curve of his chest, brushing his nipples.

Closing her eyes, she arched against Slade as his mouth found the valley between her breasts. "Y-yes."

Slade continued his gentle assault. "God, you smell and taste good. Are you sure? You sound a little doubtful."

An exquisite ache was building in her and Cat moaned, her mind fleeing as his knowing fingers gently parted her thighs. "Slade...." His name came out like a breathless prayer. "Love me, just love me. Now. I need you so much..."

With a smile, Slade brought a hardened nipple into his mouth and sucked gently, feeling Cat press against him.

A cry of pleasure tore from her as Slade moved one hand down across her belly, finding the rich carpet below to coax the smoldering fire to life within her. She sagged against him, jolts of such magnitude rushing through her that she was helpless in his arms. The ache intensified and Cat moved against his palm.

"Yes," Slade said in a rough whisper near her ear, "show me how much you need me. Show me, my lovely lady…"

The shattering gift of fulfillment rippled through her, and afterward, Cat lay in Slade's arms, unable to move as wave after wave of melted heat flowed through her. Her lips curved into a smile and she barely opened her eyes. The immense satisfaction on Slade's face reflected how she felt and Cat weakly lifted her arms, pulling him on top of her. "Let me give to you as much as you've given to me," she whispered huskily.

Slade's smile was pure male as he slid his hand beneath her hips and watched her eyes close as he slowly moved into the depths of her warm, rich body. His fingers froze against her hips as her fire touched him and drew him more deeply into her. His breath was torn from him, followed by a groan born deep and low in his chest. Sunlight, she was sunlight on the cool water's surface, he thought raggedly. Then reality became a blur as Slade fell beneath Cat's magical spell. Never had another woman loved him so thoroughly or with such consuming passion. Like the handfuls of warm soil he had held so often in his hand, she reminded him that she was of the earth: warm, fertile and all-encompassing. With a groan, Slade gripped

her in release. Sunlight and earth once more touched as
he reemerged in the magic that was Cat.

Spent, he lay against her damp breast, aware of the
uneven beat of her heart. Sweat trickled down his jaw,
but Slade didn't care. Gently, he ran his hand up her
torso, and cupped her breast. Cat's fingers moved slowly
through his hair, and he closed his eyes in contentment.
Words were useless for what he felt toward Cat. Instead,
he held her for a long time, caressing her and letting her
know just how much he loved her.

Finally, Slade rose. On his return, Cat smiled and
curled up again in his arms. He moved his fingers along
the satin curve of her back.

"Every time we love, it's better," he told her.

"Every time is like the first time," Cat whispered,
kissing his stubbled jaw. "You make me feel like the
earth touched by rain and sunlight: a rainbow of colors
and sensations."

"You're the earth, sweetheart. Giving and holding the
warmth within you and giving it back when I need it."

"I never thought this kind of love or contentment was
possible, darling."

"Neither did I."

Slade settled one hand behind his head and stared
up at the gray ceiling. "Matt once told me he didn't believe in dreams ever coming true. Kai changed his mind,
of course. But in a lot of ways, I was like him. I never
thought the woman of my dreams would ever become
a reality."

"But you dreamed, Slade. And that was important."

He grinned. "But both of us doubted our dream would
come true." He sat up and leaned against the headboard,
bringing Cat into his arms. "And we were wrong."

"Men," Cat muttered darkly. "Can't live with 'em…"

"Now, now, be kind and patient to us Neanderthal types. We might be a bit slow, but once we're taught, we come around."

Cat sat up facing Slade. He looked so young. There was a rebellious lock of hair on his brow, as usual, and his cobalt eyes were bright and warm with amusement. "Neanderthal," she chortled. "You're hardly that. A smooth operator would be closer to the truth."

Slade raised his hand against his heart, trying his best to look wounded. "I'm Texan. That says it all."

She gave him a dirty look. "That's barely scratching the surface. Coming out of the bathroom and saying the robe was too small was a rotten trick, Slade Donovan, and you know it!"

A grin edged his mouth. "That was the easiest way I could think of to get you out of that robe and into my arms."

"Did you ever stop to think that asking might have gotten the same result?"

He quelled a smile and shrugged. "I didn't think you'd leave that steak for anything."

"Well, you were probably right. I was hungry."

Slade gave her an impish smile, obviously pleased with the success of his escapade. Cat got off the bed and pulled on a robe. As she handed him the other one, she noted the one-size-fits-all tag on the inside. With a shake of her head, she moved the table. Slade grabbed her hand and pulled her back into bed with him.

"Come here," he growled, wrestling with her until she was effectively trapped beneath him. "I'm not done with you, my proud lady."

Cat laughed, hotly aware of his naked body against

her. "Now what have you got cooked up? I see that look
in your eyes."

Slade rolled off her and kept a restraining hand on her
while he reached in the drawer of the bed stand. "See?
There you go again accusing me of being up to something."

Cat waited expectantly as he settled a folded piece
of tissue paper the size of a quarter on her robed breast.
"You've got that gleam in your eye again, Slade. What
do you expect me to think? What's this?"

"Open it and find out. Careful…it might bite you."

Meeting Slade's smile, Cat slowly unwrapped the
white tissue paper. It crinkled between her fingers. She
glanced up at Slade's expectant features. "You're such a
rogue, Slade Donovan."

"And you love me for it."

"Yes, I do." Cat pushed aside the outer wrapping.
There was a second layer of paper. "What did you do?
Spend hours wrapping this?"

"You'll see why," Slade said, his hand resting on her
hip.

Cat's eyes widened as she pulled the last of the paper
away. There, nestled in the center, was a thick gold ring
set with a long, rectangular emerald. She gasped and
struggled to sit up. Slade removed his hand so that she
could.

"Slade…"

He leaned over her, resting his chin on her shoulder.
"Like it?"

Cat ran her fingers lightly over the emerald. "Like it?
My God, it's huge and beautiful and priceless! Look at
the clarity!" She held it up for him to see.

"Of course it's clear. It's from our mine. The first

Verde emerald we discovered." Slade glanced at her, tenderness in his blue gaze. "And it's priceless, like you are to me, Cat."

With a cry, Cat turned, throwing her arms around Slade. "You wonderful romantic. I love you so much!"

Slade held her tightly. "You and I, sweetheart, are going to have one hell of a happy life together. You know that, don't you?"

Cat smiled, kissed his cheek, then eased away from him. Tears made her eyes luminous as she met and held Slade's sober expression. She held the ring between them. "You and I will live life as never before," she promised. "Because now, we've added love to our existence. I'm looking forward to each new day with you, Slade."

His heart wrenched and he cradled Cat's face gently between his palms. "Green fire can't compare to how you've set my soul on fire, my love. You've captured my heart. Forever."

* * * * *

USA TODAY bestselling author **Barb Han** lives in north Texas with her very own hero-worthy husband, three beautiful children, a spunky golden retriever/standard poodle mix and too many books in her to-read pile. In her downtime, she plays video games and spends much of her time on or around a basketball court. She loves interacting with readers and is grateful for their support. You can reach her at barbhan.com.

Visit the Author Profile page
at Harlequin.com for more titles.

TEXAS ABDUCTION

Barb Han

All my love to Brandon, Jacob and Tori,
the three great loves of my life.

To Babe, my hero, for being my best friend,
greatest love and my place to call home.

I love you all with everything that I am.

Chapter 1

When you reach the end of your rope, tie a knot in it and hang on.

Cheyenne O'Connor couldn't count the number of times her mother had repeated the line from a past president, but the one that had stuck in her memory happened moments before her mother closed her eyes for the last time. This morning, as Cheyenne pulled the covers over her head, not yet ready to face another day, guilt racked her for letting her mother down. She needed to figure out a way to get out of bed despite the feeling of heavy weights on her ankles that made moving her legs seem impossible. Not even the promise of caffeine or the shining beams of sunlight streaming through the mini blind slats could break those shackles. Or the fact that her friend was probably home from working the night-shift at the hospital with a ready smile and the promise of a fresh brew. Ally Clark had been a lifeline.

Cheyenne glanced down at her stomach and the bump that was no longer there. Big mistake as emotions brimmed and a devastating sense of loss filled her. Crying wouldn't change a thing and yet she prayed for the sweet release it could give.

It was strange someone she'd never actually met could cause this much pain when she was gone. Except that Cheyenne had known her baby. She'd felt movement right up until the day of her delivery—a delivery that she'd been told had gone horribly wrong.

All she had left now was a drug-induced blur where there should be memories, and empty arms where there should be a bundle of joy.

Shouldn't she feel something if the life force that had been growing inside her was suddenly snuffed out? Shouldn't she *know* her little girl was gone? Shouldn't she somehow sense it? She'd never put too much stock in a mother's intuition until now, when she'd become one. *Almost*, a little voice in the back of her mind reminded.

"Take care of my little girl," she said under her breath as she fingered the ladybug bracelet on her left wrist, a final gift from her mother.

Cheyenne reached for a pillow and hugged it to her chest, trying to find a way to fill the void. Her body ached to hold the little girl she'd imagined meeting so many times over the past eight months. What would she look like? What color would her eyes be? Would she inherit Cheyenne's blue eyes or Riggs's mocha brown? Bar none, Riggs O'Connor had the best eyes. She could stare into them all day. She'd wanted her daughter to get those from him. Mocha brown eyes with Cheyenne's blond locks. Now, that would be a combination.

Keep lying here thinking about it and you'll run out of rope.

Cheyenne forced herself to sit up. She glanced over at the two-carat princess-cut diamond ring next to her cell phone. Habit had her reaching for it first thing. She stopped herself midgrab, diverting to her cell instead. She'd shut down her phone before bed last night, too lazy to get the charger from the next room.

Staring at the screen while her eyes tried to focus, she hit the power button. A few seconds later, the screen came to life. The first thing she noticed was a text from Ally.

On my way. b ready. I have news. There was a firework icon beside the last word. Ally always did that when she thought something would blow Cheyenne's mind. Using it in this context left Cheyenne with an unsettled feeling in the pit of her stomach.

When did Ally send the message?

An hour ago.

Strange. Cheyenne hadn't heard her best friend come in and Ozzy would have barked until the cows came home. The little yapper went off at just about anything that moved, and she herself woke at every noise. Two weeks had already passed. She still wasn't used to living here.

Cheyenne figured it best to get up, splash some water on her face and track her friend down to find out what Ally was talking about.

After freshening up—and avoiding the mirror as best she could—Cheyenne walked into the hallway. She stood in front of a closed bedroom door. Ally had a habit of closing her door when she left for work but normally left it open when she was home, even when she was sleeping.

Cheyenne knocked and leaned in so she could hear as Ozzy came gunning down the hall full force, his tiny legs working double time. He barked his greeting and maybe disapproval that Cheyenne was standing at the door of his fur mom's room.

There was no response on the other side of the door. Since the message indicated urgency, she cracked the door open and called out. Again, there was no response.

Ozzy was at her ankles, losing his mind from barking.

"Okay, little guy. Calm down." She was a dog lover, but he didn't exactly fit the bill. He was more purse accessory than anything else. And yes, he was adorable with the little blue bow on his head, but he was also the most annoying creature she'd ever come across.

Her head raged at the spot right between her eyes—eyes that were so dry they were the equivalent of west Texas dirt.

"Shhhh." She bent down to pick him up. The hospital was less than half an hour's drive from here. Twenty minutes at this time of day. Shouldn't Ally be home by now?

A quick tour of the two-bedroom bungalow revealed Ally was nowhere to be found in the house. Her car wasn't outside on the parking pad, either. Had she taken a detour on the way home? Gotten distracted? How important could her message be if she didn't race home?

Cheyenne's mind snapped to a darker possibility. She gasped.

What if Ally *was* speeding home and got in a wreck? Terrible things kept happening to the people she loved. Why should this time be any different?

She retrieved her cell phone and responded to the text. Ally always had her phone tucked inside her pocket. She would either answer in a few seconds or a few minutes, depending on whether or not she was delayed by a patient. But she always answered and a glance at the clock said her nursing shift was already over.

When five minutes ticked by with nada, Cheyenne's heart raced and her concern level shot through the roof.

Could this year get any worse?

Riggs O'Connor gripped the steering wheel of his pickup a little tighter as he navigated through traffic, thinking of everything that had befallen. He'd lost his wife a couple of weeks ago after losing their daughter during childbirth. Since the events happened within hours of each other and were 100 percent related, he lumped them in the same category—utter devastation.

Before that, his father had been murdered on the very cattle ranch he'd built as a family legacy. His father received a medical diagnosis that meant his days were numbered. Because of this eventual death sentence, he'd decided to reopen an investigation into his daughter's kidnapping, and was killed in the process. Digging into the case, Riggs and his brothers realized their father had opened a deadly can of worms by renewing a thirty-year-old search to find out what happened to his daughter. Caroline had been the only O'Connor girl born into a family of seven kids.

Although four of Riggs's brothers worked in law enforcement, leads on finding their father's killer had been drying up until his brother Garrett uncovered a link to an alpaca farm that was a front for an illegal adoption ring that had since been raided. Progress on the investigation was still slow.

Life didn't discriminate when it delivered a bad hand. Even good folks were thrown unfortunate circumstances and sometimes the biggest jerks got off scot-free. Riggs wasn't much for self-pity. Anger—now, there was an emotion he could relate to. But this general lack of enthusiasm for doing something as routine as getting out of bed in the morning was foreign.

"Long on questions, short on answers" pretty much described his entire existence. A few nagging questions wouldn't quit, though. Why had an otherwise healthy baby been born "sleeping" as they'd called it? Why had Cheyenne pushed him away after suffering the devastating loss? He couldn't think of a time when they'd needed each other more. Cheyenne's best friend, Ally Clark, had been working in the hospital that night in the ER. He'd assumed Cheyenne moved in with Ally after telling him *he* would be better off without her in the long run. Did Cheyenne really believe that? He'd been informed of her plans to divorce him via a text message. *A text message.*

She'd returned none of his calls. And then, out of the blue, Ally had reached out to him an hour ago. She'd asked him to stop by, saying something about important news that she needed him to hear directly from her. She also asked him not to tell anyone she'd contacted him. He was still scratching his head over that part. Then again, much of his life was one big question mark lately.

He parked on the pad in front of the two-bedroom bungalow, debating whether or not this was still a good idea. The sedan that belonged to his wife—soon to be ex-wife, once she filed the papers in court—was parked around the side of the home, confirming his suspicion that Cheyenne was with Ally. It was only a matter of time before he heard from her lawyer. If she wasn't grieving so hard, and he didn't doubt for one second that she was, he probably would have already. It frustrated him to no end that he couldn't speak to her one-on-one. Not that there was anything he could do to help her, especially while he was burning up with anger for being shut out in the first place.

The soft spot he had—the one that had him wishing there was something he could do to ease her pain—was another question mark. He shouldn't care what happened to her now that she'd turned her back on their marriage. He didn't even know if he could help her other than to accept the fact she didn't want to be married to him anymore.

And yet, part of him believed there was a solid reason she never returned his texts. To his thinking, she knew that if she faced him, she couldn't hold the line, which gave him hope she didn't want to dissolve the marriage in her heart of hearts. Was it ego talking? An ego that couldn't accept a hardline rejection from someone he loved? Maybe.

There wasn't much he could do if she wouldn't speak to him. It took two people to make a marriage. His parents had been successful at it, and he'd hoped for the same in his union to Cheyenne, despite the rushed circumstances. Rushed to marriage and now he'd be rushed to divorce, he thought wryly.

Ally's car wasn't outside, so he sat in his truck with the engine running. Curiosity was getting the best of him and he wanted to know why she'd asked him to come. Cheyenne wouldn't be happy to see him. He issued a sharp sigh as he glanced over at the door. His gaze skimmed the car seat in his truck he didn't have the heart to remove and the baby blanket draped over that his mother had knitted.

He owed it to his little girl to find out what happened

at the hospital two weeks ago. Administration was still conducting an internal investigation into the ordeal and why there was no body to bury. Mistakes happened, they'd said, promising to get to the bottom of it.

Biting back a string of curses, he cut off the engine and then exited the pickup. A moment of hesitation made him pause as he stood on the porch. And then the anger that had been burning him up inside raged. He flexed and released his fingers a couple of times to work off some of the tension.

He took a step forward and fired off three rapid knocks. Ozzy went nuts, barking up a storm on the other side of the door. For a little dog, he had big lungs. He also disappeared a little too fast, which meant someone was home. His guess was Cheyenne.

Did Ally set them up to try to get them in the same room together so they could talk? Nah. She wouldn't surprise her best friend like that. The two were close enough for Ally to know Cheyenne wouldn't want to be ambushed.

No matter how much he wanted to speak to her, there was no amount of talking that could change a mind that was already made up. Frustration caused his hands to fist. Frustration from being so angry at her that he wanted to shout from the top of his lungs. Frustration from feeling sorry for her because he knew, without a shadow of a doubt, she'd been looking forward to the baby as much as he was, if not more. Frustration from the overwhelming feeling that he was letting her down in some way by not figuring out how to get her to talk to him.

No one came to the door.

Wasn't she a little bit curious as to who was outside? At least one of his questions was answered quickly when the curtain moved. His chest squeezed. His heart turned out to be a traitor because it beat a little faster at the thought of her being so close.

The door, however, didn't budge.

Riggs knocked again to no avail. He didn't drive all the way out here only to turn around without knowing what was so important Ally had him cut out of work in the middle of the workday and make the drive over. It was eight o'clock in the morning and he'd already been up and at it since four.

He reached up to knock again, figuring he'd give it one more shot before giving her a call, when the door cracked opened.

"Riggs," she said. Her eyebrows drew together and stress lines formed on her forehead. She was clearly caught off guard by his presence. "What are you doing here?"

All the anger that had been building inside him for the past two weeks took a back seat the minute he saw the depth of pain in her pale blue eyes. All the arguments died on his tongue as to why she should tell him exactly what happened that night. All his frustration over the way she'd told him about her plans to divorce him fizzled out feebly.

Standing in the doorway was a beautiful woman who was doing her level best to keep it together and be strong.

"I got a text from Ally," he said by way of defense. His tone was stiffer than he'd intended.

She stood there, mouth open, shock stamped on her features.

Chapter 2

"Ally hasn't come home from work yet. And now I'm seriously worried about her." Cheyenne frowned despite how fast her pulse raced at seeing Riggs standing not five feet in front of her. It wasn't like her best friend to pull a stunt like this. Ally would never ask Riggs to come over without running the idea past Cheyenne first.

Seeing him standing there, all six feet three inches of male glory, sent Cheyenne's pulse racing. Sweaty palms. Butterflies in stomach. The feeling like she'd just dived off the face of a mountain with nothing more than a bungee cord around her ankles engulfed her. He was excitement and sexual chemistry times a hundred. All of which explained how fast she'd fallen for him and how far down the rabbit hole she'd gone once she did.

As much as she wanted to blame stress for her body's reaction to him, she couldn't. Riggs had always had that effect on her.

Ozzy was going crazy at her heels, barking rapid-fire, and that wasn't helping her headache one bit.

"Cheyenne," he said in the low timbre that had a way of reverberating through her and disarming her defenses. "What is all this about?"

Since that was a loaded question, Cheyenne decided to take a step back without answering. She cracked the door open a little bit more. "You can come in and wait for her."

Without waiting for a response, she opened the door a little more before turning around and walking away. Seeing him again was doing a number on her senses.

Besides, her coffee was getting cold in the kitchen and she figured half the reason for her headache was a complete lack of caffeine. She brought her hands up to her temples and tried to massage some of the tension out.

No sound came from behind her except for Ozzy. No way would Riggs be afraid of that little yapper.

Cheyenne turned around, despite wondering why she hadn't heard the screen door open yet. In the sliver, Riggs stood there like he was debating whether or not he should come inside. His cell phone was out and he was staring at the screen like his life depended on him memorizing the contents.

Her heart surged. It would be so easy to get caught up in the man standing on the other side of the screen. It had been so easy to forget how cursed her life was before she met him. Too easy? The whole fling had felt like the fairy-tale version of life. Girl meets down-to-earth and ridiculously gorgeous and almost obscenely wealthy rancher. Falls in love instantly—something she never once believed was possible for anyone before. But this guy is different. He's tall and muscled with rough hands from working outside. He's grounded. So much so that it became too easy to forget he was one of the wealthiest bachelors in Texas, and that was saying something in this state.

Not only that, but he had the kind of billboard-model good looks that made her pinch herself when he'd asked her out. And that was just the outward appearance. The physical attributes that got noticed when she first met someone. An initial appraisal that ticked all the boxes.

Talking to him had rocketed the attraction into a whole new stratosphere. He was quick-witted. He was funny. He was compassionate despite a tough exterior. He lived by a cowboy code that set him apart from other guys she'd dated. Combine all those qualities, wrap them up with his devilish charm, and he was irresistible.

Reality was settling in now, and it was a hard, cold one. He deserved so much more than she would be able to give. She could see that clearly now. Looking at him as he stood there, she knew without a doubt that short-changing him wasn't an option. Not once in the past year had she stopped long enough to think about what being in a relationship with her might do to him. How the dark cloud following her would rain on him, too. She'd been caught up in a whirlwind fantasy and wanted to blindly trust that everything would magically work out.

Life had handed her a different reality. One she must've known she had coming, because fairy tales weren't real and men like Riggs didn't exist. And the rare few who did? They deserved something better than the bad luck that stalked her.

She'd also neglected to assess how devastating the consequences might be for her when she left after giving away her heart.

He glanced up before reaching for the handle. Her

heart skipped a couple of beats when he stepped inside the living room. And all she could think to say was, "There's coffee if you want some."

An awkward silence filled the room before he finally said, "Yes, please."

His manners had always been spot-on, but she knew him well enough to realize anger brimmed under the polite surface.

"You can come on in and find a seat," she said, motioning toward the bar stools and then the kitchen table. "Sit wherever you like."

"I can't stay long," he said, and her chest deflated. She had no right to be disappointed. In fact, she should celebrate because her resolve to keep him at arm's length wouldn't last long if he tried to get close to her.

Rather than dwell on it, she fixed him a cup of coffee and walked it over to the counter in between the living room and kitchen.

"I got a text from her, too. She said she had news and to be ready, but she didn't explain. She said we'd talk about it when she got home and the news would blow my mind." Cheyenne palmed her own cup.

Riggs thanked her and then stared at the cup in her hand for a long moment before finally asking, "Since when did you start drinking coffee?"

"Recently." She shrugged, not ready to admit the real reason.

Riggs eyed her suspiciously before picking up the cup, and took a sip. He set his phone down presumably where he could keep an eye on it in case Ally called or sent another text.

"When did she contact you?" Cheyenne asked.

"About an hour ago." He confirmed what she already suspected.

"Same here," she said.

"You don't think she would be trying to get us to…" His voice trailed off when he seemed to think better of finishing the sentence.

"No. I don't." Cheyenne was clear on that point. Her best friend would never pull a stunt like this to shock her out of her funk. "Something is wrong. I can feel it."

The last time she said those words, she'd ended up in the ER and then in labor and delivery. An icy chill raced down her spine at the memory. She shrugged in an attempt to shake it off.

"We can take a ride up to the hospital to see if she's still there and got sucked into working another shift," he offered without meeting her gaze. Riggs O'Connor wasn't afraid a day in his life, so she doubted he was scared to make eye contact. Was he trying to shield himself from the disappointment their relationship must represent to him now? She wouldn't blame him one bit. She also took note that he hadn't so much as looked at her stomach. Was it too painful a reminder?

"I don't know," she hedged, not wanting to be in close quarters with the one man who caused a dozen butterflies to release in her chest without doing much more than glancing at her.

"I'm fresh out of ideas, then." His frustration came through in his tone. "We can sit here as long as you like but she might be on the side of the road somewhere."

"Okay," she said without thinking it through. If Ally was stranded, she would call. If she had access to a phone, she would return a text. If she was going to be stranded at work, she would let them know. Plus, the two of them were struggling to talk as it was, despite a growing piece of her that was comforted by his presence. Riggs was like that. He was the sun, and everything else orbited around him, drawn to his warmth.

"Ready?" He cocked an eyebrow.

"Yes." These one-word conversations ranked right up there as the worst. They were a stark contrast to all the nights they'd missed sleep while lying in each other's arms and talking about the future they were going to build together. A future that died alongside their daughter.

"I'll wait in the truck."

She nodded. At least they were up to five words now. It was her fault. She'd been the one to tell him she was going ahead with a divorce, breaking the promises they'd made to each other. This might be best for Riggs, but it sure left a hole in her heart the size of Texas.

She would learn to get by. Hadn't she always picked herself up by her bootstraps and forged ahead? Hadn't she always found a way to keep going even when it felt like the world was crashing down around her, grabbing hold of the rope, tying the knot and then holding on for dear life?

She instinctively reached for the ladybug bracelet that was her mother's favorite piece of jewelry. Fingering the delicate lines and jewels brought her heart rate down to a decent level after panic caused her pulse to jump.

Reminding herself to breathe always helped in these situations. She watched, unable to move, as Riggs walked right out the front door.

Breathe.

Ozzy ran to the door and back. He ran circles around

her feet. It took a second, but she finally caught on to what he was trying to tell her. He wanted to go outside.

"You're a smart doggo." She reached down and picked up all six pounds of him and brought him nose to face. "Okay. You're in. Only because Ally will be so happy to see you and not because you're starting to break down my resolve to not get too attached to you."

She realized she'd just had a longer conversation with a dog than with the man she'd promised to spend the rest of her life with. That pretty much summed up how her life was going these days.

Setting him down, she fed him before letting him out in the small backyard. She took another sip of coffee before moving down the hallway. She threw on her favorite yoga pants and cotton shirt, and then pulled her hair up in a ponytail. Socks and tennis shoes were next. So, basically, the most nondescript clothes she could find. The dark colors matched her mood.

She grabbed the leash on the way out the door before shouldering her purse and locking up.

Riggs sat in the driver's seat, engine running, as another dark-cloud-hanging-over-her-head feeling nailed her. She held Ozzy a little closer to her chest, and then hopped off the porch, figuring this was going to be the longest drive of her life despite the hospital being less than half an hour away.

Riggs was used to being with folks who didn't feel the need to fill empty air with meaningless words. But the chilly twenty-plus-minute ride to the hospital with no conversation ranked right up there with one of the most awkward moments of his life.

What was he supposed to say to someone who was

hurting so much she couldn't speak? It was impossible not to feel like he'd let her down in some way. Then there was his own anger to consider. Anger that had him chomping at the bit to release all the fury he held inside. At least they hadn't found Ally in a ditch somewhere unconscious and therefore unable to call.

"She usually parks on the east side of the lot," Cheyenne finally chimed in as the hospital building came into view.

"It's the closest to the road leading home." His voice came out a little gruffer than he'd intended. His finger itched to reach over and touch Cheyenne again. But what would he say to her? There were no words that could cover their loss, and the divorce he knew was coming was nothing more than insult to injury.

Even so, he couldn't rightly walk away without knowing there was no chance of a reconciliation. Anger or not, he'd made a commitment he didn't take lightly. Based on the look on her face and her closed-up body language, she'd rather move on.

As much as he wished things had turned out differently, he wouldn't try to convince her to stay with him when she so clearly couldn't wait to be as far away from him as possible. As it was, she sat so far on the opposite side of the bench seat that her right shoulder pressed against the door.

"Do you see her car?" The parking lot was less than half-full, about thirty cars and trucks mostly huddled up toward the entrance. He drove up and down each aisle, searching for the cherry red Mustang Ally drove. He'd met her a few times and had been threatened to within an inch of his life if he ever hurt Cheyenne.

He'd promised not to and that was the second promise he broke. The first was to love and protect her. Not being able to protect her from the kind of pain that would cause most to curl up in a fetal position and give up had his hands tightening around the steering wheel.

Guilt racked him for not being in the room with his wife when she'd had their child. He'd been called out onto the property after someone spotted poachers. She'd gone into early labor. He was in an area without cell coverage, none the wiser. So yeah, he felt like a jerk for not being there for his…for her.

"It's not here," she finally said after studying each vehicle like she was going to be tested on it later.

"Does she ever park anywhere else?" he asked. Being back at the hospital where she'd lost their child two weeks ago caused stress lines to crease her forehead.

"I suppose it's possible." She frowned.

"We can take a lap around the hospital. Check the other lots." He navigated around the white-and-glass building, not ready to leave empty-handed. There were four lots and he drove each aisle as concern mounted for Ally with every minute that ticked by.

Cheyenne had been right earlier. Her friend wouldn't call them together and then ditch.

"I can call my brother and ask if there have been any accidents in the area," he offered. They would have seen something on their way over, though. There was only one main road from Ally's house to the hospital and a couple of side streets, so it wasn't like there were a lot of options.

"Okay." There was a lost quality to Cheyenne's voice that nearly ripped his heart out. She was holding Ozzy close to her chest with one arm while chewing her thumbnail to bits on her right hand.

He pulled out to the edge of the lot and parked, leaving

the engine running. Colton's number was programmed into the truck, so all Riggs had to do was press the screen on his dashboard to call.

"Hey, what's up?" Colton answered on the first ring, barely covering the concern in his voice. It came as no shock that everyone was worried about Riggs and he appreciated his brothers for their concern. The O'Connor family was a tight-knit bunch. Always had been and always would be. Even their rogue brother Garrett had come around recently after their father and family patriarch's death.

"You're on speaker. I'm with Cheyenne and we were supposed to meet her best friend after work. You remember Ally?"

The line was dead quiet for more than a few uncomfortable beats.

"Yes," Colton finally said, not masking the confusion in his tone as well as he probably thought he was.

"She requested a meetup. Gave us the impression it was important and that she had news to deliver that had to be kept hush-hush," he said to his brother, the sheriff.

"And you believe this information is related to your daughter." Colton was sharp. There was no doubt in Riggs's mind his brother would catch on to the implication without spelling it out for him.

"I do." He didn't want to speak for Cheyenne. Although she was nodding, hunkered over in the corner. "She didn't show up at her residence. We're at her place of employment and her vehicle is nowhere to be found. We didn't observe any accidents between her home and usual route to work."

"Which is?" Colton was all business now. This was his territory, and he was good at his job.

Riggs rattled off street names after giving both her address and the name of the hospital.

"I can be there personally in—"

"No need." Riggs appreciated his brother for wanting to show up for him. But he really did just want to know if any accidents had been reported.

The click-clack of a keyboard sounded.

"Hold on a second," Colton said in a distracted voice. He was no doubt staring at the screen, waiting for results.

"Nothing in your area has come up on the radio and I'm not getting anything in the system, either," Colton reported. "Have you spoken to anyone inside the hospital yet?"

"No."

"Someone might have needed to borrow her car last-minute." Colton's suggestion was a reach. Ally would have her cell phone on her and would have contacted either Riggs or Cheyenne.

"I can ask around, but it doesn't seem like she'd leave us hanging like this," Riggs said.

"Hold on for a second." Colton must've muted the call because he went radio silent.

After a few tense moments, his brother returned to the line.

"No accidents reported. I'm sending a deputy over to make the drive and I've contacted a group that volunteers to use drones in searches." He exhaled. "With the information we have right now, I'd say she probably stopped off somewhere along the way for a drink to force the two of you in a room together. Or it's possible she ran into the grocery store and happened into an old chatty friend."

Riggs compressed his lips to stop from refuting his brother's ideas. Colton was coming at this from a seasoned law enforcement officer's point of view. In many cases, he was probably right. He also probably wouldn't even send a deputy or dredge up drones if he wasn't talking to a trusted source. Riggs needed to keep perspective and hold his frustration in check. He was already ticking through possible stop-offs along the route home. If they had to visit every business to find her or convince his brother she was missing, so be it.

"I appreciate your help," he finally said.

"This is just a starting point. There are other things I can do if she doesn't turn up from these efforts," Colton assured him. His wheels were turning, apparently.

Riggs thanked his brother and ended the call.

"She wouldn't do this on purpose." Cheyenne tapped her fingers on the armrest. "She's in some kind of trouble and it's somehow related to us. Ally would never just disappear like this without contacting us first."

The thought was sobering.

"Where do you want to start?" he asked, figuring they could backtrack but also needed to check out any of her favorite haunts.

"Anywhere but the same hospital…" She didn't have to finish the sentence. He didn't want to go inside the place they'd lost their daughter, either.

Chapter 3

There was one grocery store, three restaurants and two gas station/convenience stores in between Ally's house and the hospital. Cheyenne remembered one of the gas stations as Ally's favorite, and the convenience store where she herself had stopped for coffee the other day. And yes, she'd started drinking coffee two weeks ago instead of her usual chai tea.

Ally's red Mustang was nowhere to be found. Hers was distinguishable by the color and the personalized license plate, IAM NRSE.

An hour and a half later, they were right back where they'd started, in the hospital parking lot. Pulling up to the hospital building, knowing she was about to walk through those cold, white-tiled corridors again, filled her with dread. She wasn't sure what to do with herself, let alone Ozzy.

"Think I can get away with putting him in my purse and sneaking him inside?" she asked, motioning toward her best friend's dog.

"Might as well try." Riggs had been quiet along the way, which was never a good sign. In the short time she'd gotten to know him, she realized how often he closed up when he was frustrated.

Then again, he wasn't her business anymore. After they located Ally, he would go back to the ranch and she would figure out her next step. The timeline and the circumstances of the pregnancy hadn't been ideal, but Cheyenne was surprised at how quickly she'd adapted to the news and pivoted to welcoming full-time motherhood. Now she needed a job. The nearby community college where she'd worked as an admissions counselor had already replaced her. Her emergency funds would only get her through the next three or four months, and there was no way she was asking for any of Riggs's money. Seeing him again had already stirred up feelings she needed to keep at a safe distance. Safe? There was nothing safe about Riggs O'Connor when it came to protecting her heart.

The time had come to tie a knot in the rope.

Shouldering her purse, she tucked Ozzy inside so that only his head peeked out. Staring down the building was the hardest thing for her to do. But she hadn't survived this long by hiding from things that might hurt her. She would have to face this pain at some point. Was she ready? No. But Ally was worth it.

With a deep breath meant to fortify her, she exited the truck. While wrestling with her own thoughts, it hadn't occurred to her how much this might be affecting Riggs.

A quick glance at him was the equivalent of a punch in the solar plexus.

His chin was jutted out, and his gaze was focused on the entrance as he stood there waiting for her to come around the truck. He was strength and courage personified, so to see him struggle, even for a brief moment, was a direct hit to the heart.

She stood there, just out of sight, giving him a minute of privacy.

"Ready?" he asked after glancing over at her.

"Yes." She couldn't muster enthusiasm and she couldn't stop the flood of emotions engulfing her. She didn't cry no matter how much she wanted to. Instead, she tucked her chin to her chest and took it one step at a time. She could take a step. And then another. She could cross the circular road and then step up on the curb. She could walk inside the double doors that opened with a swish.

Her heart pounded with every forward step until it felt like it would bust through her rib cage, but she could take a step onto the sterile white tile.

"May I help you?" An older voice, a gentle voice, caused Cheyenne to look up.

A four-foot-high counter separated her from a lovely older lady. The woman, whose name tag read Grey, had the warmest smile. Her long white hair was pulled up in a bun on top of her head like she was an aging ballerina. She had the kindest pale blue eyes, which stood out against age-worn skin.

"We're visiting a friend who works here," Cheyenne piped up. She could only hope Ozzy would behave in her handbag and not start barking. He had a habit of getting in trouble, and yet strangely, he seemed to have settled in there.

"Do you know the floor?" Grey asked. Cheyenne had become fascinated with names while trying to find the perfect one for her daughter.

"Yes," she said.

"Have a good day," Grey said.

Cheyenne started to walk away and then stopped. "You have an unusual name. Do you mind me asking what it stands for?"

Grey smiled and it warmed her face. "Greyson. My daddy wanted a boy. He got four girls. He'd planned on giving a boy my name." She laughed and it filled the space with more of that warmth. "Everyone calls me Grey for short."

"It's a beautiful name." Cheyenne loved rare or unusual names with a story behind them.

"Thank you." The older woman beamed.

Cheyenne smiled before casting her eyes to the floor, and then headed toward the elevator bank. She'd go anywhere but labor and delivery on the seventh floor. Lucky for her, Ally worked on three.

The bell dinged. A set of elevator doors opened, and Riggs put his hand in to keep them from closing. He nodded toward Cheyenne to go first. He'd always been a gentleman. She thought of him more as a Renaissance man. His Southern manners, which gave a lady the option to go first, were always appreciated in her book. Did she need someone to open doors for her? No. She was capable of doing that for herself. And yet there was something nice about having the option, about being spoiled just a little bit. It was one of the perks of living in Texas among cowboys and ranchers, and she hoped it stayed in style.

She pushed the number three, thankful they had the elevator to themselves. She wasn't one for crowds on a good day, preferring curling up in bed with a good book over drinks at a crowded bar or dinner at a busy restaurant.

Ozzy tried to climb out of her bag.

"No. No. You're okay," she soothed.

The little guy jumped out before she could stop him. Riggs caught Ozzy before he crashed to the ground.

"Hey, there, little guy. You need to stay put and keep your head down so you don't get us kicked out of this place. We're trying to find your mama." His voice caught on the last word and he seemed to notice how it sounded. He cleared his throat and whispered an apology. He'd always had the kind of deep timbre that threaded right through her, traveling over her and through her.

Even now, when she couldn't afford to let it.

The elevator bell dinged, indicating they'd reached their floor as Riggs tucked the little dog in Cheyenne's bag. He pulled back his hand the minute it grazed Cheyenne's creamy skin—skin he couldn't afford to think about for how off-limits she was.

The doors opened and he waited for her to go first. He didn't have the first idea how to talk to her about what had happened on a different floor inside these same walls. She might have been the one to close that door, but he didn't know what to say anyway.

In the first couple of days, he'd naively believed she needed time. She'd refused to take his calls, so he gave her the space she needed. Was that a mistake? Would it have made a difference if he'd shouted from the rooftops that he wanted to be there for her? That she didn't have to go through any of this alone? An impenetrable wall had come up around her, a fortress he'd had no idea how to break down or break through.

Riggs held out his hand to keep the elevator doors from closing. Then he followed her.

Ozzy's ears peeked out. Cheyenne was doing a good job of keeping the squeaky little barker under wraps. As long as the little guy cooled it, they should be fine.

Cheyenne walked up to the nurse station where three nurses were working on separate tasks. One studied a computer screen. She was facing them but so engrossed in what she was doing she didn't look up. Another stood with her side to them, writing in a file. And the third stood at the back of the station with her arms folded, looking down at the tile.

Cheyenne waited for someone to acknowledge them, rather than draw attention. The old saying it was easier to catch bees with honey than vinegar came to mind. Interrupt the nurses while they were deep in thought or busy doing their jobs, and they might be uncooperative.

Rude people rarely ever got more than base-level information or service. Besides, these were Ally's coworkers. He didn't want to appear a jerk and he was certain he could speak for Cheyenne on that front.

The one mesmerized by the computer screen broke her trance and then looked up. "Oh. Sorry. I…uh…can I help you?"

Her eyebrows drew together and an emotion passed behind her eyes that he couldn't quite pinpoint. Shock? Fear?

Couldn't be.

He was probably seeing things. He didn't know this woman from Adam. She had no reason to be afraid of him.

"We're looking for Ally," Cheyenne said. "We were

supposed to meet for breakfast and figured she got caught up here."

The nurse shrugged. "I didn't see Ally today when I started my shift. I can ask around, but I doubt she's still here."

"That would be great, if you wouldn't mind," Cheyenne said. Ozzy started moving around inside the purse and he might get them booted out if they weren't careful.

The nurse didn't seem enthused about the request.

"Sorry to bug you about our friend." Riggs stepped forward and placed a hand on Cheyenne's lower back. The nurse locked onto Riggs and her face flushed, a reaction he'd never get used to.

She smiled and brought a hand up to tuck her hair behind her ear, a sign of flirting that would have upset Cheyenne a while back. Now she didn't seem to care who looked at him or when. Crazy how the tide could turn on a dime.

Much like a rogue spring thunderstorm, Cheyenne's feelings had changed course in a flash. Again, there wasn't much he could do if she was unwilling to sit down and talk about their future. To be fair, she'd said she didn't see one for them anymore. And yet, part of him couldn't believe she meant those words. Couldn't believe or couldn't accept? an annoying voice in the back of his mind asked. Because there was a big difference. None of which mattered at the moment. His priority had shifted. He wasn't much for worrying, but Ally's disappearance was troublesome. He also made a mental note to ask Cheyenne about Ally's personal life. He wanted to know if she had other friends, a boyfriend, or had started a new relationship. While he was at it, he wanted to know if she'd had any disagreements with anyone recently, a falling out or a breakup. Riggs's brothers who worked in law enforcement were beginning to rub off on him.

"It's not like her to leave us hanging." He leaned an elbow on the bar-height counter and smiled.

The cheesy move worked, because the nurse winked at him before rolling her chair back a couple of feet.

"Hey, Sherry. Have you seen Ally today?" she asked.

"Not me." The nurse didn't look up from her file. Her name tag read: Renee.

"How about you, Becca?" she asked the nurse at the back of the station without making much of an effort to make eye contact.

Becca continued to study the tile but shook her head.

Renee rolled her chair back to its original position. "Doesn't look like anyone here knows where she is."

Funny. Cheyenne hadn't asked if anyone knew where her friend was. She'd asked if anyone had seen her today.

A coincidence? Or was the nurse holding something back?

Chapter 4

"Thank you for your time." Cheyenne knew when she was being stonewalled and saw no point in sticking around the hospital. She turned to leave when a nurse rounded the corner. The young woman froze in her tracks, a horrified expression on her face.

Riggs seemed to catch on. He started to say something when the nurse glanced up at the camera in the corner of the hallway before scurrying off.

He took Cheyenne's hand in his and then gave a quick squeeze. On instinct, she jerked her hand back. She didn't dare look up at him. She couldn't look into those eyes one more time—eyes that showed pain no matter how well he tried to cover.

"Let's get out of here," he said low and under his breath. His voice had the same gravelly quality she loved. Correction, *used* to love. She couldn't afford to love anymore.

"Okay." There was no point in waiting there when the nurses seemed determined not to give them any information.

She followed him down the hallway, into the elevator, and out the same door they'd come in twenty minutes ago. As they walked to the parking lot, she caught sight of the nurse from the hallway a few minutes ago.

Of course, the nurse would know a quicker way down to the parking lot. She would also know where Ally parked and might have guessed they would do the same. These were a lot of assumptions and yet they were logical.

The mystery nurse pulled something from her pocket. Metal glinted in the bright sun. For a split second, Cheyenne's pulse leaped into her throat. On instinct, she grabbed Riggs's arm. He stepped beside her, using his considerable size to block Cheyenne from the nurse. And then he almost immediately sidestepped so Cheyenne could see the woman had pulled out one of those electronic cigarettes. She gave a weary look, glanced from side to side, and then waved them over.

Cheyenne wasn't 100 percent certain the woman could be trusted, especially with the way she kept checking the parking lot every time the wind blew. They were short on options, though. Mystery nurse was their best shot at progress.

It was then she realized the woman stood in the blind spot of a pair of cameras attached to the building. Riggs must have noticed the same thing because he nudged Cheyenne with his elbow and then made eyes toward the cameras.

"You can stay here or head to the truck. You don't have to go with me," he said quietly.

"I'm good now that I know she's not carrying," she

said, careful not to squeeze her bag since Ozzy was still inside. The half-demon dog turned into an angel inside a handbag. Maybe that was where he felt the most secure. Everyone should be so lucky to have a place that made them feel safe. Cheyenne would have said she had Riggs's arms before…

She didn't want to go there while they approached the nurse. Being with Riggs already caused the world to tip on its axis and Cheyenne needed to check her balance, not throw it off even more. *Tie the knot, Cheyenne.*

The woman stood a little shorter than Cheyenne and had mousy brown hair in a ponytail that swished from side to side as she moved her head. She was of petite build and had an oval-shaped face. She kept twisting her hands together and searching around, looking like she'd jump out of her skin if someone said, "Boo."

As Cheyenne and Riggs neared, the doors swished open. A woman came out. Face down, she barely acknowledged the two of them. The nurse, however, tucked the e-cig back inside her pocket, mumbled an apology, and then scurried past them and back into the hospital.

They stood there for a moment, frozen, not wanting to draw attention. When the woman walking toward her vehicle in the parking lot turned toward them, Riggs pulled Cheyenne into an embrace and then kissed her. His lips still tasted like dark roast coffee, just like she remembered. Her favorite flavor.

Her breath caught and her pulse skyrocketed. His lightest touch caused her stomach to free-fall.

Kissing her had been a maneuver. Something to deflect attention from the woman walking by. It was a smart move on Riggs's part. And yet, so dangerous for Cheyenne's resolve. Because she could get lost in his arms.

She loved the way his lips felt when they moved against hers. And she loved breathing in his spicy scent.

Her hands fisted at her sides. She knew exactly what *she* wanted. It would be so easy to be selfish right now. It would be so easy to be with Riggs again. It would be so easy to tell herself the only thing that mattered was the here and now. Would that be the best thing for Riggs? The long answer was no. The short answer was no. No. No. No.

Pulling on all her willpower, she took a step back. Glancing to her right, she saw the back of the woman's head as she climbed into her sport utility.

Riggs didn't immediately move, and she could only guess what must be running through his mind right now. Hers raced.

"Think we should head back to the truck?" she asked, thinking there wasn't much more they could do.

"My first thought was to follow the nurse back inside." He shook his head. "Wouldn't do any good, though."

"As much as I want to march inside the hospital and demand answers, I agree with you." Based on her experience with Renee, Sherry and Becca, doing that would be as productive as planting summer crops in December. With a sharp sigh, she walked back to the truck with Riggs.

Inside, he didn't seem in a hurry to start the engine or pull out of the parking lot.

"Cameras are probably watching us as we speak," Cheyenne pointed out. Her nerves were shot. She checked the sky for the drones Colton had promised and didn't see any. She reminded herself it would take time to get resources in the air.

"Let them. We aren't doing anything wrong in sitting

here. A deputy will be here in a little while, and he'll be on our side." His voice was a study in calm. In fact, he was too calm. It was the calm before the storm.

She shifted to one side and then back to the other. Ozzy peeked his head out of her purse and she reached over to scratch him behind the ears. He ducked in time to miss contact, back to his old tricks. Little squirt. Or maybe he *should* recoil at her touch. Did he know on instinct to keep a distance from her? Did he have a sixth sense for cursed people? Because she had to be cursed. No one had this much bad luck in one lifetime.

"Who does Ally socialize with from work?" He pulled out his cell phone and she assumed the reason was to take down names.

"To be honest, I have no idea." The admission stung. Cheyenne should know who her best friend had been hanging out with. "I've been so wrapped up in my own life for the past year and getting ready for the baby that I haven't been staying in touch as much as I should have."

He nodded.

"Do you know if she was seeing someone?" There was no judgment in his voice.

"She used to date someone in Dallas, but I don't remember his name and I think it was a long time ago." Cheyenne blew out a frustrated breath. There were fuzzy memories of Ally coming home in the mornings after work, coming into Cheyenne's room to check on her. Her friend talked about her shift as Cheyenne drifted in and out. "Look. I haven't been the best friend to her lately. I got so caught up in my relationship with you and then the pregnancy that she and I didn't talk as much as we used to." She threw her hands up in the air. "There was a time when she was going back and forth to Dallas for a guy, but I couldn't tell you if that was still the case and for the past two weeks all I've wanted to do is stay in bed twenty-four seven, so it's not like we've been having sleepovers to catch up."

She blew out a breath and apologized.

"I'm frustrated with me, not you. Please don't take what I'm saying the wrong way," she said. "I remember something about work… I can't remember what, though."

"It happens to friendships," he said and his attempt to comfort her shouldn't make her even more frustrated. "And it was probably just her needing to talk about her shift."

"It shouldn't, though. I care about Ally. I just never really worried about our friendship before. It's not like we talk every day. We've gone weeks, sometimes months, without talking. Then we just pick up where we left off. Except this year has been the longest break we've ever taken." And she wanted to add it was her fault. She also wanted to remember who Ally complained about from work. A doctor? It would be another angle they could follow up on. And yet nurses grumbling about how a doctor treated them wasn't exactly new.

"I'm sure you two would have picked up again once the baby was born." Again, his attempt to let her off the hook shouldn't infuriate her more. Except that was exactly what it did.

"How? From everything I read, babies are more than a full-time job," she said with a little more heat than she'd intended. She pinched the bridge of her nose to stem the headache threatening. "I would have just let our long-standing friendship slip away. And now, something might have happened to her and it's because of…"

She stopped herself right there before she went all in

blaming herself. This wasn't a pity party by any means. She had a very real sense of annoyance that she'd let her friend down—a friend who had been there for Cheyenne during her darkest days.

"I won't pretend to know your friendship with Ally, or how it works. All I can say is that I'm guilty of the same thing with my brothers." He didn't have to tell her how close his family was. She'd seen it firsthand while living at KBR, Katy Bull Ranch. "It can be easy to take the ones we care about most for granted." He put his hand up before she mounted an argument. "I'm not saying we have to do it that way, but it's more common than it should be."

He wouldn't get an argument from her there.

"Why is that, Riggs?" She leaned her head against the headrest. The headache from earlier threatened to return.

"You tell me and we'll both know," he said. It was one of his favorite sayings while they were together. A smile ghosted her lips at the memory. There were others that tried to follow but she shut them down.

"All I know is that she's out here somewhere and if I was a better friend, I'd know where. I'd be able to find her and help her," she admitted before she had time to reel those words back in.

Riggs didn't immediately respond. In fact, he took so long she slowly opened her eyes and turned to look at him. When she did, she saw something else…

Movement in the background caught her attention. The mousy-haired nurse was back, and she was standing in the same spot as before.

"Well, look at that." Cheyenne nodded toward the woman.

"She must have something she wants to say to us," he said.

"What if she was just trying to bum a lighter?" Cheyenne couldn't afford to get her hopes up.

"I don't think e-cigs work that way but I don't exactly have personal experience to draw from," he said. Then he turned to lock gazes with Cheyenne. "Only one way to find out."

"True." She opened the door, exited the vehicle, and met him around back.

They approached the nurse together. She had the same e-cig out. Cheyenne figured a smoke break must be her excuse to leave the building while on duty.

"Come closer." She took a drag off the e-cig before glancing around again. "I need this job and I'll get fired if I'm seen talking to either of you."

"Why us?" Riggs took the lead.

"Don't you know?" The nurse's name tag wasn't on her left pocket like everyone else's. Had she removed it?

"I'm drawing a blank here." He threw his hands in the air for emphasis.

"Your friend is in trouble," she said like it was plain as the noses on their faces.

"Why?" Cheyenne asked.

"Because of you. She went poking around where she shouldn't, and now she disappeared just before her shift was over. Have you seen her?" the nurse asked with a cocked eyebrow.

"No. I haven't," Cheyenne said. "I was hoping you could tell me where she was."

The woman shook her head. "That's not a good sign."

"Her car is gone," Cheyenne pointed out. "Did she leave on her own free will?"

"All I know is that she was poking around in the files on your birth, asking around about Dr. Fortner," the nurse said. "Then she was gone, and Sherry, the head nurse, starts asking if anyone can fill her shift tomorrow."

Sherry knew?

Riggs reached over and squeezed Cheyenne's hand.

"Is there anything else you can tell us?" Cheyenne asked. "Please. My friend might be in danger. Anything you can tell us might save her life."

The nurse's eyes widened to saucers. She pushed past them and tucked the e-cig inside her pocket. "I gotta go."

"That's it?" Cheyenne asked. "What about Ally?"

"I've already said too much. I'm sorry. I have to worry about me and my kid." She twisted her hands together.

"Can I ask why you're here talking to us, then?" Riggs asked.

"Yeah. Because any one of us could be next." She stormed off and disappeared around the corner into the building.

"She knows more than she's telling us," Riggs said.

"I know." Cheyenne reached in her bag and pulled Ozzy out. He immediately started barking. She placed him back inside, figuring she was right about him feeling the most secure there. She might not be able to help Ally right now, but she could take care of Ozzy.

They headed to the truck with the confession spinning in Cheyenne's thoughts. Riggs walked her to the passenger side and opened the door for her. She could open it for herself but her hands were busy with Ozzy, and she appreciated the gesture.

She thanked him and then climbed inside the cab. After situating the dog and securing her seat belt, she exhaled. "Something sinister is going on here."

"It sure is." He started the engine and then put the gearshift in Reverse.

"Something about the birth." She couldn't bring herself to say the words *our daughter*, despite them sitting right there on her tongue. After feeling like her heart had been ripped from her chest, she couldn't dare to hope there'd been some kind of mistake. Although rare, mistakes did happen. Could their daughter have been sent home with someone else by accident? Babies switched at birth? Those kinds of things made the news. As tragic as it was for all parties, mistakes happened.

"Yes," he agreed, clearly not wanting to get his hopes up, either. They would be crazy to, and both seemed to realize it.

"Which doesn't mean there's a different outcome," she quickly said. "It could be something as simple as Ally figuring out someone messed up the birth. That it wasn't all my fau—"

"Hold on there a second." Riggs hit the brake. "These things happen in life. And as awful as they are, no one person is to blame."

Did he really believe that? Because she didn't. She was the one in the hospital in early labor. She was the one who was supposed to be able to give birth like so many other women did every day of the week. And *she* was the one who'd lost their daughter.

The black cloud hung over *her* head, not his.

Judging from his reaction, telling him so wouldn't change his mind and there was nothing he could say to change hers. So she left it at that, figuring it was time to redirect the conversation back on track.

"Where do we go next, Riggs?" she asked, hoping he would let it go.

He sat there silent, with the engine idling for a long moment before shifting into Drive, looking like he had a whole lot to say. He seemed to decide on, "Let's go back to the house. She might be there waiting already."

"Do you really believe that after what the nurse just said?" Cheyenne asked.

"Not really, but I'm grasping at straws as much as you are," he admitted.

"I'm not saying I don't believe the nurse. But it wouldn't be the first time Ally's cell died after a long shift." Evidence pointed to the contrary, but she wasn't ready to embrace the thought something permanently bad had happened to Ally. "On second thought, do you think we should circle back and try to get more information out of E-cig Nurse?"

The woman had disappeared a little too fast. She knew something she wasn't sharing.

"If it's true that she has a kid, she won't tell us anything else. She barely told us anything as of now. And we don't even know her real name." He navigated out of the parking lot and onto the roadway back toward Ally's bungalow. "We'll give Colton an update. The nurse will talk to law enforcement and so will Sherry. I'd like to hear her explanation as to why she seems to know Ally won't be coming back to work in the next few days."

The obvious answer was that Ally was going somewhere and asked for time off. But Ally wouldn't. She didn't. And yet Cheyenne couldn't prove it.

"I'd like to be a fly on the wall when the nurses talk to law enforcement." The thought of going back to the bungalow to wait for Ally with Riggs made breathing a challenge. *Slow down. Breathe.*

Tie the knot. Hold on. Her new mantra had to work because Riggs was most definitely going home with her.

She couldn't turn him away when the investigation involved finding out what had happened to his daughter.

Cheyenne picked up her handbag and held Ozzy to her chest. Instead of trying to snap at her, he leaned his head against her neck and nuzzled her.

"You like car rides?" She kept her voice quiet. Talking to the dog was one thing. Figuring out what to say to her soon-to-be ex was a whole different ball game, especially since her pulse pounded so loudly he had to be able to hear it.

Being around Riggs did things to her heart she couldn't afford right now. She needed all of her determination and resolve to find out what had really happened to her daughter. To *their* daughter. The unfairness of shutting him out slammed into her. She'd been so caught up in trying to protect him that she'd hurt him even more.

Cheyenne took in a deep breath. She had to figure out a way to find the words to talk about what had happened.

Riggs deserved to know.

Chapter 5

"No sign of your friend." Riggs pulled onto the parking pad in front of Ally's place for the second time that day. A few thoughts circulated through his mind and a picture was emerging as he hopped out of the driver's seat after cutting off the engine. Cheyenne blamed herself for losing the baby. He suspected it was at least part of the reason she'd told him that he would be better off without her. There could be more to it, but something told him this statement carried most of the weight.

"No." The sadness in her voice nearly cut a hole in his chest.

The passenger door swung wide open before he made it halfway around the front of the pickup. She'd been quiet on the ride back. Too quiet for his liking. It meant she'd gone inside herself again and he had no idea how to reach her. It had happened twice during the early months of their relationship. The first time wasn't too long after she'd told him she was pregnant. He'd given her space and she'd come around after two long weeks. The second came midway through the pregnancy, when she'd shut down on him. Again, he'd given her space, and she'd come around with a little bit of time. This time seemed different.

Riggs headed toward the bungalow as Cheyenne shut the door to the truck. She stopped on the porch and turned to face him. The way she bit the inside of her cheek before she launched into whatever she was about to say caused a knot to form in his gut.

She shifted her weight from one foot to the other and her fingers traced the house key in her hand. A sense of dread for what might come next tightened the knot.

"Is there any chance you can stay for a while?" she asked, not making eye contact.

Cheyenne's question caught him off guard.

"I can and planned to," he said. Nothing inside him wanted to get back inside his truck and drive away while there were so many unanswered questions anyway.

"Good." She turned around before unlocking the front door. "We need to talk."

The second surprise struck with her last comment.

Riggs closed, then locked the door behind him and nodded toward the kitchen. "Mind if I get a fresh cup of coffee?"

"Be my guest." She shrugged. Tension radiated off her in waves. "I can get it for you. It wouldn't be any trouble."

"I sort of remember where everything is," he said, figuring he needed something to do with his hands as much as the caffeine boost.

Cheyenne followed him into the next room. Ozzy was

still tucked inside her purse and he seemed to like it there. He'd stopped yipping, so that was a step in the right direction.

"You want a cup?" he asked.

"Sure." Cheyenne kept her distance, looking like she was working up her nerve to tell him something. If he moved toward the fridge, she took two big steps backward. Five feet seemed to be her "safe" distance from him.

Hell, it wasn't like he was going to bump into her despite the small space. He had no plans for intentional contact. Granted, the kiss from the parking lot still sizzled on his lips. But he didn't foresee the need for a repeat. It had gotten them out of a tricky situation.

Telling her to relax would most likely increase her stress levels, so he let it be, forcing himself not to think about the fact they normally couldn't be in the same room without near-constant contact even if it was just outer thighs touching while seated on the couch.

Riggs fixed two cups and handed one over. Their fingers grazed, causing a familiar jolt of electricity to shoot straight to his heart. He stared at the cup for a second longer than he'd intended, and she seemed to do the same.

After taking a sip and then a breath that was apparently meant to fortify her, Cheyenne apologized.

"It's not easy for me to talk about that night," she continued, referring to the birth. "But that's no excuse. It has dawned on me that you deserve to hear what happened."

He nodded as she glanced at him. Suddenly, the rim of her coffee cup became very interesting to her.

"I panicked when I couldn't reach you," she said.

"Why didn't you grab someone else at the ranch?" he asked.

"Because I wasn't there." She started working the ladybug bracelet her mother had given her, another sign her stress levels were climbing.

"The doctor didn't think it was a good idea to be away from the r—"

"I'm aware," she cut in, her voice laced with more of that sadness. "I should have been home and probably in bed. At the very least somewhere with my feet up."

She flashed her eyes at him.

"I was going stir-crazy at home by myself and I don't know the rest of your family well enough to—" she took in a slow breath before continuing "—to ask someone to go to my mother's favorite place with me."

"You hiked Harken Falls alone?"

"There were technically park rangers there, but yes." Another emotion was present in her voice. Shame?

"What made you decide to go there?" This wasn't the time to pour on more guilt, so he checked his frustration.

"I knew the baby was coming soon and I—" her voice dipped low "—missed my own mom, so I went to the place we spread her ashes."

"It's understandable." He knew her mother had died many years ago. Other than that, Cheyenne didn't say much about her family. Any time the subject came up, she got quiet.

"Is it?" she quipped. "My water broke and I went into labor. There was no one around to help and I had to hike down the falls area. I ran in between contractions. Once I got in cell range, I called 911, but it was irresponsible of me to go there by myself."

She'd tried to call him almost a dozen times. He'd missed every single attempt. Reminding her of that now didn't seem like it would help much. So he held his tongue.

"You couldn't have known that would have happened, Cheyenne. We both know you would never do anything on purpose to hurt the baby." His words didn't seem to sink in. She appeared determined to punish herself for the mistake.

"The EMT gave me oxygen and I was in pretty bad shape by the time I got to the hospital. I guess I dehydrated out there faster than I realized I would." She turned her face away from him and it took every ounce of strength inside him not to walk over to her and offer comfort. "That's about as much as I remember. I was too far along for the epidural and then there were complications with the birth. The rest is all like a nightmare. I have fuzzy bits of being told the baby was breech. Another of a masked doctor leaning over me right before everything went dark."

Riggs sat there, listening to what had to have been one of the worst moments of his wife's life. Knowing full well that he should have been right beside her. Guilt was a knife stab in the center of his chest.

"People make mistakes, Cheyenne," he said after a few thoughtful minutes. "You never would have done anything to hurt her," he repeated, hoping this time he could convince her what happened wasn't her fault.

She glanced up at him with red-rimmed eyes. Her chin quivered but not a teardrop fell.

"You did everything right. You couldn't have known how events would unfold. What happened isn't your fault," he said in a low voice. He couldn't deny that he was being a hypocrite. He absolutely believed everything that had gone wrong with the birth and his marriage had to be his fault.

She wiped away a rogue tear and stood up straighter. A sip of coffee seemed to be what she needed to regain control of her emotions. "I owed you that conversation, Riggs. But now I'd like to move on to talk about Ally before it's too late."

Everything Riggs wanted to say died on his tongue as her walls came up again.

"You don't really believe what you said about Ally earlier, do you?" he asked, wishing they didn't have to move on from the first real conversation they'd had about that night.

Her eyebrow shot up as she took a sip of coffee.

"That her phone is turned off or ran out of battery." He figured the subject of the baby was off-limits from here on out and this didn't seem the right time to ask why she'd pushed him away after losing their little girl. Cheyenne was right about one thing. All of their attention needed to go toward finding Ally.

"Wishful thinking," she admitted. "I'm at a loss as to where she could be, though."

"Without her cell phone records, we don't know who she spoke to or texted with other than what she sent us," he said. "The nurses aren't talking but they are covering for someone. E-cig Nurse brought that point home."

"My guess is the doctor who delivered…" she flashed eyes at him before continuing "…made some kind of mistake and they don't want word to get out."

"Tight-knit communities have a habit of sticking together," he pointed out. He should know. He'd grown up in one. Katy Gulch was a cattle ranching community that had each other's backs. Not to say there weren't disagreements or that people always got along. It was a lot like having siblings. They might mess with each other from time to time but no one else could. Period. Riggs had five brothers who would prove his comment true and he felt the same about them. Even his most troubled brother, Garrett, had come back into the fold recently. Now that their father was gone, they needed all hands on deck in order to run KBR, as well as be there for their grieving mother.

Granted, Margaret O'Connor was one of the strongest people he'd ever known. She would balk at the idea of needing help and would never ask Riggs or his brothers to give up their lives to work the ranch out of obligation. And that was one of the most beautiful things to come out of everything that had happened. Each brother had come home because he wanted to and was wrapping up other work obligations to transition into working the ranch full-time.

Riggs had always stayed at KBR. There'd never been another job for him. He loved the family land and had a great deal of pride working in the family business. His side job as a volunteer firefighter was something he did to give back to the community.

But there'd never been a question in his mind of where his heart truly was. And clearly, that was all he knew in life because it was the only thing that made sense to him now.

"I know nurses stick together. Ally has mentioned they have to, with some of the doctors who can be jerks," she said, breaking into his thoughts. "Now that I think about it, there was a traveling doctor who could be a real horse's backside."

"He probably didn't think he had to worry about making nice if he only worked there to cover for other doctors," he said.

An idea he couldn't afford was forming in his head. One that gave him a sliver of hope there was a mistake somewhere that meant his daughter was still alive. Riggs shut it down before it had time to take hold. The ache in his chest and the hole in his heart told him he couldn't bear to lose her twice. He'd already lost her mother. Based on the dead look in Cheyenne's eyes, there was no hope of resurrecting their marriage.

Shame, he thought. He might have been doing what he considered to be "the right thing" by asking her to marry him six and a half months ago, but he took the vow he'd made seriously. Sickness and in health. Richer or poorer. 'Til death do us part.

That was the deal.

Cheyenne had to make that decision for herself. She'd been clear that she'd only married him because of the pregnancy, despite convincing him otherwise when she'd taken the ring—a ring that was no longer on her finger, he noticed. He couldn't make her want to stay married to him. And to be honest, his ego didn't want to have to.

Riggs's cell buzzed. He fished it out of his pocket and checked the screen. "It's Colton."

Cheyenne moved a few steps closer, still keeping him at arm's length as she white-knuckled her coffee mug.

"Hey, what's up?" he asked Colton.

"I have news." The sound of Colton's voice caused Riggs's stomach to drop.

"Let me put you on speaker," Riggs said with a quick glance toward Cheyenne. She was chewing the inside of her jaw, a nervous tic he'd noticed during their marriage.

He held the phone in between them and hit the screen. "We're both here."

"You might want to sit down first," Colton warned.

Cheyenne didn't argue. She immediately walked over to the small dining table next to the kitchen, and then sat down. She removed her handbag from her shoulder, placing it on the back of the chair. Ozzy seemed content to stay inside, not bothering to peek out.

Riggs took the opposite seat, breaking the five-foot rule Cheyenne seemed to have imposed on their proximity. He couldn't help it. The café table wasn't but two feet around.

"We're sitting," Riggs said to his brother.

"Community Friends Hospital came up in connection with the alpaca ranch we've been investigating." Colton paused, letting those words sink in.

A baby ring connected to the hospital where Riggs's daughter was born.

Cheyenne looked more confused than ever, so he gave her the quick rundown that his brother Garrett had been investigating their father's murder and was led to an alpaca farm that was a front for an illegal adoption ring.

"Does that mean there's a possibility she's alive?" Cheyenne immediately asked.

"I don't know what it means yet. I won't stop investigating until we find out, though," Colton said.

"Ally's text message was hopeful," Cheyenne said, her voice laced with some of that hope. "She said my mind would be blown. I assumed it meant I would be happy."

Hope was dangerous. Losing their child had knocked her completely on her backside once. Riggs didn't want to give false hope and yet he couldn't bring himself to quash the only life he'd heard in her voice since the birth.

"And I remember hearing her cry in the labor and delivery room," she added. "The nurse said I probably wasn't remembering right because of the medication I was under, but I swear I heard my baby cry."

Hearing those words for the first time was a gut punch. The air in the room thinned. The hole in his chest widened. Without realizing, he'd fisted his hands. Cheyenne had heard their daughter cry?

The little girl could very well be alive.

Chapter 6

"Do you remember the name of the nurse who assisted with the birth?" Colton asked.

Riggs wondered if the information would be on her discharge papers.

"There was a shift change. I think. My mind isn't so clear on the order or some of the details. Okay, most of the details," Cheyenne admitted. She stared at the phone on the table like it was a bomb about to detonate. "But that doesn't mean what I do know isn't true."

"If it's any consolation, I believe you," Colton said.

"So do I," Riggs agreed.

"It means more than you could know." Chin up, she brought a hand up to cover her heart.

Riggs didn't want to point out there wasn't a judge in the state who would take the word of someone who'd been given enough drugs to make her thoughts blurry and lose the chain of events. She'd be deemed an unreliable witness and any decent attorney would have a field day with her in court if she pursued a civil case against the hospital. Most prosecutors would refuse to take on the case to start with.

Riggs had access to the best lawyers in Texas and he'd have no qualms about draining his bank account if it meant bringing his child home alive or making certain this didn't happen to another family. It was clear something was up with the hospital and the nursing staff. He didn't have to be in law enforcement to suspect Ally must have uncovered something others didn't want to get out. E-cig Nurse had confirmed their fears there.

The question lingered in the back of his mind. Could his child be alive?

Was that the reason for the medication? Had Cheyenne really needed it? Or was she given it to numb her mind and dull her senses? It sure was a convenient excuse. It gave the hospital an out, too, because all anyone had to say was that she was under the influence and her memories couldn't be trusted. Now that he really thought about it, he should bring in the family attorney to put some heat on the hospital's internal investigation.

"Didn't you say your regular doctor wasn't on call the night of the delivery?" Riggs asked.

"That's right. I asked them if we could wait but everything was already happening so fast the nurse said we had to get going or risk losing the baby." Cheyenne exhaled and her shoulders slumped forward.

Riggs had to fight every instinct inside him not to reach out and be her comfort. He quickly reminded himself his touch was the last thing she would want. She'd been clear where the two of them stood. Divorce.

The kiss didn't change anything.

He tried to convince himself the only reason he wanted to protect her came down to the same basics of why he would try to help anyone or anything in need. It was ingrained in him to help someone who was suffering. His family always went out of their way to offer aid. It was part of Riggs's DNA—a part he had no qualms with.

"Do you remember what the nurse on duty looked like?" Colton asked.

"Not really. I think I remember hoop earrings. Like from the 1970s." She squeezed her eyes shut like she had to block everything else out to concentrate. When she opened her eyes, she frowned. "Sounds like someone from a hallucination, doesn't it?"

"Don't be hard on yourself. Every memory is important. All it takes is one detail to blow a case wide open," Colton said reassuringly.

Cheyenne nodded and compressed her lips. She was clearly frustrated with herself.

"Can you make a guess as to her age?" Colton asked.

"Not young," she said quickly. "Not too old, either. I'd say somewhere in her late thirties to early forties."

"Good." Colton was quiet for a few seconds. "What do you remember about the doctor on duty?"

"Sandy-blond hair. He had blue eyes, cobalt," she explained. "He was definitely older. Maybe early to mid-forties. His name was Dr. Fortner and he only works at the hospital on a rotating basis. He'll be easy enough to look up on my discharge papers."

"Does that mean he works at other hospitals, as well?" Colton asked.

"I believe so. Honestly, once I was told my baby died, I blanked out on everything else going on. I went into a state of shock that I seriously doubt I've recovered from yet." She chewed on the inside of her cheek while staring at the phone.

A hammer slammed into Riggs's chest at hearing the details. He did his level best not to let his anger show. Right now, he needed a clear head. Flying off the handle had been Garrett's gig. Riggs used to have a temper, too. He'd watched how it could destroy relationships between friends and brothers, and had forced himself to get his temper under control. This situation tested his resolve.

In fact, he wanted nothing more than to plant his fist through a wall to release some of the tension that pulled his shoulder blades taut. A blinding pain hit square in between his eyes as white-hot anger engulfed him at the thought there could be foul play when it came to his child.

The pain Cheyenne must have been in during that moment wasn't lost on him and he suddenly understood the dark circles cradling her eyes. He still didn't like the fact she'd pushed him away in the process but at least he was developing an understanding of the depths of her pain.

He'd lost a child, too. And a wife in the process. So he knew about pain.

"Is there anything else you remember about the hospital, the staff or the birth?" Colton continued.

Part of Riggs wanted to stop this conversation right here and now. Watching Cheyenne relive what had to be one of the worst moments of her life twisted the knot in his gut. Not being able to take away her pain or make a difference messed with the knot even more. He'd asked for a meeting with hospital administration and that was still pending their internal investigation. His lawyer should be able to get things moving.

No one should have to watch someone they cared about recount the loss of something so wanted, so loved.

Strangely enough, it was Riggs who'd had to talk Cheyenne into keeping the baby. Early on, she'd brought up adoption as an alternative. He still remembered the moment she'd told him she was pregnant, like it was yesterday. The look of shock on her face was still etched in his thoughts. She'd sat on his couch, her feet tucked underneath her sweet round bottom.

"I have to tell you something and I have no idea how you're going to react."

He'd set a cold beer down in front of her, her favorite longneck. Instead of picking it up, she'd stared at it with a look that said she wished she could partake but wouldn't be for quite some time.

The move had puzzled him.

That was when he'd really looked at her. There'd been something different about her from the moment she'd walked into his house, weeks before that, too. Something he couldn't quite pinpoint. Glow wasn't the right word. Although, looking back, it wasn't a bad place to start, either. There was a flush to her cheeks that made her even more beautiful. Her eyes looked a little tired but that only made her more attractive to his thinking.

Then it had dawned on him. *Pregnant.*

He'd let her tell him the news in her own time. It had taken her twenty more minutes to work up the courage. He'd reassured her that everything happened for a reason and a baby was always a good thing. No, it wasn't planned or expected. In fact, they'd been careful to avoid this very thing. Birth control had failed and he figured he shouldn't be having sex with someone he couldn't handle the risks with.

So yes, it came out of the blue. Yes, it was a huge surprise. But no, it wasn't a bad thing.

In fact, he'd been planning to tell her for days by then that he'd fallen in love with her. After hearing the news, he'd figured he might as well go all in and ask her to marry him. They were stupidly in love. At least he was.

The second she'd thrown her arms around his neck and told him she loved him he'd been hooked. Hooked on her. Hooked on getting married. Hooked on starting a family. And the same candle that had burned so brightly burned out just as fast.

Cheyenne couldn't risk hope.

There was no way she was going to nurse the possibility of her baby being alive before getting absolute, undeniable proof. And yet, her heart argued against such caution. It wanted to believe the baby had somehow survived. But that also meant she'd been taken from Cheyenne. In a hospital. With multiple people either directly involved or looking the other way. White-hot anger boiled her blood as she suspected a conspiracy.

Strange as it sounded, she'd heard stories on the news that made this seem not just plausible but likely. Or was that her heart running after what it wanted to be true? She settled on likely.

Riggs filled his brother in on their encounter at the nurse station and then the nurse who met up with them outside the building. Colton promised to follow up.

"A deputy is almost at the hospital. He got sidetracked on a call earlier. I'll update him before he arrives." Colton didn't hesitate and she appreciated her brother-in-law's fast action.

She blew on the surface of the hot coffee, watching the

steam form a sail before returning right back to where
it started. She welcomed the burn on her throat as she
took a sip of the fresh brew. Coffee was a funny thing in
times of stress. She hadn't started drinking it until two
weeks ago. Strangely, it had given her something to do
and made her miss Riggs a little less. *Put on a pot of coffee* had been her mantra recently. Maybe it was time to
adopt a new routine. Take up tea drinking again. Something needed to change, because her mind was wandering
into dangerous territory, speculating her daughter could
have lived, and she needed to shake things up.

She glanced over at Riggs. She'd been unable to look
at him much of the time when she was speaking to his
brother. The way he clenched his back teeth and his hands
fisted, she realized how much he must be hurting, too.

The realization hit hard. She had somehow been able
to convince herself he would be relieved that she was letting him out of the marriage. She had told herself that he
wouldn't be as devastated about losing their child. Well,
now she really did feel like a jerk.

Of course, he would be hurting. Based on the look on
his face now, she had hugely underestimated how much
he would be affected. Didn't change the fact she knew
in her heart of hearts he'd be better off without her in his
life. Despite her heart trying to play devil's advocate, she
wouldn't go back on her decision to let him out of the
marriage commitment.

Riggs ended the call with a promise to let Colton know
if by some chance Ally showed up.

"I feel like I should be doing something more," she
said to Riggs.

"You are," he said. "You're here, taking care of Ozzy
while we figure out our next move."

Her stomach growled despite feeling like she wouldn't be able to get a bite of food down.

"The other thing you can do is make sure you're keeping up your strength," he said without missing a beat. "Is there anything in the fridge to work with?"

"To be honest, I haven't really checked," she admitted. "I've been kind of checked out ever since leaving the hospital. In fact, I could probably use a shower."

"Why don't you go clean up while I poke around in the kitchen to see if there's anything in here to throw together for a meal." He stood up and walked over to the fridge, moving with athletic grace. She forced her gaze away from his strong back—a back that she'd memorized. Every curve and scar was forever etched in her mind.

Rather than let herself continue down that road, she pushed to standing and headed for the shower. She stopped in the hallway. "You'll come get me if anything happens, right?"

"Of course. Take your time. I'm here. I've got nowhere else to be," he reassured.

Somehow, she doubted that. His family ranch boomed with activity and he'd been checking into his father's murder along with the others. Finn O'Connor was a great man. She wished she'd spent more time getting to know him. Now she wished she'd had more time with her father-in-law.

"Thank you," she said. "For sticking around. I don't have a right to ask anything of you, so it means a lot that you're willing to stay."

The look of disappointment on his face as he nodded got her feet moving in the opposite direction. She needed to put some distance between them before she let her guard down even more. Being around Riggs was dangerous. Just being in the same room with him started chipping away at her carefully constructed walls.

No good could come of making herself vulnerable. Nothing about their situation had changed. She was done with trying to have a family and Riggs was just getting started.

Twenty minutes later, she was showered, toweled off, and dressed in something besides joggers. The sundress hugged her curves and fell midcalf. She threw on a little lip gloss and concealer. With just those two moves, she started feeling better. There was something about getting out of bed and putting on a little makeup that lifted her spirits even just a tiny bit. She reminded herself that when this was over and she and Riggs went back to their separate lives, she needed to force herself to get out of bed and get moving. Tie the knot. Hang on.

That, of course, could only happen if Ally turned out to be all right. Where could she be? It was well past four o'clock and her friend was still missing.

They'd driven past all the possible stop-offs. It was already coming up on dinnertime and there was still no word. Part of Cheyenne wanted to sit down at the table with her phone and call every business up and down the roads leading to the hospital.

Colton was a good sheriff. She had to give him time to do his job. She trusted him. All the O'Connor men were trustworthy, even Garrett, whom she knew the least. From everything she'd seen and heard, he was a good person underneath his tough exterior. Of course, he'd met the love of his life according to Riggs, and that had caused him to turn a new leaf. Good for him.

Cheyenne ran a brush through her still-damp hair before straightening her dress. This was as good as it got, she thought, before joining Riggs in the kitchen.

"I noticed you barely touched your coffee. I can heat it up or grab a glass of water for you instead." He motioned toward the full mug.

"It's okay." She took in a deep breath. The smell of food was actually making her hungry despite the nausea she'd felt in the shower a few minutes ago. "Something smells amazing in here."

"It's a breakfast skillet. My mother used to make these when we were little. You basically throw any chopped vegetables you can find along with some spinach and green onion into a pan of eggs and sausage."

"We have sausage?" she asked.

"You had ham, so I made that work."

This reminded her of all those late Sunday morning breakfasts shared out on the back patio. Or in bed. The latter was her favorite. Then there was the homemade pizza in bed after a long session of making love.

She sighed. She'd really tucked those memories down deep in the last couple of weeks. Seeing Riggs in the kitchen, watching him as he moved so effortlessly, caused her chest to squeeze. She thought about the phone call she needed to return from her divorce attorney to keep the ball rolling. She couldn't make her hands move to pick up the phone if her life depended on it. There was too much going on, and it didn't make sense to push things forward until they knew what happened to their daughter and brought Ally home safely.

So she made a decision. There was no harm in asking if Riggs was on the same page. She would respect his position. Either way, she needed to know.

"I was thinking that while we're investigating this...

situation…maybe it's for the best if we put the divorce on hold," she said and then held her breath.

He didn't turn around, so she couldn't see his reaction. He stopped what he was doing for a few moments and she had second thoughts about what she'd just said. The last thing she wanted to do was cause him additional pain. They were already knee-deep in it.

"Look, I didn't mean that we should stop altogether, it's just…" She couldn't find the right words.

"The investigation seems more important right now." His tone was unreadable. "Is that how you really see it?"

She searched for any signs of judgment in his voice and decided she couldn't find any. He had his poker face on.

"Yes. But we don't have to wait. I was just thinking out loud," she said. More like she was speaking on impulse.

"I didn't have any interest in divorcing in the first place. This has all been your idea." He shrugged a shoulder like it was no big deal. Was that true? She couldn't imagine it being so. And yet it felt like someone sucked all the air out of the room.

"Okay," she said.

"Okay," he confirmed.

The divorce dropped in priority. Nothing was more important than joining forces to find out if their daughter was still alive. Could she risk hope?

Chapter 7

"There you go." Riggs plated his culinary masterpiece and set it down on the counter-height bar along with a bottle of sriracha. Cooking had distracted him for a few minutes from all the thoughts circling in his mind. Concentrating too hard on one subject was the fastest way to stay stumped. He always did his best thinking out on the land, away from distractions. Out there, his mind cleared all the clutter and answers came to him.

"Would you mind handing me a fork?" Cheyenne asked. He couldn't count the number of times she'd said the same thing when he'd cooked breakfast on the ranch.

"Where are they?" Walking down memory lane was probably a bad idea.

"Second drawer. Or you could just grab one from the dishwasher." She fidgeted in her seat like when she was out of her comfort zone. Any time he'd tried to do something for her in the past year she'd done the same. He understood on some level, considering she was one of the most independent people he'd ever met. She'd been an only child with working parents and had learned to do things for herself early on. But they were a couple and couples did little things for one another.

He located the drawer, grabbed two forks and then handed one over. Once again, when their fingers grazed, electricity shot through him. He chalked it up to residual attraction and did his level best to put it out of his mind, which was difficult with her in the room.

During their marriage, he'd made a vow to himself that he would get her used to letting someone else do for her every once in a while. Although she was one of the most giving people he'd ever met, he'd been caught off guard at how bad she was at receiving. He'd attributed it to her fierce need for independence and left it at that.

Now he wondered if there wasn't something more to the story. Because she seemed downright uncomfortable accepting help, which would make sense if he was a stranger. Not so much considering they'd signed up to be partners in life.

Then again, if they saw life through the same lens, she wouldn't be asking for a divorce in the first place. When times were tough, the O'Connors came together. Garrett was living proof that no matter how far someone strayed from the fold, he or she would travel as far as necessary to come home and help out during a crisis. It was as much in their DNA as chivalry and working the land.

He fixed his own plate, opting to stand in the kitchen and eat.

"I didn't think I could eat a bite and here I've cleaned

my plate," Cheyenne said after a few minutes of silence. "At least let me do the dishes."

True enough, her plate was empty.

"It's no trouble," he said. There were only two plates, a couple of forks and a skillet. "Won't take but a second to rinse these off and put them in the dishwasher."

"It's clean," she said.

He cracked a smile and shook his head.

"Don't tell me you emptied it…"

"I was looking for a pan." A tiny burst of pride filled his chest that she sounded pleased. He'd been brought up to be self-sufficient just as his brothers had. He shouldn't want to make her happy and told himself it was nothing more than reflex.

"Well, thank you. You didn't have to do that." Cheyenne moved from her bar stool and then brought her plate around.

In the tiny kitchen he could breathe in her clean and citrusy scent. To clear his head, he moved past her and managed to bump into her in the process. Not his best move. More of that electricity rocketed through him, awakening parts that needed to stay dormant.

What could he say?

He was affected by Cheyenne. It was half the reason he'd gone ahead and proposed to her the minute after finding out she was pregnant. Had he been freaked out? Yes. Did he know what to say or do? No. He'd gone with his heart and the fact that he'd never met a woman who could knock him off balance with one look before. The instant he'd laid eyes on her, he knew she was going to be important in his life.

People talked about love at first sight and he used to believe they were crazy. Then he'd met Cheyenne. He'd been hit with something so different there wasn't anything to compare the feeling to. He'd tried and failed numerous times. There was no rhyme or reason to the heart.

Looking at her was the equivalent of a lightning strike on a sunny day. Actually, more than that, but he struggled to put the feeling into words. Riggs was a man of action. So he'd gone out on a limb and asked her to marry him.

Being married to Cheyenne had been heaven on earth. At least on his side. Clearly, she felt differently. It might be pride talking, but he didn't want someone to stay married to him out of obligation. Their relationship had been the real deal to him.

"I better let Ozzy outside," she said, exiting the kitchen as fast as humanly possible after loading her plate into the dishwasher. She scurried over to the table and pulled him from her handbag. She must have as much rolling through her thoughts as he had, especially after the news about the alpaca farm.

The little dog started yelping.

"You need to do your business," she said to him, holding him tightly to her chest. She walked out the side door and immediately heard the sound of tires burning rubber.

Riggs jumped into action, bolting toward the door. Adrenaline kicked in and his pulse thumped.

Cheyenne dove inside and he caught her before she landed, softening her fall with his body. For a split second, their eyes met and locked. Hers were a mix of fear and something else…regret? Or maybe Riggs saw what he wanted instead of what was really there. It could explain their marriage and recently paused divorce. Ozzy had been spared from being accidentally tossed across the room by Riggs's fast thinking.

Not wanting the vehicle to get away, Riggs rolled onto

his side. Cheyenne scrambled off him and comforted the little dog, who stood there shaking. No need to take him outside again. Ozzy had done his business right then and there.

Riggs hopped to his feet in one swift motion. He bolted to the window. Swiped the curtain to one side with his right hand. Too late. There wasn't a car or truck in sight.

One good thing to come out of this situation was that no one was hurt.

He fished for his cell phone and updated Colton via text.

"Someone is watching the house," Cheyenne said. Her voice was stilted. Shock?

"I should have seen this coming," Riggs said along with a few choice words he didn't care to repeat in mixed company.

Colton's response was instant. Get out of the house.

"No one tried to shoot." He'd expected to hear a shotgun blast.

"That was my first thought, too." Cheyenne picked up the little dog and took him to the sink. She gently cleaned him before returning him to her handbag.

By the time she returned to the living room, Riggs was already on his hands and knees cleaning up after the little guy.

"Here. I can—"

"It's not a big deal, Cheyenne. Seriously. Cooking up a little breakfast and cleaning a pan and a pair of plates are nothing to make a fuss about, either." The words came out a little more bitter than he'd intended. What could he say? He was taking the breakup of his marriage hard and his mind was reeling after all the new information they had.

"Oh." She stopped in her tracks.

"Stay below the window line in case someone comes back on foot." He motioned toward the front windows.

"Right." She dropped down almost immediately. "I wasn't trying to offend you, by the way. It's just…"

"What? Weird for the man you married to make a meal for you?" He sat back on his heels. He shouldn't have said that. It was out of bounds. Their situation was complicated, and he didn't want to make it worse. For the time being, they were working together. "Forget I said that, okay?"

"I can't." She folded her arms across her chest like she was defending herself from the world. "Like I can't forget a lot of things said between us in the past few weeks."

"What has been said between us? You haven't given me the time of day in case you hadn't noticed. I've been told I'm getting a divorce and I'm still scratching my head as to why you went down that road." He issued a sharp sigh, needing to get a handle on his outburst. It sure as hell wouldn't make anything better between them and he didn't want to ruin all the ground they'd been making today.

But what could he say? He couldn't exactly take any of it back and wouldn't want to anyway. Part of him needed her to know exactly how he felt. It wasn't like he'd been given the chance to clear the air before the call from his attorney came to let him know what was going down.

"Mind if we have this conversation at a later date? Right now, all I can think about is finding my friend and possibly getting answers to what happened to our daughter." There was no anger in her words, just resolve.

"Why not." It wasn't like he had any easy answers, either. Even if they could get back together and that was a laughable *if*, how would he ever believe her again?

* * *

Cheyenne got on her hands and knees beside Riggs and finished wiping up Ozzy's mess. Being this close to Riggs was a problem, but she needed to learn to deal with it. If she wasn't attracted to him or didn't feel a pull so strong her body ached to touch him, she would be worried. There'd been enough attraction and chemistry between them for her to throw all logic aside, decide to have a baby together, and get married.

Thinking all that would dissipate overnight would be downright crazy. Even now, her stomach clenched and her chest squeezed in his masculine presence.

Taking in a deep breath, Cheyenne tried to rebalance but only ushered in his scent. He was all outdoors, campfires, and dark roast coffee. Speaking of the latter, it had always tasted better on his tongue. He was the reason she'd taken up coffee drinking because she missed tasting it on his lips so much her heart ached.

"Where do we go now?" she asked sitting back on her heels.

"We could go back to our house."

She started shaking her head before he could finish. It was one thing to be around him for the foreseeable future. It was quite another to go back to the home they'd shared on the ranch that belonged to his family, a ranch she'd loved.

"Hotel. There's a decent one over by the highway that has suites. We could rent one of those just until we get answers or Ally contacts us," he offered.

"I'll leave her a note…in case." She stood. "I've already sent a few texts, so no need to go down that road again. Once she turns on her cell, she'll know I've been trying to reach her. I know the odds of that happening aren't great, but I have to find some reason to hope she'll turn up."

It was wishful thinking on Cheyenne's part to believe it could be that simple. That Ally would somehow magically realize her cell was off, turn it on, and return home with one of her you-won't-believe-how-stupid-I-can-be stories. Ally had managed to lock her keys in the car while it was still running. She was probably half the reason most new cars made it impossible to do that now.

Riggs nodded.

"There was this time Ally decided to cook Thanksgiving dinner," Cheyenne started. "She invited me and this guy she had a crush on to eat with her. She wanted to do everything and wouldn't even let me bring dinner rolls. So I walk in with a bottle of wine that I could barely afford because we were being grown-ups, and I couldn't figure out why her house didn't smell like the holiday. You know?"

He cocked an eyebrow, clearly confused as to where this conversation was going. It was one of the many things she appreciated about him before. She could come out of the blue with a topic and he would go along with it until she made sense.

"I couldn't figure out what was missing. There were a few familiar smells, but it wasn't as if I walked in and was hit with the amazing food aromas like when my mom was alive and we did Thanksgiving. I chalked it up to my memory being faulty." She paused long enough to finger the charm on her bracelet. "At Ally's there was corn heating on the stove, and she'd bought a pumpkin pie for dessert. She'd made the green bean casserole the night before. The stuffing was in the bird, so I just went with it. Then she goes to take the turkey out of the oven and realizes she never turned it on."

She chuckled as a stray tear streaked her cheek at the bittersweet memory.

"And that's Ally, you know?" she continued. "When she was on duty at her job, she was on point. Nothing got past her, and she was there for her patients. Sure, a couple of doctors gave her a hard time now and then but that was the nature of her work. Once she walked out of that hospital, totally different story. So much so, that early on I refused to allow her to bring candles in our dorm room in college for fear she would burn the entire building down because she forgot to blow one out."

Riggs studied her thoughtfully. There was no judgment in his eyes now. Just a hint of compassion.

"You're hoping this is one of those times despite what we already know," he finally said, catching her drift.

"Maybe she got sidetracked or forgot to tell us that she was still with the guy in Dallas. Maybe he called and she's on her way there. Maybe the battery ran out on her phone." Chin to chest, she tried to hide the tears that rolled down her face. The thought anything bad might have happened to her best friend ripped her insides out. The fact Ally was trying to help Cheyenne wasn't lost on her. The weight of it was crushing.

In the next second, Riggs was there. He looped his arms around her and hauled her to his chest, where she felt the most at home she'd ever felt. "I've never been one to believe in miracles, but I sure wouldn't be against being proven wrong this once."

Cheyenne nodded. She wiped away a few more rogue tears as they sprung from her eyes.

The sound of a car pulling into the gravel drive broke

them apart too soon. Riggs's movements were smooth and predator-like as he bolted to the window. Crouching low, he peered through the window, barely moving the curtain.

"Someone's using the drive to turn around," he said. "It's a sedan loaded up with a family."

Cheyenne let out the breath she'd been holding. A miracle was probably too much to hope for.

Wherever they were going, they needed to get to it. The thought someone had been watching the house and could still be sent an icy chill down her spine.

She wondered if they had been followed home from the hospital?

"I find it interesting that someone started watching the house after our visit to the hospital," she said to Riggs.

"I'd like to know what Renee, Sherry, and Becca have to say to law enforcement." Riggs walked over to the kitchen and drained his coffee cup. "Pack up whatever you need and let's head out of here. Colton requested the place be looked after by local police. Manpower is limited and there's only so much cooperation he can get while also requesting his deputy be permitted to interview nurses."

"As sheriff, can't he investigate anyone he wants to?" she asked.

"He's certainly able to follow a lead wherever it takes him, but gaining local support gives him more resources to work with." He set the coffee cup down and gave her the look she recognized as needing to get a move on.

"I'll be five minutes." She circled back to her bedroom and, true to her word, had an overnight bag filled in the time she'd promised. She closed the door to her bedroom and paused in front of Ally's room. It dawned on her there might be a clue inside.

The door was ajar from the time she'd opened it this morning. It seemed wrong to go snooping around in her best friend's bedroom, but if she could find one clue, it would be worth a few minutes of discomfort.

Inside was dark, with the blackout curtains still closed. Ally flipped on the light thinking her roommate would be all kinds of angry if she walked through the front door about now. Since the probability of that happening was about as high as Colonel Sanders pulling up out front to personally deliver a bucket of chicken, she shut down the guilt and pushed ahead.

The bed wasn't made. No surprise there. Ally normally jumped out of bed and ran straight to the shower. Her habits hadn't changed all that much. Her laptop sat on top of her bed.

Cheyenne walked over and tucked it inside her bag. She might be able to figure out the password. Guilt got the best of her, so she pulled out her cell and tried to text Ally one more time.

I'm going through your room.
Sorry.
Taking your laptop.
Pls respond.

No response came. Cheyenne issued a sharp sigh. At least some of her guilt for going through Ally's personal belongings eased after reaching out.

A dark thought someone might have Ally's cell phone and be reading the texts struck. It wouldn't be a good idea to lay out their plans. Cheyenne decided not to mention anything about leaving.

A handwritten note would do the trick.

She moved to Ally's dresser and found a scrap of paper along with a pen. She clicked the pen and scribbled a message. *Leaving for a few days. Call me. Text me. I'm worried.*

The note was cryptic enough not to broadcast Cheyenne's next steps and yet got the point across. The creepy feeling someone could break into the house and read the note raised goose bumps on her arms. The whole situation was surreal. This kind of thing only happened in the movies. It didn't happen to normal, law-abiding citizens.

And yet, she knew on some level crime didn't discriminate. Criminals were everywhere and would take advantage of anyone. But an O'Connor? Surely the name would be a deterrent.

It dawned on her that she was still using her maiden name. Would that make a difference? No one would mess with an O'Connor baby. Or would they? She thought about what had happened to Riggs's sister.

Wouldn't the person be in touch to demand some type of ransom by now if that was the case?

Chapter 8

Riggs caught himself tapping the toe of his boot on the beige tile in the kitchen. Impatience edged in when Cheyenne didn't return after the promised five minutes. Ten passed before the toe tapping had started. He realized he was gripping the bullnose-edge granite like a vise at the fifteen mark.

Fighting the urge to traipse down the hallway and see what was taking so long, he started whistling. The next thing he knew, Ozzy scampered over and sat at his feet. Looked like the little yippy dog had some training after all.

Riggs bent over to pick up the small animal. Ozzy growled before backing away.

Maybe not.

Riggs's thoughts shifted to the events of the day. He had no idea what Ally's personal life was like. Cheyenne had mentioned her best friend a few times before arranging a meetup. His impression of Ally had been good. She promised to be an amazing godmother after Cheyenne had asked.

Ally had the kind of personality most would describe as bubbly. Cheyenne joked that only happened after a decent amount of caffeine, which Riggs could relate to. The three of them had chatted easily about plans for the baby. Cheyenne had apologized to her friend for what felt like a dozen times for not having a traditional wedding or having Ally as maid of honor.

To make up for it, Cheyenne had asked Ally to be godmother to their child. Ally accepted and did nothing but support Cheyenne as far as Riggs could tell. He'd had a good feeling about his wife's best friend, and he was usually spot-on with his assessments when he met people. Ally was what most would call a pure soul. The thought of something bad happening to her was a gut punch. Not just because she was Cheyenne's best friend, although that was part of it. Because Ally was a good person who deserved the life she wanted.

He stopped himself right there before he got too far ahead of himself. They didn't know anything for certain despite his gut telling him this situation had gone south. The chilly reaction he and Cheyenne had received at the nurse station and then with E-cig Nurse outside drove home the point. Not to mention the fact Ally had gone off the grid. No cell phone contact after sending the texts to him and Cheyenne. No witnesses so far. No sightings.

And now the vehicle that had been watching the house.

So yeah, he expected the worst when it came to news about her and prayed like the dickens he was wrong. Despite her strength, Cheyenne could only handle so much. There was a something in her past that he hadn't been able to break through while they were together. He'd figured they had a lifetime to get to know the nuances of each other's personalities.

When they'd first met, she'd reacted more like a wounded animal who needed protection and was the last to know it. Every time he got close to her, she backed away. It was okay. He understood being broken after her mom's death. He understood needing time. And he certainly understood needing space. The last thing he'd wanted to do was spook her away by trying to get too close too fast. Because he also knew in his heart that when she truly opened up to him, she would absolutely be worth the wait.

"I found her laptop." Cheyenne bounded into the room and patted her weekend bag. She no longer looked like she'd jump out of her skin at the slightest noise. It was progress and he'd take it. Getting her to relax and trust him might just get her talking about why she thought she was protecting him by pushing him away.

"Any chance you know the passwords, too?" He walked over and took the bag so she wouldn't have to carry that and her purse once she put the devil dog in it.

"I wish. I know her personal information like her birthday and first pet name. Maybe I can make an educated guess," she offered as Ozzy started running around her ankles, threatening to nip. "What's wrong with him?"

"No clue. I whistled and he came. When I tried to pick him up, he went psycho." Riggs was normally good with four-legged critters. Dogs were his favorite and there were several on the ranch who preferred living in the barn and bunkhouse. He didn't have time for one of his own. Maybe someday he would. He'd been thinking of surprising Cheyenne with a puppy once the baby came.

"Ready when you are," she said, picking up the devil dog and then tucking him inside her handbag where he settled.

Riggs took note of the behavior. Dogs were den animals, and this guy must feel out of his element now, with Ally gone and a strange male in the house. Not to mention the fact he didn't seem too keen on Cheyenne being there. Based on what she'd said so far, it didn't appear like she'd left her room much except to heat a leftover or grab a cup of coffee or take the occasional shower.

Under the circumstances, Riggs would cut the little guy some slack.

"Keep the dog in your purse. He settles down inside there. I'll go start the pickup truck and then text you when it's safe to come out."

She cocked her head to one side but then nodded with a confused look on her face.

Good. That meant she hadn't caught the underlying meaning in what he was saying. Yes, it was dangerous to leave the house. It was also risky to start his vehicle and he planned to perform a couple of safety checks before hopping in and starting the engine.

"I won't be but a minute." He waited for the okay, which she gave, before heading outside.

First, he stepped outside and beside his truck to block anyone's shot from the road. There were a few cars on the street zipping by. For his taste, this was a busy street, but he lived on a ranch where he didn't have to see another vehicle or person for days on end if it suited him.

By town standards, the street would probably be considered normal. Nothing looked out of the ordinary, but he'd learned a long time ago not to trust appearances. If someone wanted to climb on top of a roof and hide behind a chimney, he could be picked off without ever knowing what hit him.

He ran his hand along the bottom of the truck, feeling for anything out of the ordinary. If someone wanted the two of them dead, a bomb would do the trick. It would be messy, but it would blow up the evidence along with them. He rounded the front and then popped the hood.

A quick check gave him the confidence to take the driver's seat and risk starting the engine.

It hummed to life as he listened for any unusual sounds that might come right before a big boom. When he was certain it was safe, he palmed his cell and fired off a text for Cheyenne to join him.

She came out of the house so fast she forgot to lock the door behind her. Once she settled into the passenger seat, he asked for the house key.

She blinked at him and then embarrassment heated her cheeks. She was even more beautiful with her face flushed, but this wasn't the time to get sentimental or take another trip down memory lane. Their relationship was in the rearview. For now. They had come together as interested parties in an investigation. He needed to remember that when he was staring into those blue eyes or noticing how beautiful she was.

"Right. I didn't even think…" She placed the key on top of his opened hand. "Are you sure you want to get out of the vehicle?"

He didn't say better him than her. Instead, he went for "I got this."

Cheyenne held her breath waiting for Riggs to return. Her nerves were shot, and she couldn't even go there about something bad happening to Ally. The thought alone gutted her. But this was also the first time she'd felt alive in days. Weeks?

Riggs did that to her. Being around him again reminded her how much she enjoyed his company and how safe she felt around him. This situation was far from ideal, yet it felt right to do this together.

Of course it did. He was the father of her baby. An annoying voice in the back of her mind reminded her that he deserved to know what happened as much as she did. It was, after all, the reason he was here.

Being near him again also reminded her of all the things she could never have. Not because she didn't want them but because her life just wasn't designed that way. Call it destiny or fate but having a happy homelife—with kids running around and a husband who adored her even when she woke up first thing in the morning and was a hot mess—wasn't in the cards.

And, man, did Riggs deserve all those things. Even now, he stood beside her, opened doors for her and took the heavy bag so she could walk a little lighter. He was kind, considerate and wicked smart. He wasn't hurting in the looks department, either. The man was pure billboard-worthy hotness. And the only reason she thought about any of those things right now was to remind herself he deserved much more than she would ever be able to give him.

How many times had he teased her, saying he wanted enough kids to field a football team? More than she could count. He even had names for half a dozen of them already picked out despite swearing he'd never thought a day about having his own children until her pregnancy.

How could she rip his dreams, his future, out from underneath him? Because she didn't ever want to have kids again. What kind of a selfish person did that to another human being, especially one she loved?

Loved?

Did she love Riggs? It had been so easy to convince herself she did while pregnant with his child. Living together had been the definition of perfection. She'd found herself opening up to him little by little only to have it all ripped out from underneath them by losing the baby. Without a doubt, Cheyenne knew she would never try to have another child after what happened.

What if her daughter was alive, though?

Cheyenne couldn't go there yet. Not now. It was too soon. She would pull herself up by her bootstraps and soldier on. She would get back into her career as a college admissions counselor, the career she'd put on hold to have a baby. She would force herself to get out of bed every morning and get back into life.

Strange that she'd only known Riggs for less than a year and yet the thought of a life without him nearly broke her. He was that special. More proof that he needed to be with someone who could give him a football team of kids. He needed someone who could fill the ranch property with little ones running around, and maybe even a dog or two. As much as she might care for him, that person would never be her. She was fine with it, except for the part about having to walk away from Riggs forever. That was the tricky part.

"Now we're ready." Riggs reclaimed his seat.

"I forgot Ozzy's food." Cheyenne was most definitely not used to taking care of an animal.

"Keep your cell in your hand and have 911 on speed dial," he instructed. "Make the call if you see anything suspicious."

"Got it." She fished her cell out of her handbag and made sure she was ready.

"Lock the door behind me. I'll leave the truck running in case," he said.

She locked the door the second he exited. The street was quiet. There were no pedestrians and only a few cars that occasionally zipped past.

She searched for any signs of movement near houses or in the landscaping. A cat stepped out of shrubbery and she nearly jumped out of her skin.

She gripped the cell so tight she had to remind herself to relax her fingers for fear she might crack the screen. The area was almost too quiet. A few minutes ago, there'd been almost too much activity.

A second wave of relief washed over her the minute the door opened and Riggs slipped out. He locked it before returning to the truck with a small grocery bag in hand.

"This should keep him fed for a couple of days," he said as he checked the neighborhood one more time before slipping the gearshift into Drive.

A couple of days? The reality of the situation pressed down on Cheyenne. She would, at a minimum, be with her soon-to-be ex for the rest of the day. At a maximum, she might be looking at several days. The pull toward him was difficult enough to resist in the short term.

All she had to do was remind herself that her actions were for his own good. What she wanted wasn't important. All she could think about was how selfish she would be to trap him in the marriage now. The pain he might be experiencing from the loss would be temporary. In a few months, he'd be recovered and a whole lot better off.

Short-term pain for long-term gain. That would be her new mantra.

Chapter 9

The suite hotel off the highway was basically two rooms and a bathroom. It came standard with a full-size sofa bed, a kitchenette and a square-shaped dining table. The bedroom housed a king-size bed with a decent-sized bathroom attached that included four rolled-up towels, face soap and shower supplies.

The place had a decently modern vibe and smelled clean, which was a bonus she hadn't been sure she could expect when they'd pulled into the lot. The recent renovation was advertised in the lobby with a large sign. Although it fit the bill of what they needed for now, there was nothing homey about the place. The suite would meet their needs, but it also made her realize how much she missed the ranch.

A growing part of her prayed her phone would ring and Ally's name and picture would fill the screen. The ache in the pit of her stomach said she wouldn't.

"Is there anything else we can do?" Today felt like a week instead of a day. A lot had happened, and it was already getting dark outside. Her hopes of this all somehow being a big mistake were dashed.

"Afraid not," he said. "We have to give Colton a chance to work the investigation. Right now, no one at the hospital is talking to us and I'm pretty certain the one nurse who did would run the other way if she saw us again, especially since a deputy is probably finishing up interviews as we speak. I've already updated Colton on what happened at Ally's house before we left."

"Sitting here and doing nothing is awful." Cheyenne twisted her hands together. Then she remembered the laptop. "Hold on." She grabbed it out of her bag and moved to the kitchen table. She opened it and powered up, realizing she'd forgotten the power cord.

The battery was almost fully charged. Thank heaven for small miracles. It would give her time before she had to figure out a plan B. Going back to the house without Ally seemed wrong and dangerous. It was clear the place was being watched and they could probably buy another one. Had Riggs's truck being parked out front deterred a would-be assailant? A shiver raced down her spine at the thought, and an idea sparked.

"Here's hoping I can find something on her laptop to make sense of all this." She glanced at Riggs before exhaling and testing the waters. "How many tries do you think I'll get before I'm blocked?"

"I'm probably not the right person to ask about technology. My best days are spent out of cell range." He seemed to catch himself when he shot her a look of apology. He'd been out of cell range when she'd gone into labor. "I think it's three tries before you'll get locked out."

Three tries. Great. That sounded right.

The first attempt netted a zero. Same with the second. She chewed on the inside of her jaw and tapped her fingers on the edges of the keyboard. If he was right, and she figured he was, this would be her last try.

"What have you done so far?" he asked, seeming to pick up on her hesitation to go for what might end up a third strike.

"I played around with her birthday and her name," she said.

"Try Ozzy," he offered.

"Would it be that simple?" she asked, typing in the name and then hesitating before hitting Enter.

"It's possible."

Inspiration struck before she dropped her right pinky finger on the button. "Her lucky number is six. I remember her saying something once about her passwords always being plus 06."

"It's worth a try." Riggs sat down next to her and she could breathe in his spicy scent, which reminded her of campfires and home. It reminded her of late Saturday nights lying in his arms. And it reminded her of having felt for a while that she might not be cursed after all.

Cheyenne typed in 06 after the dog's name and squeezed her eyes shut.

"You're in," Riggs said, his voice traveling over her and through her.

"Seriously?" She risked opening her eyes. He was right. "Yes." The first win in what felt like a very long time was sweet.

"Let's see if she left any clues," he said.

"First off, I think we should check her email." She figured it was an easy place to start.

Riggs nodded.

There were more ads than anything else in Ally's inbox. If she was dating anyone in particular, they didn't exchange messages over email. But then, everything was on the phone these days. Text. Social networks.

"Oh. I should check her social media page," she said. "See if I can find anything there."

"And her browser history," he added.

"Good idea."

The browser didn't reveal much. Ally mostly shopped online with her laptop. She must live off her phone. Come to think of it, the laptop was old, whereas Ally got a new phone every couple of years. Okay, so there might not be anything here to work with.

She moved on to social media. Ally's page hadn't been posted on in months. Her relationship status was single.

"What about those apps that text certain people," Riggs said.

"I'm not on those, so I wouldn't know." Cheyenne had ditched those years ago. She couldn't blame Ally for lacking a social media presence. Cheyenne was in a similar boat. She didn't live her life online like some. But then, she'd always been the quiet type, preferring one close friend to several surface-level acquaintances. She had no judgment about people who liked a big circle. She just didn't have time to keep up with one. She'd never been the join-a-sorority type, either. Then again, she'd never been much of a joiner of anything. A simple life was all she craved. So much so that her only real wish was to own a horse someday. She'd much rather be on horseback than in a car, despite not having ridden much in far too many years.

"She didn't use this a lot," Cheyenne said as she closed the laptop, figuring she needed to save battery for the time being. "Give me her phone and we'd be talking about another story. That thing was practically glued to her hand."

"I don't think most folks even own a laptop anymore unless they use one for work," Riggs admitted. "I wouldn't have one if not for keeping records. Plus, it just seems easier than staring at my phone or setting up a desktop in my house."

"You never did like bringing work home anyway," she said, smiling at the memory. He'd explained much of a cattle rancher's life was spent doing paperwork.

"Home is sanctuary in my book. Once you step inside the front door, you have to learn to leave the rest of the world behind," he said. Then added, "Easier said than done during calving season."

She laughed out loud. It wasn't even that funny, but the stress of the day was catching up to her and she needed a release.

His eyebrows drew together in confusion.

"Sorry. Calving season isn't funny except that all it made me think about was how many places I found you asleep while fully dressed. And once buck naked." Again, she laughed. "I think the last count was eleven."

"Very funny. And it was twelve if I remember correctly." His face broke into a wide smile in a show of perfectly straight teeth. He had the kind of mouth that had never known braces, and confounded dentists. Perfect white teeth. But it was his lips that had always drawn her in. Lips she didn't need to be thinking about right now.

"You're right. Then there was that one time I found you sitting on the porch, passed out. Who were you waiting for?" she asked.

"Cash, I think. Who can remember? Calving season is a blur."

"And there was the time I found you snoring standing up. You were leaning against the wall in the bathroom with the shower running. I walked past and there you were. Door open. Buck naked. Dead asleep." She laughed so hard she snorted.

And the embarrassment didn't end there. She laughed so hard about snorting that she double-snorted.

Riggs was already holding his side, trying to gain his composure. He lost it after the double-double.

This was the first time she'd laughed in what felt like a really long time. Everything at the ranch had become tense after his father was murdered and then found on the property. She barely knew Finn O'Connor but he'd accepted her and the pregnancy without hesitation. Losing him was a blow the family found difficult to deal with and accept. She tabled that thought, too. It didn't seem right to think about his father when the two of them couldn't stop being silly.

After they'd laughed so hard literal tears fell down her cheeks, Cheyenne took in a few slow, deep breaths. "I don't know what it is about stress that can make you laugh."

"Better than the alternatives. Holding it in makes you sick. Crying...well, that's never been my thing," he said.

"Is it weird that I'm exhausted right now? Mentally. Physically. And every which way." She'd been that way since losing the baby.

"Not at all." His voice was full of reassurance. "In fact, it might do some good not to think about the current situation for a little while."

"How do you propose we do that?" she asked.

"We could watch TV. See if we can find a movie," he offered.

"Turning it on might be a useful distraction." Her mind was spinning out and she needed to think about something else for a little while.

It didn't take more cajoling to get her up from the table and onto the sofa. She settled on the couch as Riggs grabbed the remote and figured out how to find a movie. Easy-peasy, considering there was a room charge.

"Before we get started, Ozzy probably should be taken out." She started to push to standing but Riggs waved her off.

"I got this." He grabbed the bag and produced a pad. "I'm guessing that's what this is for."

"Your guess is as good as mine." She had no idea. Wow, had she really been in that much of a funk that she didn't know what food Ozzy ate or if he used one of those pads on a regular basis?

The short answer? Yes.

Cheyenne slipped off her shoes as Riggs set up the pee pad by the door on the small patch of tile. She curled up with a pillow on her side and settled in to watch the movie.

"Mind if I join you?" he asked.

"Be my guest," she said.

They settled on something light and she barely remembered the beginning before she conked out. By the time she opened her eyes again, the sun was up.

How many hours had passed? Her vision was blurry, and she felt like she was in a fog. Nothing seemed familiar. Where was she?

Cheyenne sat bolt upright as fear gripped her.

* * *

"You're all right." Riggs reached over to touch Cheyenne's leg out of instinct. He wanted to ground her to reality after what must have been a shock, waking up disoriented with memories flooding back.

"What time is it?" She gasped for air and clutched her chest, clearly in distress.

"It's early. The sun is barely rising and I'm right here with you. You haven't missed anything," he reassured.

She searched his gaze with wild eyes. Then she eased back to sitting.

"Where's Ozzy?" she asked.

"He's inside your handbag again. I set it on the floor so he could come and go. He seems to be more comfortable in there and I'm guessing it has to do with being a den animal," he said. Watching her wake up in a complete panic sent his blood boiling. She shouldn't have to wake up scared. They should be at home instead of in this suite, together with their newborn.

Wishful thinking. Dangerous territory, too.

The past twenty-plus hours had planted a seed of hope inside him. One that he knew better than to water. After all, there wasn't a piece of solid evidence yet that pointed to their child being alive. Foul play was a whole different story.

"Is that coffee I smell?" she asked, still sounding a little hazy.

"Fresh brewed fifteen minutes ago." He regretted making the noise now. It was probably the reason she had woken up. "Is everything okay? Did you have a dream?"

She nodded. "I need caffeine first."

"Stay put. I don't mind. Besides, I never did get up to pour mine." He stood, ignoring the electricity lighting his fingertips on fire on the hand where he'd made contact with Cheyenne.

Electricity had never been a problem for them. Sex had never been a problem for them. He was beginning to realize he didn't know her as much as he'd convinced himself that he had. And he was paying a price for it.

Not that he would go back and do anything differently if he could. He couldn't regret the past year with Cheyenne. Or the baby. Both had brought happiness to him like he'd never known, and pain to depths he never wanted to hit again.

The question still burned in the back of his mind. Was their daughter alive?

His cell buzzed, causing Cheyenne to nearly jump out of her skin.

"It's okay," he tried to soothe as he scooted off the couch to retrieve the phone that sat on the table. He checked the screen. "It's Colton."

Cheyenne sat ramrod straight. Her right hand came up to cover her lips as she seemed to stop breathing. The look on her face told him she was desperate for good news and yet too afraid to want it too badly.

"Good morning," he said to his brother. "What's up?"

"I'm afraid I have news." Those words combined with the compassionate tone in Colton's voice sent Riggs's blood pressure racing. His back was to Cheyenne and he didn't turn around on purpose, not until he knew exactly what he was dealing with, for fear she would be able to read him.

"Go on," Riggs urged, realizing his brother's hesitation meant one of his worst fears was about to be realized. He sucked in a sharp breath.

"It's Ally Clark. She's been found." The finality in Colton's voice sent fire through Riggs's veins.

Chapter 10

"And?" Riggs's tone caused Cheyenne's stomach to clench. His silence was not good.

No. No. No. Cheyenne had a sinking feeling the news was going to be crushing. The fact Riggs hadn't turned to face her had been her first clue.

Riggs was quiet. He nodded his head a couple of times and said a few uh-huhs into the phone while Cheyenne prepared for the worst.

It only took a few seconds for him to end the call. A couple more for him to deliver the news that shattered her heart into a thousand pieces. Ally's vehicle had been found in the field near the hospital with Ally inside.

Cheyenne's hands fisted at her sides as she stood up and crossed over to the window. She flexed and released her fingers several times before pulling back the curtain to look out over the highway.

So many people zipping up and down the road, busy with their lives. Many without a care in the world, driving to or from work. It struck her as strange how life just went on. The first time she'd had the thought was after losing her mother. The second occurred when she'd been told her daughter was gone. Her world had stopped and yet others kept on, going about their day like nothing had happened. It had been a strange and surreal realization both times and one she wasn't ready to embrace again.

So many emotions threatened to consume Cheyenne. She could easily let them burn her from the inside out. Anger surfaced first. Disbelief was a close second. She wanted to question what she knew deep in her gut had to be true.

So many feelings were bearing down on her all at one time. It would be easy to give in, curl up on the sofa and block out as much of the world as possible.

There was one very big reason why she could never allow herself to do that. Ally. Her best friend deserved justice. Letting emotions rule, despite the tears rolling down Cheyenne's face at the moment, wouldn't be fair to her friend. Cheyenne needed a clear head and she needed to stay as logical as possible. She'd gone emotional after losing her daughter and had made bad decision after bad decision. Yes, blocking Riggs's pain out of her mind had been a huge one. There'd been others, too. Most involved her treatment of her hus—soon to be ex-husband.

Pulling on all the strength she had left, Cheyenne wiped away the tears and took in a deep breath to calm her racing pulse.

"Hey," Riggs said from close behind her. He was so close, in fact, she could feel his presence before he spoke.

"I'm fine," she said.

He brought his hand up to her shoulder. "It's okay if you aren't."

"I have to be." She sniffed back a tear. It would be so easy to lean into him right now and let him be her strength.

And then what?

How would she be able to go back to the way it was a few minutes ago? To the place where she managed to keep enough of a distance to hold her emotions in check? To the place where she would be able to walk away from him permanently once this was all said and done?

"I want to go to the scene," she said, tensing up for the argument that was sure to come.

"I know." There was a whole lot of resolve in his voice.

The fact he didn't argue showed how well he knew her. There was nothing, short of being called away to find their daughter, that would keep her from that crime scene.

"I'll let Colton know we're on our way, then," he said.

"Thank you." She was half-surprised he hadn't already told his brother they'd be there as fast as possible. She turned to find Ozzy standing next to the door like he wanted to go out. Did he know they were talking about his owner? Ally said he was the only responsibility she ever planned on having other than being a godmother.

Ally.

A few deep breaths and Cheyenne walked over to pick up Ozzy. She nuzzled him to her chest despite his low warning growl. "I won't abandon you, little guy. I'll take care of you."

Ozzy continued to growl but he was all bark and no bite. She wondered how much dogs picked up on human emotions. Probably more than anyone would ever know.

And then Ozzy settled down, nuzzling his head

against her. She walked over to her handbag, picked it up and placed him inside. Shouldering the bag, she grabbed her cell phone and then headed to the door without another word.

Riggs picked up his wallet, keys, and phone before following her out the door. After a quick coffee stop, he drove off the main road onto a side road near the hospital. The road dead-ended and then there was nothing but a field that seemed to go on forever. Had Ally been this close to the hospital the whole time?

There were half a dozen emergency vehicles around. There was an area at the back of the field, a heavily treed part that was cordoned off with yellow police tape. The scene made her head spin. And yes, Ally's cherry red Mustang was parked in the field.

A law enforcement officer had all the doors open, including the trunk. He was making his way around the vehicle, snapping pictures from just about every angle. One minute he was on his feet, the next he was on his back, snapping pics from underneath.

She spotted Colton, who was making a beeline toward them as they exited the truck. His serious expression confirmed what she already knew even though she didn't want to accept it as truth. This whole scene was going to take time to process. Answers would have to wait.

Riggs met her at the front of his truck, reached for her hand and then linked their fingers. She ignored the electricity shooting up her arm from contact as it was quickly replaced by warmth.

Colton immediately brought his brother into a bear hug. She'd always admired how close the O'Connor men were. They were tight knit before their father's murder and had only become more so since his death.

Colton surprised her by bringing her into a hug next. "I'm sorry about your friend."

She nodded, taken aback by the show of kindness. She wasn't sure what she'd expected from Colton. Anger? Defensiveness? Definitely not this.

"Thank you," was all she could say as she reached for the comfort of Riggs's hand after hugging his brother. The second their fingers linked she could exhale again.

If Colton was shocked by the move, he hid it well.

"A teenager called it in. Raven was riding her bike across the field to go to the convenience store for breakfast tacos when she came upon the scene. She'd stayed up all night playing video games online with a friend who was supposed to meet up," Colton said. His gaze moved from Cheyenne to Riggs and back like he was checking to make sure it was okay to keep going.

Riggs nodded as Cheyenne skimmed the small crowd of people for the teenager. She must have been so shocked to come up on a crime scene like this…being the one to find a…

Cheyenne couldn't bring herself to finish the sentence. It was too horrific.

Her gaze stopped on a woman who looked to be in her early forties and was wearing jogging pants and a sweater. She was leaning against a deputy's sport utility, smoking. Inside the SUV, a young person sat hunched over with a blanket around her shoulders. Her shoulders shook like she was crying, and it took everything inside Cheyenne not to march right over there and bring that poor kid into a hug.

"She was out without her mother's permission, wasn't she?" Cheyenne asked. "Raven."

"Her mother claims so, but the teen said she does this all the time," Colton said.

"The mother is embarrassed?" she asked.

"That's my guess," Colton said. "She doesn't seem to want to admit to allowing her daughter free access to come and go as she pleases."

Shame.

"Did she see the...?" Again, Cheyenne couldn't bring herself to finish the sentence. Her stomach clenched so tightly she was nauseous.

"Yes," Colton confirmed. "She dropped her bike and ran to the hospital. She came screaming into the ER and one of the orderlies immediately called 911."

Cheyenne thought about the kind of mark that would leave on this teenager.

"They tried to give her something to calm her nerves, but she refused to take it. Said it would interfere with her Adderall," he continued.

The medication sounded familiar. Then it came to her. She had a friend in middle school who used to take it for attention deficiency disorder. It also explained why the teen might have been up all night. What day was it anyway?

Cheyenne realized it was Saturday. Wow. She'd lost track of the day of the week. Hell, she'd lost track of the month, too. All time had stopped in the past two weeks.

"Is she going to be okay?" Cheyenne hated the fact this would scar this teenager for the rest of her life. At the very least, for many years to come. The mother didn't seem like she was being a whole lot of help, either.

Normally, Cheyenne would mind her own business when it came to a parent-child issue. This was sticking in her craw for reasons she couldn't explain.

Riggs squeezed her hand for reassurance and more of that warmth shot through her. She took a slow, measured breath. The move meant to calm her did its job. Her pulse kicked down a couple of notches. Her heart went out to the teen. Same for her gratitude.

"She was in hysterics at the hospital but she's doing better now. Her father is on his way. The minute she got him on the phone, she started calming down. Apparently, the parents divorced and it was hard on her. She lives with her father by choice and spends every other weekend with her mother. I get the impression the relationship is contentious on a good day," Colton admitted.

Cheyenne couldn't help but think about her relationship with her father. How they had drifted apart after her mother's death. How she barely knew what to say to him anymore now that he'd remarried a woman named Virginia and gone off to tour the country in an RV. And how it had taken him almost a week to respond to her text letting him know his granddaughter was gone. A surprising tear sprang to her eye. She coughed to cover.

A girl never stopped needing her father, even if he wasn't perfect.

Riggs kept a careful eye on Cheyenne. She was stronger than just about anyone else he'd ever had the pleasure to meet. Too strong at times and it made her stubborn. She had the kind of strength that also made her try to fix all her own problems, like she didn't want to trouble anyone else even if they volunteered. And yet everyone had a breaking point. Was losing their baby hers? Or would it be losing Ally?

Her eyes were sharper today, not like the distant stare she'd had when he first saw her at Ally's house. This also meant she was tucking her feelings somewhere down deep. He could be accused of doing the same thing far too often. Talking out his feelings wasn't something that normally ranked high on his list.

Except with Cheyenne. He missed talking to her every day in the two weeks since she'd been gone. He missed waking up beside her, that long blond hair of hers spilling all over her pillow and his. He missed the warmth of her body against his first thing in the morning and when he went to sleep at night, and the sense of the world being right when she was in the room.

"How long before her father gets here?" Cheyenne asked. Her motherly instincts seemed to have kicked into high gear. She looked poised and ready to fight off a bear if it got in the way. She was going to make an amazing mother someday despite her many arguments to the contrary.

Colton checked his watch. "Soon. He should be here in the next fifteen minutes or so. He's working the grave-yard shift over at the meatpacking plant as security to keep up two houses so Raven's mother doesn't have to move out of the place they shared."

The teen's father sounded like a real stand-up guy. Someone who could use a hand but probably would never take one. Riggs made a mental note to circle back to get information about the man's character. If he turned out to be the person Riggs believe him to be then Riggs planned to set up an anonymous donation to pay off the man's mortgages. He would set up a college fund for the teen, as well. There was no use in having all the zeroes in his bank account that came with the last name O'Connor if he couldn't use the money to help out decent people—

people who would never ask for a dime and yet deserved to hold the world in their hand.

He squeezed Cheyenne's fingers and she rewarded him with a small smile. It was in the eyes more than anything else. Those serious blue eyes that reminded him of the sky on a clear spring morning. Eyes that he'd loved staring into.

"You should know the scene looks as though it's been staged." Colton made eye contact with each of them.

"What does that mean exactly?" Cheyenne asked.

"There are empty beer cans loose in Ally's vehicle. All over the floorboard in fact," Colton supplied.

"Ally doesn't drink beer," Cheyenne said without missing a beat.

"Ever?" Colton asked.

"Nope. She likes those fruity wines and she's recently been into Prosecco. She raves about it." Cheyenne seemed to catch her almost smile at the memory before it could take seed.

"Interesting." Colton pulled out his favorite notebook from the pocket of his shirt and took down the note. "This whole scene has been made to look like she had a rendezvous with someone, a male."

"She texted to meet up with us," Cheyenne said. Riggs confirmed with a nod. "There's no way she would change plans."

"Is it possible she was trying to get the two of you in the same room together?" Colton asked.

"We already considered it," Cheyenne said, "but dismissed the idea. There's no way she would do that to us. And there's no way she would text us and then secretly meet up with some random guy."

"Did she ever do any online dating?" Colton asked.

"Not that I know of." Cheyenne shrugged. "But to be one hundred percent honest, I can't say that for sure. She could have. It doesn't sound like her, though."

"She never mentioned it?" Colton asked.

"Not to me. I've been wrapped up in my own situation for the past year, though. Still, I feel like Ally would have told me at some point," she said. "She wouldn't have felt there was anything wrong with online dating, but she was afraid of her own shadow. She wouldn't meet up with a stranger who wasn't carefully vetted first. We had friends in college who used to try to set her up on blind dates with acquaintances and she wouldn't consider it. Not unless the person had a long history."

"What about dating at work?" he asked.

"I don't think she was against the idea." Cheyenne snapped her fingers like she was trying to recall something that was just out of reach. "I think I remember her complaining about a visiting doctor and I can't remember if he was hitting on her or just being a jerk."

"I'll follow up with her coworkers to see if she mentioned it to any of them." Colton stood there for a moment like he was debating his next question, which caused Cheyenne's pulse to pound in her throat.

"I apologize in advance for the question as we shift gears." Colton locked gazes. He must've decided to go for it. "Did you actually see your daughter when she was born?"

Cheyenne searched her memory. She shook her head and gasped.

"I was shown something wrapped in a blanket. It's all fuzzy." The possibility she'd been lied to, tricked, pressed heavy on her chest. She hated not having clear recall with someone so important. She remembered the blanket. It

had been pink. And the nurse who dipped down to give
Cheyenne a glimpse of the bundle but…

"No. I didn't see her clearly. All I remember being
shown was the pink blanket," she finally realized.

Riggs squeezed her hand. She looked up at him and
saw all the questions forming behind those mocha eyes.

Chapter 11

Riggs wished he'd been the one to ask Cheyenne the question about whether or not she'd actually seen what was inside the pink blanket. The chance, however remote it might be, that their daughter was still alive slammed into him with the force of a runaway train.

Questions raced through his mind. Thoughts he had to shelve for now while Colton finished the interview with Cheyenne. Riggs would have to circle back later when he was alone with Cheyenne and could really talk.

Colton jotted down a couple more notes before locking eyes with Riggs and nodding. "My deputy spoke with the nurses. It's clear to me there's foul play here. I don't for a minute believe Cheyenne's friend was murdered while on a random date. The evidence says otherwise." He paused. "In fact, it almost shouts it from the rooftop."

"Too obvious?" Riggs asked, but it was more statement than question.

"Yes. The beer cans, for one. Someone Ally's size and weight wouldn't have been able to knock down all these. There are flowers, too. Roses. The kind anyone can pick up at the supermarket without much trouble. She was found inside the vehicle in a way that was very unnatural. She was stabbed by a kitchen knife, which indicates pre-meditation. Forensics will piece together more of what happened yesterday morning when Ally left from work, her time of death…" Colton apologized for his bluntness when Cheyenne sucked in a breath. "Based on the texts she sent the two of you, the possibility exists that she was killed because she discovered information someone didn't want leaked out of the hospital."

She exhaled slowly, and then urged him to continue.

"What about the flowers?" Riggs picked up on something in his brother's voice when he mentioned the roses.

Colton's gaze flashed to Cheyenne, who had brought Ozzy up against her chest. She was speaking quietly in his ear, no doubt whispering reassurances to the dog. The little dog was growing on Riggs. Or maybe it was just his situation. He no longer had a caregiver. The one person who'd promised to care for him was gone through no fault of her own. It wasn't the animal's fault or Ally's. Bad luck.

Ozzy wasn't the best fit for ranch life, but Riggs figured he could find a home for the guy if Cheyenne couldn't take him. Damn, it was strange to think of Cheyenne and his separation as permanent. He would respect her wishes, though, no matter how much it gutted him. There wasn't much of an alternative. He shouldn't have to convince his wife to stay with him.

Watching her while she took in the news their child might be alive, no matter how small the possibility, he could see how guarded she was being. No one wanted to be crushed twice, not with this kind of pain.

"They were 'arranged' in a heart shape around her face and torso to look like someone was obsessed with her." Colton's gaze dropped to the ground. He shook his head.

"I didn't find anything on her laptop to indicate she was seeing someone," Cheyenne chimed in. "Did you find her phone?"

"Not yet. The whole scene feels off," Colton admitted. "We'll follow the evidence and see where it leads. Word of warning, though. Investigations take time. It's not like on TV where answers pop up almost instantly. Of course, I do get the occasional gift of speed. I just don't want either of you to count on it."

Riggs knew this firsthand, having several of his brothers work in law enforcement. The statement was aimed at Cheyenne. Of course, Colton wouldn't want to get her hopes up. Not once he took a look at how hard she was taking the losses. Losses that were stacking up.

"She knew something," Riggs said. "She requested my presence at her home ASAP. By the time I arrived, someone had made certain she would never make the meetup."

"Interviews with security haven't revealed that she left work with anyone," Colton admitted.

"The cameras," Cheyenne stated. "The ones aimed at the parking lot. E-cig Nurse seemed afraid to be seen on them. She stood in a blind spot when she waved us over."

"That's right," Riggs confirmed.

"The images are blurry, and even if they weren't, security doesn't keep the videos overnight. The system resets at midnight. Otherwise, there'd be way too much recording to keep track of plus space on the system. The hospital doesn't have the most storage, so the head of security said it gets deleted every night," Colton said.

"Why have cameras at all, then?" Riggs couldn't for the life of him figure out how any of it made sense.

"According to security, it's meant for backup if there's an immediate situation. The team can pull the data and hold onto it. They just don't do it routinely," Colton admitted.

"What about the nurses? What did they have to say?" Riggs needed to hear from his brother what he already feared. The interviews came up with nothing.

"Not as much as I would have liked. I think I know which nurse you're talking about when you say E-cig Nurse. Her hair is mousy brown, and she has a small, pointed nose. Right?" Colton asked.

Cheyenne confirmed with a nod.

"She wouldn't talk, and she seemed scared," Colton said. "We've told the nurses that we'll be arranging for a lie detector test just to give them something to chew on."

"Is it possible someone got to her? Maybe even threatened her?" Riggs asked.

"It is likely," Colton confirmed. "I got the impression she wanted to talk but someone or something was causing her to hold back."

"She's a single mom," Cheyenne pointed out. "Said she needed this job."

"Is it possible someone threatened her child?" Riggs added.

Colton nodded before taking down notes.

Cheyenne shifted her weight from one foot to the other as she waited. He reached out to link their fingers to stop her from twisting her hands together. She rewarded him with a smile so brief he almost questioned whether or not he'd seen it at all.

"I'll check into it personally," Colton finally said.

"Any chance you'll let me walk over to Ally's car?" Cheyenne asked. Her voice shook and her hands trembled.

"I would if I could." Colton issued an apology. "I can't allow witnesses on a crime scene. It might seem like my deputy is being careless by moving around so much but he's methodical and the best forensic investigator I have. Plus, there's a lot of blood and you'll never be able to unsee the scene."

Cheyenne nodded despite her frown.

"It probably wouldn't be good for Ozzy anyway." She exhaled and her chest deflated.

Riggs needed to get her out of there as soon as possible.

"Is there any chance the person in the vehicle wasn't Ally?" Cheyenne didn't look up at Colton when she asked. This was her tell she wasn't 100 percent certain she wanted to know the answer to the question. She would never make it in a card game, which was another reason Riggs couldn't accept the fact she didn't love him anymore.

Pride could be to blame for his reasoning and yet deep down he felt like he would have known if their relationship had been fake. And no, he wouldn't be better off without her despite what she seemed to believe. No matter how rushed their marriage might have been, he'd never been more certain of anything in his life.

Was it pride keeping him from telling her how he really felt?

"I'm afraid Ms. Clark has been positively identified

by a co-worker. There's no possibility of mistaken identity." Colton lowered his head in reverence. "I'm sorry for your loss, Cheyenne."

"What about her parents? Do they know?" She ducked her head, chin to chest, and turned her face away. Riggs took note of the move she'd done a couple of times already. Was she hiding tears?

"Yes," Colton confirmed.

Cheyenne coughed before lifting her face to Riggs.

"Can we go now?" she asked.

Riggs shot a look toward his brother, who nodded.

"I'll check in with you later," Riggs said to Colton. He needed to find out from Cheyenne what was causing her to need to leave right away.

Emotions were getting the best of Cheyenne and she needed to leave the place before she lost it. The morning had started to wear thin and all she could think about was going somewhere safe so she could lie down. Some of her best thinking came when she slowed down. The morning slammed into her like a train going a hundred miles an hour.

Riggs walked beside her, hand in hand, back to his truck. He took her over to the passenger side and then waited while she took Ozzy out of her purse to let him do his business. The little dog glanced back at her before bolting toward the crime scene.

"Ozzy, no," she shouted after him.

"I'll get him," Riggs said, chasing after the little guy as Cheyenne stood there feeling useless.

Since that was about as comfortable as wearing wet clothes in church, she did the same. Ozzy zigzagged across the field, diverting left at the last minute.

He ran another five yards outside of the crime scene area that had been cordoned off and then stopped.

"What is it?" Cheyenne asked through labored breaths. She'd been way too inactive lately to run as fast as she had without her sides hurting and her lungs screaming for air.

"A piece of cloth." Riggs stopped, bent over and studied the ground. "A bandanna." He put a hand up to stop her from coming all the way over. "There's blood on it."

Cheyenne moved close enough to scoop Ozzy up and hold him to her chest. He was breathing heavy and his eyes were wild, which made her believe Ally's scent might be on the bandanna. The blood most likely belonged to her, as well. Cheyenne thought she might be sick. It was one thing to know her friend had been murdered and quite another to see the evidence, the blood.

Riggs motioned for his brother to come over. Colton set off jogging toward them almost immediately.

This seemed like a good time to take a couple of steps toward the truck. Cheyenne backpedaled as Colton reached the spot. He pulled a paper bag out of his pocket and a pair of tongs. He picked up the bandanna and examined it.

Nausea nearly doubled Cheyenne over as anger filled her. So much senseless loss. A spark of determination lit a fire inside her. Ally's death would not be in vain. There was no way Cheyenne planned to let the jerk who did this get away.

The person responsible had set this up to look like a date gone wrong. Why? What issue could a person possibly have with Ally other than the one that came to mind… Cheyenne's baby and a secret someone was willing to kill to protect.

Thoughts raced through her mind about what kind of person would do this. Dr. Fortner came to mind. He'd been there in the delivery room. Were there other possibilities?

This person would be someone who had something to lose. Was a career or family on the line? The latter begged the question as to whether or not Ally would engage in an affair with a married man. Cheyenne would bet against it. Internet dating was out. One of those swiping apps wouldn't surprise Cheyenne but the circumstances weren't right. All roads led back to Cheyenne and the baby.

"Excuse me, Colton." The answer to this question was one that couldn't wait. "You said Ally's phone is nowhere to be found, right?"

"That's correct," he confirmed.

Whoever killed her would probably be smart enough to take it and dispose of it. She glanced around the ground, figuring the perp might have dropped it, too. Or thrown it.

Cheyenne remembered what Colton had said about not stomping all over the crime scene. She figured the perimeter had just expanded with the find.

"Let's get you out of here," Riggs said, and she wondered what else the lawmen might have spotted.

Fighting the urge to argue, she walked next to him on the way to the truck. Both were careful to stick to the same path that had brought them to the bandanna.

"Ozzy might have just discovered an important piece of evidence," Riggs said as she climbed into the passenger seat. He reached over and patted Ozzy's head. His fingers grazed her neck and she ignored the electric impulses rocketing through her at his lightest touch. All her senses were on high alert. She chalked her body's over-reaction to that and did her best to move on.

Her cell buzzed in her purse. She gasped before digging her hand in to locate the noisemaker. For a split second, she thought it might be Ally. She reminded herself to breathe as reality struck. It was a cold, hard reminder her friend would never call again.

Cheyenne could so easily get lost in the sea of emotion that came with losing her best friend. She couldn't allow herself to go down that path. For Ally's sake. Cheyenne needed to keep a clear head because the person who killed her best friend needed to be brought to justice. She realized she was gripping her cell so tightly that her knuckles had turned white. She checked the screen as Riggs reclaimed the driver's seat.

Unknown caller.

Didn't those two words send a chill racing up her spine? She fumbled to touch the green button on her screen. A click sounded, and then a recording came on the line telling her she needed to extend her vehicle warranty.

White-hot anger filled her. "It's bad enough these jerks call our personal cells. First of all, that information should be ours and ours alone. No one, and I mean *no one* should be able to telemarket us on our personal phones. It's wrong and someone should put a stop to it."

As anger raged through her, Riggs sat in the driver's seat as calm as anyone pleased.

Suddenly, she was mad about that, too.

Rather than let her words rip unchecked, she clamped her mouth shut and felt her face warm. He probably thought she was crazy at this point and she probably shouldn't care as much as she did.

"You don't have to stop on my account," he said quietly.

"Stop what?" The words came out a little too harshly.

"Ranting," he said and there was no judgment in his voice.

"Is that what you think I was doing, because I can tell you one thing… You're dead wrong. And I mean no one has ever been more wrong in their life than you are right now if you think I'm rantin—"

Cheyenne stopped herself right there. He was right on target. And she had so much more frustration built up she didn't know what to do with. One thing was certain. She couldn't hold her tongue any longer.

"Okay, fine. You sure you want to hear this?" She asked the question infusing as much indignation in her voice as she could. He needed to know what he was getting himself into.

"One hundred percent," came the confident response. It was all the urging she needed.

"I am mad as hell Ally is dead because of me." Those words stung. The truth hurt.

"She isn't—"

"Come on, Riggs. You don't actually believe that, do you?" she bit out.

He didn't respond. He just sat there patiently.

"If I hadn't called Ally or brought her into this, she would be alive right now. If I hadn't run to her instead of going home like I should have after the baby was born, she would be home sleeping off a long shift. If I hadn't been so selfish, Ozzy would have her instead of being stuck with me for the rest of his life." Those last words broke her. She released a sob before sucking in a breath and holding her head high. *Chin up* had been her motto when her mother died. It would get her through this rough patch, as well. It had to, despite how much the losses were stacking up.

Tie a knot in the rope, Chey.

Riggs continued to stare out the front window even though his hand found hers. His fingers covered hers, causing a sense of warmth to spread through her. That was just Riggs. He was always a steady calm no matter how rough the waters became. He had a rare ability to make her feel like the world might not fall apart despite evidence to the contrary. Cutting herself off from him had been about survival on her part because she would never be able to walk away while he was her life raft in a raging storm.

"I'm sorry for—"

"Don't be," he said, cutting her off. He shook his head as though for emphasis. "I'm the one who should apologize."

Now she really was confused.

Chapter 12

"Hear me out." Riggs had had no idea, until now, how much Cheyenne blamed herself for the loss of their child, until he heard how pent up her emotions were. "I should have done better by you."

The look she shot him said she thought he was crazy. He'd seen that look before, so he put a hand up to stop her from objecting.

"You are carrying around the weight of the world on your shoulders, Cheyenne."

"Which isn't your fault," she defended.

"I needed to be a better husband to you. I wasn't," he admitted. "I got caught up in the surprise of becoming a father and husband, and volunteered for extra work on the ranch rather than come home and figure out how to talk to you about what you were going through. I told myself that if I just kept my head down and worked, everything would magically work out between us. That we'd figure out how to talk to each other and everything would be hunky-dory. Believe me when I say that I'm usually not that naive."

"The pregnancy news came out of the blue. We were just getting to know each other, Riggs. You're being too hard on yourself." The words rolled off her tongue like she didn't even have to think about them.

"Am I?" He didn't think so. In fact, he wasn't being nearly hard enough on himself.

"Yes. The whole marriage and family idea takes some getting used to," she said.

"Did you get used to it?" For some reason, it mattered.

"Not really," she admitted. "We rushed into it. I guess I expected a transition but then with a baby it seemed like being an instant family was going to be a tough hill to climb."

"Yeah." He couldn't have said it better himself. "I'll be one hundred percent honest right now. I wasn't ready to be a father. Not when I first heard the news and not a few weeks ago before the…"

He stopped himself before saying *the birth*.

"And now all I can think about is her…*us*. I'd give my right arm to go back to the way things were before," he admitted.

"What would you do different?" she asked.

"I'd be there for you in the way you needed me to. I'd be a helluva lot more excited about the birth. You would not have been in an ER alone," he said.

"I wasn't alone. I had Ally," she pointed out.

"You should have had me." He started the truck and put the gearshift in Reverse, backing out of the field.

No one spoke for half the ride back to the motel room.

And then Cheyenne said, "I'd like to go back to the ranch if the offer still stands."

Few words could have shocked him as much as those.

"It's your home, Cheyenne. You'll always be welcome," was all he said in response. Despite her arguments to the contrary, he should have been a better husband. There was no excuse in the book good enough as far as he was concerned. But at least the two of them were talking now and he'd let go of some of the pride that kept him from telling her how he really felt. "Anytime you need to get something off your chest, talk to me."

He shouldn't have let it build up to the point she was ready to explode.

"I appreciate it, but—"

"No 'buts' about it. If we'd talked more about what we were really feeling while we were married, then we probably wouldn't be talking about divorce now," he said. The words came out a little more aggressive than he'd planned, and he regretted it, but they needed to be said. It might be too late for them to reconcile, even though his heart argued the opposite, but he'd needed to say his piece.

"Okay, then. Honesty it is." She surprised him with the response.

"And full disclosure," he insisted.

She nodded.

"We might not have made the marriage thing work, but I'd like to stay friends." He had no idea how she would react to his request. He had no idea how two people went from the kind of sexual chemistry that would light a house on fire in the rain to casual acquaintance, but he couldn't stand the thought of losing her, either.

"Friends it is." There was no conviction in her words.

He appreciated them just the same. Trying counted for something and she was making an attempt to build a bridge over the river between them.

The rest of the ride to the motel was silent. They picked up her things and tossed them in the back seat of the truck. The drive to the ranch went by surprisingly fast. Riggs's thoughts were all over the map. He kept circling back to one question. Was Ally killed because she'd discovered his daughter was alive? And if so, where was his little girl? The text she'd sent to Cheyenne indicated mind-blowing news.

Cheyenne had to be wrestling with the same thought. She seemed unable to fully discuss the possibility. At least she'd raised her voice earlier and let out some of her frustrations. She'd been like a teakettle about to blow, before the outburst.

Riggs parked in the garage of their two-story log-style cabin. He hadn't truly taken possession of this place until Cheyenne came along. Before, he'd been content to sleep in the bunkhouse with the other men during the week. He only came here on Sundays. The place was far too big for one person.

There was an open-concept living room and kitchen. An office and the master suite rounded out the ground floor. The upstairs had a game room with a flat-screen TV that practically covered one wall. There was a nursery and two other bedrooms. Cheyenne had decorated one of the rooms as a guest room for her father and his wife. They'd promised to come for a visit soon and that was the last he'd heard of it. They made an excuse to miss the wedding and he had yet to meet his father-in-law.

The place had been decorated to Cheyenne's liking and Riggs wouldn't have it any other way. He wanted her to be comfortable in her new home. It was already asking a lot to have her live at his family's ranch. He'd wanted this place to be her retreat. Thankfully, she liked soft colors and couches big enough to sink into. Her taste had been a perfect fit for him. To be fair, though, he'd lived there with not much more than a leather sofa downstairs, a couple of bar stools at the granite island, and a king-size bed in the bedroom. He hadn't taken the time to pick out dressers or coffee tables, let alone linens and knickknacks. All he really needed was a shower, bed and a stocked fridge. And a flat-screen.

To be honest, the place had never felt like home before Cheyenne moved in. Before he got too sentimental, he cut the engine. After hopping out of the driver's seat, he grabbed her belongings.

When he'd first listened to the message from her on his phone saying she was in labor and headed to the hospital, an image had flashed in his thoughts. It was an image he couldn't erase no matter how hard he tried, the snapshot of his family. The first thought he'd had was the next time they walked through these doors, they would be parents.

In that moment, he'd realized how ready he was to become a father. Much to his shame, he hadn't been so sure before. He knew that he'd fallen hard for Cheyenne. There was something deep inside that told him she was going to be important to him when they'd first met, something he couldn't explain if he tried. It was more of a feeling than an instinct. Instinct told him the best place a poacher would make camp on the property. This was more like his world had clicked into place—a place he'd never known before.

The sensation had intrigued him from the get-go. The news she'd become pregnant had caught him off guard, but the next step seemed as natural as breathing. She was special. He'd known that from day one. He didn't want to be with anyone else and he assumed the feeling would last forever. Most of the experience was a mystery.

If one of his brothers had asked him if he believed in love at first sight before Cheyenne, he might have laughed. Now he'd changed his mind. The instant he set eyes on her something new and different had stirred in his chest. It would be too easy to chalk it up to attraction or lust. And it would also be wrong. It was so much more.

"Mind if I take the couch?" She interrupted his deep thoughts as he followed her into the kitchen.

"You can have the master." He had no problems sleeping upstairs in the guest room when the time came.

She hesitated, looking like she wanted to say something but decided against it.

"If you don't tell me what you're thinking, I'll never know." Those words covered so much more than this conversation.

One look into her eyes said she caught on to the deeper meaning.

Cheyenne stood there for a long moment without speaking, in the kitchen of the home she'd created for their family. For a split second, she thought about closing up and going inside herself again. But what good would that do?

Her marriage had already been destroyed and the child she loved more than life itself was gone. Now she'd lost her best friend. Staying quiet held little appeal.

"I don't like to admit to being afraid…" She took in a fortifying breath before continuing. "So, if you plan to sleep upstairs tonight, I'd like you to teach me how to load the shotgun before you go."

"I'm not going anywhere this minute. It's just now

noon, but I thought you'd be more comfortable in our...
your bed. And I didn't think you wanted me anywhere
near while you slept," he said with brutal honesty.

The truth hurt but she was also learning that staying
quiet destroyed.

She walked over to the granite island and sat on one
of the bar stools. She'd already forgotten how uncomfortable this chair was right up until sinking into it. She put
her elbow on the island for leverage because exhaustion
threatened to land her on her backside.

"Tell me what you want, Cheyenne." He set the bags
down and walked over to the vacant chair beside her.

She slid the band of her handbag onto the chair. Ozzy
was curled up inside. He blinked his eyes open when the
purse was no longer against her body. She reached down
and ran her hand along his back to soothe him.

"I'd rather you be close to me, if that's okay," she
said to Riggs. "The reason is stupid because there's no
safer place on earth than the ranch. I know that logically.
And yet, when I think about being down here alone and
you upstairs—" she flashed eyes at him "—I can hardly
breathe."

Riggs brought his hand to cover hers and the instant he
made contact, more of that warmth spread through her.

"I know," he started and then stopped like he was
searching for the right words. "Relationships change.
They take different forms. But I hope you know that I
will always be here for you. If you ever need anything,
just ask."

She nodded. His kindness washed over her. And
maybe it was the losses that were racking up or the fact
that her only living relative still hadn't made her a prior-

ity that had her thinking she wanted to be back in Riggs's arms if only for a few moments.

"I have a question." She couldn't meet his gaze because suddenly she felt vulnerable. With him, and for the first time since losing her mother and her family breaking up, she didn't feel alone.

"I told you. Ask anything," came the quick response. His gravelly voice traveled over her and through her.

There were plenty of reasons she shouldn't continue…

"Kiss me."

Riggs leaned toward her and brought his hand around to cradle the back of her neck. His thumb drew circles around the sensitized skin there. He issued a sharp sigh before bringing his forehead to rest against hers.

"You have no earthly idea how much I want to." He paused and she braced herself for the rejection. "Is this a good idea?"

She let a few moments of silence sit between them.

"Probably not," she finally said. "But it is what I want."

That seemed to be all the encouragement he needed. Before she could talk herself out of it, his lips gently pressed to hers. He sucked in a breath before his tongue teased her mouth. A dozen butterflies released in her chest and her stomach dropped in a free fall.

The world tilted on its axis in that moment and everything seemed like it was going to be okay. She'd had that sensation very few times in her life and didn't take it lightly. Right now, though, she wanted to focus on how tender his kisses were and how much each one caused the tide of emotions welling in her chest to gain momentum until a tsunami was building. She wanted to shut out all her sorrows and frustrations and get lost in Riggs. It was so very easy when all she had to do was take in a breath to fill her senses with his spicy male scent.

She spun her legs around to face him, planting her feet on the stool's footrest. In the next second, she brought her hands up to rest on his muscled shoulders—shoulders she'd mapped and memorized a hundred times when they made love.

Sex with Riggs was the best she'd ever experienced. There was something out of this world about the moment they joined together and the perfect way their bodies fit before her belly grew big and uncomfortable.

Without a doubt, she would never find another person who fit her to a T. Logic said there was no way the chemistry would last and yet her heart argued the opposite. Some stars burned bright, not out.

Why couldn't they be the first kind?

Not that any of that mattered now. And she didn't want to focus on anything but the way his tongue excited her as it dipped inside her mouth. Or the way she felt when his teeth scraped across her bottom lip.

Before she could debate her next actions, she moved to standing in between his powerful thighs. Her body was flush with his. Her breasts against a muscled chest. She ran her fingers across the edges and grooves of his shoulders and chest.

He released a low growl when she let one of her hands drift down to the snap on his jeans. She rested her finger on the warm metal.

Cheyenne shut down logic because it wanted to argue that nothing had changed. That this moment happening between them would make it next to impossible to walk away when the investigation was over and they both needed to go back to their lives.

Heat rushed through her body, making it impossible to think. The fog that was Riggs O'Connor encircled her in the best possible way, so she let go. In his arms, everything else faded. All the stress. All the loss. All the pain. Nothing broke through except the two of them and the sensations rocketing through her body. Sensations that created a firework show that would rival any Fourth of July.

With his mouth moving against hers and his tongue delving inside, she could taste the hint of coffee from earlier still on his lips.

And then his cell buzzed, breaking into the moment. Panic this could be more bad news gripped her.

Chapter 13

For a split second, Riggs considered not answering his phone. Pulling on all the strength he could muster, he scooted his chair back and stood up. His breathing made it seem like he'd run a marathon.

"Hey, Colton. What's going on?" Riggs asked in between breaths, hoping his brother would let it slide and not question why it sounded like Riggs had just sprinted to the phone.

"You might want to come to my office and bring Cheyenne with you." The sound of his voice sent a chill racing down Riggs's back.

"What's this about?" Riggs asked.

"No time to explain. Meet me there?" Colton asked.

"Okay. We're on our way," he promised.

Cheyenne's eyebrow arched as she reclaimed her seat. Her chest heaved at the same pace as his. She reached down to check on Ozzy and Riggs figured she was going to be better with that dog than she realized.

"Colton wants us to meet up at his office. He didn't say why," he told her.

She frowned before jumping into action, securing her handbag on her shoulder with Ozzy inside. "Do I have time to feed this guy and give him some water?"

"We'll make time," he said.

Cheyenne took care of the little dog while Riggs grabbed a couple of sandwiches for the road. His stomach was growling, and she needed to keep up her strength. He threw in a couple of pieces of fruit to give her options along with a pair of power bars he kept with him while out on the land.

Ten minutes later, they were out the door and inside his truck. He set the lunchbox he'd packed in between them and told her to help herself.

"I'm not sure I could eat anything if I tried," she admitted.

"Will you at least try? I'd be happy if you could get down a banana," he urged. It might not be his place to take care of her anymore, but he couldn't erase from his thoughts the months they'd belonged to each other.

Cheyenne nodded as he pulled out of the garage and onto the gravel road leading past the main house. She pulled out a banana and polished it off with surprising speed. Not a minute later, she reached in and grabbed a sandwich. In the half hour it took to exit KBR, they'd cleaned out the lunchbox.

After Cheyenne suppressed her third yawn, he said, "Feel free to lean your head back and rest on the drive over."

"That's a good idea. I think better when I power down anyway." She tilted the seat back and then closed her eyes.

He had to fight the urge to take his hand off the wheel and reach out to her. They were talking again. This time, they were sharing their frustrations and what was on their minds. They'd talked about something real instead of walking on eggshells or tiptoeing around a hard conversation. Or working longer than he had to in order to avoid dealing with conflict. He'd take the progress. They were taking small steps.

Besides, he liked talking to Cheyenne. Before her, Riggs wouldn't categorize himself as one for long-drawn-out conversation. He said what needed to be said and then got out of there. With her, he wanted to know the details. He wanted to know what she was thinking. He wanted to hear how something made her feel. The more drawn out, the better.

Go figure.

Pride swelled in his chest that she had food in her stomach and looked to be resting peacefully in his truck. After hearing the account of what had happened at the hospital and witnessing firsthand how shifty the nurses were being, he could only imagine what Cheyenne must be experiencing. It was obvious she blamed herself for losing the baby—a baby who might be alive.

The thought burned him from the inside out. The implication that a doctor, or nurses, or both could have drugged Cheyenne and taken their baby sent another hot poker through his chest.

He was reminded of one of his father's favorite sayings—*What happened in darkness always came to light*. It was the line Finn O'Connor had fed his children from a young age as to why honesty was always the best policy.

Even when people thought they were getting away with something, they rarely were. They might for a time, but there'd be a reckoning. The saying proved gospel time and time again.

Finn O'Connor had never been able to expose the darkness that led to his baby daughter, firstborn and only girl, disappearing from her crib more than three decades ago. Right up until his death, he was trying to shine a light on what had happened.

Now that Riggs had become a father, he better understood the devastation of losing a first child. He could relate to the intense pain of losing a daughter. And he could not allow history to repeat itself.

A deer leaped from behind a tree and then darted across the road. Riggs slammed on the brake. His seat belt caught, stopping him from smacking his head into the steering wheel.

"What happened?" Cheyenne gasped. She grabbed the strap on her seat belt, clearly shocked.

"Deer. It's okay." His pulse skyrocketed and his heart jackhammered against his ribs despite the verbal reassurance meant as much for him as for her.

Cheyenne took one look at him and said, "Pull over."

There were no vehicles on this stretch of roadway, so he complied with her request. He put his blinkers on to give others fair warning from a distance.

She wrestled with the seat belt for a few seconds after it had locked on her. She managed to finagle out of it and then scooted over to him.

"What are you doing?" he asked as she wrapped her arms around his neck.

"Tell me what's going on with you right now," she said. Those pale blue eyes of hers were filled with so much compassion. "And I don't mean what just happened on the road. I mean in here." She pointed to the center of his chest.

Revealing the parallels between his family's greatest tragedy and their situation didn't seem like the best move right then. Him making the link was bad enough. He felt ten times worse at the thought his daughter might have been kidnapped right out from underneath them. Much like in the case of his sister, no ransom note had shown up. Much like his sister, the baby seemed to have disappeared into thin air. Much like with his sister, there were far more questions than answers.

Opening up to Cheyenne might cause her even more pain. The last thing she needed was to hear the thoughts rolling around in his head. They would only upset her. However, a voice in the back of his mind warned against holding back the truth.

On balance, he'd hurt her enough. He couldn't continue, not when he wanted to protect her more than he wanted to breathe.

"I'm running through all the times my brother had the same tone in his voice and trying to figure out just how bad this news might be." It had been his first thought, so he wasn't being dishonest. He was simply neglecting to tell her where his thoughts had gone next.

She stared at him and for a few seconds he felt like she could see right through him. Hope followed by something that looked like disappointment colored her eyes. A wall came up and it was too late to go back and recapture the moment.

"What did you decide?" She moved back to her side of the cab and clicked on her seat belt.

"I can't figure it out." Again, he was being honest

despite not sharing the whole of his thoughts. The small voice in the back of his mind told him he'd just messed up royally. There'd been a window of opportunity to really talk to her and he'd lost it. There was no backtracking now as he turned off the emergency flashers and put the gearshift in Drive.

He navigated back onto the roadway.

"We'll know soon enough." The disappointment in her voice struck him square in the chest. *Too late* were his least favorite pair of words.

Cheyenne drummed her fingers on the armrest. She'd miscalculated the moment with Riggs. There'd been a time when she had a better handle on what he might be thinking. She'd lost her touch. Or maybe losing the baby had changed their connection.

Her mind snapped to Colton and the fact they were barreling toward his office after what could only be described as one helluva morning. Powering down had only caused her to go over her last conversation with Ally repeatedly, trying to remember any and every detail about what had transpired. There was a whole lot of day left and she was already exhausted.

"I keep thinking about Ally's parents and how they had to learn their daughter was murdered today. And how much I want to contact them to offer my sympathies and support, but I don't think I can pull it together long enough when I hear their voices." She pinched the bridge of her nose to stem the headache threatening.

"I can't imagine the pain they must be experiencing," he agreed. "No parent should have to lose a child." He seemed to realize what he'd said and how much it applied to their current situation when he shot a look of apology.

"You don't have to be sorry, Riggs," she said. "When I lost her, I blamed myself and shut everyone out, including you. I convinced myself that I was protecting you by not letting you see me in the state I was in, which was pretty awful."

"What changed?" he asked.

"Thanks to Ally, you showed up at the door. Then, talking to you. Realizing that you were in just as much pain as me, and that not talking about her with you wasn't going to make me feel any better. I can't protect you from the hurt that comes with losing a child." She paused for a long moment before continuing. "And I realized I was punishing myself even more by shutting you out. I didn't think I deserved your compassion or kindness."

"You suffered a loss, too. I'd argue yours was bigger than mine, considering I had yet to meet her and she'd been growing inside you all along. You were already connected to her in ways that I hadn't experienced yet," he said.

Those words were balm to a wounded soul.

"Thank you, Riggs." That was all she said. All she needed to say. She meant those words and he seemed to know it.

"I've said it before, but I couldn't be sorrier for not being there for you, Cheyenne." This time, she didn't try to stop him. Saying the words out loud probably helped him in some way.

He pulled into the lot of his brother's office where a dozen or so vehicles were parked. He found a spot and started to exit when she reached over to him, placing her hand on his forearm.

"I know you are, Riggs." She knew he would never make the same mistake if given the chance, which was the kicker. The dark cloud over her head wasn't going anywhere and there was no way she could try to have another child. "We'd both do things a lot different if we could go back."

He nodded.

"But we can't." Those words hurt more than she wanted to admit. She picked up her handbag and held it against her chest, securing Ozzy.

Riggs exited the truck and came around to her side as she climbed down. He held onto her arm to steady her before closing the door. For a minute, they stood there, staring into each other's eyes. He searched her eyes as if to see if she was truly ready for whatever waited for both of them inside.

She did the same, nodding when she found what she was looking for—confirmation.

After a deep breath, she hooked her free arm around Riggs's and headed into the building.

The lobby had a desk on the left, where she knew Gert Francis, Colton's secretary, sat, and a long counter on the right. There were glass doors that required a special ID badge for entry. Once behind those doors, they were in a building shaped like a U. Colton's office was to the right and down the hall. The route to the interview room was behind another locked door to their left, as best as Cheyenne remembered. She'd been here once before with Riggs.

Gert rounded her desk to greet them. She was in her late sixties and had been described as lively by Riggs and the others. She definitely had a twinkle to her brown eyes and a grandmotherly smile that could be disarming. Behind her back, folks had nicknamed her Oprah for her ability to get people to spill their secrets, like the popular TV host Oprah Winfrey.

After a round of hugs, Gert led Cheyenne and Riggs through the locked doors and down the hallway to the witness room, which was roughly the size of a walk-in closet.

The lights were dim and there was a small speaker with a box and a button. She presumed the button was used to communicate orders to the people inside the interview room, which was on the other side of the two-way mirror.

"I'll let your brother know you're here," Gert said with a wink before ducking out of the room.

"Why are we here?" Cheyenne asked quietly. All she saw was a young girl, who barely looked old enough to be in puberty, sitting opposite Colton. She recognized Garrett standing next to her, but not the woman on the other side of the girl.

"Missy?" Riggs asked under his breath. "What's she doing here?"

"Isn't that the girl from the alpaca farm?" Cheyenne tried to piece together why she and Riggs needed to be present at what looked like the questioning of the young lady. The girl sat there, twisting her hands together. She looked to Garrett and then to the woman.

"Yes. Garrett and Brianna are foster parents to Missy. She'd been locked up and made to go without food for the slightest infractions," he said. Those words nearly gutted Cheyenne. Her hands fisted at the thought of anyone abusing this timid child.

"How old is she?" she asked.

"Sixteen," he said.

Sixteen? Cheyenne could scarcely believe the number

was true. Her stomach twisted in a knot as she thought about the cruelty of some people.

"Rest assured the people who held her captive will live out what's left of their very long lives in jail, where they belong. Justice will be served." Riggs's reassurance didn't stop her heart from hurting for this kid. "A private search is being conducted to find her parents."

"She was kidnapped?" she asked.

"Seems so. Several children have already been re-united with their families from that farm," he said.

"Didn't you say that your father was investigating a kidnapping ring when he was murdered?" The connection started to sink in. Colton would never have called them there if the news coming out of Missy's mouth didn't apply to both of them. He hadn't asked for Riggs to come alone. He'd asked for her, too.

And that must mean he'd found out something about their baby.

Chapter 14

Gert knocked on the door of the adjacent room before poking her head in. She nodded and Colton immediately turned to glance at the window before turning back to Missy.

"Can you repeat what you told me over the phone?" Colton asked. His body language indicated he was calm and relaxed.

"Yes." Missy's voice shook. She looked like she was suddenly back in grade school and had been called on to read when she wasn't ready.

"Take your time," Colton said in a tranquil voice Riggs rarely ever heard. His brother was a damn fine sheriff and had a pair of twin boys who lit up any room with their smiles. He was also a solid investigator whom Riggs trusted with his life.

Missy looked down at her feet. She twisted her hands

together a few times before taking in a breath. Brianna took one of the girl's hands in hers and she exhaled like she was taking a breath for the first time. It was impossible not to feel sorry for the kid even though Riggs didn't normally do pity. Most folks made their circumstances and needed to learn to live with the consequences. Kids were the exception. They didn't have control over their lives, not until they were old enough to go off to college or work. Some ran away, which he didn't condone but certainly understood in extreme cases. There'd been a few ranch hands over the years who said they were of age but clearly weren't.

This kid looked like she had a heart of gold and that frustrated him even more. No child deserved to be abused or taken advantage of. White-hot anger roared through him, so he decided to force his thoughts in a different direction. When it came to families, this kid had just hit the jackpot. Garrett and Brianna were devoted to her. She was receiving counseling. She had a good home now and would be getting plenty of food and nurturing. Brianna was going to make an amazing mother someday, just like Cheyenne would have.

Might still get the chance to, a voice in the back of his mind pointed out. All hope was not lost when it came to their daughter.

"There was a newborn who came through the farm about a week ago," she admitted, turning her face toward the floor again like she'd done something wrong. Kids had a habit of blaming themselves for everything that happened, he'd noticed. Thinking back, he'd probably done the same. His brothers, too. Like they might have done something differently and their sister would come back to them.

It was a strange thought to have and yet he knew how common it was. The truth didn't have nearly enough influence when it came to kids and their emotions. After experiencing his own loss, he also realized how strong his parents were. His mother had been a rock over the years despite never giving up on Caroline coming home one day. Did that keep his mother going? Would Riggs fall into the same thinking if his daughter proved to be alive? Or would despair dig a hole too deep to crawl out of?

Pain. He hated it.

Both he and Cheyenne sat up a little straighter at the news.

"She wasn't more than a week old at the time," Missy continued with Brianna's encouragement.

"Can you describe her?" Colton asked.

"She was tiny, like usual. This little girl didn't cry. They said she was born early, and we needed to take special care of her." She squirmed in her seat.

"How premature did they say she was?" Colton's voice was a study in calm whereas Riggs's pulse was climbing.

"A few weeks. Maybe four," she said. "They don't really tell us very much. I listened behind the door to find out any information I could to help the baby."

"That was very brave of you to do. You could have gotten into a lot of trouble," Colton pointed out.

The compliment rolled off her as though she didn't think she deserved any praise. It broke Riggs's heart a little bit more to imagine her situation and what she'd endured.

"It was the only way to be sure I could keep the baby alive. I mean," she glanced up at Brianna and then Garrett, like she was looking for permission to continue. She started working the hem of her shirt in between her fingers of her free hand. "They didn't care. Not really. They called them 'goods' and talked about 'transactions.' They didn't look at them...*us*...as real people with families."

Missy stopped talking and stared at the wall. Her gaze became unfocused, like she'd gone inside an invisible shell where she was lost. Riggs's hands fisted at his sides. He flexed and released his fingers a couple of times to work out some of the tension.

Cheyenne must've picked up on his mood because she reached for his hand and slipped hers inside. He clasped his fingers around hers, needing the connection more than he cared to admit to her or anyone else.

How ironic would it be if the investigation into Caroline's kidnapping led him straight to the place his daughter had been taken? He thought back to Ms. Hubert's death a couple of months ago and how that opened the door, just a crack, for investigators to use. Ms. Hubert was the local who was murdered in her front yard. The investigation into her death prompted questions about Caroline's kidnapping.

Had his father been right all along? The investigator Garrett had hired to look into his sister's disappearance had tracked down a connection to the alpaca farm. Now, three decades after Caroline's abduction, could the same farm be in business? The short answer was yes. It might not have been an alpaca farm all these years, but Riggs would put money on someone making certain that the farm was transferred to a person or couple in on the scheme.

He didn't want to think about how frustrating it must be for law enforcement to know this operation had been running thirty-plus years at a minimum.

More hope his daughter was out there somewhere both

safe and alive took seed. Cheyenne had been clear about her position. She couldn't afford hope. Riggs understood that on some level. But he'd watched from the sideline with his family's ordeal and had realized hope was all they had to go on for most of it. Life also had to go on, he realized. He had even more respect for his parents after realizing how damn hard that must've been.

But then what were the options?

Fold up the tent and stop living? His mother had soon found out she was pregnant with Cash. She was far too strong a person to let her child suffer. No, his mother was the type to pluck up the courage to keep moving. When he really thought about it, Cheyenne would have done the same. She wouldn't have stayed stuck and miserable. It was a knife stab that she'd intended to go on without him...

A thought struck. He'd been protecting his pride by not sharing his feelings with her earlier. He'd tried to convince himself that he was doing it for her benefit. Was that true?

Hard questions deserved real answers.

"When was the last time you saw the little girl?" Colton asked.

Missy shook her head. "She was in and out. I overheard them say she got a high price because she came from a good family. They said something about good breeding and revenge..."

The young woman stopped and took in a breath. A pin drop could be heard for how quiet both rooms became.

"They said she wouldn't be missed because the parents got married to save face anyway." Missy dropped her face into her hands, breaking the connection she had with Brianna.

"You didn't do anything wrong, Missy," Colton soothed.

The young girl's shoulders shook, and she refused to look up.

Brianna wrapped an arm around the young girl's shoulder before locking gazes with Colton.

"She's done for now. Okay?" Brianna's expression could best be described as tense and tortured. On the one hand, she wouldn't want to let Riggs and Cheyenne down. On the other, she had taken on the responsibility for the young girl who was anguished by what she'd been through. Asking her to talk about anything connected to her past must be a trigger.

"It's okay," Missy said with a little more umph than he'd heard from her so far. She straightened her back and took in another breath. "I can't let them win."

Those words sent a fireball raging through Riggs's veins. He tightened his grip on Cheyenne's hand, realizing for the first time that she was trying to be his support. Guilt slammed into him for not telling her what was on his mind earlier. He made a promise to himself to do better if given another opportunity.

Would there be a next time?

The link with Riggs was one of the only things keeping Cheyenne calm as she listened to the account from the young girl. Sixteen wasn't so young, and yet it was difficult to believe the girl sitting at the table in the next room was a teenager, let alone a sophomore in high school. She barely looked old enough to babysit and yet it was clear she'd been forced to care for newborns. Had the young girl held Cheyenne and Riggs's baby?

More of those dangerous seeds of hope blossomed inside her chest. Could her child…*their* baby…be alive?

Deep in her bones, she believed the answer to be yes. Now her attention turned to finding her daughter.

"I heard them talk a lot about someone named Miss H," Missy continued. "This new baby was supposed to be revenge."

"After my dad's diagnosis, he reopened the investigation," Riggs said quietly. "I think he wanted to give my mom peace of mind before he died. At that point, he had time left."

Cheyenne squeezed Riggs's fingers before nodding.

"Miss H might refer to Ms. Hubert. She was part of the kidnapping ring linked to Caroline's disappearance," Riggs said. He issued a sharp sigh. "Looks like this crime has come full circle."

"Someone took our child to get back at your father?" Cheyenne couldn't hide the disbelief in her voice.

"It's possible." He turned to her and locked gazes. "I'm so sorry you got caught in the middle of all this."

Before she could answer, Colton asked, "To your knowledge, is the baby still alive?"

"I'm not sure," Missy admitted. "She was when I last saw her."

"Do you know what happened to her?" Colton continued.

"She was most likely sent to her new home. Austin, I think. But I'm not sure. They didn't all make it to their homes. One…" Missy started crying. "We lost one and I never found out who it was before the raid."

Cheyenne's pulse was through the roof. Her heart pounded the inside of her rib cage as disbelief tried to take hold. She shoved it aside for Ally, for the baby, and for Riggs. She needed to keep a clear head. She'd been blaming herself all this time for what had happened.

Hearing the shame and guilt in Riggs's voice just now made her second-guess being so hard on herself.

One of the kidnapped children didn't make it. Her heart literally cracked in half at the thought. Didn't mean it was hers and didn't have to be for her to be broken about the loss of life or the fact someone's child had died.

"Do you know what happened to the baby who lost its life?" Colton was calmer than Cheyenne could be. As it was, her hands trembled.

"They always took them away separately. Bert and Ernie came to get them." She looked at Brianna and then Garrett. "Those weren't their real names. They liked to talk in code and said never to reveal the truth."

"Did you ever see Bert or Ernie?" Colton continued.

"Yes." Her body shivered at the admission.

"Can you give a physical description of them?" Colton asked.

Missy nodded. She went on to describe a pair of men who were similar height and weight. One had brown hair and the other golden brown. The two looked like they could be brothers with their sharp noses and beady brown eyes.

Colton scribbled notes feverishly. "Did someone different drop off the babies?"

"Most of the time, they came in at night when I was asleep. I'd be told to get up and then I'd be handed a child to care for," she revealed. "There was one guy, though. He came a few times but his visits were always spaced out. I was sure he brought babies but I never saw him carry one inside the building."

"I'd like to bring in a sketch artist," he said to Missy when she was done. He glanced at Garrett before turning his head toward Brianna. "Would that be okay with the two of you?"

Brianna seemed to be thinking seriously. Cheyenne understood the need to protect someone so young, who clearly had been traumatized. Under normal circumstances, she wouldn't want to push for more information. But her child's life might be hanging in the balance. "Okay."

"I know she cried," she said quietly. The echo of her baby's cry rang in her ears.

"You were right all along. Not that I doubted you." Riggs's words offered more comfort. She wasn't ready to cool down just yet, because a fire raged inside her. She was angry at the lies from the nurses and hospital staff. And she was exhausted. Her emotions were wrung out. Bed sounded amazing even though she doubted she could get a wink of sleep.

At this point, her body ached. This was the most physical exertion she'd had since delivering her daughter. *Alive*, a little voice in the back of her head stated loud and clear.

"Are you finished with questioning for now, Colton?" Brianna asked, a torn look on her face.

"Yes, I am." He turned to Missy. "The information you've given me here right now is very important. You've made a big difference in my investigation and I know none of this is easy for you. Thank you for coming down here in person to talk to me."

Missy's bottom lip quivered, and Cheyenne had to fight the urge to barge into the next room and bring the girl into a hug. It wasn't her place to, and Brianna beat her to the punch anyway.

Cheyenne teared up to see Missy enfolded in Brianna's loving arms. Brianna was clearly going to be a very protective and nurturing mother someday. It warmed Cheyenne's heart to see the tenderness among the trio in the next room. Garrett looked like he'd strangle anyone who tried to hurt Missy or Brianna. Who would have thought the wildest O'Connor brother would turn out to be a family man?

He came from good genes, she thought. Granted, he couldn't come close to Riggs in comparison, but she was happy to see Garrett looking so natural as part of a family, and so protective over his fiancée and Missy.

"Are you ready to get out of here?" Riggs asked and she realized he'd been studying her as she stared at his family.

"Yes."

Chapter 15

Riggs had a lot to think about on the drive home. Cheyenne was quiet. Ozzy was still content in the handbag. The little yapper wasn't as bad as Riggs had chalked him up to be when he'd first met Ally.

He couldn't go there about her murder. He'd overthink it until the cows came home. Chew on it over and over again, which wouldn't do any good. In fact, he needed to take a step back in order to clear his thoughts.

More times than not, the answers to any problem came to him while he was distracted. Normally, that meant working extra hours on the ranch. He was also a volunteer firefighter but had put that job on hold during the pregnancy.

Before he realized, he was pulling into the garage.

"How's the tiny tot in your purse? Does he need to go out?" he asked as he cut the engine off. "I can take him."

"I can go with you," Cheyenne offered, and he realized how much the dog meant to her. Ozzy was the last she had of her best friend. The way she held on to her handbag meant someone couldn't pry that dog out of her hands with a crowbar.

"Someone should stay with him at all times because of the coyotes and I'd enjoy your company." There were other dangers for an animal of that size, none of which needed spelling out tonight. It had been a long day by any measure. The dark circles underneath Cheyenne's eyes said she needed to sleep.

Riggs kept the garage door open and walked beside her to the grassy patch of lawn in front of the house. She lifted Ozzy out of her handbag and then set him on the ground. He did his business almost immediately. Two seconds later, he pranced over to Cheyenne and looked up at her expectantly.

Cheyenne picked him up before nuzzling him against her cheek. She mumbled something about making sure he would be well taken care of. The whole scene struck a nerve in Riggs for reasons he couldn't explain. A question arose. Was it seeing Cheyenne dote on the dog that reminded him what an amazing mother she would have been…*correction*…was going to be when they located their daughter? Because he was now more convinced than ever that she was still alive.

On a sharp sigh, he turned and walked toward the garage. Her footsteps sounded on his heels and a wave of comfort washed over him that she didn't hesitate to follow.

"You take the master if you want to try to rest. I'm fine sleeping on the sofa tonight," he said before reassuring her, "I won't leave you alone downstairs."

"Thank you, Riggs. It means a lot that you're willing to be there for me even after everything that's happened between us," she said.

He wanted to tell her that in his mind she was still his wife. Would that bring up more walls between them? No one should have to *ask* their wife to stick around. The vow they'd taken should have implied it.

Rather than let his pride run wild, he nodded.

"I'll always be here for you, Cheyenne. All you have to do is ask." He meant it, too. She could leave when this was all over. He didn't like the idea, but it was true. She could walk away from him and he would still be here for her if she came back and asked for a favor. It was the vow he had taken and had no intention of breaking. Call it cowboy code, or whatever. Riggs O'Connor wasn't brought up to renege once he gave his word.

Cheyenne stopped. She bit her lip like she was trying to stop herself from saying what was on her mind. And then she headed toward the master.

Riggs needed a shower and there was only one on the first level. He would give her a few minutes to get settled before knocking. He didn't want to startle her or catch her getting ready for bed.

The interview with Missy rolled around in his thoughts as he took a bottle of water out of the fridge and downed it. The terrified look on her face would haunt him. The kid had been through a tough ordeal, to be sure. She'd been taken from her family some time before the age of four, according to Colton. For some reason, she was kept at the alpaca farm. An adoption gone bad? Had she been returned by adopted parents who'd decided they didn't want her after all? She had no memories of the events, according to what Colton had said. Just fuzzy details here and there, confused by a child's developing mind.

Was it possible his child would suffer the same fate?

Missy had been neglected and treated poorly physically. There'd been no signs of sexual abuse, which was the lone bright spot in her situation other than the help she was getting now. Brianna and Garrett had pledged to get her the help she needed and find her family. Garrett of all people would know how important that was. It was unimaginable to think a young child had been separated from her parents this long. Riggs clenched his back teeth. He couldn't fathom going sixteen years without knowing what had happened to his child.

Fanning the flames of anger would only serve to distract him from what needed to be done to find his own child. So, with heroic effort, he managed to shove his feelings down deep and focus. There was no way he could rest under the circumstances despite not sleeping a wink last night, so he might as well use the time to be productive.

He retrieved his laptop and made a cup of instant coffee. He had one of those rarely used fancy machines in the kitchen that Cheyenne had fallen in love with. She'd taken to waking up at three thirty in the morning to make him a cup of coffee before he headed out to work for the day. It was something she'd insisted on doing despite the fact he was fully capable of figuring out the machine and making his own brew.

She'd told him not to worry. Her favorite part of the day was kissing him goodbye with the taste of coffee still on his lips. And then it dawned on him. Was that the reason she'd taken up drinking coffee in the last two weeks?

Did it mean she missed him more than she was letting on?

Deciding that was another trail he didn't need to go down, he set up his laptop at the granite island and took a seat. The kiss they'd shared at this spot had him getting up to retrieve another drink of water.

Riggs wasn't really sure what he was looking for online. Sitting around doing nothing would have him pulling his hair out. He sent a text to Garrett thanking Missy for bravely coming forward. The response from his brother was almost instant.

We'll find her.

Riggs set his phone down and stared at it, unable to believe history was repeating itself in his family. Colton needed to be left alone so he could continue to conduct his investigation. He'd call the minute there was another development. Plus, two investigations had kicked into high gear. There were three actually. The murder of Ally Clark was one. The disappearance of their sister, Caroline, was another. And now the abduction of Riggs's daughter.

Three intertwined cases.

It wasn't lost on Riggs that Ally had been killed within a stone's toss of the hospital where she worked. No doubt Colton had already received the reports from his deputy. E-cig Nurse from the other day was afraid of someone. She had information that could be damaging to one of the people she worked with, or for, but clearly, she also had a conscience, or she never would have called Riggs and Cheyenne over in the first place.

Not that it had done any good. E-cig Nurse had panicked when a woman walked out of the hospital and clamped her mouth shut after. So there was a whole lot of haze around what had really happened when Cheyenne was in the hospital.

E-cig Nurse had a kid. She was trying to protect her child. With investigators swarming the building after the discovery in the field, was the nurse in real danger?

Riggs made a mental note to follow up to make sure she and her kid were safe. There wasn't much he could do at this point. He picked up his coffee cup and took a sip. Cold. He nearly spewed the contents. Lots of folks loved iced coffee. He didn't see the appeal. Give him a hot brew any day.

Opening the laptop, he sent an e-mail to the family attorney to research Raven's dad and if he checked out to set up an anonymous fund to pay off the nightshift security guard's pair of mortgages and a college fund for the teenager who'd chanced upon Ally's body.

Cheyenne must've fallen into a deep sleep, because he didn't hear so much as a peep from the master bedroom as he paced in the kitchen. Dinner came and went. He heated up leftovers. He fed Ozzy and saw to it the dog did his business outside. Then he returned to the bar stool.

How long had he been sitting there churning over his thoughts? After forcing himself to get up and make another cup of coffee, he glanced at the clock on the wall. Two thirty in the morning. In an hour, several of his brothers would be waking for the day. An hour after that, the ranch would be kicking into gear. Assignments would be given out and everyone would disperse.

Riggs loved the ranch. He loved being an O'Connor. What he didn't appreciate was the burden that sometimes came with his last name. The thought his daughter was abducted in order to get back at his father for investigating Ms. Hubert was a knife stab straight to the heart.

Whoever killed Ms. Hubert was responsible for kidnapping his child. He'd long considered his last name a blessing. The thought of it being a curse nailed his gut.

He couldn't let himself go down that road. There were pros and cons to everything. He'd always been proud of his family name. He prayed Cheyenne could forgive him for it. He couldn't read the look on her face when they'd learned the crime was linked to his family. Had she convinced herself this was all somehow her fault?

He'd seen her touch the ladybug bracelet several times during the interview and since. It was a go-to move in times of stress. Did she even realize she did it?

Colton was most likely asleep at this point, but Riggs needed to send his brother a text asking him to get in touch when he could. He wanted to know what Colton had learned from the interviews with the nurses and he needed to get E-cig Nurse's name out of his brother if he could. The person who murdered Ally might go after the nurse next. She deserved protection. Riggs couldn't allow any more bloodshed of innocent people tied to this case.

He picked up his phone and sent the text to Colton. Riggs's cell immediately vibrated, indicating a call. With the device still in his hand, he checked the screen. Colton.

"Hey. What's going on?" There had to be news, or his brother wouldn't have called in response to a text.

"I've been wanting to call all night but didn't want to wake you." Colton's voice had the spark that said he was making progress on the investigation.

"I'm wide-awake. Couldn't sleep. What did you find out?" he asked.

"The coroner reported the time of death. Seven thirty yesterday morning," Colton supplied.

"The text from Ally came in twenty minutes prior,"

he said quietly. This confirmed she was murdered after she reached out to him and Cheyenne. It was as close as they'd been so far to being able to link her murder with whatever she'd found out.

"There's more. The flowers have been traced to a nearby grocery store. They were sold at quarter to nine," Colton reported.

"The killer bought them *after* he killed Ally," Riggs said out loud. The perp must have figured out Ally's plans and decided to get rid of her on the fly. "He had time to wash the blood off and change his clothes. He had to have resources close by, like a shower and change of clothes."

"Gert is on the phone to area motels, asking for single male registrants. A man is the only one who would be strong enough to move her body. He would have rented a place that didn't require him to walk through a lobby with blood on him."

"Makes sense," Riggs said. "Is it possible the perp worked at the hospital? He might have access to a back-door that isn't widely used."

"I've been doing a lot of digging into the visiting physician who delivered your daughter. Two nurses at hospitals where Dr. Fortner has worked came forward last night to say they believe there have been suspicious circumstances around births he's attended," Colton supplied.

Riggs needed a minute to absorb what he was hearing. His heart hammered his ribs.

"Is that so?" he finally asked.

"Yes. They're willing to come in and speak to me or one of my deputies. Dr. Fortner doesn't fit the description Missy gave of the farm visitor or the one given by the clerk at the grocery store who remembered selling flowers to a tall guy in a hoodie," Colton said. Then he added, "I don't want you to be discouraged, though. This case is blowing open, Riggs. We'll get to the bottom of what really happened sooner rather than later. I promise."

"Do you believe my daughter is alive?" Riggs had to ask the question outright.

"I hope she is. I can't confirm either way, except to say I have questions about what really happened that night." Colton never pulled any punches and Riggs was grateful for the honesty.

"What about the flowers? Do you have a name?" Riggs asked, figuring the perp might have used a credit card.

"No, the perp paid with cash."

Of course, he would. The murderer wouldn't want to leave a trail.

"Do you have any idea what Dr. Fortner looks like?" Riggs asked. "Cheyenne didn't remember much about his face. She said the details were fuzzy."

"I do. I'll send over the photo from his badge the hospital provided," Colton promised. "Or, if you want it faster than that, his photo is on the web."

"Right. Good point." He should have thought of that sooner. "What about the nurse who tried to talk to us outside? The one I told you about. She panicked and stopped talking real fast. With what you're telling me now, I believe she's in danger."

"Let me see." There was a paper-shuffling noise in the background for a few seconds before Colton's voice came back on the line. "Loriann Fischer is her name."

"Are you sending someone over to protect her?" Riggs asked, figuring he already knew the answer to his question.

"I don't have the resources." Colton's voice was low. It was obvious he didn't like it any more than Riggs did.

"What about her number? Can you give it to me? I'd like to check up on her and make sure she's okay. Maybe get her to a safe place until you catch this guy," Riggs said.

"I can't—"

"She mentioned a kid, Colton. What if the perp goes after one or both of them?" Riggs couldn't live with himself if he didn't do everything in his power to ensure their safety.

"I doubt she'd appreciate a call in the middle of the night," Colton argued.

"What if she isn't sleeping? The way she looked yesterday morning when Cheyenne and I were talking to her…you should have seen it. She was afraid, Colton. And now Ally's body has been found. That has to be all over the hospital grapevine by now."

"How about this. I'll give her a call and ask if you can check up on her. I can volunteer your phone number, but I can't promise she'll use it," Colton reasoned.

It wasn't exactly what Riggs had asked for, but it was better than nothing.

"Can you call her as soon as we get off the phone?" Riggs asked.

"That I can do."

"Then I guess I'll talk to you later," Riggs said.

Colton hesitated. "This is really important to you, isn't it?"

"It is," Riggs admitted.

"Then you didn't get this number from me. And please don't let it come back to bite me." Colton supplied the number.

"I'm not sure how I'll ever repay you, but—"

"Just try not to get me fired," Colton shot back. His joke lightened the mood.

"Yes, sir," Riggs teased, appreciating the break in tension. It wouldn't last long.

"Let me know if she needs protection," Colton said. "I might be shorthanded, but I'll figure something out."

"Will do." Riggs could do one better than that. He had every intention of seeing to it personally.

The brothers ended the call. Riggs glanced at the clock again. Twenty minutes had passed since the last time he looked. For most folks, this was a ridiculous hour. Not so for ranchers, bakers and people in a handful of other jobs that required early mornings or twenty-four-hour days.

Besides, if E-cig Nurse, aka Loriann Fischer, was as stressed as she had been earlier, there was no way the woman was asleep. She might not answer a call from an unknown number in the middle of the night, though. So he sent a text first, telling her exactly who he was and why he planned to call. Despite the late hour, he had a hunch she might not be able to sleep. Acting on it, he tapped her number into the keypad. Loriann picked up on the first ring.

"How did you get this number?" she asked with a shaky voice.

"I needed to make sure you and your kid were all right." Riggs intentionally didn't answer her question.

"Oh." She sounded suspicious. "How did you find out my name?"

"Through the investigation of the murder of my wife's best friend." It wasn't a lie.

"Sad about what happened to the other nurse. I shouldn't be talking to you right now," she said. The panic in her voice was palpable. "It's not safe."

"Have you already spoken to investigators?" He knew the answer. He was trying to get her to see reason. Folks in a highly charged emotional state weren't known for making the best decisions. Based on the sound of her voice and the fact she was up in the middle of the night, he figured she'd been chewing on yesterday's events.

"Yes," she conceded.

"Then you need additional protection for you and your child," he stated like it was as plain as the nose on his face.

"Where am I supposed to get that?" Her voice trembled with fear.

"I'm here to help. I apologize for not introducing myself yesterday morning. My name is Riggs O'Connor," he said.

"I know that n…" She drew out the last consonant. It was like bells were going off inside her head and she couldn't figure out why.

"Go ahead and look me up. I'll wait," he urged.

"Hold on." The line got quiet for a couple of minutes and he was pretty sure she'd used the mute function. When she came back to the line, he could hear her breathing for a moment before she spoke. "Why would someone like you help me?"

"Because you helped us. Your statement will help nail the person who killed my wife's best friend and, more important, it's the right thing to do." He meant every word.

Loriann was quiet. Stunned? A question hung in the air. Would she accept his offer?

Chapter 16

"That's mighty nice of you, Mr. O'Connor, but I don't think—"

"Accept my help for your child," he interrupted before she could get too much momentum on the rejection.

"I don't know," she hedged but he could tell his statement had made the impact he'd hoped for.

"Do you have a boy or a girl?" he asked.

"Boy," came the response.

"How old, if I may ask?" He'd learned a long time ago that he got more done with honey than vinegar, as the old saying went.

"Six years old." She blew out a sharp breath.

"I'm guessing he's asleep right now," he continued.

"Yes, that's right. He is," she acknowledged.

"Let me help you keep him safe, Loriann. My wife and I would like to come pick the two of you up and bring you to my family's ranch, where you'll both be protected until the person who murdered our friend is locked behind bars. No one at the hospital who is willing to speak up against him is safe until that happens and you know it." He'd made his plea. He couldn't and wouldn't try to force her to take the help. At this point, he could only hope she would see reason.

"I wish I could. But I have to work tomorrow." The anguish in her voice caused his heart to bleed for every single parent who had to balance being able to put food on the table versus ensuring the safety of their child.

"What if you could come to work on the ranch? Get paid what you normally make at the hospital to help out around here?" he asked.

"Well, I guess that could work. But I'd lose my benefits if they fire me," she said. Based on the change in her tone, he was making progress.

"What if I told you my family could ensure that didn't happen? If going back there would cause you any discomfort, we could set you up in a new position at another hospital," he said, doing his best to radiate confidence. For his plan to work, she needed to believe him. Most wouldn't trust a random stranger but the O'Connors had built a strong legacy of honesty. One that he was hoping to capitalize on now.

"You can do that?" She nearly choked on her words. Then she said, "Of course, you can. I'm not used to keeping company with people who can make a difference like that."

Riggs was never more reminded how fortunate he was being an O'Connor, and how rare it actually was to grow up in a household with two loving parents who had the financial means to move mountains if need be.

His folks had had an admirable marriage. One he'd believed he could repeat with Cheyenne despite the rushed nature of their wedding.

"We don't take our privilege lightly," he reassured her. It was true. Being an O'Connor meant honor and holding up the family name—a job he'd been born to do and welcomed with open arms. "And it would be a waste if we couldn't use our resources to help others who deserved it."

The line was quiet. He could tell that Loriann was proud and not the kind to take what she would view as handouts from others lightly. This situation was different, but he respected her for her convictions.

"You say you'll keep my boy safe until this situation is sorted out," she finally said.

"Yes, ma'am," he said quickly. She needed to know how serious and committed he was. No hesitation.

"Do you know where I live?" she asked.

"No. I do not," he responded.

She rattled off her address before saying, "It might be my imagination running wild but I'm pretty sure a two-door gray sedan has circled the building three times since we started talking. Get here as quick as you can."

"On my way, but it'll be about an hour. Call the law and report a suspicious vehicle." He didn't want to wake Cheyenne, but he would look in on her and leave a note beside the bed for when she woke. "You have my number now. Call me if anything changes."

"Okay."

The line went dead. The gray sedan might be nothing, but he wasn't taking any chances. He grabbed his shotgun from his gun cabinet in the closet underneath the stairs. And then decided his holster and 9mm wouldn't be a bad choice, either.

A couple of seconds later, he scribbled out a note to Cheyenne and then headed to the master. He tiptoed inside the room, praying he wouldn't disturb her, and then he realized that wouldn't do. He'd promised not to leave her alone while she rested and she'd been asleep a long time. Plus, he'd told Loriann that he and his wife would be picking her up.

The light flipped on as his resolve to wake her grew. Cheyenne sat up, hugging her knees to her chest.

"Where are you going?" She blinked a couple of times like her eyes needed a minute to adjust to the light.

"To pick up the nurse we spoke to yesterday morning. Both she and her child might be in danger. I convinced her to come to the ranch for protection until Ally's killer is behind bars." There was no reason to hold back. "I wrote a note explaining but I planned to wake you up and tell you. Make sure you were okay with me leaving."

"I'm coming with you." Cheyenne threw the covers off. He forced his gaze away from those long silky legs of hers revealed by the sleeping shirt she wore, which was one of his old T-shirts.

He picked up a pair of her favorite joggers that she'd left behind during the move, no doubt by accident, and then tossed them over to her.

"Thanks." She caught them and shimmied into the pair.

He opened her dresser and threw a pair of socks next, realizing the movers had left quite a bit behind in their haste. But then, she might have instructed them to grab what they could see and get out.

No one had checked the laundry room when he'd stood

by and watched drawers be emptied one by one in their bedroom. He wasn't about to point out places that had been missed. The memory caused his gut to clench. He chalked it up to one of the worst days of his life.

In the span of two weeks, he'd lost a child and a wife. And in the last twenty-four hours the world had shifted again. To say life was unpredictable would be the understatement of the century. It had more twists and turns than a multimillion-dollar roller coaster and all the ups and downs to go with it.

Cheyenne finished dressing, turning her back to him when she changed her shirt and put on a bra. He respected her privacy.

"Ready." She hopped on one foot as she slipped on her second tennis shoe.

She gathered up Ozzy and tucked him inside her handbag. He figured he'd buy her one of those carriers to make them both more comfortable once this was all over.

In a surprise move, she reached for his hand at the door. He didn't pull away even though he probably should have. There was no reason to confuse the issue of why she was staying there and why they were together... Ally. In fact, if Cheyenne's friend hadn't reached out, the two of them wouldn't be in the same room right now. Add random to the list of life's attributes. Without that arbitrary idea of Ally's to have the two of them listen to her at the same time, Cheyenne would still be at her friend's house and Riggs would be working at the ranch.

The thought struck hard. He wanted his wife to be home because she couldn't stay away. This was a good reminder to keep his feelings in check. At present, they were all over the map. As levelheaded as Riggs normally was, this situation couldn't be more extreme. The stakes couldn't be higher with his wife and child hanging in the balance.

This time, he'd give himself a break for the slip that had him wanting to bury himself deep inside the woman he'd married and not let go of her again.

He released her hand as they entered the garage. She shot a questioning look, but he didn't acknowledge it. Keeping himself in check was his new marching order.

Cheyenne pushed down the hurt from Riggs's action with the realization the two of them were wading through shark-infested waters. It was good to keep guards up and some distance. She respected his boundary, figuring it wouldn't hurt for her to strengthen her walls, as well.

If they were going to be parents, and she hoped they would with everything inside her, she realized the baby showing up wasn't a magical fix. Their relationship had been strained over the past few weeks. She'd asked for a divorce and no matter how confusing life had become, neither could go back and pretend none of it had happened.

He was right to pull back, even though it stung.

On the drive to Loriann's apartment building, he filled her in on his conversation with his brother and how he'd convinced Colton to let him have Loriann's cell number.

"The gray sedan is worrisome," she said when he was finished.

"Let's hope it's a coincidence. I doubt Loriann is usually up at this time of night looking out the window, so it might not be as strange as she thinks," he said.

He was right.

"We both know I can't watch a scary movie before

bed," she agreed. "Plants too many ideas in my imagination and it just runs with it."

"Like the time you thought there might be a ghost in the laundry room," he said. "Which turned out to be a squirrel that had gotten in through an opened window earlier in the day."

"How was I supposed to know the little guy was in there? We didn't exactly have any pets," she defended.

"You'd just watched one of those horror movies... which one?" He tapped the steering wheel with his index finger. It was a habit she'd missed in the two weeks they'd been apart. It was crazy how much she missed the little things about her husband. The first kiss in the morning before either got out of bed. It wasn't romantic so much as sweet. Or the way he always picked a single flower for her while they were in season before he walked in the door. She'd set it inside a jar on the table, keeping a constantly growing and changing bouquet.

Relationships were a lot like that. Leave a spoiled flower in the jar too long and suddenly the water was moldy. They took constant pruning, especially in the early years, according to her mother. Cheyenne thought about how much her mother would have loved Riggs. And she would have been blown away by the ranch. The place was glorious by anyone's standards, and her mother had been one of the least picky people on the planet.

Her mother had loved the little things in life. A ladybug crawling on a blade of grass. Ladybugs had been her favorite, thus the bracelet.

"What are you thinking about?" Riggs's deep, masculine voice washed over her and through her.

"My mom." She fingered the ladybug, rolling it around in between her thumb and forefinger.

The next thing she knew, the delicate clasp broke and the bracelet fell apart. Pieces of it flew in opposite directions, on her lap and on the floorboard. Cheyenne's chest hurt as she tried to breathe, realizing she'd just ruined her mother's legacy.

She gasped and probably cursed but she couldn't be 100 percent certain. All she could think about was the loss.

"No," she said loudly. She fisted her right hand and then slammed it on the armrest, drawing it back the minute she connected. Pain shot through her pinky.

Riggs put on his turning signal and hit the brake.

"No. No. Keep going. I'll find the pieces later. We can't stop now," she said.

"Cheyenne, are you sure?"

"Yes. It's too late." Those words were knife jabs to the center of her chest. She repeated them over and over again in her thoughts as she bent forward to find what she could.

"Use your phone. The dome light won't do much good," Riggs urged.

She reached for her cell, disturbing Ozzy, who made no secret of how unimpressed he was with the move.

"Okay, okay. Settle down, little guy." Breaking her promise to her best friend wasn't on the table no matter how much the dog overreacted. "You're good." She lightened her tone and Ozzy responded by curling up and lowering his head to rest on the side of her handbag. He'd warmed up to her and yet she couldn't help but think he was in survival mode.

His eyes—those sad eyes that made her want to cry—stared up at her brokenly.

If ever there was a time for wisdom, this would be it.

Except that none came. She patted Ozzy on the head and then scratched behind his ears until he went back to sleep.

There was no way she was leaving this truck without finding the ladybug. The rest of the bracelet could be replaced.

She ran her fingers along the floorboard. The piece she was looking for was so tiny and the cab of the truck was so big. It didn't help that this was a work truck, so it wasn't exactly empty. There were rags and a couple of empty water bottles on the floorboard in the back. And there were clumps of dirt. One fooled her into thinking she'd found what she was looking for as she reached underneath the seat.

"I hate to stop what you're doing, but we're here and I need you to take something." Riggs pulled into a parking spot and then handed over a 9mm handgun. "Can you handle this?"

"I can," she assured him, figuring she better qualify the statement. "My parents took me to a shooting range when I was a teenager, so I'd know what to do if I encountered a gun at a friend's house. Shotguns are a different story. I've never used one. And I didn't load any of the weapons I shot that day."

It felt strange that she hadn't told him that story before or that her husband didn't know all the little things about her. After discovering the pregnancy and then jumping into marriage, they'd gone straight to getting ready for the baby mode. They'd only been dating a short time before the pregnancy news came.

Riggs nodded.

"I have to find the charm first," Cheyenne said.

He seemed to catch on immediately. This was important to her. He gave a quick scan of the parking lot before taking hold of the cell while she resumed her search.

Cheyenne reached for the chair release lever. Her fingers landed on a button. She played with it until she figured out how to move the seat back. Then she moved onto all fours to be eye level with the floor.

"I can't find it, Riggs." She didn't bother to hide the desperation in her voice.

He moved the flashlight around, and then she saw it.

"There." She reached underneath the seat. Warmth spread through her as she picked it up and held it on the flat of her palm.

Tap. Tap. Tap.

The metal barrel of a gun beat out a staccato rhythm against the driver's-side window.

Chapter 17

Riggs froze. His back was to the driver's-side window where the taps came from.

"Gun," was all Cheyenne said as her eyes widened in shock and fear. She quickly dropped the ladybug inside her handbag.

The 9mm was still in his right hand. He'd used his left to hold the light for Cheyenne. Could he turn fast enough to surprise the person on the other side of the glass?

It was a risky move. Too risky. One wrong flex of a finger and disaster could strike. The sound behind him was at too close a range to miss and it would take Riggs a couple of seconds to swivel enough to get off a shot.

"What does he look like?" he asked Cheyenne.

She put her hands in the air as she rose to her knees. "I can't tell. His face is covered, and he has on a dark hoodie."

The same description of the rose buyer from the grocery store. For a fraction of a moment Riggs thought about drawing down on the guy. But Hoodie was already in position to fire and the second or two it would take Riggs to position his weapon could cost Cheyenne her life.

After issuing a sharp sigh, he released his grip on the 9mm, letting it tumble onto the seat and then put his hands in the air before slowly turning around. A gun wasn't the same MO as Ally's murder, which meant multiple people could be involved or the original perp could be getting nervous. Ally had been stabbed, a bloody and personal way to die. It fit with the date-gone-wrong ruse.

Riggs's thoughts immediately jumped to Loriann and her kid. This person couldn't be random. He had to be connected to the case. Nothing else made sense.

Was this the guy from the gray sedan?

Hoodie took a step back into the shadows and motioned for them to exit the truck. It looked as though he was working alone and that would give Riggs and Cheyenne a possible advantage. Two against one were numbers he'd like better if he was the one in possession of the firearm.

If he could get close enough to the bastard to safely take him down, he wouldn't hesitate.

"Can I count on you to stay behind me?" Riggs asked Cheyenne.

"Yes." There was no conviction in her response, but this wasn't the time to dig around for clarification.

Keeping his hands in the air, he motioned toward the door handle. He would have to lower his right hand out of the perp's view to open the door. Again, he tried to figure out a way to capitalize on the opportunity but came up blank.

The perp also had on dark pants…slacks? He had on surgical gloves. Dr. Fortner? Or someone else from the hospital?

"Does this guy seem familiar at all?" he asked Cheyenne quietly.

"I can't see anything," she said.

The perp stepped forward and opened the driver's-side door before moving approximately fifteen back. The guy had on surgical gloves. He was too far away to make a move but even at this distance Riggs could see the perp's hand shaking.

"Come out," came the demand. Riggs didn't recognize the voice.

Did he plan to shoot them outside the truck? Make it look like a robbery gone wrong? Or set up some other scene like the one he'd tried to use to cover Ally's murder?

Murder-suicide?

The silencer on the end of his gun would minimize noise. Folks wouldn't be any the wiser as they slept through the night. Except Loriann, who was waiting for Riggs and Cheyenne. He couldn't let his mind go to a place where this jerk had already gotten to her and her son. Anger ripped through him. She'd been watching out the window. Was she now?

He'd parked across the lot from her building so he wouldn't run into the driver of the gray sedan.

As he was about to climb out of the truck, Cheyenne reached for his door. She held it where he couldn't move. It only took an instant for him to realize she meant to use it to shield them as she brought the 9mm around and aimed at the perp.

A second later, Riggs felt the shotgun being shoved at

him. He gripped it and took aim as the perp darted between vehicles, firing a wild shot. A warning?

Riggs was momentarily torn between chasing after the guy and checking on Loriann. Her safety won out. That, and the fact he didn't want Cheyenne chasing a guy with a gun, and she would insist on coming with him. Not to mention the fact he couldn't very well leave her in the truck.

The sounds of screeching tires came a second before a gray streak shot out of the lot and in the opposite direction. At this point, Riggs was at a full run to get to Loriann and her child. He vaguely remembered slamming his truck door closed and locking the vehicle.

Cheyenne was right behind him, gripping her handbag with Ozzy inside, as they raced to Loriann's unit. Her apartment was on the second floor. Riggs made as little noise as possible as he took the steps two at a time. As he and Cheyenne made it to the door, it swung wide open and a scared-looking Loriann stood on the other side.

Relief he couldn't begin to describe washed over him.

"Come in quick." She ushered them both inside, then closed and locked the door behind them. "The gray sedan couldn't get out of here fast enough. Now I know why. He was coming for me, wasn't he?"

"Yes. We got here as fast as we could," Riggs said as he tried to catch his breath.

"I'm just thankful we got here in time," Cheyenne added.

"Me, too." Loriann stepped forward and brought Cheyenne into a brief hug. "I called the police to report a suspicious vehicle like you said, but the dispatcher didn't seem too thrilled. She said they'd been getting calls about teenagers joyriding, and I couldn't prove any different, so I just let it go."

"You did the right thing," Riggs reassured. "The guy in the gray sedan had a gun with a silencer on it and he wore surgical gloves. I doubt he was planning to let you leave here alive."

Loriann shook visibly.

"What was he waiting on?" she asked. Something passed behind her eyes that Riggs made a note to ask about later. Right now, all he could think about was getting her and her son to safety.

"My guess?" Riggs asked. "An opportunity."

"Makes sense." She shook her head like she was trying to shake off the creepiness of the close call. "I packed a bag for me and Zachary." She looked from Cheyenne to Riggs. "I wasn't real sure how long we'd be gone."

"We can get whatever else you need at the ranch," Riggs said. "Let's get out of here before he decides to come back."

As it was, they got lucky. The perp must have realized he was outnumbered. Cheyenne's move had been brilliant. There was no way Riggs could have pulled it off while the guy was focused on watching him, viewing him as the bigger threat. The man never saw Cheyenne's move coming and, to be honest, neither had Riggs. His wife had always been strong and quick-witted, so he wasn't shocked. His admiration for her grew leaps and bounds, though.

Cheyenne O'Connor was a force of nature. One he admired and respected for her strength and courage, which wasn't going to make it any easier when they went their separate ways. Of course, if their child was alive out there and they found her, they'd be bound together for the rest of their lives.

"Give me your suitcase. I'll run them down." Riggs handed the 9mm over to Cheyenne. "If anyone besides me walks through that door, shoot first and ask questions later."

"I should go with you for cover," Cheyenne said with a pensive look.

"I'd rather you stayed here with Loriann and Zachary." Riggs had no doubt Cheyenne's protective instincts would kick into high gear since a child was involved.

Loriann rolled a large suitcase into the room. "He has a favorite blanket and teddy, but I wouldn't be able to pry those out of his fingers if I tried."

"It's fine. We'll bring those with him," Riggs said. "Will seeing guns scare him if he wakes up?"

"I'll tell him we're playing pretend cops and robbers," Loriann offered.

"Lock the door behind me," Riggs said before heading out the door.

The look of concern from Cheyenne had him wanting to figure out another way. This was their best bet, though. Cheyenne's adrenaline was jacked through the roof as she locked the door behind Riggs.

"He's a good person," Loriann said.

"Yes," Cheyenne responded.

"A good husband, too?" Loriann asked.

"Yes." Her admission wasn't helping Cheyenne keep an emotional distance. Did she want to stay married to him? The short answer was yes. If only it was that easy. Life was complicated now that she'd pushed him away because she could never give him children, only to find out their daughter was alive.

The thought of Anya—that was to be their daughter's name—being out there somewhere with another family sent a tsunami of emotions roaring through her. She had to shove them aside to focus on getting Loriann and her son out of the apartment in one piece.

"You should probably go and get your son now," Cheyenne said to Loriann, figuring they would be on the move the second Riggs returned. She moved to the window with the view of the parking lot. She cracked it open and readied the gun. If the gray sedan came back, she wouldn't hesitate to shoot.

From this vantage point, she was able to keep watch over Riggs. When he returned, he brought the vehicle with him, blocking three parking spots so he could be as close to the stairs as possible.

Relief like she'd never known washed over her as she watched him take the stairs. She closed and locked the window. The floor creaked behind her, indicating Loriann had returned. Cheyenne dropped the barrel of the gun, hiding it behind her leg in case the little boy woke. She didn't want to frighten him and had no idea if he'd been around any type of weapon like this before.

"I can't thank you and your husband enough," Loriann said quietly. The boy in her arms was more than half her size. His head rested on her shoulder and she bounced like she had an infant in her arms. The sweetness of the mother-child scene slammed into Cheyenne's solar plexus. It hurt to breathe.

The fact Loriann kept referring to Riggs as Cheyenne's husband wasn't lost on her. There was no reason to explain how complicated their relationship was. And if she thought she could give him what he wanted...*deserved*...there'd be no talk of divorce. Make no mistake about it, Riggs O'Connor had been the best thing that ever happened to Cheyenne.

Riggs tapped on the door three times. Cheyenne raced to open it and usher him inside. After closing it behind him, she reached up on her tiptoes and gave him a kiss partly for luck and partly because recent events showed her how little was guaranteed in life.

He brought his hand up to cup her face before feathering a kiss on her lips. There was something so tender about Riggs's kiss that it robbed Cheyenne's ability to breathe.

A second later, the moment had passed, and they were wrangling Loriann and her son out of their home.

"You lead the way," Riggs said to her. "I'll take the back to ensure no one is lingering."

Cheyenne nodded and did as requested. Thankfully, it was a short trip to the truck. She opened the passenger door and helped Loriann step inside. The boy in her arms stirred, opening his eyes for the briefest moment. He had the sweetest brown eyes. His cheeks were flush and his lashes long. He had the face of a cherub.

Loriann positioned in the back and her son sprawled out on the bench seat, holding tight to his teddy. Cheyenne helped with his blanket as he rolled over. Then she hopped into the passenger side and secured her seat belt. Shotgun at the ready, Riggs reclaimed the driver's side.

The sun came up on the drive back to the ranch, giving Loriann the ability to see the full glory of KBR as they drove through security. A bunkhouse in one direction and barns in the other created a kind of grandeur that still wowed Riggs today when he slowed down.

"This is where you live?" Loriann asked, wide-eyed. The place would be considered grand by anyone's standards. A guard at a security stand controlled entrance to the paved road leading to their massive white house.

"Technically, my mom lives in the main house. Our place is another half hour's drive from here. I'd like to get the two of you situated before heading home," Riggs said to Loriann.

"Are you sure it'll be all right for us to stay here?" The wonder and disbelief in her voice was a little too familiar to Cheyenne. It was difficult to believe people who were this well off could be as kind and generous as the O'Connor family.

"Believe me when I say I had the same reaction the first time Riggs brought me home to meet the family. They'll welcome you and Zachary with open arms. No questions asked," Cheyenne said. It was true. She'd never met people like the O'Connors before. Part of her had been losing faith in the goodness in the world until Riggs.

He parked in front of the main house.

"I hope you'll be comfortable here. Like my wife said, my mother will be pleased to have the company. She's always complaining about rattling around in this big house by herself now that her children are grown," he said. That seemed to put Loriann at ease.

As they started the process of exiting the vehicle, Cheyenne's cell buzzed.

Riggs froze.

"Go on inside without me," she said. "I'll be right there."

He nodded even though he looked reluctant to leave her there. She shooed him away, fishing for her cell phone inside her handbag. Besides, she had to give Ozzy a chance to stretch his legs.

Being at the main house brought back a whole slew

of memories. His family had been nothing but welcoming. It was impossible not to feel like she let them down in some way. She hoped they realized she was hanging onto the end of her rope as best she could.

A quick check of the screen told her that her father was on the line. She caught the call right before it headed into voice mail.

"Hey, Dad," she said. "Is everything okay?"

"I came as soon as I could," her father said. His voice had lost the spark it once had. Hearing it again shocked her into the reality of what her future might look like without Riggs.

"Hold on a sec. What did you just say?" she asked.

Chapter 18

"I'm here, knocking on your door. I see your car right there." Cheyenne's father spoke like she was standing on the porch with him and he was pointing it out.

"I texted you two weeks ago," she said as panic gripped her. He'd come to Ally's place?

"I'm sorry I couldn't drive any faster," he explained.

"You should have texted me back or called." What if the driver of the gray sedan was watching Ally's house? He might be expecting Cheyenne to come home where he could ambush her.

"Listen to me very carefully, Dad," she began. "Leave right now. Okay?"

"What? Why?" Her dad's confusion wasn't helping with her fried nerves.

"You have to get out of there. It's not safe," she warned, praying he would listen to her and not question it. She might be overreacting, but she wasn't willing to take a chance.

"What's not safe, honey?" There was real concern in her father's voice and she appreciated him for it.

"I don't have time to explain right now. Get in your RV and start driving. You can come out to the ranch or—"

"What are you doing at the ranch? I thought you were staying here. Is everything all right between you and Riggs?" Her father sounded confused.

"Yes," she said for lack of something better. It would be easier to explain once she got her father on the road and away from Ally's place. "Drive right now. I need to see you."

"Oh. Well, then. I'll just get off the porch here, and walk back to the RV. I'm parked on the street." As he'd gotten older, he'd developed a habit of giving her a play-by-play in situations like these.

"Yes. Hurry. It's been too long since we've seen each other, and I need my father right now." She let the emotions coursing through her play out in her tone. It was a ploy for his sympathy, but she didn't have time to explain. She would do or say just about anything to get him out of harm's way. The two of them might not be as close as they once were but she couldn't risk anything bad happening to another person she loved.

"What's the address?" he asked.

"Get in the RV and then give the phone to Virginia. I'll direct you once you get on the road," she urged.

"Well, all right. If it's that important to you we'll head on over," he conceded.

"It is, Dad. It's the most important thing you could ever do for me." She wasn't afraid to pour it on thick.

She heard him tell Virginia to stay in the RV. Virginia grumbled but she went along with what he said.

It was impossible in times like these not to compare Virginia to her mother. The two might resemble each other in looks but they couldn't be more different when it came to their personalities.

Cheyenne let Ozzy run onto the lawn while she waited for her stepmother to pick up the phone. Rustling came over the line before the sound of the engine kicking over. She sighed with relief when she heard the two of them arguing about where they were going. She shouldn't be surprised and yet it made her sad. Her parents had had one of those magical relationships. They rarely ever disagreed. Their house was filled with laughter and her mother's happy squeals as she was being taken for a spin around the kitchen after supper.

She didn't recognize her father's life anymore. Now that she'd experienced loss, she didn't blame him for wanting to fill the void. It struck her as strange how the two of them reacted in completely opposite ways to their grief. When Cheyenne was told her daughter was gone, she'd decided never to try to have children again, whereas her father had married the first woman he came across who looked like the wife he'd lost. While she couldn't fathom trying to replace her child, she suddenly wondered if they were both equally wrong. Had they gone to opposite extremes?

"Hello, Cheyenne?" Virginia sounded like she half expected someone else to be on the line.

"Hi. Yes. It's me," Cheyenne responded, never quite sure how to speak to her stepmother.

"I'm sorry about your…*situation*." Virginia sounded sorrowful.

"Thank you." Cheyenne realized it was the first time she'd spoken to Virginia since losing the baby.

"I lost a pregnancy once and couldn't get out of bed for a month," her stepmother continued. "It's awful."

"I'm sorry to hear." Cheyenne appreciated the sentiment. Virginia spoke more sincerely than she usually did. "You're right about one thing. It's the worst feeling."

"It sure is." The cold edge that had always been in Virginia's voice softened.

The thought occurred to Cheyenne that it couldn't possibly be easy to step into another woman's shoes. And her dad was far less sad now that he was remarried. He'd been gutted after his wife's death.

"Sounds like you guys are on the road now." Cheyenne needed to change the subject and steer the conversation back on track. "This is going to sound like a strange question. I promise to explain later."

"Go on," Virginia urged.

"Is there a gray sedan anywhere near you?" Cheyenne held her breath while waiting for the answer.

"Let's see." There was a moment of silence before Virginia said, "No. Not one in sight."

Cheyenne released the air in her lungs with a slow exhale. She rattled off the address of the ranch and told her dad to call when GPS said he was getting close. He mumbled something about finding an RV park first. She ended the conversation, picked up Ozzy and then turned to face the main house. Her chest squeezed.

Riggs's mother must be inside. Margaret O'Connor was about the nicest woman Cheyenne had ever had the pleasure of meeting. The thought of hurting someone who had already experienced the worst possible pain didn't sit well.

If Margaret gave Cheyenne a chilly reception, she wouldn't be surprised or place any blame. It would be nothing more than just desert for hurting Riggs and letting the family down.

With a heavy heart, she marched to the front door. As she arrived, it burst open and Margaret stood on the other side, arms wide open.

"It's so good to see you," Margaret said as she brought Cheyenne into an embrace.

Shock robbed her voice. This warmth was so unexpected and, to be honest, felt undeserved. All Cheyenne could say in response was, "I'm sorry."

Margaret pulled back and shooed the comment away. "There's no reason for apologies. You're here now and I don't want to waste a minute."

Cheyenne couldn't stop the smile from curling the corners of her lips.

"Who do you have here?" Margaret motioned toward the handbag.

"This is Ozzy." He popped his head out as though he knew he was being talked about.

"Oh my goodness. What a sweetheart." Margaret cooed at the little dog and Cheyenne could have sworn he made the same noises back.

"Do you still like to drink that chai tea?" Margaret asked, returning her gaze to meet Cheyenne's.

"Coffee is my drink of choice now," Cheyenne admitted.

"How about a cup?" Margaret asked. "I can figure out how to work the machine while Riggs gets our new houseguests set up in one of the guest rooms."

"Sounds good to me." Everything about being back

at the ranch felt right. A couple of weeks away suddenly felt like an eternity.

Arm in arm, she walked with Margaret into the expansive kitchen. She'd rarely come to the main house during her pregnancy and yet the place felt like home. Her house with Riggs was the same. She'd moved around a lot as a kid, so it surprised her how much she fit at the ranch the minute she arrived.

Ozzy whimpered inside the handbag.

"What's wrong, little guy?" Cheyenne freed him.

He wiggled like a baby who didn't want to be held.

"Okay if he runs free for a few minutes?" Cheyenne asked Margaret.

"Fine by me," came the response as the older woman went to fix the brew.

Cheyenne set Ozzy down on the tile floor. She squatted next to him. "Is that better? Do you need to stretch your legs?"

Ozzy half ran, half hopped over to Margaret, and then lay down by her feet.

Riggs closed the door to the guest suite where Loriann and Zachary were settling in. The little boy was still asleep and Loriann was unpacking their suitcase when he left. Riggs would be lying if he didn't admit to taking a hit at seeing the mother and son together. Loriann's love for her son made him wonder what it would be like to hold his own child in his arms.

As it was, he could only imagine how powerful a moment that might be. He had yet to meet his daughter and he already knew he'd move heaven and earth to make her comfortable.

They had to find her. Period. There was no other out-come in his mind.

Riggs had learned a long time ago to shut out all other possibilities when he went after something. Whether it applied to work or a personal goal, the same tactic came into play. Singular vision gave him clarity.

Whoa. He thought about that for a moment and applied it to his relationship with Cheyenne. When she'd told him about the pregnancy, he'd set his sights on becoming a family. Technically, that wasn't the same as becoming a good husband. A strong relationship required com-munication. And what had he done when she'd seemed stressed? Given her space. He figured everything would magically work out once the baby came. That was as real-istic as cooking an egg on a December sidewalk in Texas.

He could say the same for when she tried to talk to him in the cab of his truck. He'd decided telling her the whole truth would cause more harm than good. Part of his thinking was meant to protect her. But she needed to know what was on his mind. Otherwise, they'd never get to know each other on a real level. He'd lost some of her trust when he didn't communicate. He'd seen the change in her eyes the minute he lost her. The eyes never lied. He had some work to do to gain her trust again. His mistakes were racking up.

Riggs veered into the kitchen. The smell of fresh cof-fee quickened his pace.

When he stepped onto the tile, his heart squeezed. There his mother stood nuzzling Ozzy, chatting easily with his wife. His two favorite people in the world looked like they were old friends. A growing part of him wanted to fight for his marriage no matter what else happened with the investigation.

The annoying voice in the back of his mind picked that time to point out she'd pushed him away when they needed each other most. What would stop her from doing it again?

Again, the concept of communication came to mind. Looking back, he could have done a better job.

"Are either of you hungry?" his mother asked. She had a special radar for when one of her boys walked into a room. There was no hiding from Margaret O'Connor. Maybe that was the by-product of bringing up six rowdy boys. He smirked, figuring he owed her a couple of apologies for some of their antics as kids.

Cheyenne turned toward him, and it was like the sun breaking through the clouds after weeks of rain.

"We should do what we can to up our strength," he said, figuring he needed to catch his mother up to date with all the new information.

"Take a seat at the table and I'll whip up something," she said like it was nothing.

"Why don't the two of you grab chairs and let me stumble around in the pantry for a change," he offered.

"I'll take you up on that after fixing a cup of tea." His mother beamed. She'd brought up all of her boys to be able to fend for themselves in the kitchen when necessary. Her guidance had come in handy all those times he had nothing but a skillet and a campfire as tools and a small bag of groceries to sustain himself when tracking poachers.

"Let me get the tea. You have your hands full already." He motioned toward Ozzy and one word came to mind… traitor. The little dog was as happy as a lark. He'd come alive. Cheyenne didn't seem to mind the slight despite becoming closer with the little yapper after Ally's death.

Speaking of which, Riggs went over the basics in his mind as he heated the stove and grabbed enough ingredients to make breakfast tacos. Eggs were basically his staple and he hoped Cheyenne wasn't tired of them yet.

Cheyenne had finally rested. Before coming home, he doubted she'd slept more than a few hours. Based on what she'd said so far, he didn't get the impression she was getting a whole lot of quality rest for the past couple of weeks. He could attest to the fact she hadn't been sleeping well in the last month of her pregnancy. The middle-of-the-night trips to the bathroom had multiplied. So had the back pain and cramps. Pregnancy didn't seem to be for the faint of heart.

And yet, every time she talked about the baby, she brought her hand down to gently rub the bump. Was that her subconscious at work? He figured so. Long before the child would come into the world her mother had bonded with her.

Riggs didn't have that same instant connection, but he would be ready to love the child once he met her. She was still an idea in his mind. Not real until he held her in his arms, a move he'd been anticipating more and more the closer the due date got.

Breakfast was served and eaten in a matter of minutes. Cheyenne bit back three yawns while praising his cooking, despite having conked out for almost twelve hours at the house before he woke her at three o'clock this morning. Almost four hours later, he wondered if he could get her to rest while Colton did his job.

"What do you think about grabbing one of the guest rooms here at the main house and taking a quick nap?" he asked, clearing the table.

She stood up and joined him before glancing down at Ozzy.

"My father and stepmother are coming, and I doubt I'd be able to sleep while waiting for them," she said. "They did say something about finding an RV park first, so I'm not sure when they'll be here."

Riggs wouldn't mind meeting his in-laws for the first time.

"I'd be happy to take care of this guy to give you a break," his mother said before cooing at Ozzy again. The dog practically purred. "You could relax at the very least."

"I'll take you up on the offer for Ozzy," Cheyenne said with a half smile.

"Good," his mother said.

"I'll get you settled and then come back for the dishes." Riggs prided himself on his self-sufficiency. Had he gotten too used to living alone? Taking care of himself and letting no one else in?

"You'll do no such thing," his mother said. "You fed me. And quite well if I do say so. Dishes are the least I can do."

He opened his mouth to argue but Margaret O'Connor was having none of it. She shooed him out of her space like he was a fly buzzing in her ear.

"Okay, I'm going," he said, appreciating a little levity in what had been some of the heaviest days of his life. He'd given his mother the two-cent version of what had happened, and she'd told him Colton had been sending updates. Thankfully, Riggs didn't have to go into it in detail.

Mentally, he was whipped, and he could use some down time to process. He also wanted to think about his next move. He knew full well investigations took time. His brother was working this case on steroids, throwing as many resources as he could toward it. There would be a breakthrough. There *had* to be one. Progress was being made.

The thought of Riggs's daughter, if she'd lived, sleeping one more night away from her parents, from her home, caused anger to rip through him. Did the family who had her know the adoption was illegal? He shook those questions out of his thoughts as he walked Cheyenne to his old bedroom on the second floor.

"This is it. I think you'll be comfortable." He stopped at the door. "Use anything you want. The bathroom is attached. I'll be in the room across the hall if you need anything else."

She grabbed a fistful of his shirt and tugged him toward her. Those pale blue eyes of hers locked onto his, sending heat swirling through him in places he knew better than to think about with her standing so close.

"Will you stay?" Her voice was steady. And yet he realized she wasn't trying to hit on him. There was a lost quality to her, too, and he figured she didn't want to be alone with her thoughts.

He wrapped his hand around the doorknob and twisted. "I'm right behind you."

Chapter 19

"Thank you for sticking around." Cheyenne meant it. "Everything you're doing for me is above and beyond and I wanted you to know that it's not going unnoticed or unappreciated."

"You deserve it." He waved her off like it was nothing.

Her cell buzzed in her purse. The call was from her dad. She fished her phone from her purse and answered. "Everything all right?"

"Yes, honey. It's fine. You told me to call you when we get close. We found a nice little park where we can hook up the RV. We've been driving a long time and I thought it might be best if we rest and come to you refreshed," her father said. Was he avoiding facing her?

The thought sent a dagger into the pit of her stomach. From all accounts, he hadn't been identified as her relative, so a park should be safe. And honestly, she could use a couple of hours to gather herself.

"If you think you'll be more comfortable," she said, figuring arguing wouldn't do any good.

"We will." The emphasis her father placed on the word *we* made her think this might be his wife's idea.

Either way, Cheyenne could use some rest of her own, so she wouldn't argue.

"Call me when you feel up to it," she said before ending the call and then staring at Riggs.

"What was that all about?" he asked.

"He's not coming," she said.

Riggs took a step toward her, closing the gap between them. He cupped her face in his hands before pressing a tender kiss to her lips. "I'm sorry."

Those two words spoken with conviction eased so much of the hurt inside her.

"He was an amazing dad at one time," she said by way of defense.

"What do you think happened?" Riggs asked, taking her by the hand and leading her to the bottom of the bed where he sat down and tugged her onto his lap. He encircled his arms around her waist and then waited.

"My mom died, and it shattered him." She'd never said those words aloud. Some of the pressure that had been weighing on her shoulders lifted. "She was the glue that kept our family together."

"He still had you," Riggs said.

She sat there for a long moment without speaking. How could she make him understand? *Show him.*

"Have I ever shown you a picture of my mother?" she asked.

"No, I don't believe you have." His dark brow arched.

Phone still in hand, she pulled up a photo of the three of them.

"You're the spitting image of her," he said. "She was a beautiful woman."

"Inside and out," she said.

And then it seemed to dawn on him.

"Every time your father looks at you, he sees her," Riggs said, catching on.

"It's the only reason I can think of for him to take off with his new wife and leave me behind," she admitted. A rogue tear welled in her eye. "We talk on the phone, but it's not the same as being face-to-face. I don't doubt that he loves me. Or, at least I didn't until recently."

The tear escaped and Riggs thumbed it away.

"I can tell you that he's missing out on an amazing person," he said, his voice low and gravelly.

The air grew charged around them. Their chemistry had always been off the charts.

"He doesn't seem to be too bothered," she said. And that was the last time she was going to feel sorry for herself. "But it is what it is. I can't change other people no matter how much I wish I could." She paused and waited for Riggs to respond. Part of her expected him to judge her.

He didn't.

"I just miss having a family sometimes. You know?" she said.

"You have a family," he responded, sounding a little hurt. "Me. My brothers. My mother. We're your family now."

"Until—"

"There's no expiration date, Cheyenne. I'm not wired that way. The two of us had a child together. One I very much hope to bring home and raise together. I respect your wishes to do that from separate residences but that doesn't change the fact I'm your family now."

Those words spoken with such reverence literally raised goose bumps on her arms. She hadn't known that kind of unconditional love in far too long. Then again, it had been right under her nose with Riggs and she hadn't even realized the depths of it.

"I don't know what to say, Riggs. But I'll start with thank you." She could only pray their daughter was alive and well, and somewhere they could find her. "And I want very much to find her and bring her home. This child will be so loved between the two of us and your family."

"She will," he agreed. His belief was so strong that it gave Cheyenne hope. "Right now I need you to rest. This might be a long game, and you should know there is no length to which I won't go to find her and bring her home. At the very least, I will find out what happened to her if she didn't survive. Either way, we'll know. That much I promise you."

Cheyenne had no idea how she would sleep under the circumstances. He was right, though. They might be in this for the long haul. The first step of the journey was figuring out who killed Ally. That would lead them to the person who took their child. Was it Dr. Fortner? All signs pointed in his direction.

It felt almost too easy.

But then, sometimes solving a crime was as plain as the nose on a face. What had Colton said? *Follow the evidence.*

Would a wealthy traveling doctor drive a gray sedan? Surely he could afford a much more expensive vehicle? It was probably just her being naive, but she believed doctors made a whole lot more money than that. Of course, he could also use this cheaper car to mislead people.

Those thoughts needed to be tabled for now. Rest.

Riggs toed off his boots and she followed suit, kicking off her tennis shoes. He pulled back the covers and slipped out of his shirt and jeans. Ripples of muscles on his stomach provided plenty of eye candy. She'd mapped every line, every ridge. Fear she would lose him and everything good that had happened to her was a pit bull constantly nipping at her heels.

It was an exhausting way to live her life. Could she set it aside and just be in the moment? Not constantly figure out an exit plan or a way to deal with the disappointment when he realized his mistake and took off?

She made a promise to herself right then and there to get out of her head and into the present. More of the weight lifted and, for the first time, she didn't feel like the world would crumble at the snap of a finger.

Cheyenne decided to keep her clothes on but she curled her body around Riggs's the way she did when they used to sleep together. It was strange not having a huge belly in between them and also kind of nice for a change.

He wrapped his arm around her and closed his eyes.

The next thing she knew, there was movement beside her. She sat straight up, disoriented. A night-light emanated from the adjacent room.

"Hey, it's just me." Riggs's husky voice radiated calm in a storm.

"What time is it?" She rubbed blurry eyes.

"Noon," he said quietly.

"I slept five hours?" She shoved the covers off and

hugged her knees into her chest. Tremors rocked her body as she slowed her breathing.

The mattress dipped underneath Riggs's weight. He moved beside her and brought her into an embrace.

"What's going on, Cheyenne? Tell me what to do to help," he said. His voice alone soothed more than he realized.

"It's okay. I'm fine." She could hear the shakiness in her own voice. "It'll pass."

He sat there holding her for more minutes than she cared to count before her body obeyed her request to calm down.

"It happens sometimes. Since…"

"Having the baby?" he finished for her.

"Yes. There are all kinds of fun things that come after…" She didn't feel the need to go into it all now. "It'll pass."

How many times had she heard the phrase? Dozens? More? *This too shall pass* were her least favorite words.

"Should we call your doctor?" he asked.

"No. It's nothing worth worrying over. My body has been through a lot of stress with the birth. That's all." She didn't want to go into the mental duress the whole ordeal had caused. And yet, part of her thought she would do it all again if things had turned out differently. "Anya."

Riggs shot her a worried look.

"We never say her name," she said.

"We need to change that," he agreed. Then came, "Anya."

Their daughter's name spoken out of his mouth was the sweetest thing Cheyenne had ever heard. He would be an amazing father whether the two of them lived under the same roof or not.

Speaking of fathers...

Hers was supposed to reach out to her. "What did I do with my phone?"

"I put it on the nightstand. Why?" he asked.

"My dad. I told him to call once he was settled," she said.

Riggs reached for the phone and she tried not to notice the flex and release of his muscles as he moved. His body was athletic grace in motion, and sinning-on-Sunday worthy.

She stopped herself from reaching out and seeking comfort. It would be temporary, at best. Damn good. But stoking the flames of the heat between them would only complicate matters even more. No need to tempt fate further. So why was it getting more and more difficult to fight what her body wanted and her mind knew better than to go for?

Riggs handed over the cell, then sat by and watched the disappointment play out on Cheyenne's face.

"No messages and no attempts to call," she said, tossing the phone on top of the duvet.

There was nothing he could say to ease her pain. Rejection hurt like hell. He could only imagine how awful it would be coming from a parent.

"I'll never do that to my children," she said low and under her breath.

"Why don't you call him?" he asked, noting it was the first time he'd heard her mention the possibility there could be more kids since reuniting. Was she having a change of heart? Would she reconsider her position on the status of their relationship?

"You said the two of you were close once," he said.

"That's right," she confirmed.

"Have you tried to talk to him about how you're feeling?" he asked.

"Well…" She paused for a long moment. "No. Not really. I guess I figured that as the parent, he should know. I'll just text to make sure he's okay." She did. Confirmation came back a few seconds later with no additional explanation.

"I don't disagree with you, but if the relationship is important to you, I think you owe it to yourself to talk to him."

She lowered her eyes to the duvet and gave a slight nod.

"Any child would be lucky to have you as a mother, by the way," he said to her.

"Do you really think so?" She exhaled a shaky breath. "Because I'm not so sure that's true."

"Based on our talks during the pregnancy, you had a clear idea of the kind of mother you wanted to be," he said. "You agree the most important thing for a child to receive is unconditional love. Your priorities have been clear."

"True." As confident as she was, everyone needed reassurance now and then.

"There's not a question in my mind," he said and meant it.

Cheyenne twisted the edge of the blanket in her fingers. "When I believed she was gone…it shredded me inside and out."

"Because you love her," he said. "Anya."

"Our Anya might be alive, Riggs." She brought her eyes up to meet his. Hers had an equal mix of heartbreak and hope.

"Yes," was all he could manage to say. As much as he didn't want to get either of their hopes up, after hearing Missy's statement, he had, for the first time, let himself go to the place where his daughter was really alive, and he might have the chance to hold her.

"We could get her back," she continued.

"That's the hope," he said.

"I know we can't exactly pick up where we left off and pretend the past couple of weeks didn't happen. I know that would be asking too much," she said.

"What if the news about Anya isn't what we're hoping, Cheyenne? What happens then? Do you move on with your life just like you'd planned, or do you try to come back home?" Those were fair questions that deserved answers.

She worked the hem of the duvet a little harder. "I guess I haven't thought that far ahead."

There'd been a determination in her eyes to keep him at arm's length from the get-go. Riggs couldn't stand to lose his child and Cheyenne twice. If he was going to seriously entertain the possibility of giving their relationship another shot, he needed reassurance that she wouldn't bolt if they got bad news.

"As much as I don't want to go down this road, there's a decent chance we won't get what we want, Cheyenne."

She put her hand in the air to stop him from going further, like she couldn't fathom it now that she'd dared to allow herself to believe their daughter might be alive.

"I think I know what you're going to say, and I completely understand where you're coming from." She dropped the material and clasped her hands. "My emotions get the best of me sometimes. You know?"

"It's understandable, after what we've been through."

"The truth is that I can't go through another birth if Anya's gone." Her admission caused more confusion.

"I understand not wanting to jump back on the horse in a manner of speaking, but why cut yourself off from the possibility of ever having a family because it didn't work out the first time?" He didn't even go into how hurt he was that she didn't view him as enough in a marriage.

"You want kids, right?" she asked.

"I haven't changed my plans to have a family when the time is right, if that's what you're asking." He saw the writing on the wall. Cheyenne refused to continue with plans to have a family if she lost Anya. Riggs might not like it, but at least he knew where he stood.

"I just don't see a middle ground here, Riggs."

Shame, he thought. Because he'd believed she was the one. And now? He couldn't fathom devoting his life to someone on condition.

Chapter 20

"We should think about something else."

Riggs wasn't wrong. And yet Cheyenne wanted to keep talking until they figured out a way to stay together. The disappointment in his tone told her just how badly she'd wounded him.

She hated it. But if she stayed married to him and refused to have children, he would resent her even more. Worse than that, he'd be denied having the family he was so ready for. The news of the pregnancy might have caught him off guard, as it had her, but he sure had risen to the occasion. Was he perfect? No. But then, neither was she.

They were both taking shots in the dark and coming up to the good more often than not. No matter what her heart wanted, she couldn't be selfish when it came to denying Riggs a child.

"I need a drink." She moved into the adjacent room

and then splashed water on her face. When it came to her father, Riggs was right. She needed to have a conversation with him in private, just the two of them. She exited the bathroom after brushing her teeth. "Do you mind if I let a little sunlight in?"

"Not at all."

He grabbed a fresh outfit of jeans and a T-shirt from his dresser, and then threw them on.

Cheyenne stared outside, transfixed by the beauty of the land as he moved beside her.

"It's amazing you grew up here. Do you ever take it for granted?" she asked.

"Not me. I love this place. Of course, I'd prefer to sleep in my own bed but the view from the main house still takes my breath away." There was so much reverence in his tone.

"My mother would have loved waking up to this sky," she said, wishing her mother was alive to see it from this perspective.

"Texas is known for its incredible sunrises and sunsets." He put a hand on the small of her back and then seemed to catch himself when he pulled it back. He mumbled an apology and said something about muscle memory.

"I have decided to talk to my father." She wanted Riggs to know he was right about coming forward with her feelings. "In fact, I'm going to text him right now."

"For what it's worth, I'm proud of you." Riggs took a step back.

"What you said made a lot of sense. If he doesn't know how much I'm hurt by his actions he won't change them. If he does know and doesn't change them, I'll be able to move on," she said with conviction.

"If he's half the man I think he is, I have a feeling he'll do the right thing by you, Cheyenne."

"I hope you're right," she said on a sigh. Rejection was never fun but when it came from a parent it was devastating. She sent the text to her father asking for a meetup. The response came immediately.

When and where?

She blinked at her phone. "He wants me to pick a time and place."

"I'd feel better if he came on property for security reasons," Riggs said.

"That's probably a good idea. I'd hate for him to feel ambushed, though." She wanted her father to be as comfortable as possible during a conversation that might be anything but.

"How about if I drive you to him? That way, I can sit in the truck and keep watch. Make sure no one followed us or finds him," he said.

"When should I say? Half an hour? Forty-five minutes? I'd like to freshen up and grab coffee before we leave," she said.

"And a sandwich at the very least," he insisted.

"Deal. I'll just clean up." A shower sounded like heaven about now.

"Hand me your clothes and I'll run them through a quick wash-and-dry cycle. My mom has been bragging about her new machines that wash and dry a load in ten minutes each." His smile didn't reach his eyes.

"You have to find out if that's true. Hold on." She darted into the bathroom, undressed and then wrapped herself in a towel. Handing over her dirty clothes, including undergarments, should probably feel awkward. Except this was Riggs and he had a way of making her feel comfortable in any situation.

So she ignored the fact she had a towel wrapped around her when she cracked the door open and tossed her clothes toward him…clothes he caught on the first try.

"Thank you, Riggs." She realized she'd been saying those words often. Did he know how much she valued his help?

A quick shower revitalized her. Finding a new toothbrush and toothpaste in the top drawer made her want to pump her fists in the air from joy. She was learning to appreciate the little things—things she'd once taken for granted.

Realizing she'd taken the ladybug charm out of her handbag and tucked it inside the small key pocket in her jogging pants caused her heart to skip a few beats. It was small. Would it get lost?

Panic seized her as she searched for a robe in the attached closet. Most secondary bathrooms didn't have walk-in closets but then most homes didn't belong to an O'Connor. A hotel-sized white robe was folded up and tucked into a cubby. It was large enough to fit Riggs, so she wasn't worried about coverage. Running through the house with it on made her chest squeeze.

As she swung open the door to the bedroom, she nearly charged into Riggs's chest.

"Whoa there," he said. "Everything all right?"

"The ladybug charm…"

Before she could finish her sentence, he held his hand up, palm out. "I grew up with five brothers. My mother taught me to check pockets."

"Oh, thank heavens." She exhaled a shaky breath, trying to get her nerves under control. As it was, she seemed to go from normal to raging faster than a roller coaster could plummet down the first hill only to rise again a few seconds later. "I know I've said this a million times but I'm not sure what I would do without you, Riggs."

He stood there for a moment as the air around them grew charged. Then he turned and walked away without so much as a peep.

The move was probably for the best and yet it still stung. Besides, they needed to get on the road. As much as she dreaded having the conversation with her father, a growing piece of her wanted to get it over with.

Twenty minutes later, she'd washed and brushed everything that needed it, dressed, and then joined Riggs in the kitchen where a sandwich waited.

"My mom offered to take care of Ozzy today," he said.

"She's good with him." The little dog seemed to like Margaret O'Connor better than he liked Cheyenne. To be fair, she hadn't made much effort with him until losing Ally.

Cheyenne gobbled down the burrito and drained a cup of coffee in record time, eager to get out the door. She settled in the passenger seat as Riggs's cell buzzed.

"It's Colton," he said after checking the screen.

Riggs put the call on speaker as he navigated onto the road leading to the ranch's exit.

"Hey, Colton. What's going on?" Riggs explained that he was in his truck and that his brother was on speaker.

"Good. I want Cheyenne to hear this, too," Colton said. "I was able to track down Dr. Fortner and interview him."

"And?" Riggs and Cheyenne asked in unison.

"He started talking, expressing a suspicion he's had about one of the traveling ER docs he sometimes works alongside. Turns out they work for the same company and go wherever there's a shortage," Colton informed. "It wasn't uncommon for him."

"Ally worked in the ER," Cheyenne offered. "She would have worked with him at the very least. Did Dr. Fortner give a name?"

"Kyle Douglas," Colton supplied. "Sound familiar?"

Cheyenne smacked the armrest. "It sure does. He's the one who tried to hit on Ally a couple of times. I remember she thought he was cute, but something warned her against getting too close to him."

"Well, I learned another interesting fact about him. He drives a gray two-door sedan while traveling for work. He leaves his sports car at home in favor of something more practical, according to Dr. Fortner," Colton said. "I asked for a description and he matches both the one Missy provided and the one given by the clerk from the grocery store. He's our guy."

"What about the other nurses who came forward at other hospitals?" Riggs asked.

"Gert is on it but has confirmed the crossover in at least two instances," Colton said. "The hitch is that he wasn't working in the hospital the night Cheyenne gave birth."

"I'm betting Becca or Sherry was," Cheyenne said, remembering the two nurses she'd chatted with when she was trying to find Ally.

"That's right. I have a deputy on the way to pick Becca up for questioning at my office," Colton supplied. "I have no doubt in my mind about her involvement. In fact, I'm working the angle with the other hospitals, too. My best guess is that he has a network of nurses he cuts in on the deals."

"But Dr. Fortner was my attending," Cheyenne said. "How do you explain the amount of medication I was given? Or the fact I remember seeing him?"

"He was called away moments before the delivery and then told the baby didn't make it," Colton supplied.

"That's not how I remember it." Cheyenne blew out a frustrated breath.

"Given the amount of medication you were on, that isn't surprising. Dr. Fortner is calling for a review of the case. By the time he got back to your room the nurse said the baby had already been born. He said he had no reason to doubt her word," Colton added.

"Any idea where Douglas is now?" Riggs asked.

"None. The service he works for has been reaching out to him and he hasn't returned any calls yet." Colton white-knuckled the steering wheel as they thanked Colton before ending the call.

Disbelief and a sense of being violated caused anger to rip through Cheyenne. How could anyone do this to another human being?

Riggs pulled into the RV park, his mind spinning.

"We have a name," Cheyenne said. "And all the confirmation I need to know our daughter lived."

He didn't remind her of the fact one of the babies had died. The newborn very well could have been Anya. There was no way he could dash the hope and resolve in Cheyenne's voice.

"Which one belongs to your father?" There were half a dozen RVs sprinkled throughout the park.

She pointed to a white and orange number that looked straight out of the seventies. Riggs made a loop and pulled up alongside the vehicle. He could watch the entrance from this vantage point.

Cheyenne grabbed the door handle. "Are you coming with me?"

"I thought I'd stay out here to keep an eye out," he admitted.

She chewed on the inside of her cheek. "I'm not sure I can do this without you."

The RV door opened and a man who looked to be in his late fifties stepped out. He wasn't tall by Texas standards, coming in around five feet ten inches if Riggs had to guess. A tiny woman who, oddly, resembled Cheyenne's mother stepped out with him. She waved. Cheyenne's father had made an excuse about why he had to miss the wedding, so this was the first time Riggs was able to look his father-in-law in the eye.

Riggs thought about the irony of a man not wanting his own daughter around because she looked too much like her mother but then marrying someone who did. Maybe Cheyenne's assessment was misguided.

"Hello, Dad." Cheyenne got out of the truck, but she didn't make a move to hug her father and vice versa. Instead, she leaned against the truck and folded her arms.

Riggs joined her so he could keep an eye on things.

"Cheyenne," was all her dad said in response.

Riggs walked up to his father-in-law and extended a hand. When her father took the offering, Riggs realized the man's palms were sweaty. He shot a look of fear and regret at Riggs.

"Good to meet you, sir," Riggs said.

"Same to you," her father said.

"Hi, Virginia." Cheyenne introduced Riggs to her stepmother.

"Ma'am," he said after a hearty handshake.

"I'll leave you alone. I just wanted to come out and say hello," Virginia said.

Riggs started toward the driver's side of the truck and

was stopped by Cheyenne's hand. So he moved closer to her and noticed the tight grip she had on his fingers.

"Dad, I need to get something off my chest," Cheyenne started after sucking a breath.

"Oh," her father said.

"I still need you in my life and you're gone all the time. Most of the time, I can't reach you and when I do leave a message you don't get back to me for weeks. I've been married more than half a year, and this is the first time you're meeting my husband. I just have one question… why?" She'd clearly done her best to stay calm, but her words rushed out anyway.

"Because I can't stand seeing the disappointment in your eyes and not knowing what to say or do to make it better—just like when your mother died. I felt like I failed you by letting her die and I'm failing now." He threw his hands up in the air. "Renting the RV was supposed to help me heal from losing the love of my life, but I've learned one thing. I can't outrun the pain."

"Then, stick around and deal with it. Be here for me and I'll do the same for you." Her voice hitched on the last few words.

Her father stood there for a long moment before making eye contact with her.

"Is there any chance you can forgive a foolish old man?" he asked. "Because I feel like I lost the two great loves of my life when she died. Her and you."

Cheyenne released her grip on Riggs's hand before charging toward her father and wrapping him in a hug.

"It's never too late for forgiveness, Daddy."

Riggs wondered if the same could be true for their relationship.

Chapter 21

"Can you stick around?" Cheyenne's father asked when she finally released him. The torment in his eyes when she'd first seen him had softened. It was crazy how much they were able to clear up in one short conversation. Being face-to-face helped. It was so good to see her father's face again.

"We have to take care of something first. But I promise to spend as much time together as you can stand once we clear something up," she said. Her answer seemed to satisfy her father.

"I'd like to invite you and your wife to camp on the ranch. There's plenty of room and you'd be closer to your daughter," Riggs offered. It was a sly move because he would want her father in a secure location. She also believed Riggs was being honest about the two of them being closer. "I can call ahead and get you set up through security."

Her father's gaze bounced from Riggs to her and back. "What do you think, honey?" he asked.

"I'd like it very much, Daddy."

Now it was her father's turn to beam. "Then, that's what we'll do."

Cheyenne sighed with relief.

"I'll get your father set up with directions if you'd like to say goodbye for now to Ms. Virginia," Riggs said.

Right again.

Cheyenne disappeared into the RV after first knocking. Riggs was a whole lot better at navigating family. Of course, with five siblings, he had more experience.

"I'm really happy to see you, Virginia," Cheyenne said.

"Well, it's good to be here." Virginia smiled through her surprise at the gesture.

Yeah, Cheyenne needed to get better about acknowledging her stepmother. Virginia made her father happy. Their relationship was different but that didn't mean it wasn't special. Cheyenne could see that now.

"I just wanted to let you know how happy you make my dad," Cheyenne said. She imagined her father would be so much worse off without his new wife.

"Do you think so?" Virginia asked and it was the first sign of insecurity Cheyenne had seen.

"Yes. I really do," she reassured her before adding, "My husband asked if you guys would like to camp at the ranch. The land is unbelievable, and I think you both would love it very much. I'd like it if you came."

Virginia smiled. "I'd like that, too."

Cheyenne said her goodbye as she exited the RV. Seeing her father and her husband standing there talking made her realize how much she wanted to be with Riggs. Could he accept her for who she was?

"We were just finishing up," Riggs said to her.

"Virginia and I will be on our way as soon as I run the idea past her," her father said.

"I just did. She was happy about it," Cheyenne assured him. "And so am I."

"We'll head out, then, since your husband has made all the arrangements," her father said.

"See you later." Cheyenne gave her father one last hug before claiming her seat on the passenger side.

Riggs got behind the wheel and put the gearshift into Drive.

"You didn't correct my father about being my husband," Cheyenne said to Riggs. "Was that on purpose or were you just being polite?"

"I am your husband, Cheyenne. You're the only one who can change that."

"And what if this doesn't turn out the way we'd hoped with Anya? Can you live with me not wanting to have children?" she asked.

"I married you and I meant it." He barely got the words out when he slammed on the brakes. "Hold on a second."

The entrance to the RV park was barricaded.

"Stay low," Riggs warned as he slid down in his seat.

She realized he was searching for a possible shooter as he grabbed his cell and slid it onto the bench seat toward her.

"I have a group text with my brothers. Send out an SOS and let them know where we are," he said.

"My dad," she said, firing off the text.

Riggs put the vehicle in reverse and flew backward, kicking up one serious dust storm. "Text your father and tell him to get inside the RV, lock the door and stay put until you call him."

Cheyenne did that next. Riggs's phone started dinging left and right with promises of help. Her father agreed to do as she asked. And yet her pulse still skyrocketed as panic squeezed her chest.

"Do you have anything we can use as a weapon in here?" she asked.

"Not sure," Riggs responded. "There has to be something around, though."

She unbuckled her seat belt and then hopped in back. Keeping low, she rummaged around. There were tools that might come in handy. Nothing like bringing a wrench into a gunfight. *Possible* gunfight, she reminded.

"I found these." She grabbed everything hard and metal that she could find, returning to the front with a fistful of options.

Riggs came to a roaring stop in front of her father's RV. The dust cloud made visibility next to impossible.

Cheyenne's cell rang, causing her heart to drop. She checked the screen. Her father.

"Hello, Dad. Is everything okay?"

"Someone's here. He wants to talk to you and said you should come inside." There was a mix of shock and fear in her father's voice that drilled a hole in her chest.

"I'm coming. Stay put and don't do anything to make him angry. Okay, Dad?"

Before her father could answer, there was a rustling noise on the line before it went dead.

As Cheyenne reached for the door handle, Riggs touched her shoulder. She brought her hand on top of his, needing the comfort of his touch.

"I'm not letting you waltz into a trap," he said quietly. "I can't lose you, too."

His phone was blowing up, but he didn't budge.

"I don't know what else to do, Riggs. It's my dad in there," she said before issuing a sharp breath.

He nodded. "Give me a few seconds to think up a plan. Okay?"

"I don't know how much time I have. If I don't head out of here in a second, he might get trigger-happy," she said.

"He was nervous before. His hand shook. He's not used to this. I think we have time," Riggs said.

"Yeah, but are you willing to bet my dad's life on it?"

A shot fired.

On instinct, Riggs ducked. And then he snapped into action. He jumped out of his truck as Cheyenne bolted out the passenger side. Sirens pierced the air; the cavalry was on its way.

Was it too late?

Without hesitation, Riggs opened the door to the RV. Inside, Virginia was on her knees with her hands clasped behind her head. Hoodie stood behind Cheyenne's father with the barrel of his gun pointed at his temple.

There was no sign of blood and that was the first bit of good news.

Cheyenne's father had his eyes closed and he looked to be whispering a prayer. There was a look of resolve on his face, like he was ready to join his first wife.

Not today, if Riggs had anything to say about it.

"Stop," Cheyenne said from behind him.

"You've gone too far. You keep poking around where

you don't belong." Hoodie's voice had a hysterical note to it.

"You took an oath to save lives, Douglas," Riggs aid.

"How did…" The hood came off. The doctor would be considered attractive by most standards. He was a couple of inches taller than Cheyenne's father. He had sandy-blond hair and tanned skin, with a runner's build.

"Authorities know who you are, Kyle," Riggs continued. "Don't make this any worse than it already is."

The doctor's eyes were wild.

"Worse? It's a little late for that." He squeezed the trigger.

By some miracle, the bullet misfired. Riggs took advantage of the situation by diving headfirst toward Kyle. Riggs managed to shove Cheyenne's father out of the way a second before crashing into the doctor.

The gun went off in a wild shot again as Riggs struggled for control. He wrapped his arms around Kyle and body-slammed him onto the floor of the RV. The tile shook like there'd been an earthquake. Kyle tried to wiggle out of Riggs's grasp.

No dice.

Riggs clamped his arms around the guy like a vise. "You're not going anywhere but jail, where you belong."

"You'll never get her back," Kyle said through gritted teeth. He tried to point the barrel of his weapon at Riggs.

"The hell I won't," Riggs said. "My family won't rest until she's home where she belongs and you're rotting in a cell for kidnapping my daughter and killing Ally."

Cheyenne's father snatched the gun out of Kyle's hand unexpectedly. The older man took a couple of steps back before pointing the barrel at Kyle's head.

"Keep moving and I'll shoot," he warned and the tone in his voice said he meant every word.

In the next minute, the RV was flooded with O'Connors. Colton zip-cuffed Kyle and tossed him in the back seat of his service vehicle. Cash stood next to Cheyenne while she hugged her father and comforted Virginia. The afternoon had been traumatic for both of them.

Riggs walked over to his brother Colton, who stood next to Dawson.

"Why?" Riggs asked. "What would make a successful, well-paid doctor sell babies?"

"A gambling addiction for one," Colton said. "Once we got a name, we did some digging. He's in over his head in debt with men who don't take kindly to folks who can't clear their debt. And Becca was in on the take."

"Sonofabitch is willing to destroy people's lives to feed his own addiction." It had taken all of Riggs's restraint not to knock the guy out. He wanted him to be awake and aware of where he was going…jail.

"That's not all we found, Riggs. Caroline is alive and lives in Houston," Colton said.

"What? When? How?"

"Garrett hasn't stopped investigating and neither has Cash. I've been on it, too. We didn't want to say anything until we were one hundred percent certain. The trail came out of the alpaca farm. Turns out Dad was on the right trail," Colton said. "Arrests at the farm are being made as we speak."

"That's great news." Riggs was almost speechless. He thought about another mother and child who needed help. Loriann and her son would be well cared for. Riggs would put the wheels in motion with the family attorney when he headed back to the ranch.

A dirt cloud broke behind a vehicle that was moving toward them, catching their attention before Colton could answer.

Instead, he put a hand on Riggs's shoulder and said, "Go get your wife. We found something that belongs to you."

Riggs's pulse skyrocketed. He stared at his brother for a long moment before Colton urged him to get moving. He did, taking Cheyenne by the hand and bringing her to where Colton stood.

The vehicle Riggs recognized as Gert's came to a stop. His brother's assistant came out of the driver's seat. Instead of moving toward them, she went straight to the back and opened the door.

Riggs caught his brother's eye. Colton nodded. So Riggs turned to his wife.

"I love you, Cheyenne. I always will," he began, turning her away from the vehicle so she faced him.

Tears streamed down her cheeks as she looked at him the same way she had on their wedding night…with love in her eyes.

"I wouldn't care if you couldn't have children. I married *you*. Plus, there are other ways to have a family," he said before locking gazes. "I want you to come home. I want to do better by you. I want to learn to talk to you when I think something's wrong. What do you think? Is that what you want?"

He didn't finish his sentence before she wrapped her arms around his neck and kissed him.

"Yes, Riggs. I love you more than I could express in a thousand lifetimes. But I'll take this one if you'll give it to me," she said. "I don't want to hang on to the rope any longer. I want to let go and fall into your arms."

"I love you with all that I am, Cheyenne," he said. "And there's one more thing you need to know."

Confusion knitted her eyebrows together.

"My brothers found *her*," was all he said. All he had to say before recognition dawned on her. "What do you say we go meet our daughter?"

More of those tears streamed now as Cheyenne nodded.

"Yes," she said, repeating the word a few more times as he turned her around.

There Gert stood, next to her car. A pink bundle in her arms. A smile plastered on her face.

Home. Their daughter was finally home. Cheyenne practically ran to Anya. Gert immediately handed over their child. Riggs followed and his heart swelled the minute Cheyenne turned around and beamed at him. He couldn't be happier to have Cheyenne and Anya together with him where they belonged.

"Meet our daughter," she said with the sweetest smile on her face.

The baby wasn't the only one who was finally home.

Chapter 22

Margaret O'Connor sat in her library on the velvet couch. This was the place Riggs could normally find her—the place she loved most in the house. She'd said countless times how at home she felt among her books. Now that the house was filled with new life and new faces, she didn't spend as much time in the room as she used to. He saw that as progress, considering the innumerable hours she'd stayed here after her husband's murder.

He glanced at the long line of his brothers waiting behind him in the hallway, Cash, Colton, Dawson, Blake, and Garrett. They all seemed ready. He knocked lightly on the door, not wanting to surprise her or catch her off guard. Not in her sanctuary.

"Come in," her voice was less frail than it had been in the days after losing her husband. Finn O'Connor had left big shoes to fill on the ranch. Each of his sons, including Riggs, was now ready to take their rightful place on the ranch, working side by side as their father had intended when he'd built a successful cattle ranch all those years ago.

There was something very right about all of his brothers being home. Even Garrett was making the transition home with his new fiancée in a moment Riggs wasn't sure he'd ever see. His brother had always gone rogue. He'd always needed to buck convention and do his own thing. Of course, it didn't help matters that Garrett and Cash had been gas on fire for as long as Riggs could remember. Then there was Garrett's relationship with Colton, more fuel to the blaze.

"I have company." Riggs stepped inside the library, and then each of his brothers stepped inside the room. They made a half circle behind a very confused Margaret O'Connor.

No one wanted to miss this moment—a moment that had been thirty years in the making. Each of his brothers took a spot, hands folded in front of them like they were in church. This moment deserved that kind of reverence, Riggs thought, as emotion knotted in his throat. He figured his brothers were struggling just about as much as him, considering how many pairs of eyes were cast to the floor.

Finn O'Connor had died without ever knowing what happened to his daughter. Their mother would not suffer the same fate. In fact, she was about to see for herself.

"What's happening?" His very concerned mother looked around the room, a moment of panic darkening her eyes. "Is everyone okay?"

"We're fine. Never been better." Cash stepped forward. As the oldest son, he normally spoke on behalf of the family. He glanced at each of his brothers, waiting for the okay to continue. When he seemed satisfied that he got what he was looking for, he continued, "You already know Dad was trying to find Caroline when…" Cash's voice caught on the last word and he ducked his chin to his chest, no doubt to cover the emotion threatening to pull them all under. He cleared his throat and then continued, "I think we're all clear on what happened to Dad as a result of him renewing the search for our sister."

A moment of silence, of respect, passed before Cash continued, "But his efforts to find Caroline weren't in vain and we understand why he chose to pick up the search when he did. The diagnosis meant he wouldn't be around forever. Granted, he should have had more time. We wanted more time with him. But we understand why he picked the timing he did to resume the search for her. And we've all learned more than a few important lessons because of his example. No one is guaranteed time on this earth. Every day is a gift that deserves to be embraced."

"Did you? Find out what happened to Caroline?" Mother asked, her back ramrod straight now.

Cash nodded.

"And?" their mother asked.

"We think you'll be pleased with what we learned." Cash moved to the doorway and waved in their guests as their mother sat perfectly still. A pin drop could be heard from miles around for how quiet everyone had become. "And we believe you should see it for yourself."

A very pregnant Caroline stepped into view. She stopped at the threshold and her mouth nearly dropped to the floor when her gaze locked onto their mother—the mother she never knew despite being a mirror image. It was one of the many things Riggs had first noticed when he'd met his sister for the first time. It was striking just how much she took after their mother.

Mother seemed to pick her jaw up off the floor. She blinked a couple of times like she couldn't trust her eyes. And then the tears slid down her cheeks as she pushed to standing, each of her sons at the ready in case she needed a hand up. She didn't.

"Caroline?" she asked but it was more statement than question.

Caroline nodded even though she didn't call herself by that name anymore. She'd gone by the name Andrea for as long as she could remember. "I go by Andrea now."

Arms out, Mother practically bolted around the coffee table before bringing her only girl into a hug. There wasn't a dry eye in the room as their mother stroked her daughter's hair.

"It's been so long," Mother said quietly. "I was beginning to think I'd never see you again. That I'd never know what happened to my baby girl."

Andrea was crying now, too. Sniffles filled the air. No tears of sadness. Just sweet release and then joy.

Mother pulled back and then took Andrea by the hand. "Can you come sit?"

"I'd like that actually." Andrea wiped away her own tears with her free hand.

"Would one of you boys be kind enough to make us some tea?" Mother looked at Andrea before smiling at her pregnant belly. "Or whatever you and the baby would like to drink."

"Tea is good. Decaf if you have any." She practically beamed.

"I've got it," Cash said. He was standing closest to

the door. Colton volunteered to help and the two disappeared a second later.

"What? How? I..." Mother covered her laugh. "I don't even know where to start."

Andrea held their mother's hand. "I can go back as far as I remember. But I'm afraid I don't remember this or anyone from here."

"Of course, you don't." If Mother was disappointed, she didn't show it. "You were a baby when you..." She seemed like she couldn't bear to say the words.

"I had a good childhood," Andrea said as though she realized that would be important to any mother. In fact, she rubbed her belly with her free hand and Riggs wondered if the move was subconscious on her part. "I'm sure it was nothing like this. I grew up in Santa Fe and we never moved. I had two parents who are still married. We grew apart when I went off to college in Houston. I'd always been drawn to Texas and now I know why they always looked at each other strangely when I brought it up. I always wanted to come here for vacation, but they refused." She shrugged. "I never understood why and, like all teenagers, became rebellious at a certain point."

Andrea paused for a minute and took in the room, the faces.

"I grew up an only child, but it never felt right to me. You know?" she asked with a hopeful look in her eyes.

No one in the room might understand, but every head nodded. Because being an O'Connor was in the blood. Ranching was in the blood. And each brother seemed to agree something would feel off if they'd been plucked out of this life.

"Going to Houston changed everything for me. It was

a perfect fit, but it was the closest I'd ever been to feeling like I belonged somewhere," she continued.

Mother's smile was a mile wide as she hung on every word. She turned serious when she said, "A woman by the name of Ms. Hubert moved into the area about a year before you were taken from your crib."

Andrea sat there looking stunned. "It's going to take a minute for all this to set in. It must've been horrific for you."

Mother nodded as Andrea rubbed her belly again, and a look of horror overtook her face.

"How far along are you?" Mother asked, as though she realized Andrea needed a distraction from the gravity of the situation.

"Seven months." She sniffed away a few tears that seemed to be building. "Sorry. I'm just so emotional these days."

"It's understandable," Mother said without missing a beat. A kind of peace had come over her. She settled back into her seat, and her face glowed. "You don't ever have to apologize for feeling overwhelmed. This has to be a lot for you. I'm sorry we didn't find you sooner."

"Like I said, my childhood was good. I had a lot of friends. I did well enough in school to get a scholarship for college, which was good because my parents said that if I went to Texas, I'd have to figure out a way to pay for it myself." She exhaled and her shoulders slumped forward. "I think they were just scared I'd run into one of you guys and they'd be caught red-handed."

"It sounds like they loved you very much," Mother said.

Andrea nodded. "They weren't perfect by any means, but I never doubted they loved me. Not for one day. My mother became overprotective and it felt like I was being smothered. I think that's why I wouldn't consider any of the schools in New Mexico or Arizona. Too close to home."

"Do you still have communication with them?" Mother asked.

"Not really. Not since I refused to come home," she admitted.

Garrett stepped forward. "According to the investigation, her parents had no idea of the circumstances. They were high-risk for adoption because of their age and the fact Mr. Landis had a record. He spent time in a federal prison for a white-collar crime in the accounting firm where he worked. Apparently, he and one of his coworkers decided to skim money from the company accounts by padding expense reports that came in from the sales teams. The two of them got caught and he served five years."

"So they knew they were doing something illegal when they adopted me?" Andrea asked.

"They knew the adoption was shady but there's no evidence to suggest they knew you'd been kidnapped," Garrett said.

"Oh." Andrea sounded defeated. "You think you know people for your entire life and then, bam, you get hit with something like this out of the blue."

"The important thing is that they loved and cared for you, Ca—"

Mother caught herself. She couldn't finish and it seemed like she couldn't bring herself to call her daughter by another name.

"I guess," Andrea said before catching their mother's gaze. "But I can't imagine what you must have gone through as a mother. I mean, I haven't even met this little angel yet and I already wake up in a cold sweat at the thought anything could happen to her."

Mother sucked in a burst of air.

"A girl?" she asked.

"Yes." Andrea beamed.

Love was written all over Mother's features. "We have another little girl in the family now. Anya. She'll be a great older cousin. And now we have Missy." Mother's gaze shifted to Garrett. He smiled and nodded. He and his fiancée, Brianna, were a newly minted foster family. Missy had been separated from her parents at the age of four and brought into a kidnapping ring. She'd been returned when she couldn't "adjust" to the new family. When Missy was taken from her family, she'd been told her parents had gone to heaven. If that happened to be true, and no one believed it was, then she would live her life with Garrett and Brianna. But Garrett wouldn't rest until he had answers, because he knew firsthand how important it was for a child to be reunited with his or her parents if at all possible.

"But I'm getting ahead of myself, aren't I?" Mother asked. She straightened her back and continued, "You're a grown adult now. I have no idea if we fit into your life and I wouldn't judge you for a minute if you decided to go back to Houston and forget you ever knew us. You can't know what it means to me for you to be here, right now. And as much as I'd love for you to stay, you have a life that we're not part of in Houston."

Andrea waved her hand in the air like she was stopping traffic. "Right before I found out about the baby, that I was pregnant with her, my husband was killed in the line of duty. He'd been working deep nights and made what was supposed to be a routine traffic stop when it all went south. To make a long, sad story short, he was shot at point-blank range. I've honestly been wandering around ever since, not really certain what my next move was going to be. I used to work at the arboretum. I was always drawn to the outside, even when I was a kid." She smiled, but it didn't reach her eyes. "I guess now I know why."

"Why don't you move in here for the rest of your pregnancy?" Mother asked, her voice brimming with hope. "You'd have plenty of people to look after you until you gave birth and Houston isn't so far away."

"Are you sure about that?" Andrea studied their mother. "Because I'm tempted to take you up on the offer, but I really don't want to put you out or anything."

"I've never been more certain of anything in my life." Their mother was steadfast. Little did Andrea know their mother had been planning, hoping for this day since her daughter was taken from her crib where she peacefully slept. "In fact…"

Mother held her index finger in the air, indicating she'd be right back. Her face lit up like Christmas morning and the skip in her step didn't go unnoticed.

Andrea looked up at each of Riggs's brothers as Cash and Colton entered the room.

"What did we miss?" Cash handed a steaming cup of tea to Andrea while Colton placed the other one on the coffee table for their mother.

"Mom took off to get a gift for Andrea." Riggs winked at his brothers as Andrea stared at them. The wrinkle in her forehead said she was clearly confused by what was going on.

"While your…*our*…mother is out of the room, I'd like

to ask you six if you think it's a good idea for me...*us*... to stay here until she's born." She caressed the bump.

Cash made eye contact with each brother, including Riggs. Each gave a slight nod.

"I think I can speak for everyone when I say welcome to the family," Cash said. "You won't find a better bunch of people and we always have each other's back."

A tear slid down Andrea's face. She quickly wiped it away. Chin up, she smiled. "I'm looking forward to getting to know each and every one of you."

"We're a good bunch, but I wouldn't get too excited about getting to know each one of us personally. At least, not a few of us." Riggs elbowed Garrett.

"You definitely don't want to get to know this guy any better. Arm's length is good," Garrett shot back, jabbing Riggs in the side.

They both burst out laughing and the room followed suit, breaking some of the tension. Andrea laughed, too, and it was one of the best sounds. Their sister was home. Riggs let that thought sink in, which he couldn't do without thinking what a shame it was for their father to have missed this moment. If it wasn't for his investigative work, she might still be lost to them. The work had come at a heavy price and Riggs would miss his father for the rest of his days. Seeing the look on Mother's face...

It was exactly what his father would have wanted.

Mother bebopped into the room, her right hand fisted. She perched on the edge of the sofa next to Andrea. "I've been waiting a long time to give you this."

She opened her hand to reveal a key.

"You have your own house here on the property, Ca—" Mother's cheeks flamed. "Calling you Andrea is going to take some getting used to." She sat up a little taller. "But, you know, maybe it's time to move on and accept that Caroline is gone. Andrea is her own person and you're right here. And you're just as much part of this family as any one of us."

Andrea took the offering, the wrinkle on her forehead deepening. "I'm afraid I don't understand."

"Mother had a home built and decorated for each one of us. We get the key when we turn eighteen," Riggs explained.

"And do all of you live here on the property at your homes?" she asked.

"For the most part, yes," Garrett interjected. "Some of us are just now moving back home. A couple of us have always lived here. Point being, we've all made the decision to come home and take our rightful places running the family business. If you love the outdoors as much as you say, there's no better place to work and live than KBR and we'd love to have you here."

More of those tears streamed down their sister's face.

"I'd like that very much," she said.

"Welcome home, Andrea." Mother wrapped her daughter in an embrace. The brothers stood shoulder to shoulder, forming a circle around the pair of them. Each placed a hand on either their mother or Andrea's arms. There were wide smiles and overflowing hearts all around.

"It's good to finally be in a place where I feel like I belong," Andrea said.

And she did. KBR was home.

* * * * *

Get 4 FREE REWARDS!

We'll send you 2 FREE Books plus 2 FREE Mystery Gifts.

FREE
Value Over
$20

Both the **Romance** and **Suspense** collections feature compelling novels written by many of today's bestselling authors.

YES! Please send me 2 FREE novels from the Essential Romance or Essential Suspense Collection and my 2 FREE gifts (gifts are worth about $10 retail). After receiving them, if I don't wish to receive any more books, I can return the shipping statement marked "cancel." If I don't cancel, I will receive 4 brand-new novels every month and be billed just $7.49 each in the U.S. or $7.74 each in Canada. That's a savings of at least 17% off the cover price. It's quite a bargain! Shipping and handling is just 50¢ per book in the U.S. and $1.25 per book in Canada.* I understand that accepting the 2 free books and gifts places me under no obligation to buy anything. I can always return a shipment and cancel at any time by calling the number below. The free books and gifts are mine to keep no matter what I decide.

Choose one: ☐ **Essential Romance**   ☐ **Essential Suspense**
(194/394 MDN GRHV)   (191/391 MDN GRHV)

Name (please print)

Address   Apt. #

City   State/Province   Zip/Postal Code

Email: Please check this box ☐ if you would like to receive newsletters and promotional emails from Harlequin Enterprises ULC and its affiliates. You can unsubscribe anytime.

Mail to the **Harlequin Reader Service:**
IN U.S.A.: P.O. Box 1341, Buffalo, NY 14240-8531
IN CANADA: P.O. Box 603, Fort Erie, Ontario L2A 5X3

Want to try 2 free books from another series! Call 1-800-873-8635 or visit www.ReaderService.com.

---

*Terms and prices subject to change without notice. Prices do not include sales taxes, which will be charged (if applicable) based on your state or country of residence. Canadian residents will be charged applicable taxes. Offer not valid in Quebec. This offer is limited to one order per household. Books received may not be as shown. Not valid for current subscribers to the Essential Romance or Essential Suspense Collection. All orders subject to approval. Credit or debit balances in a customer's account(s) may be offset by any other outstanding balance owed by or to the customer. Please allow 4 to 6 weeks for delivery. Offer available while quantities last.

Your Privacy—Your information is being collected by Harlequin Enterprises ULC, operating as Harlequin Reader Service. For a complete summary of the information we collect, how we use this information and to whom it is disclosed, please visit our privacy notice located at corporate.harlequin.com/privacy-notice. From time to time we may make your personal information with reputable third parties. If you wish to opt out of this sharing of your personal information, please visit readerservice.com/consumerschoice or call 1-800-873-8635. **Notice to California Residents**—Under California law, you have specific rights to control and access your data. For more information on these rights and how to exercise them, visit corporate.harlequin.com/california-privacy.

STRS22R3

Get 4 FREE REWARDS!

We'll send you 2 FREE Books plus 2 FREE Mystery Gifts.

FREE Value Over **$20**

Both the **Harlequin® Special Edition** and **Harlequin® Heartwarming™** series feature compelling novels filled with stories of love and strength where the bonds of friendship, family and community unite.

HARLEQUIN
PLUS

Try the best multimedia
subscription service for romance
readers like you!

Read, Watch and Play.

Experience the easiest way to get
the romance content you crave.

Start your **FREE TRIAL** at
<u>www.harlequinplus.com/freetrial</u>.